Jonathan Swift

The Lilliputian Library, or, Gullivers Museum, in ten Volumes

Containing Lectures on Morality, Historical Pieces, Interesting Fables. Vol. VI -X

Jonathan Swift

The Lilliputian Library, or, Gullivers Museum, in ten Volumes
Containing Lectures on Morality, Historical Pieces, Interesting Fables. Vol. VI -X

ISBN/EAN: 9783744767965

Printed in Europe, USA, Canada, Australia, Japan

Cover: Foto ©Andreas Hilbeck / pixelio.de

More available books at **www.hansebooks.com**

THE
LILLIPUTIAN LIBRARY,
OR
GULLIVERS MUSEUM

IN TEN VOLUMES.

CONTAINING

LECTURES ON MORALITY	SURPRISING ADVENTURES
HISTORICAL PIECES	REMARKABLE LIVES
INTERESTING FABLES	POETICAL PIECES
DIVERTING TALES	COMICAL JOKES
MIRACULOUS VOYAGES	USEFUL LETTERS.

The whole forming

A

COMPLETE SYSTEM

of JUVENILE KNOWLEDGE

for

the AMUSEMENT and IMPROVEMENT
of all

LITTLE MASTERS and MISSES,

Whether in Summer or Winter, Morning,
Noon or Evening

by

LILLIPUTIUS GULLIVER

Citizen of Utopia and Knight of the moſt noble ordre of
human prudence

VOL. VI—X.

BERLIN
Sold by CHR. FRIDR. HIMBURG. 1782.

GULLIVER'S LECTURES

VOL. VI.

CONTAINING

THE

POETICAL

FLOWER - BASKET;

OR,

THE LILLIPUTIAN FLIGHT

TO

PARNASSUS.

PREFACE.

NOTHING can be more useful to little Masters and Misses than the perusal of well-chosen poetical pieces, since it brings them to an easy and fluent mode of reading, and gives them an idea of the harmony of syllables, far better than can be expected from the constant perusal of prose authors.

With this view, the *little* Gulliver has travelled over all the poetical regions, and has cautiously collected the choicest flowers of the Muses, and placed them in his *Flower-Basket*, to gratify the smell and taste of his pretty little pupils.

To convince my readers, that I am none of those who wishes to confine all his happiness to himself, I do hereby freely invite all the Masters and Misses of the great

city

city of London, and of all cities and towns in the whole world, to come and fmell at my *Flower-Bafket*. Thefe are not like the flowers that grow in our gardens; for they, being plucked in the morning, frequently wither befo- re night, and are too intoxicating to be kept in our chambers; whereas thofe which compofe my *Flower-Bafket* never lofe their fmell or beauty, and at no time prove offenfive; but the longer they are kept, the more beautiful they become, and, inftead of intoxicating the head, ex- pand the mind, and enlarge the heart.

THE
POETICAL FLOWER BASKET.

PART I. CHAP. I.

The Story of INCLE and YARICO.

YE Virgin train, an artless dame inspire,
   Unlearnt in schools, unbless'd with
     natal fire,
To save this story from devouring fate,
And the dire arts of faithless men relate.
A youth I sing, in face and form divine,
In whom both art and nature did combine,
With heavenly skill to mingle every charm,
As Gods of old did fair *Pandora* form.
Stranger to virtue, this deceiver held
The box of mischiefs in his breast conceal'd;
His outward form each female heart enflam'd,
His inward beauty lurking av'rice stain'd;
Insatiate love of gold, and hope of gain,
Encourag'd him to cut the yielding main.
By winds or waves, or the decrees of
     heaven,
His bark upon a barbarous coast was driven;

A 4   Possess'd

Poffefs'd by men who thirft for human blood,
Who live in caves or thickets of the wood:
Untaught to plant, yet corn and fruits
      abound,
And fragrant flow'rs enamel all the ground;
Diftrefs'd, he landed on the fatal fhore,
With fome companions which were foon no
      more;
The favage race their trembling flefh devour,
Off'ring oblations to the infernal pow'r.
Dreadfully fuppliant human limbs they tore,
Accurfed rites! and quaff'd their ftreaming
      gore.
Immortal *Jove* ftoop'd from his azure fky,
Grieving a form fo like his own fhould die,
On the fair youth mercurial fpeed beftow'd,
Swifter than thought he reach'd the moffy
      wood;
Beneath a nightly fhade he panting lies,
Screen'd by all-pitying *Jove* from hoftile
      eyes;
Yet gloomy forrows and unmanly fears
Swell'd his fad breaft, which he bedew'd
      with tears;
When lo! a negro virgin chanc'd to rove
Thro' the thick mazes of the nodding grove,
Whofe glitt'ring fhells and elegant undrefs,
With various plumes a noble birth confefs:
           With

With reverential fear the well-fhap'd maid
Thought him a God, and low obedience paid;
His face like polifh'd marble did appear,
His filken robe, and flowing flaxen hair
A'maz'd the nymph; nor lefs her fparkling
   eyes,
And naked beauty, did the youth furprife.
Low at her feet in fuppliant pofture laid,
With fpeaking eyes, he thus addrefs'd the
   maid:
O let foft pity touch that lovely breaft?
Succour a man by various ills opprefs'd;
Such finifh'd grace does through your per-
   fon fhine,
Sure 'tis enliven'd by a foul divine.
The tender negro look'd a kind reply
Thro' pearls of pity, dropping from her eye;
With hands uplifted, did the Gods implore,
That her relentlefs countrymen no more
Might ftain their native land with human
   gore.
He feis'd her hand, with tender paffion
   prefs'd,
While copious tears both love and fear
   confefs'd:
The pitying maid view'd him with yielding
   eyes,
And from each bofom mutual fighs arife:

His safety now becomes her only care,
A secret cave she knew, and hid him there;
Adorn'd it with the spoils of leopards slain,
Which other lovers ventur'd life to gain.
Through mazy thickets and a pathless wood,
She press'd advent'rous with delicious food.
Daily her hand a rich repast did bring,
Of ripen'd fruits, and waters from the spring;
But when declining t'ward the close of day,
The crimson sun sets weary in the sea,
Strait to a shady grove where fountains rise,
From woods defended and inclement skies,
Where the wing'd warblers of the air conspire,
From several boughs to form a heavenly
　　　　choir,
Adorn'd with fragrant flowers and evergreen,
She leads the youth, delightful Sylvan scene,
Where he in peaceful slumbers takes his rest,
Forgets his fears, and calms his tim'rous
　　　　breast.
In soft repose the beauteous lover lies,
While Yarico with care unseals her eyes:
With anxious fear the matchless maid attends,
Careful to save him from her barb'rous
　　　　friends.
The flowing curls, which o'er his shoulders
　　　　play'd
With artless beauty, pleas'd the Negro maid:
　　　　　　　　　　　　　　　　She

She thought her finger, when entangled
   there,
Like clouds encircling Berenice's hair:
The graceful youth, confessing equal fire,
Did her just symmetry of shape admire.
Oft would he say, My Yarico with thee,
My only blifs; could I my country see:
If ever I forget my vows of love,
Unblefs'd, abandon'd, may I friendlefs rove.
To thee alone I owe the vital air,
My love and gratitude for ever share;
I'll gems provide, and filks of curious art,
With gifts exprefsive of my grateful heart;
Thou in a houfe by horfes drawn shalt ride
With me, thy faithful lover, by thy fide:
The female train shall round with envy
   gaze,
Wonder, and filent figh unwilling praife.
Pleas'd with his words, defiring more to
   pleafe,
She from a craggy cliff furvey'd the feas;
A bark she fpy'd and did by figns implore,
That they would touch upon the fandy shore.
With joy she ran—my love, make hafte
   away,
A vefsel waits us on the foaming fea;
Soon he the vefsel's lofty fide afcends,
And finds them to be countrymen and friends;
      With

With lovely Yarico puts off to sea,
With equal joy they plough the wat'ry way:
When the fair youth, despairing, calls to
　　　mind
All hopes eluded of his wealth design'd;
Riches the seat of his affection seise,
And faithful Yarico no more can please.
Unhappy maid; to wasting sorrows born,
And fated evils undeserv'd to mourn.
This youth was born too near the northern
　　　pole,
Which chill'd each virtue in his frozen soul;
But near the sun the nymph her birth
　　　confefs'd,
Where every virtue glow'd within her breaft.
Thus ore lies in the earth, unfinish'd, cold,
But purg'd by fire, it brightens into gold.
Propitious zephyrs fill their swelling sails,
They make *Barbadoes*, blefs'd with pros-
　　　p'rous gales;
The planters thick'ning on the key appear,
To purchase negro slaves, if any there;
When the false youth, by cursed avarice
　　　sway'd,
Horrid to mention! fells his faithful maid.
Amaz'd and trembling, silently she mourn'd,
While speaking tears her radiant eyes
　　　adorn'd.

　　　　　　　　　　　Low

Low at his feet, the lovely mourner lay,
Nor would to words her fwelling heart give
　　way.
She grafps his knees, in vain attempts to
　　fpeak;
At length her words in moving accents
　　break;
O much lov'd youth, in tender pity fpare
A helplefs maid, my long-try'd faith revere.
From you this worft of human ills to prove,
Muft break a heart that overflows with love.
Break not my heart, nor drive me to defpair,
Left you deface your lovely image there.
Ah! do not with confummate woe undo
A foul that father, mother, country left for
　　you:
How fadly muft my tender parents mourn,
By me forfaken, never to return?
Transferr'd from them, to you my love I
　　gave;
Unjuft return, to fell me for a flave!
Oh call to mind the facred oaths you've
　　given,
Remember there are thunder-bolts in heaven.
But if the fwelling forrows in my breaft,
Your heart of adamant can ftill refift;
Yet let the infant in my womb I bear,
The blefling tafte of your paternal care.
　　　　　　　　　　　　　　He

He thruſt her from him with remorſeleſs
    hand,
For her condition rais'd his firſt demand.
Pleas'd with ſuccefs he chearfully returns,
While hapleſs Yarico in bondage mourns:
And all his friends the prudent youth admire,
That could, ſo young, a trading ſoul
    acquire.

CHAP. II.

AN ELEGY ON

The DEATH and BURIAL of

COCK ROBIN.

WHO kill'd Cock Robin?
    I ſays the Sparrow,
      With my bow and arrow;
And I kill'd Cock Robin.

Who ſaw him die?
    I ſaid the Fly,
      With my little eye;
And I ſaw him die

Who

Who catch'd his blood?
 I, faid the Fifh,
  With my little difh;
And I catch'd his blood.

Who made his fhroud?
 I, faid the Beetle,
  With my little needle;
And I made his fhroud.

Who fhall dig his grave?
 I, faid the Owl,
  With my fpade and fhow'l;
And I'll dig his grave.

Who'll be the parfon?
 I, faid the Rook,
  With my little book;
And I'll be the parfon.

Who'll be the clerk?
 I, faid the Lark,
  If 'tis not in the dark;
And I'll be the clerk.

Who'll carry him to the grave?
 I, faid the Kite,
  If 'tis not in the night;
And I'll carry him to the grave.

Who'll carry the link?
    I, said the Linnet,
    I'll fetch it in a minute;
And I'll carry the link.

Who'll be chief mourner?
    I, says the Dove;
    For I mourn for my love,
And I'll be chief mourner.

Who'll bear the pall?
    We, says the Wren;
    Both the cock and the hen,
And we'll bear the pall.

Who'll sing a psalm?
    I, says the Thrush,
    As she sat in a bush;
And I'll sing a psalm.

Who'll toll the bell?
    I, says the Bull,
    Because I can pull,
So Cock Robin farewell.

    All the birds in the air
        Fell to sighing and sobbing,
    When they heard the bell toll
        For poor Cock Robin.

CHAP.

CHAP. III.

The HARE *and* MANY FRIENDS.

By Mr. GAY.

FRIENDSHIP, like love, is but a name
   Unlefs to one you ftint the flame.
The child, who many fathers fhare,
Hath feldom known a father's care;
'Tis thus in friendfhip; who depend
On many, rarely find a friend.
   A hare, who, in a civil way,
Comply'd with ev'ry thing like *Gay*,
Was known by all the beftial train,
Who haunt the wood, or graze the plain:
Her care was, never to offend,
And ev'ry creature was her friend.
   As forth fhe went at early dawn,
To tafte the dew-befprinkled lawn,
Behind fhe hears the hunters cries,
And from the deep-mouth'd thunder flies.
She ftarts, fhe ftops, fhe pants for breath,
She hears the near advance of death;
She doubles to miflead the hound,
And meafures back her mazy round;
'Till, fainting in the public way,
Half dead with fear; fhe gafping lay.

What

What tranfports in her bofom grew,
When firft the horfe appear'd in view!
    Let me, fays fhe, your back afcend,
And owe my fafety to a friend:
You know my feet betray my flight,
To friendfhip ev'ry burthen's light.
    The horfe reply'd, poor honeft pufs,
It grieves my heart to fee thee thus;
Be comforted, relief is near;
For all your friends are in the rear.
    She next the ftately bull implor'd,
And thus reply'd the mighty lord;
Since ev'ry beaft alive can tell
That I fincerely wifh you well,
I may, without offence, pretend
To take the freedom of a friend;
Love calls me hence; a fav'rite cow
Expects me near yon barley mow;
And when a lady's in the cafe,
You know all other things give place.
To leave you thus might feem unkind:
But fee, the goat is juft behind.
    The goat remark'd her pulfe was high,
Her languid head; her heavy eye.
My back, fays he, may do you harm;
The fheep's at hand, and wool is warm.
    The fheep was feeble, and complain'd.
His fides a load of wool fuftain'd,

                                Said

Said he was flow, confefs'd his fears;
For hounds eat fheep as well as hares.
   She now the trotting calf addrefs'd,
To fave from death a friend diftrefs'd.
   Shall I, fays he, of tender age,
In this important care engage?
Older and abler paft you by;
How ftrong are thofe! how weak am I!
Should I prefume to bear you hence,
Thofe friends of mine may take offence.
Excufe me then. You know my heart,
But deareft friends, alas! muft part;
How fhall we all lament! Adieu,
For fee the hounds are juft in view.

The Fox *and the* Eagle.

   A N eagle and a fox once were
In friendfhip join'd.—The happy pair
On lodgings in one place agree,
And fix'd upon an old elm tree.
Amidft its fair wide fpreading head,
The broody eagle plac'd her bed:
A hollow near its root did lie,
Which made the fox a nurfery.
It happ'd one day, that forth fhe went
In fearch of needful aliment.

Home

Home in mean time the eagle came,
Hungry, as having mifs'd her game;
From Reynard's cabbin fhe fupplies
That lofs, then to her neft fhe flies.
The fox mifs'd them when fhe return'd,
And in a mother's anguifh mourn'd;
But, quick as thought, away fhe runs,
And with a fire-brand returns;
Then fets the neft on fire, when down
Came eagles young, with fox's own.
Now 'twas the eagle's turn to mourn,
And her to triumph in her's turn:
For as they fall, the fox, hard by,
Catches, and with an eager joy
Devours while yet alive her young.
The haplefs bird from whom they fprung,
Unable to prevent their fate,
Repents her cruelty too late.

Ingratitude's a bone of ftrife
That often fep'rates friends for life.

The Court *of* Death.

DEATH on a folemn night of ftate,
In all his pomp of terror fate:
Th' attendants of his gloomy reign,
Difeafes dire, a ghaftly train!

Crowd

Crowd the vaft court. With hollow tone,
A voice thus thunder'd from the throne:
'This night our minifter we name,
Let every fervant fpeak his claim;
Merit fhall bear this ebon wand.
All, at the word, ftretch'd forth their hand.

Fever, with burning heat poffefs'd,
Advanc'd and for the wand addrefs'd.

I to the weekly bills appeal,
Let thofe exprefs my fervent zeal,
On ev'ry flight occafion near,
With violence I perfevere.

Next Gout appears with limping pace,
Pleads how he fhifts from place to place;
From head to foot how fwift he flies,
And ev'ry joint and finew plies;
Still working when he feems fupprefs'd.
A moft tenacious ftubborn gueft.

A haggard fpectre from the crew
Crawls forth, and thus afferts his due.
'Tis I who taint the fweeteft joy,
And in the fhape of love deftroy:
My fhanks, funk eyes, and nofelefs face,
Prove my pretenfion to the place.

Stone urg'd his ever-growing force;
And next, Confumption's meagre corfe,
With feeble voice, that fcarce was heard,
Broke with fhort coughs, his fuit preferr'd.

Let

Let none object my ling'ring way,
I gain, like *Fabius*, by delay;
Fatigue and weaken every foe
By long attack, secure, tho' slow.
　Plague represents his rapid power,
Who thinn'd a nation in an hour.
　All spoke their claim, and hop'd the wand
Now expectation hush'd the band,
When thus the monarch from the throne:
　Merit was ever modest known.
What, no physician speak his right?
None here? But fees their toils requite.
Let then Intemp'rance take the wand,
Who fills with gold their zealous hand.
You, Fever, Gout, and all the rest,
Whom wary men, as foes, detest,
Forego your claim; no more pretend:
Intemp'rance is esteem'd a friend;
He shares their mirth, their social joys,
And, as a courted guest, destroys,
The charge on him must justly fall,
Who finds employment for you all.

The Sick Man *and the* Angel.

　Is there no hope? the sick man said.
The silent doctor shook his head,

And

'And took his leave with figns of forrow,
Defpairing of his fee to morrow.
When thus the man, with gafping breath;
I feel the chilling wound of death:
Since I muft bid the world adieu,
Let me my former life review.
I grant, my bargains well were made,
But all men over-reach in trade;
'Tis felf-defence in each profeffion:
Sure felf-defence is no tranfgreffion.
The little portion in my hands,
By good fecurity on lands,
Is well increas'd. If unawares,
My juftice to myfelf and heirs,
Hath let my debtor rot in jail,
For want of good fufficient bail;
If I by writ, or bond, or deed,
Reduc'd a family to need,
My will hath made the world amends;
My hope on charity depends.
When I am number'd with the dead,
And all my pious gifts are read,
By heav'n and earth 'twill then be known,
My charities were amply fhown.
An Angel came. Ah friend! he cry'd,
No more in flatt'ring hope confide.
Can thy good deeds in former times
Outweigh the balance of thy crimes?

What

What widow or what orphan prays
To crown thy life with length of days?
A pious action's in thy power,
Embrace with joy the happy hour.
Now, while you draw the vital air,
Prove your intention is fincere.
This inftant give a hundred pound;
Your neighbours want, and you abound.

But why fuch hafte? the fick man whines;
Who knows as yet what heaven defigns?
Perhaps I may recover ftill;
That fum and more are in my will.

Fool, fays the vifion, now 'tis plain,
Your life, your foul, your heav'n was gain.
From ev'ry fide, with all your might,
You fcrap'd, and fcrap'd beyond your right;
And after death would fain atone,
By giving what is not your own.
While there is life, there's hope, he cry'd.
Then why fuch hafte? fo groan'd and dy'd.

The Painter *who pleafed* Nobody *and* Everybody.

SO very like a painter drew,
That every eye the picture knew;
He hit complexion, feature, air,
So juft, the life itfelf was there.

He

He gave each mufcle all its ftrength;
The mouth, the chin, the nofe's length,
His honeft pencil touch'd with truth,
And mark'd the date of age and youth.

He loft his friends, his practice fail'd;
Truth fhould not always be reveal'd;
In dufty piles his pictures lay,
For no one fent the fecond pay.
Two buftos, fraught with ev'ry grace,
A Venus and Apollo's face,
He plac'd in view; refolv'd to pleafe,
Whoever fat, he drew from thefe,
From thefe corrected ev'ry feature,
And fpirited each aukward creature.

All things were fet; the hour was come,
His pallet ready o'er his thumb,
My lord appear'd, and feated right,
In proper attitude and light,
The painter look'd, he fketch'd the piece,
Then dipp'd his pencil, talk'd of Greece.
Of Titian's tints, of Guido's air;
Thofe eyes, my lord, the fpirit there
Might well a Raphael's hand require,
To give them all the native fire;
The features fraught with fenfe and wit,
You'll grant are very hard to hit;
But yet with patience you fhall view
As much as paint and art can do.

Obferve

Obferve the work. My lord reply'd,
'Till now I thought my mouth was wide:
Befides, my nofe is fomewhat long;
Dear fir, for me 'tis far too young.
  ¿ Oh! pardon me, the artift cry'd,
In this, we painters muft decide.
The piece ev'n common eyes muft ftrike,
I warrant it extremely like.

My lord examin'd it a-new,
No looking-glafs feem'd half fo true.

A lady came, with borrow'd grace:
He from his Venus form'd her face.
Her lover prais'd the painter's art,
So like the picture in his heart!
To ev'ry age fome charm he lent;
Ev'n beauties were almoft content,

  Through all the town his art they prais'd,
His cuftom grew, his price was rais'd.
Had he the real likenefs fhown,
Would any man the picture own?
But when thus happily he wrought,
Each found the likenefs in his thought.

  Thus flatt'ry never feems abfurd;
The flatter'd always take your word:
Impoffibilities feem juft;
They take the ftrongeft praife on truft.
Hyperboles, though ne'er fo great,
Will ftill come fhort of felf-conceit.

The

The Setting Dog *and the* Partridge.

THE ranging dog the ftubble tries,
And fearches ev'ry breefe that flies;
The fcent grows warm; with cautions fear
He creeps and points the covey near;
The men, in filence, far behind,
Confcious of game the net unbind.

A partridge with experience wife,
The fraudful preparation fpies;
She mocks their toils, alarms her brood!
The covey fprings, and feeks the wood!
But ere her certain wing fhe tries,
Thus to the creeping fpaniel cries.

Thou fawning flave to man's deceit,
Thou pimp of luxury, fneaking cheat,
Of thy whole fpecies thou difgrace,
Dogs fhould difown thee of their race,
For if I judge their native parts,
They're born with open honeft hearts;
And, ere they ferv'd man's wicked ends,
Were gen'rous foes or real friends.

Epitaph

Epitaph on a Dormouse, *really written by a little* Boy.

I.

IN paper cafe,
Hard by this place,
Dead a poor dormoufe lies;
And foon or late,
Summon'd by fate,
Each prince, each monarch dies.

II.

Ye fons of verfe,
While I rehearfe,
Attend inftructive rhyme:
No fins had Dor
To anfwer for,
Repent of yours in time.

True Riches; *or,* Virtue *its own* Reward.

STILPO, of Stoick caft, who firft
Stoutly refus'd to fear the worft;
Who knew no ill could e'er befall,
Where confcious virtue's *all in all;*
When old Antigonus's fon,
So oft a king, fo oft undone,
Like a tempeftuous whirlwind came,
And fet Megara in a flame;

Stripp'd

Stripp'd of his all, half naked went
To feek the haughty victor's tent:
The tyrant fmil'd; but mov'd to fee
Merit expos'd to mifery,
Order'd the captains of his hoft
To give him back the goods he'd loft.
Stilpo the ufelefs boon deny'd;
Forbear, miftaken prince, he cry'd;
I've nothing that I value loft:
Wifdom and virtue ftill I boaft
Triumphant in my foul, the reft,
Mere joys of life, are all a jeft.
Th' aftonifh'd monarch blufh'd with fhame,
Confcious of Stilpo's brighter fame:
This man, he cry'd, has conquer'd more
By *virtue* than I have by *pow'r.*
Cities may burn, and empires fall,
But virtue triumphs over all.

The Shepherd *and the* Philofopher.

REMOTE from cities liv'd a fwain,
Unvex't with all the cares of gain;
His head was filver'd o'er with age,
And long experience made him fage;
In fummer's heat, and winter's cold,
He fed his flock, and penn'd the fold;

His

His hours in chearful labour flew,
Nor envy nor ambition knew;
His wifdom and his honeft fame
Through all the country rais'd his name.

A deep philofopher, whofe rules
Of moral life were drawn from fchools,
The fhepherd's homely cottage fought,
And thus explor'd his reach of thought.

Whence is thy learning?   Hath thy toil
O'er books confum'd the midnight-oil?
Haft thou old Greece and Rome furvey'd,
And the vaft fenfe of Plato weigh'd?
Hath Socrates thy foul refin'd,
And haft thou fathom'd Tully's mind?
Or, like the wife Ulyffes, thrown,
By various fates, on realms unknown,
Haft thou through many cities ftray'd,
Their cuftoms, laws, and manners weigh'd?

The fhepherd modeftly reply'd,
I ne'er the paths of learning try'd;
Nor have I roam'd in foreign parts,
To read mankind, their laws and arts;
For man is practis'd in difguife,
He cheats the moft difcerning eyes;
Who by that fearch can wifer grow,
When we ourfelves fhall never kow?
The little knowledge I have gain'd,
Was all from fimple nature drain'd;

Hence

Hence my life's maxims took their rife,
Hence grew my fettled hate to vice.
  The daily labours of the bee
Awake my foul to induftry.
Who can obferve the careful ant,
And not provide for future want?
My dog, the truftieft of his kind,
With gratitude inflames my mind:
I mark his true his faithful way,
And in my fervice copy Tray.
In conftancy and nuptial love,
I learn my duty from the dove.
The hen who from the chilly air,
With pious wing protects her care;
And ev'ry fowl that flies at large,
Inftruct me in a parent's charge.
  From nature too I take my rule,
To fhun contempt and ridicule.
I never with important air,
In converfation over-bear.
Can grave and formal pafs for wife,
When men the folemn owl defpife?
My tongue within my lips I rein;
For who talks much, muft talk in vain.
We from the wordy torrent fly:
Who liftens to the chatt'ring pye?
Nor would I with felonious flight
By ftealth invade my neighbour's right.

Rapacious animals we hate:
Kites, wolves, and hawks deferve their fate.
Do not we juft abhorrence find
Againft the toad and ferpent kind?
But envy, calumny, and fpite,
Bear ftronger venom in their bite.

    Thy fame is juft, the fage replies;
Thy virtue proves thee truly wife.

    Thus ev'ry objeƈt of creation
Can furnifh hints to contemplation;
And from the moft minute and mean,
A virtuous mind can morals glean.

The Spaniel *and the* Camelion.

    A Spaniel, bred with all the care
That waits upon a fav'rite heir.
Ne'er felt correƈtion's rigid hand;
Indulg'd to difobey command,
In pamper'd eafe his hours were fpent:
He never knew what learning meant.
Such forward airs, fo pert, fo fmart,
Were fure to win his lady's heart.
Each little mifchief gain'd him praife;
How pretty were his fawning ways!

    The wind was fouth, the morning fair,
He ventures forth to take the air.

He

He ranges all the meadow round,
And rolls upon the fofteft ground:
When near him a cameleon feen,
Was fcarce diftinguifh'd from the green.

    Dear emblem of the flatt'ring hoft.
What, live with clowns, a genius loft?
To cities and to courts repair;
A fortune cannot fail thee there:
Preferment fhall thy talents crown,
Believe me, friend, I know the town.

    Sir, fays the Sycophant, like you,
Of old, politer life I knew:
Like you, a courtier born and bred;
Kings lean'd their ear to what I faid,
My whifper always met fuccefs,
The ladies prais'd me for addrefs.
I knew to hit each courtier's paffion,
And flatter'd ev'ry vice in fafhion.
But Jove, who hates the liar's ways,
At once cut fhort my profp'rous days;
And fentenc'd to retain my nature,
Transform'd me to this crawling creature.
Doom'd to a life obfcure and mean,
I wander in the fylvan fcene.
For Jove the heart alone regards,
He punifhes what man rewards,
How diff'rent is thy cafe and mine!
With men at leaft you fup and dine;

While

While I, condemn'd to thinneft fare,
Like thofe I flatter'd, feed on air.

The Poet *and the* Rofe.

AS in the cool of early day
A poet fought the fweets of May,
The garden's fragrant breath afcends,
And every ftalk with odour bends.
A rofe he pluck'd, he gaz'd, admir'd,
Thus finging as the mufe infpir'd.

Go rofe, my Chloe's bofom grace;
  How happy fhould I prove
Might I fupply that envy'd place
  With never-fading love!
There, phoenix like, beneath her eye,
Involv'd in fragrance, burn and die!
Know, haplefs flower, that thou fhalt find
  More fragrant rofes there;
I fee thy with'ring head reclin'd
  With envy and defpair!
One common fate we both muft prove
You die with envy, I with love.

Spare your comparifons, reply'd
An angry rofe which grew befide.

Of

Of all mankind you fhould not flout us;
What can a poet do without us?
In ev'ry love-fong rofes bloom;
We lend you colour and perfume.
Does it to Chloe's charms conduce,
To found her fame on our abufe?
Muft we, to flatter her, be made
To wither, envy, pine, and fade?

The Agreeable Lady: *or* Virtue *the greateft*
Beauty.

THE things that make a virgin pleafe
The fair who feeks will find are thefe:
A beauty without art complete,
Who, from her toilet fimply neat,
The golden tiffue can defpife,
And wears no brilliants but her eyes.
Soft blended in her eyes fhould meet,
Defiring love and fparkling wit;
And in her dimpled fmiles be feen
A modeft though a chearful mien;
With fuch wife lowlinefs endu'd,
That neither can be mean or rude;
The virtue that does her adorn,
By honour guarded, not by fcorn;

C 3   An

An undiffembled innocence,
Apt not to give or take offence;
And whofe religion's ftrong and plain,
Not fuperftitious or profane.
With fuch a virgin, fuch a wife,
Who would not wifh to fpend his life.

CHAP. IV.
The HAPPY PAIR.

THRICE happy is a married life,
   As fages gravely fay,
With mutual aid, when man and wife
   Agree to draw one way.
Then honeft Ned, who keeps the Bear,
   And rofy Kate his fpoufe,
Muft be allow'd a happy pair:
   Both draw——and both caroufe.
When Ned's awake, he feldom' refts,
   But drinks, and tends the tap;
And Kate will draw and pledge her guefts,
   Whilft landlord takes his nap.
Thus partners both in joy and care,
   The load of life moves quicker;
For Ned and Kate each draw their fhare,
   And——drink their fhare of liquor.

The

The COBLER.

YOUR fage and moralift can fhow,
Many misfortunes here below,
A truth which no one ever mifs'd,
Tho' neither fage nor moralift;
Yet, all the troubles, notwithftanding,
Which fate or fortune has a hand in,
Fools to themfelves will more create,
In fpite of fortune and of fate.
Thus oft are dreaming wretches feen
Tortur'd with vapours, and with fpleen;
Transform'd, at leaft in their own eyes,
To glafs, or china, or goofe pies.
Others will to themfelves appear
Stone dead as WILL *the Conqueror,*
And all the world in vain might ftrive,
To face them down that they're alive.
Unlucky males with child will groan,
And forely dread their lying down;
As fearing, that to eafe their pain,
May puzzle doctor *Chamberlain.*
Imaginary evils flow,
Merely for want of real woe;
And when prevailing whimfies rife,
As monftrous wild abfurdities
Are, ev'ry hour, and ev'ry minute,
Found without Bedlam, as within it;

C 4 Which

Which if you further would have shown,
And leisure have to read—read on.

There liv'd a gentleman, possess'd
Of all that mortals reckon best:
A seat well chose in wholesome air,
With gardens and with prospects fair:
His land from debt and jointure free,
His money never in South-Sea:
His health of body firm and good,
Tho' past the hey-day of his blood:
His consort fair, and good, and kind;
His children rising to his mind:
His friends ingenuous and sincere;
His honour, nay his conscience clear.
He wanted nought of human bliss,
But pow'r to taste his happiness.

Too near, alas! this great man's hall,
A merry Cobler had a stall;
An arch old wag as e'er you knew,
With breeches red, and jerkin blue;
Chearful at working, as at play,
He sung and whistled life away:
When rising morning glads the sky,
Clear as the merry lark, and high:
When ev'ning shades the landskip veil,
Late warbling as the nightingale.
Tho' pence came slow, and trade was ill,
Yet still he sung and whistled still;

Tho'

Tho' patch'd his garb, and coarse his fare,
He laugh'd and caſt away old care.

    The rich man view'd, with diſcontent,
His tatter'd neighbour's merriment,
With envy grudg'd, and pin'd to ſee
A beggar pleaſanter than he:
And, by degrees, to hate began
Th' intolerable happy man,
Who haunted him, like any ſpright,
From morn to eve, both day and night.
It chanc'd when once in bed he lay,
When dreams are true, at break of day,
He heard the Cobler at his ſport,
Amidſt his muſic ſtopping ſhort:
Whether his morning draught he took,
Or warming whiff of wonted ſmoke,
The 'ſquire ſuſpected, being ſhrewd,
This ſilence boded him no good;
And, 'cauſe he nothing ſaw nor heard,
A Machiavilian plot he fear'd.
Straight circumſtances crowded plain
To vex and plague his jealous brain:
Trembling in panic dread he lies,
With gaping mouth and ſtaring eyes:
And ſtraining wiſhful both his ears   ⎤
He ſoon perſuades himſelf he hears   ⎬
One ſkip and caper up the ſtairs;   ⎦

Sees

Sees the door open quick, and knew
His dreaded foe in red and blue,
Who with a running jump, he thought,
Leap'd plum directly down his throat,
Laden with tackle of his ftall,
Laft, end, and hammer, ftrap, and awl:
No fooner down than with a jerk,
He fell to mufic and to work.
If much he griev'd our Don before,
When but o'th' outfide of his door,
How forely muft he now moleft,
When got o'th' infide of his breaft:
The waking dreamer groans and fwells,
And pangs imaginary feels;
Catches, and fcrapes of tunes he hears,
For ever ringing in his ears.
Ill-favour'd fmells his nofe difpleafe,
Mundungus ftrong, and rotten cheefe:
He feels him when he draws his breath,
Or tug the leather with his teeth,
Or beat the fole, or elfe extend
His arms to th' utmoft of his end:
Enough to crack, when ftretch'd fo wide,
The ribs of any mortal's fide.
Is there no method then to fly
This vile inteftine enemy?
What can be done in this condition,
But fending for a good phyfician!

The

The doctor, having heard the cafe
Burft into laughter in his face;
Told him he need no more than rife,
Open his windows and his eyes,
Whiftling and ftitching there to fee,
The cobler as he us'd to be.
Sir, quoth the patient; your pretences
Shall ne'er perfuade me from my fenfes:
How fhould I rife? the heavy brute
Will hardly let me wag a foot:
Tho' fceing for belief may go,
Yet feeling is the truth you know:
I feel him in my fides I tell ye:
Had you a cobler in your belly,
You fcarce would fleer, as now you do;
I doubt your guts would grumble too:
Still do you laugh? I tell you, Sir,
I'd kick you foundly, could I ftir;
Thou Quack, thou never hadft degree
In either Univerfity;
Thou mere licentiate, without knowledge,
The fhame and fcandal of the college;
I'll call my fervants, if you ftay;
So, doctor, fcamper while you may.
One thus difpatch'd, a fecond came,
Of equal fkill and greater fame;
Who fwore him mad as a March hare,
For doctors, when provok'd, will fwear.

To

To drive such whimsies from his pate,
He dragg'd him to the window straight.
But jilting fortune can devise
To baffle and out-wit the wise;
The Cobler ere expos'd to view,
Had just pull'd off his jerkin blue,
Not dreaming 'twould his neighbour hurt,
To sit *in Fresco* in his shirt.
Ah! quoth the patient, with a sigh,
You know him not so well as I,
The man who down my throat is run,
Has got a true-blue jerkin on.
In vain the Doctor rav'd and tore,
Argued and fretted, stamp'd and swore;
Told him he might believe as well
The giant of *Pantagruel*
Did oft as break his fast or sup,
For poach'd eggs swallow windmills up;
Or that the Holland dame could bear,
A child for ev'ry day i'th' year.
The vapour'd dotard, grave and sly,
Mistook for truth each rapping lie?
And drew conclusions such as these,
Resistless from the premises.
　　I hope, my friends, you'll grant me all,
A windmill's bigger than a stall.
And since the lady brought alive,
Children three hundred sixty five:

Why

Why fhould you think there is no room
For one poor cobler in my womb?
Thus ev'ry thing his friends could fay,
The more confirm'd him in his way: .
Further convinc'd by what they tell
'Twas certain, tho' impoffible.
　　Now worfe and worfe his pitious ftate
Was grown, and almoft defperate:
Yet ftill the utmoft bent to try,
Without more help he would not die.
An old phyfician fly and fhrewd;
With management of face indu'd;
Heard all his tale; and afk'd with care,
How long the Cobler had been there?
Noted diftinctly what he faid:
Lift up his eyes, and fhook his head,
And grave accofts him, on this fafhion;
After mature deliberation,
With ferious and important face,
Sir, your's is an uncommon cafe:
Tho' I've read Galen's Latin o'er,
I never met with it before;
Nor have I found the like difeafe,
In ftories of Hippocrates.
Then, after a convenient ftay, ——
—— Sir, if prefcription you'll obey,
My life for your's, I'll fet you free
From this fame two-legg'd tympany.
　　　　　　　　　'Tis

'Tis true, you're gone beyond the cure
Of fam'd Worm-powder of *John Moore*:
Befides, if downwards he be fent,
I fear he'll fplit you're nether vent:
But then your throat, you know is wide,
And fcarcely clos'd fince it was try'd;
The fame way he got in 'tis plain,
There's room to fetch him out again:
I'll bring the forked worm away
Without a Dyfenteria;
Emetics ftrong will do the feat,
If taken *quantum fufficit:*
I'll fee myfelf the proper dofe,
And then Hypnotics to compofe:
The wretch, tho' languifhing and weak,
Reviv'd already by the Greek.
Cries, what fo learn'd a man as you
Prefcribes, dear doctor, I fhall do.
The vomit fpeedily was got,
The cobler fent for to the fpot,
And taught to manage the deceit,
And not his doublet to forget.
But firft the operator wife ⎫
Over the fight a bandage ties, ⎬
For vomits always ftrain the eyes. ⎭
Courage! I'll make you difembogue,
Spite of his teeth, th' unlucky rogue;

I'll

I'll drench the rascal never fear,
And bring him up or drown him there.
Warm water down he makes him pour,
Till his stretch'd guts could hold no more;
Which doubly swoln, as you may think,
Both with the Cobler and the drink,
What they receiv'd against the grain,
Soon paid with int'rest back again.
Here come his tools, he can't be long
Without his hammer and his thong.
The Cobler humour'd what was spoke,
And gravely carried on the joke:
As he heard nam'd each single matter,
He chuck'd it souse into the water:
And then not to be seen as yet,
Behind the door made his retreat.
The sick man now takes breath a while,
Strength to recruit for farther toil:
Unblinded, he with joyful eyes,
The tackle floating there espies,
Fully convinc'd within his mind,
The Cobler could not stay behind,
Who to the alehouse still would go,
Whene'er he wanted work to do:
Nor could he like his present place,
He ne'er lov'd water in his days.
At length he takes a second bout,
Enough to turn his inside out;

With

With vehemence so sore he strains,
As would have split another's brains.
Ah! here the Cobler comes, I swear!
And truth it was, for he was there,
And, like a rude ill-manner'd clown,
Kick'd with his foot the womit down.
The patient now grown wond'rous light,
Whipp'd off the napkin from his sight,
Briskly lift up his head, and knew
The Breeches red, the Jerkin blue;
And smil'd to hear him grumbling say,
As down the stairs he run his way,
He'd ne'er set foot within his door,
And jump down open throats no more;
No; while he liv'd, he'd ne'r again
Run, like a fox, down the red lane.
. Our patient thus, his inmate gone,
Cur'd of the crotchets in his crown,
Joyful his gratitude expresses,
With thousand thanks, and hundred pieces;
And thus, with much of pain and cost,
Regain'd the health he never lost.

MORAL.

Taught by long miseries, we find
Repose is seated in the mind;
And most men soon or late have own'd,
'Tis there, or no where to be found.

This

This real wifdom timely knows,
Without experience of the woes.
Nor needs inftructive fmart, to fee
That all on earth is vanity.
Lofs, difappointment, paffion, ftrife;
Whate'er torments or troubles life,
Tho' groundlefs, grievous in its ftay,
'Twill fhake our tenements of clay,
When paft, as nothing we efteem;
And pain like pleafure is but dream.

---

the L A D Y *and the* W A S P.

AS Doris, at her toilette's duty,
    Sat meditating on her beauty,
She now was penfive, now was gay,
And loll'd the fultry hours away.
As thus in indolence fhe lies,
A giddy wafp around her flies.
He now advances, now retires,
Now to her neck and cheek afpires.
Her fan in vain defends her charms;
Swift he runs, again alarms.
    She frowns, fhe frets. Good gods; fhe
        cries,
Protect me from thefe teafing flies!
Of all the plagues that heav'n hath fent,
A wafp is moft impertinent.

The hov'ring infect thus complain'd
Am I then flighted, fcorn'd, difdain'd?
Can fuch offence your anger wake?
'Twas beauty caus'd the bold miftake.

　Strike him not, Jenny, Doris cries,
Nor murther wafps like vulgar flies:
For though he's free, to do him right,
The creature's civil and polite.

　In ecftacies away he pofts;
Where-e'er he came the favour boafts.
Brags how her fweeteft tea he fips,
And fhows the fugar on his lips.

　The hint alarm'd the forward crew,
Sure of fuccefs, away they flew.
They fhare the dainties of the day,
Round her with airy mufic play;
Nor were they banifh'd, till fhe found
That wafps have ftings, and felt the wound.

　What whifpers muft the beauty bear!
What hourly nonfenfe haunts her ear!
Where e'er her eyes difpenfe their charms,
Impertinence around her fwarms.
Did not the tender nonfenfe ftrike,
Contempt and fcorn might look diflike;
Forbidding airs might thin the place,
The flighteft flap a fly can chafe.
But who can drive the num'rous breed;
Chafe one, another will fucced.

Who

Who knows a fool muſt know his brother;
One fop will recommend another;
And with this plague ſhe's rightly curs'd,
Becauſe ſhe liſten'd to the firſt.

 Ladies who are with coxcombs great,
Mourn their ill conduct ſoon or late.

The WILD BOAR *and the* RAM.

AGAINST an elm a ſheep was ty'd,
 The butcher's knife in blood was dy'd:
The patient flock, in ſilent fright,
From far beheld the horrid ſight.
A ſavage Boar, who near them ſtood,
Thus mock'd to ſcorn the fleecy brood.

 All cowards ſhould be ſerv'd like you.
See, ſee, your murth'rer is in view;
With purple hands, and reeking knife,
He ſtrips the ſkin yet warm with life.
Your quarter'd ſires, your bleeding dams,
The dying bleat of harmleſs lambs,
Call for revenge. O ſtupid race!
The heart that wants revenge is baſe.

 I grant, an ancient Ram replies,
We bear no terrour in our eyes;
Yet think us not of ſoul ſo tame,
Which no repeated wrongs inflame;

   Inſenſi-

Infenfible of ev'ry ill,
Becaufe we want thy tufks to kill.
Know, thofe who violence purfue,
Give to themfelves the vengeance due;
For in thefe maffacres they find
The two chief plagues that wafte mankind.
Our fkin fupplies the wrangling bar,
It wakes their flumb'ring fons to war;
And well revenge may reft contented,
Since drums and parchment were invented.

The Univerfal APPARITION.

A RAKE, by ev'ry paffion rul'd,
　　With ev'ry vice his youth had cool'd;
Difeafe his tainted blood affails;
His fpirits droop, his vigour fails;
With fecret ills at home he pines,
And, like infirm old age, declines.

　　As, twing'd with pain, he penfive fits,
And raves, and prays, and fwears by fits;
A ghaftly phantom, lean and wan,
Before him rofe, and thus began.

　　My name, perhaps, hath reach'd your ear;
Attend, and be advis'd by Care.
Nor love, nor honour, wealth, nor pow'r,
Can give the heart a chearful hour,

When

When health is loft, be timely wife;
With health all tafte of pleafure flies.
　Thus faid, the phantom difappears.
The wary counfel wak'd his fears:
He now from all excefs abftains,
With phyfic purifies his veins;
And, to procure a fober life,
Refolves to venture on a wife.

　But now again the fprite afcends,
Where'er he walks his ear attends;
Infinuates that beauty's frail,
That perfeverance muft prevail;
In other hours fhe reprefents
His houfehold charge, his annual rents,
Increafing debts, perplexing duns,
And nothing for his younger fons.

　Straight all his thought to gain he turns,
And with the thirft of lucre burns.
But when poffefs'd of fortune's ftore,
The fpectre haunts him more and more:
Sets want and mifery in view,
Bold thieves, and all the murth'ring crew;
Alarms him with eternal frights,
Infefts his dream, or wakes his nights.
How fhall he chafe this hideous gueft?
Pow'r may perhaps protect his reft.
To pow'r he rofe. Again the fprite
Befets him morning, noon, and night;

Of

Talks of ambition's tott'ring feat,
How envy perfecutes the great.
Of rival hate, of treach'rous friends,
And what difgrace his fall attends.

The court he quits to fly from care,
And feeks the peace of rural air:
His groves, his fields, amus'd his hours;
He prun'd his trees, he rais'd his flowers.
But Care again his fteps purfues;
Warns him of blafts, of blighting dews,
Of plund'ring infects, fnails, and rains,
And droughts that ftarv'd the labour'd plains,
Abroad, at home, the fpectre's there:
In vain we feek to fly from Care.

At length he thus the ghoft addrefs'd:
Since thou muft be my conftant gueft,
Be kind, and follow me no more;
For Care by right fhould go before.

The Farmer's Wife *and the* Raven.

BETWIXT her fwaggering panniers load
A farmer's wife to market rode,
And jogging on, with thoughtful care,
Summ'd up the profits of her ware;
When, ftarting from her filver dream,
Thus far and wide was heard her fcream.

That

That raven on yon left-hand oak,
Curse on his ill-betiding croak,
Bodes me no good.. No more she said,
When poor blind Ball, with stumbling tread,
Fell prone; o'erturn'd the panniers lay,
And her mash'd eggs bestrew'd the way.

She, sprawling in the yellow road,
Rail'd, swore, and curs'd, Thou croaking
      toad,
A murrain take thy bawling throat!
I knew misfortune in the note.

Dame, quoth the raven, spare your oaths,
Unclench your fist, and wipe your clothes.
But why on me those curses thrown?
Goody, the fault was all your own;
For had you laid this brittle ware,
On Dun, the old sure-footed mare,
Though all the ravens of the hundred,
With croaking had your tongue out-thunder'd,
Sure-footed Dun had kept her legs,
And you, good woman, sav'd your eggs.

The Fox *at the* Point *of* Death.

A FOX in life's extreme decay,
Weak, sick, and faint, expiring lay;
All appetite had left his maw,
And age disarm'd his mumbling jaw.

His

His num'rous race around him stand
To learn their dying sire's command:
He rais'd his head with whining moan;
And thus was heard the feeble tone:
Ah, sons! from evil ways depart:
My crimes lie heavy on my heart.
See, see, the murther'd geese appear!
Why are those bleeding turkies there?
Why all around this cackling train,
Who haunt my ears for chicken slain?

The hungry foxes round them star'd,
And for the promis'd feast prepar'd.

Where, Sire, is all this dainty cheer?
Nor turkey, goose, nor hen is here.
These are the phantoms of your brain,
And your sons lick their lips in vain.

O gluttons! says the drooping sire,
Restrain inordinate desire.
Your lick'rish taste you shall deplore,
When peace of conscience is no more.
Does not the hound destroy our pace,
And gins and guns betray our race?
Thieves dread the searching eye of pow'r,
And never feel the quiet hour.
Old age, which few of us shall know,
Now puts a period to my woe.
Would you true happiness attain,
Let honesty your passions rein;

So

So live in credit and esteem,
And the good name you lost, redeem.
  The council's good, a fox replies,
Could we perform what you advise.
Think what our anceftors have done;
A line of thieves from fon to fon:
To us defcends the long difgrace,
And infamy hath mark'd our race.
Though we, like harmlefs fheep fhould feed.
Honeft in thought, in word, and deed;
Whatever hen-rooft is decreas'd,
We fhall be thought to fhare the feaft.
The change fhall never be believ'd:
A loft good name is ne'er retriev'd.
  Nay, then, replies the feeble fox,——
But hark! I hear a hen that clocks;
Go, but be mod'rate in your food;
A chicken too might do me good.

The Father *and his* Children.

A PEASANT on his dying bed,
Thus to his fons attending faid:
  A treafure in my vineyard lies,
Dig deep, and you will find the prize.
Cries one, But father, where's the fpot?
He fighing, dies, and anfwers not.

Scarce

Scarce was the burial service o'er,
Than all hie home, and straight explore
Each inch of ground: leave none unturn'd;
For now with thirst of wealth they burn'd,
With hoe and mattock, rake and shovel,
They dig the soil, and sift and grovel.
They search'd the vineyard round and round,
And though no real hoard was found,
Soon as the summer's close drew near,
A double vintage crown'd the year.
See! says the peasants wisest son,
Our father's legacy is known;
In yon rich purple grapes 'tis seen,
Which but for digging ne'er had been.

From hence we may observe with pleasure,
Industry is a real treasure.

Plutus, Cupid, *and* Time.

AS Plutus, to divert his care,
Walk'd forth one morn to take the air,
Cupid o'ertook his strutting pace.
Each star'd upon the stranger's face,
'Till recollection set 'em right;
For each knew t'other but by sight.
After some complimental talk,
Time met 'em, bow'd, and join'd their walk.

Their

Their chat on various ſubjects ran,
But moſt, what each had done for man.
Plutus aſſumes a haughty air,
Juſt like our purſe-proud fellows here.

 Let kings, ſays he, let coblers tell,
Whoſe gifts among mankind excel.
Conſider courts: What draws their train?
Think you 'tis loyalty, or gain?
That ſtateſman hath the ſtrongeſt hold,
Whoſe tool of politics is gold.
By that, in former reigns, 'tis ſaid,
The knave in power hath ſenates led,
By that alone he ſway'd debates,
Enrich'd himſelf, and beggar'd ſtates.
Forego your boaſt. You muſt conclude,
That's moſt eſteem'd that's moſt purſu'd.
Think too, in what a woeful plight
That wretch muſt live whoſe pocket's light.
Are not his hours by want depreſs'd?
Penurious care corrodes his breaſt.
Without reſpect, or love, or friends,
His ſolitary day deſcends.

 You might, ſays Cupid, doubt my parts,
My knowledge too in human hearts,
Should I the power of gold diſpute,
Which great examples might confute,
I know, when nothing elſe prevails,
Perſuaſive money ſeldom fails;

That

That beauty too, like other wares,
Its price, as well as conscience, bears.
Then marriage, as of late profefs'd,
Is but a money-job at beft.
Confent, compliance may be fold:
But love's beyond the price of gold.
Smugglers there are, who, by retail,
Expofe what they call love, to fale,
Such bargains are an arrant cheat:
You purchafe flatt'ry and deceit.
Thofe who true love have ever try'd,
The common cares of life fupply'd,
No wants endure, no wifhes make,
But 'ev'ry real joy partake.
All comfort on themfelves depends;
They want not power, nor wealth, nor
        friends.
Love then hath ev'ry blifs in ftore:
'Tis friendfhip and 'tis fomething more.
Each other every wifh they give,
Not to know love, is not to live.
: Or love, or money, Time, reply'd,
Were men the queftion to decide,
Would bear the prize: on both intent,
My boon's neglected or mifpent.
'Tis I who meafure vital fpace,
And deal out years to human race.

Though

Though little priz'd, and seldom fought;
Without me, love and gold are nought.
How does the mifer time employ?
Did I e'er fee him life enjoy?
By me forfook, the hoards he won,
Are fcatter'd by his lavifh fon.
By me all ufeful arts are gain'd;
Wealth, learning, wifdom is attain'd.
Who then would think, fince fuch my pow'r,
That e'er I knew an idle hour?
So fubtle and fo fwift I fly,
Love's not more fugitive than I.
Who hath not heard coquettes complain
Of days, months, years mifpent in vain?
Thofe who direct their time aright,
If love or wealth their hopes excite,
In each purfuit fit hours employ'd,
And both by time have been enjoy'd.
How heedlefs then are mortals grown!
How little is their int'reft known!
In ev'ry view they ought to mind me;
For when once loft they never find me.

He fpoke, The gods no more conteft,
And his fuperior gift confeft,
That Time, when truely underftood,
Is the moft precious earthly good.

CHAP.

CHAP. V.

The disappointed MILK-MAID.

HOW poorly your projectors fare,
  Who build their castles in the air!
Still tow'ring on from scheme to scheme,
They top Olympus in a dream;
But waking find, nineteen i'th' score,
Themselves far lower than before,
Of these the instances are many,
And this will serve as well as any.
It happen'd on a summer's day,
A country lass, as fresh as May,
Deck'd in a wholesome russet gown,
Was going to next market town;
So blithe her looks, so simply clean,
You'd take her for a May'day queen,
Save 'stead of garland, says my tale,
Her head bore Brindy's loaded pail.
As on her way she pass'd along,
She hum'd the fragments of a song;
She did not hum for want of thought,
Quite pleas'd with what to sale she brought;
And reckon'd, by her own account,
When all was sold, the whole amount,

                              Thus

Thus fhe — in time, this little ware
May turn to great account with care:
My milk being fold for fo and fo,
I'll buy fome eggs as markets go,
And fet them — at the time I fix,
Thefe eggs will bring as many chicks;
I'll fpare no pains to feed them well,
They'll bring vaft profit when they fell.
With this I'll buy a little pig,
And when 'tis grown up fat and big,
I'll fell it, whether boar or fow,
And with the money buy a cow;
This cow will furely have a calf,
And there the profit's half in half;
Befides there's butter, milk, and cheefe;
To keep the market when I pleafe:
All which will fell, and buy a farm,
Then fhall of fweethearts have a fwarm.
Oh! then for ribbands, gloves, and rings!
Ay! more than twenty pretty things.
One brings me this, another that,
And I fhall have — the Lord knows what.
Fir'd with the thoughts, the frantic lafs,
Of what was thus to come to pafs,
Her heart beat ftrong, fhe gave a bound,
And down came milk-pail on the ground,
Eggs, fowls, pig, hog, ah! well-a day,
Cow, calf, and farm — all fwam away.

A Modern Morning.

AT four on Monday morn, 'tis said,
The Dawn fprung from his truckle bed,
And in a paffion with old Night,
Unbarr'd the rofy gates of Light;
When out his father Phoebus flew,
With fuch amazing force he drew
Almoft unto his higheft noon,
Ere Celia rofe—it was fo foon,
But up fhe rear'd, and rang the bell, ⎫
When in came dainty miftrefs Nell,   ⎬
Oh dear, my lady, e'ent you well?   ⎭
Well!—yes—why what's o'clock?—oh
        heaven! yawning,
A little bit a paft eleven.
No more! why then I'll lay me down;
No, I'll get up child, bring my gown:
My eyes fo ache I fcarce can fee;
Nelly, a little ratifia.
Well now I'll fleep again, begone, ⎫
And get my chocolate by one: ⎬
No; bring my gown, I'll put it on, ⎭
For fee the paltry fun-beams come,
And there's no bearing of the room!
So up fhe rofe, gaping and yawning,
Whilft Nelly waited on her fawning.
Well, Ma'me, your ladyfhip's quite right,
Oh night! the glorious charms of night!

People

People of tafte, who rout and play,
Abhor the odious glare of day:
And, Ma'am, if you approve the night,
The day'll be out of fafhion quite.
Huffy, you flatter me, begone,
And fend my chocolate by John.
Nay, Ma'am.—Then curt'feying, exit Nell;
My lady laughs, and all is well—
When enters John, and bows his head,
And brings the chocolate to bed.
But here the mufe is much to blame,
Stop, Pegafus—oh fy for fhame!
Such tales as thefe you fhould not tell
Ev'n to knowing miftrefs Nell;
Enough is faid by way of jeft,
In fecret filence wrap the reft.

    Then Celia to her toilet goes,
Attended by fome favourite beaux,
Who fribble it around the room,
And curl her hair, and clean the comb,
And do a thoufand monkey tricks,
That you will think difgrac'd the fex.
Nelly! why where's the creature fled?
Put my poft-chaife upon my head.
Your chair and chairmen, Ma'am, is brought.
Stupid! the creature has no thought.

And Ma'am, the milliner is come,
Sh' has brought the broad wheel'd waggon
   .   home,
And 'tis the prettieſt little thing,
Upon my honour.——Bring! bring! bring!
How can you ſtand and talk about it!
You know I die, I die, without it.
In broad wheel'd waggon thus array'd
By beaux and milliner, and maid,
Dear Celia treads the toilet round,
In her fair faithleſs glaſs 'tis found,
And ſo employs her every ſenſe,
'T would take a team to draw her thence.

The Butterfly *and the* Snail.

AS, in the ſunſhine of the morn,
A butterfly, but newly born,
Sat proudly perking on a roſe;
With pert conceit his boſom glows;
His wings all, glorious to behold,
Bedropt with azure, jet, and gold,
Wide he diſplays; the ſpangled dew
Reflects his eyes, and various hue.
   His now forgotten friend, a ſnail,
Beneath his houſe, with ſlimy trail

Crawls

Crawls o'er the grafs; whom when he
    fpies,
In wrath he to the gard'ner cries:
    What means yon peafant's daily toil,
From choaking weeds to rid the foil?
Why wake you to the morning's care?
Why with new arts correct the year?
Why grows the peach with crimfon hue?
And why the plumb's inviting blue?
Were they to feaft his tafte defign'd,
That vermin of voracious kind?
Crufh then the flow, the pilf'ring race;
So purge thy garden from difgrace.
    What arrogance! the fnail reply'd;
How infolent is upftart pride!
Hadft thou not thus with infult vain,
Provok'd my patience to complain,
I had conceal'd thy meaner birth,
Nor trac'd thee to the fcum of earth.
For fcarce nine funs have wak'd the
    hours;
To fwell the fruit, and paint the flow'rs,
Since I thy humbler life furvey'd,
In bafe and fordid guife array'd;
A hideous infect, vile, unclean,
You dragg'd a flow and noifome train;
And from your fpider-bowels drew
Foul film, and fpun the dirty clue.

I own my humble life, good friend;
Snail was I born, and snail shall end.
And what's a butterfly at best,
He's but a catterpillar, dress'd;
And all thy race, a numerous feed,
Shall prove of catterpillar breed.

All upstarts insolent in place,
Remind us of their vulgar race.

CHAP. VI.

The Power *of* Innocence.

A NORTHERN pair, we wave the name,
Rich, young, and not unknown to fame,
When first the nuptial state they try'd,
With fabled gods in pleasure vy'd.
New to the mighty charm they feel
A joy that all their looks reveal.
We love whate'er has power to please,
So nature's ancient law decrees;
And thus the pair, while each had pow'r,
To bless the fond sequester'd hour,
With mutual love enraptur'd glow,
And love in kind complacence show.

But

But when familiar charms no more
Infpire the blifs they gave before,
Each lefs delighting, lefs was lov'd,
Now this, now that was difapprov'd;
Some trifling fault, which love conceal'd,
Indiff'rence every day reveal'd.
Complacence flies, Negle&t fucceeds;
Negle&t, Difdain and Hatred breeds.
The wifh to pleafe forfakes the breaft,
The wifh to rule has each poffefs'd,
Perpetual war, that wifh to gain,
They wage, alas! but wage in vain.
Now hope of conqueft fwells the heart
No more—at length content to part;
The rural feat, that fylvan fhade,
Where firft the nuptial vows were paid;
That feat attefts the dire intent,
And hears the parting fettlement.
This houfe, thefe fields, my lady's own,
Sir John muft ride to town alone.
The chariot waits—they bid adieu;
But ftill the chariot waits in view.
Tom tires with waiting long in doubt,
And lights a pipe—and fmokes it out—
Myfterious! wherefore this delay?
The fequel fhall the caufe difplay.
One lovely girl the lady bore,
Dear pledge of joys fhe taftes no more;

The

The father's, mother's darling fhe,
Now lifp'd and prattled at their knee.
Sir John now rifing to depart,
Turn'd to the darling of his heart,
And cry'd with ardour in his eye,
"Come, Betfey, bid mama good-bye."
The lady, trembling, anfwer'd, No —
"Go kifs papa, my Betfey go.
"Sir John, the child fhall live with me."
"The child herfelf fhall choofe," faid he.
Poor Betfey look'd at each by turns,
And each the ftarting tear difcerns.
My lady afks, with doubt and fear,
"Will you not live with me, my dear?"
"Yes," half refolv'd, replied the child,
And, half fupprefs'd her tears   fhe fmil'd.
"Come, Betfey, cried Sir John, you'll go,
"And live with dear papa, I know."
"Yes," Betfey cried — the lady then
Addrefs'd the wand'ring child again.
"The time to live with both is o'er,
"This day we part to meet no more:
"Choofe then" — her grief o'erflow'd her
        breaft,
And tears burft out too long fupprefs'd.
The   child,   which   tears   and   chiding
        join'd,
Suppos'd papa difpleas'd, unkind;

                                And

And try'd with all her little skill,
To sooth his oft relenting will.
"Do, cry'd the lisper, papa! do,
"Love dear mama!—mama loves you!"
Subdu'd the force of manly pride,
No more his looks his heart bely'd,
The tender transport forc'd its way,
They both confess'd each other's sway;
And, prompted by the social smart,
Breast rush'd to breast, and heart to heart.
Each kiss'd their Betsey o'er and o'er,
And Tom drove empty from the door.

———————

PART II.

*A Collection of little Nosegays for the further
Ornament of the* FLOWER-BASKET.

CHAP. I.
The Miser *and the* Mouse.

AS Pedro stalk'd around his house,
   The jealous miser spy'd a mouse.
How now! cries he, what dost thou here? —
Sir, says the mouse, dismiss your fear;
I came not with the hopes of food,
But for the sake of — solitude.

To an affected Old Maid.

THO' papa and mama, my dear,
   So prettily you call;
Yet you, methinks, yourself appear
   The grandmother of all.

A Character.

Sometimes to sense, sometimes to nonsense
      leaning,
And always blund'ring round about his
      meaning.

On

On Snow *that melted on a* Lady's *Breast.*

Those envious flakes which came in haste,
    To prove her breast so fair;
Grieving to find themselves surpass'd,
    Dissolv'd into a tear.

A logical Epitaph *on Mr.* Foote.

Here lies one Foote, whose death may
    thousands save,
For Death has now one Foote within the
    grave.

Sauce for Incivility.

I often bow; your hat you never stir;
So, once for all, your humble Servant — Sir.

The Wonder.

Both Man and Wife, as bad as bad can be;
I wonder they no better should agree.

The Smithfield *Wedding.*

When Loveless married Lady Jenny,
Whose beauty was the ready penny;
He chose her, as you do old plate,
Not for the fashion, but the weight.

Old Time *to the* Antiquarian.

Plague on't! says Time to Thomas Hearn,
Whatever I forget, you learn.

On.

On a Company of bad Dancers to good Music.

How ill the motion with the music suits!
So Orpheus fiddled, and so danc'd the brutes.

On an Opera.

An op'ra, like a pill'ry, may be said
To nail our ears down, but expose our head.

A droll Epitaph in Grantham Church-yard.

John Palfryman, who lieth here,
Was aged twenty-four year:
And in this place his mother lies;
Also his father, when he dies.

On a man eating Rotten Cheese.

Jack eating rotten cheese, did say,
Like Sampson I my thousands slay.
I vow, quoth Roger, so you do,
And with the self same weapon too.

On the Death of an Undertaker.

Subdu'd by death, here death's great herald
        lies,
And adds a trophy to his victories;
Yet sure he was prepar'd, who while he'd
        breath
Made it his business still to look for death.

CHAP.

CHAP. II.

The contented Farmer.

I Eat, drink and sleep, and do what I please:
The King at St. James's can do only these.

On one who made long Epitaphs.

Friend! for your Epitaphs I'm griev'd,
   Where still so much is said;
One half will never be believ'd,
   The other never read.

On a Collar of a Dog, presented by Mr. Pope
to the Prince of Wales.

I am his Highness' dog at Kew;
Pray tell me, Sir, whose dog are you?

Mr. Pope's Epitaph. *By himself.*

Heroes and Kings! your distance keep;
In peace let one poor poet sleep,
Who never flatter'd folks like you:
Let Horace blush, and Virgil too.

Mr. Prior's Epitaph. *By himself.*

Nobles and heralds, by your leave,
   Here lies the bones of Matthew Prior,
The son of Adam and of Eve;
   Let Bourbon or Nassau go higher.

Mr.

Mr. Gay's Epitaph. By *himself.*

Life is a jest, and all things show it;
I thought so once, but now I know it.

On a Butcher's *marrying a* Tanner's *Daughter.*

A fitter match than this could not have been,
For now the flesh is married to the skin.

A modern Dinner.

With lace bedizen'd comes her man,
And I must dine with Lady *Anne:*
A silver service loads the board;
Of eatables, a slender hoard.
"Your pride, and not your victuals, spare?
"I came to dine, and not to stare,"

On our imitating the French *Fashions.*

The formal ape endeavours, all he can,
With antic tricks, to imitate a man:
Parisian fops, no less ambitious, seem
To have a face, an air, a tail like them.
From whom our taste thus only disagrees,
These mimic apes—and we but mimic these.

On a Lady with fine Eyes and a bad Voice.

Lucetta's charms our hearts surprise,
    At once with love and wonder:
She bears Jove's lightning in her eyes,
    But in her voice his thunder.

The

The Lovers *Conteſt.*

My love and I for kiſſes play'd;
    She wou'd keep ſtakes; I was content:
But when I won, ſhe wou'd be paid;
    I angry, aſk'd her what ſhe meant?
Nay, ſince, ſays ſhe, you wrangle thus in
       vain,
Give me my kiſſes back, take your's again.

To an angry Rival.

'Tis not the fear of death, or ſmart,
    Makes me averſe to fight;
But to preſerve a tender heart,
    Not mine, but Caelia's right.
Then let your fury be ſuppreſs'd,
    Not me, but Caelia ſpare;
Your ſword is welcome to my breaſt,
    When Caelia is not there.

On Sir John Vanbrough, *the Poet and Architect.*

Lie heavy on him, Earth! for he
Laid many a heavy load on thee.

On Leonidas *and his three hundred* Spartans.

To ſtop the Perſian monarch's ſway,
    In vain the ſwelling ocean roſe;
In vain his progreſs to delay,
    The lofty mountains interpoſe.

                        Rous'd

Rous'd by the Spartan chief to fight,
　　When lo! his slender band obeys;
These turn'd th' unnumber'd host to flight,
　　Blush then, ye mountains and ye seas!

Fast *and* Loose.

Colin was married in all haste,
　　And now to rack doth run;
So knitting of himself too fast,
　　He hath himself undone.

To Avaro.

Thus to the master of a house;
Which, like a church, would starve a mouse;
Which never guest had entertain'd,
Nor meat, nor wine, its floors had stain'd
I said — Well, Sir, 'tis vastly neat;
But were d'you drink and where d'you eat?
If one may judge, by rooms so fine,
It costs you more in mops than wine.

The Virtuoso.

What, to the valiant knight of Spain,
　　Was Donna del Tobofo; —
Such is the idle of his brain
　　To every virtuofo.

Don

Don Quixote to a goddeſs lifted,
    An home-ſpun country laſs;
Each grain of corn the damſel ſifted,
    With him for pearls could paſs.

Whate'er the curious deifies,
    It thus his fancy warms,
And gives to ſhell and butterflies
    Imaginary charms.

But let not thoſe that look more grave,
    Themſelves their wiſdom pride on;
Since every man muſt ſometimes have
    His hobby-horſe to ride on.

CHAP. III.

A Caution to the Credulous.

WHEN dukes in town aſk thee to dine,
    . To taſte their roaſt, and ſmack their
      wine;
Or take thee to their country-ſeat,
To break their dogs, or bleſs their meat —
Ah! dream not on preferment ſoon —
Thou'rt not their friend — but their buffoon.

                    Mutual

Mutual Pity.

Tom, ever jovial; ever gay,
　　To appetite a flave,
Still rakes and drinks his life away,
　　And laughs to fee me grave.

'Tis thus that we two difagree:
　　So diff'rent is our whim;
The fellow fondly laughs at me —
　　While I could cry for him.

The Stage of Life.

Our life's a journey in a winter's day;
Some only break their faft, and fo away:
Others ftay dinner, and depart full fed,
The deepeft age but fups and goes to bed:
He's moft in debt that lingers out the day;
Who dies betimes, has lefs and lefs to pay.

True Riches.

Irus, tho' wanting gold and lands,
　　Lives chearful, eafy, and content; —
Carvus unblefs'd, with twenty hands
　　Employ'd to count his yearly rent.

Sages of Lombard; tell me which
　　Of thefe you think poffeffes more?
One, with his poverty, is rich,
　　And one, with all his wealth, is poor.

O.

On one who died of the Hip.

Death, by a conduct strange and new,
Prov'd here th'effect and motive too:
Ned met the blow he meant to fly;
And dy'd, becaufe he fear'd to die.

On the Clerk of a Country Parish.

Here lies, within this tomb, fo calm,
   Old Giles: pray found his knell;
Who thought no fong was like a pfalm,
   No mufic like a bell.

On the Sexton of a Country Parish.

Come, let us rejoice, merry boys, at his
       fall;
For, if he had liv'd, he'd have buried us all.

On a Bee ftifled in Honey.

From flow'r to flow'r, with eager pains,
   See the blefs'd bufy lab'rer fly;
When all that from the toil fhe gains,
   Is in the fweets fhe hoards to die.

'Tis thus, would man the truth believe,
   With life's foft fweets, each fav'rite joy,
If we tafte wifely, they relieve:
   But, if we plunge too deep, deftroy.

C H A P. IV.

On Dancing: *to a Lady.*

MAY I prefume in humble lays,
　My dancing fair, thy fteps to praife?
Whilft this grand maxim I advance,
That all the world is but a dance.

　That human kind, both man and woman,
Do dance, is evident and common.
David himfelf, that godlike king,
We know could dance as well as fing:
Folks, who at court would keep their
　　　ground,
Muft dance attendance the year round:
Whole nations dance, gay frifking France
Has led the Englifh many a dance!
And fome believe both France and Spain
Intend to take us out again.

　All nature is one ball, we find,
The water dances to the wind:
The fea itfelf, at night and noon,
Rifes and dances to the moon:
The moon around the earth does tread
A Chefhire round, yet ne'er looks red;
The earth and planets round the fun
Still dance, nor will their dance be done,
　　　　　　　　　　　　Till

Till nature in one blaſt be blended,
Then may we ſay, the ball is ended.

On a Fan.

Flavia the laſt and ſlighteſt toy
Can with reſiſtleſs art employ.
This fan in meaner hands would prove
An engine of ſmall force in love:
Yet ſhe, with graceful air and mine,
Not to be told or ſafely ſeen,
Directs its wanton motion ſo,
That it wounds more than Cupid's bow,
Gives coolneſs to the matchleſs dame,
To ev'ry other breaſt a flame.

To Chloe *weeping.*

See, whilſt thou weep'ſt, fair Chloe, ſee
The world in ſympathy with thee.
The chearful birds no longer ſing,
Each drops his head, and hangs his wing.
The clouds have bent their boſom lower,
And ſhed their ſorrow in a ſhow'r.
The brooks beyond their limit flow,
And louder murmurs ſpeak their woe:
The nymphs and ſwains adopt thy cares,
They heave thy ſighs, and weep thy tears.
Fantaſtic nymph! that grief ſhould move
Thy heart obdurate againſt love.

Strange

Strange tears! whofe pow'r can foften all,
But that dear breaft on which they fall.

On Mifs Gunning.

Cupid, one day, to fhow his cunning,
Laid by his bow and took to *Gunning.*

On the Marriage of on Old Maid.

Caelia, a coquette in her prime,
 The vaineft, fickleft thing alive;
Behold the ftrange effects of time,
 Marries, and dotes at forty-five.
Thus weather-cocks, that, for a while,
 Have turn'd about with every blaft;
Grown old, and deftitute of oil,
 Ruft to a point, and fix at laft.

The Dart: *to the Lady* L——M——.

Whene'er I look, I may defcry
A little face peep thro' that eye:
Sure that's the boy, who wifely chofe
His throne among fuch beams as thofe;
Which, if his quiver chance to fall,
May ferve for darts to kill withal.

CHAP.

CHAP. IV.

Upon a Path on a Lady's Face.

THAT artful fpeck upon her face,
 Had been a foil on one lefs fair;
In her it hides a wounding grace,
 And fhe in mercy plac'd it there.

The true Reafon.

Selinda ne'er appears till night;
 And what won't female envy fay?
But well fhe knows, fhe fhines fo bright,
 Her prefence may fupply the day.

On the King's *Statue, placed on the top of* Bloomfbury *Steeple.*

 At Stock's-market and Charing,
 No longer ftand ftaring,
But turn your eyes this way, good people:
 For a man on a horfe,
 Is a matter in courfe:
See here is a man on a fteeple!

On the Power of Mufic.

The force of mufic beft is found,
When foul fubfervient is to found.

To a Lady *stung by a* Bee.

To heal the wound a bee had made,
    Upon my Delia's face,
Its honey to the part she laid,
    And bid me kiss the place.

Pleas'd, I obey'd, and from the wound
    Suck'd both the sweet and smart;
The honey on my lips I found
    The sting within my heart.

To the incomparable Miss ***.

As with a friend on Sunday last,
    I tripp'd along the Mall,
Sniggering at each powder'd beau,
    And gazing at each belle;

A sudden buz ran through the croud,
    With "There! that's she in green!"
I could not for my soul devise,
    What all the noise did mean.

At length, advancing farther on,
    Where still the hum increas'd,
I saw you, lovely maid—I did,
    And then my wonder ceas'd.

On

On Peter White.

Peter White will ne'er go right;
   Wou'd you know the reason why:
Where'er he goes, he follows his nose,
   And that ftands all awry.

On a virtuous *and* beautiful *Lady.*

Underneath this ftone doth lie,
As much virtue as could die;
Which, when alive, did vigour give,
To as much beauty as could live.

On Mary *Countefs Dowager of* Pembroke.

Underneath this marble hearfe,
Lies the fubject of all verfe:
Sidney's fifter, Pembroke's mother.
Death ere thou haft kill'd another,
Fair, and learn'd, and good as fhe,
Time fhall throw a dart at thee.

On Mrs. Corbet, *who died of a Cancer in her Breaft. By Mr.* Pope.

Here reft a woman, good without pretence,
Blefs'd with plain reafon and with fober fenfe.
No conqueft fhe, but o'er herfelf, defir'd,
No art effay'd, but not to be admir'd:
Paffion and pride were to her foul unknown;
Convinc'd that virtue only is our own:

So

So unaffected, fo compos'd a mind,
So firm, yet foft; fo ftrong, yet fo refign'd;
Heav'n, as its pureft gold, by tortures try'd;
The faint fuftain'd it — but the woman dy'd.

On *Mr*. Craggs. *By Mr*. Pope.

Statefman, yet friend to truth! of foul
    fincere,
In action faithful, and in honour clear!
Who broke no promife, ferv'd no private
    end;
Who gain'd no title, and who loft no friend!
Ennobled by himfelf, by all approv'd,
Prais'd, wept, and honour'd — by the mufe
    he lov'd.

On *Sir* Ifaac Newton.

Approach, ye wife of foul, with awe divine,
'Tis Newton's name that confecrates this
    fhrine!
That fun of knowledge, whofe meridian ray
Kindled the gloom of nature into day!
That foul of fcience, that unbounded mind,
That genius, which ennobled human kind!
Confefs'd fupreme of men, his country's
    pride;
And half efteem'd an angel till he dy'd:
                Who,

Who, in the eye of heav'n, like Enoch
    ftood,
And through the paths of knowledge walk'd
    with God;
Whofe fame extends, a fea without a fhore!
Who but forfook. one world, to know the
    laws of more.

On the fame. By Mr. Pope.

Nature and nature's laws lay hid in night;
Got faid, "Let Newton be!" and all was
    light.

On an Infant.

Beneath a fleepy infant lies,
    To earth her body's fent;
More glorious fhe'll hereafter rife,
    Tho' not more innocent.

When the archangel's trump fhall blow,
    And fouls to bodies join,
Millions will wifh their lives below
    Had been as fhort as thine.

F 5   CHAP.

C H A P. VI.

On thofe who die *for their* Country.

HOW fleep the brave, who fink to reft,
By all their country's wifhes blefs'd!
When fpring with dewy fingers cold,
Returns to deck their hallow'd mould,
She there fhall drefs a fweeter fod,
Than Fancy's feet have ever trod.
By fairy hands their knell is rung,
By forms unfeen their dirge is fung;
There Honour comes, a pilgrim grey,
To blefs the turf that wraps their clay!
And Freedom fhall a while repair,
To dwell a weeping hermit there.

On Stephen *the* Fiddler.

Stephen and Time are now both even;
Stephen beat Time, now Time's beat Stephen.

Infcription on an Urn at Lord Cork's, *to the Memory of the* Dog Hector.

Strangers, behold the mighty Hector's tomb!
See! to what end both dogs and heroes come.
Thefe are the honours, by his mafter paid,
To Hector's manes and lamented fhade:

Nor

Nor words nor honours can enough commend
The focial dog—nay more, the faithful
    friend!
From nature all his principles he drew,
By nature faithful, vigilant, and true:
His looks and voice his inward thoughts ex-
    prefs'd,
He growl'd in anger, and in love carefs'd.
No human falfehood lurk'd beneath his heart,
Brave without boafting, gen'rous without art.
When Hector's virtues, man, proud man!
    difplays,
Truth fhall adorn his tomb with Hector's
    praife.

An EPITAPH *on an* honeft Fellow.
To the memory
Of
SIGNOR FIDO,
An Italian of good extraction!
Who came into England,
Not to bite us, like moft of his countrymen,
But to gain an honeft livelihood.
He hunted not after fame,
  Yet he acquired it;
Regardlefs of the praife of his friends,
But moft fenfible of their love.

              Though

Though he lived amongst the great,
He neither learn'd nor flatter'd any vice.
He was no Bigot,
Tho' he doubted of none of the 39 articles.
And if to follow nature,
And to respect the laws of society,
Be philosophy,
He was a perfect philosopher,
A faithful friend,
An agreeable companion,
A loving husband,
Distinguish'd by a numerous offspring,
All which he lived to see take good courses.
In his old age he retired
To the house of a clergyman in the country,
Where he finish'd his earthly race,
And died an honour and an example to
The whole species.
Reader,
This stone is guiltless of flattery,
For he to whom it is inscribed
Was not a MAN,
But a
GREYHOUND.

Modern Charity.

So little given at the chapel-door!
This people, doubtless, must be poor;

So

So much at gaming thrown away,
No nation sure, so rich as they.
Britons! 'twere greatly for your glory,
Shou'd those who may transmit your story,
Their notions of your grandeur frame,
Not as you give, but as you game.

On a Shadow.

The sun now clear, serene the skies,
Where'er you go, as fast the shadow flies;
A cloud succeeds; the sunshine now is o'er;
The fleeting phantom fled, is seen no more.
With your bright day, its progress too does
   end;
See here, vain man! the picture of your
  friend.

On a Pale Lady.

Whence comes it, that, in Clara's face,
The lily only has a place?——
Why, 'tis because the absent rose
Is gone to paint her husband's nose.

On a young Lady's *refusing to show her* Hand.

No argument could Caelia move,
With strong reluctance still she strove,
  Her lovely hand to hide:

The

The cafe is plain; fhe was afraid,
That, plac'd in view, it might be faid,
   'Twas by her hand they dy'd.

On a bad Tranflation.

His work now done, he'll publifh it, no
   doubt;
For fure I am, that "murther will come out."

On a certain Poet.

Thy verfes are *eternal*, O! my friend;
For he that reads them reads them to *no* end.

Written on a Window, under a Vow, againft
Matrimony.

The lady who this refolution took,
Wrote it on glafs to fhow it might be broke.

On the fair Sabina.

See, fee fhe wakes; Sabina wakes!
   And now the fun begins to rife!
Lefs glorious is the morn that breaks
   From his bright beams than her fair eyes.

On a hafty Marriage.

Marry'd! 'tis well; a mighty blefling!
But poor's the joy, no coin poffefling.
In ancient times, when folks did wed,
'Twas to be one at board and bed;
               But

But hard's his cafe, who can't afford
His chamber either bed or board.

On an old Woman, who fold Earthen Ware at
Chefter.

Beneath this ftone lies Kath'rine Gray,
Chang'd from a bufy life, to lifelefs clay:
By earth and clay fhe got her pelf,
And now fhe's turn'd to earth herfelf.
Ye weeping friends, let me advife,
Abate your grief, and dry your eyes;
For what avails a flood of tears?
Who knows but, in a run of years,
In fome tall pitcher, or broad pan,
She in her fhop may be again.

On a fcolding Wife *who died in her* Sleep.

Here lies the quinteffence of noife and ftrife;
Or, in one word, here lies a fcolding wife:
Had death not took her when her mouth
       was fhut,
He durft not for his ears have touch'd the flut;

On Twin Sifters.

Fair marble tell to future days,
   That here two virgin fifters lie,
Whofe life employ'd each tongue in praife,
   Whofe death gave tears to ev'ry eye.

                       In

In ftature, beauty, years and fame,
   Together as they grew, they fhone;
So much alike, fo much the fame,
   That death miftook them both for one.

On a celebrated Mifs.

Frefh as the fpring, and like Aurora fair,
Clarinda iffues forth, the public care!
Where'er fhe moves, admiring crouds refort,
Whilft round her charms the Loves and
    Graces fport.
Her eyes the hearts of heedlefs fops beguile,
Who catch each glance — and feed upon
    each fmile:
But the blefs'd youth, diftinguifh'd from
    the throng,
Who hears th'inchanting accents of her
    tongue;
Her native wit, her more than common fenfe,
Exprefs'd with fweet, bewitching diffidence;
Owns in her mind more pow'rful beauty lies,
And fcarce obferves the luftre of her eyes.

Written by Mr. Pope, *on a Glafs, with the Earl*
of Chefterfield's *Diamond Pencil.*

Accept a miracle, inftead of wit,
See two dull lines by Stanhope's pencil writ.

END of the SIXTH VOLUME.

GULLIVER'S LECTURES
VOL. VII.

CONTAINING

THE

MERRY COMPANION;

OR,

ORACLE

OF

MIRTH AND WISDOM.

VOL. VII.   A

GULLIVER'S LECTURES

VOL. III.

PREFACE.

I AM now laying before my little Miſſes and Maſters a collection of the moſt approved jeſts and ſmart ſayings, of which, I hope, all my pretty readers will make a proper uſe; for nothing is ſo dangerous as *wit* in the mouths of either Maſters or Miſſes. I do not mean by this to diſcourage them from the peruſal of books of this kind; but I would wiſh them to obſerve, that though real wit, properly reſtrained, adds much to the reputation of the poſſeſſor, yet a miſapplication of it is ſure to procure enemies, and never ſecures a real friend.

The true uſe of wit is to entertain and amuſe the company we may happen to fall

into;

into; but it muft be ufed fparingly, and as
it is very fcarce, be brought out only on
very particular occafions. Of all things,
however, avoid fhowing your talent for wit,
if you really poffefs it, where it may give
anger to any one in company; for if your
wit hurts any one, it will make that perfon
your enemy, and that one may make you
many. The beft way to avoid offence is
to be modeft and humble, and to be cautious how you jeft with any one.

In the fecond part, I have collected the
moft celebrated maxims and reflexions from
the works of the moft approved writings
of the ancients and moderns; and thefe I
would recommend to the moft ferious attention of my little readers, as they will
not fail properly to correct their wit,
form their judgement, and improve their
heart.

PART I.
Jests and smart Sayings.

CHAP. I.

A FAMOUS punster called for some pipes in a tavern, and complained they were too short. The drawer said, they had no other, and those were but just come in. "Aye, said the other, I see your master has not bought them very long."

A conceited fellow, who fancied himself a poet, asked Nat Lee, if it was not easy to write like a madman, as he did? "No, answered Nat, but it is easy to write like a fool, as you do."

A lady being asked, how she liked a gentleman's singing, who had a very stinking breath? "The words are good, said she, but the air is intolerable."

The

The Duchefs of Newcaftle, who wrote plays and romances in King Charles the Second's time, afked Bifhop Wilkins, how fhe fhould get up to the world in the moon, which he had difcovered; for as the journey muft needs be very long, there would be no poffibility of going through with it, without refting on the way? "Oh, madam, faid the bifhop, as your grace has built fo many caftles in the air, you cannot want a place to bait at."

Notwithftanding Mr. Tagg valued himfelf much on his wit, he was frequently overmatched, and fometimes let down, even by the common people. An inftance of this I once was witnefs of, at an inn upon the road. When Tom, being informed that a carrier who ftopped at the door, was an arch fellow, thus attacked him: "Why, they tell me, my friend that you are a very wife man." "May be fo," fays the fellow. "And that you know all London, continued Tom, and every body in it. Pray, can you tell where I live?" "In Knave's-Acre," fays the carrier. "Aye, but I am about to move," fays Tom. "And that will be to Bridewell," quoth the other.

In

In a vifit Queen Elifabeth made to the famous Lord Chancellor Bacon, at a fmall country-feat he had built for himfelf, before his preferment; fhe afked him, how it came to pafs that he made his houfe too fmall for him? "It is not I, Madam, anfwered he, who have made my houfe too fmall for myfelf; but your Majefty has made me too big for my houfe."

King William III. being upon a march, for fome fecret expedition, was intreated by a general to tell him what his defign was. The king, inftead of telling him, afked him, if he could keep a fecret. The general faid, he could. "Well, anfwered his majefty, and I can keep a fecret as well as you."

Mr. T——s C——r, the comedian, one day begged of his father to let him have an hundred pounds, which he faid would make him perfectly eafy in his affairs. "Why, The', faid the father, it is very ftrange that you cannot live upon your falary, your benefit, and other advantages; when I was of your age, I never fpent any of my father's money." "I don't know that, anfwered the fon, but I am fure you have fpent a great deal of my father's money."

A gentleman, not fo remarkable for his oeconomy as his wit and humour, was one day rallying the late Peter Walters on his avarice. "For my part, quoth the gentleman, I don't know any difference between a ſhilling and a ſix-pence, for when one is changed it is gone, and ſo is the other." "Aye, ſays Peter, my old friend, you may not know the difference between a ſhilling and a ſix-pence now; but, believe me, you will, whk.n you come to be worth eighteen pence."

A notorious thief, being to be tried for his life, confeſſed the robbery he was charged with. The judge hereupon directed the jury to find him guilty upon his own confeſſion. The jury having laid their heads together, brought him in *not guilty.* The judge bid them conſider of it again: but they ſtill brought in their verdict *not guilty.* And when the judge aſked the reaſon, the foreman replied, "There is reaſon enough, my Lord, for we all know him to be one of the greateſt liars in the world."

A parcel of merry fellows, in a country town, having a mind to humbug an honeſt toping farmer, way-laid him one dark evening, on his return from a neigbouring village,

lage, where he had got exceeding drunk, and taking him off his horfe, made preten- ces of rifling his pockets of what he had, but took nothing from him, and then fet him upon his horfe again, with his face to the tail. The horfe, well acquainted with the way home, carried his mafter fafe into the yard; where the wife, hearing her hus- band's voice, went out with a candle, and feeing his fituation, haftily enquired the cau- fe. "Ah, Mary, fays the farmer, as well as he could fpeak, I have been robbed and murthered by a parcel of rogues, who have ftolen all my money, and, what vexes me more, they have cut my horfe's head off."

Young Squire Booby, juft come from his firft term at the univerfity, was willing to give his parents a fpecimen of his improve- ment there. "Father, fays he, I can chop logic." "Aye, fays his father, how is that, Tom?" "Why, fays the fon, here de zee, father, are a couple of fowls at table; I can prove there are three fowls." "How's that?" quoth the father. "Why, there is one, faid Tom, and there is two, pointing to the difh, and don't one and two make three, father."——"Well, damme, faid the

father,

father, Tom is become a conjurer: you take one fowl, and I eat the other, and let him have the third for his logic."

Dr. Heylin, a noted author, efpecially for his cofmography, happened to lofe his way going to Oxford, in the foreft of Which-wood; and being then attended by one of his brother's men, the man earneftly intreated him to lead the way; but the doctor told him he did not know the way. "What, faid the man, have you written a defcription of the whole world, and cannot find the way out of this little wood?"

A Traveller, coming into the kitchen of an inn, in a very cold night, ftood fo clofe to the fire, that he burnt his boots. An arch rogue, who fat in the chimney-corner, cried out to him, "Sir, you'll burn your fpurs prefently." "My boots you mean, I fuppofe?" faid the gentleman." "No, Sir, replied the other, they are burnt already."

An Irifh fellow, vaunting of his birth and family, affirmed, that when he came firft to England, he cut fuch a figure, that bells were rung through every town as he paffed to London. "Aye, fays a gentleman in company, I fuppofe that was, becaufe you came up in a waggon with a bell-team."

Two

Two gentlemen, the one named Woodcock, the other Fuller, walking together, happened to fee an owl; fays the laft, "That bird is very like a Woodcock." "You are wrong, fays the other, for it is Fuller in the head, Fuller in the eyes, and Fuller all over.

A countryman enquiring the way to Newgate, an arch fellow who heard him, faid, he'd fhow him the way immediately; "Do but crofs the kennel, faid he, to yon goldfmith's fhop, and move off with one of the filver tankards, and it will bring you thither prefently."

A certain captain, who had made a greater figure than his income would bear, and his regiment not being paid as they expected, was forced to lay town part of his equipage. A few days after, walking by the road-fide he faw one of his foldiers loufing himfelf under a hedge; "What are you doing there?" faid the captain. "Why faith, Sir, anfwered the foldier, I am following your example; getting rid of part of my retinue."

CHAP.

C H A P. II.

A Lord Mayor waiting upon King Charles the Second, who happened to be at that time in the park feeding the ducks with his hat in his hand, the mayor defired he might not fpeak till his majefty was covered; "Phoo, phoo, fays the king, you may go on very fafely, it is to the *ducks* I pull my hat off."

A gentleman, going to take water at Whitehall ftairs, cried out, as he came near the place, "Who can fwim?" "I, mafter," faid forty bawling mouths; when the gentleman obferving one flinking away, called after him; but the fellow turning about faid, "Sir, I cannot fwim." "Then you are the man, faid the gentleman, for you will at leaft take care of me for your own fake."

A very ingenious man was walking along Cheapfide, whom a hectoring blade meeting, thruft from the wall, faying, he did not choofe to give every faucy jackanapes the wall. "But I do," faid the gentleman, and fo paffed on.

A

A country farmer was observed never to be in a good humour when he was hungry, which caused his wife to watch carefully the time of his coming home, and always to have dinner ready on the table. One day he surprised her, and she had only time to set a mess of broth ready for him. He, according to custom, began to open his pipes, and maunder over it, forgetting what he was about, and burnt his mouth to some purpose. His wife, seeing him in that condition, comforts him in the following manner; "See how it is now; had you kept your breath to cool your pottage; you had not burnt your mouth, John."

One gallopping over some ploughed land, meeting a country fellow, asked him if that was the way to *Tame;* "Yes, says he, to tame your horse; if he was as wild as a buck."

Two country fellows meeting, one asked the other, What news? He answered he knew no other news but that he saw a very great wind last Friday. "See a wind," says the other. "Yes, see it," replied he again. "Prithee, what was it like? said he. "Like, said the other, why, it was like to blow my house down."

A

A gentleman riding down a fteep hill, and being afraid the foot of it was boggifh, called out to a clown that was ditching, and afked him if it was hard at the bottom. The fellow replied, "Aye, aye, 'tis very hard at the bottom, I'll warrant you." Which encouraged the gentleman to ride very confidently down the hill; but in fix or feven yards ftepping, his horfe funk up to the belly in a bog, which made the gentleman kick and whip, and curfe and fwear at the fellow, who was ftill within hearing; and to whom he called out, "You country rogue, did not you tell me it was hard at the bottom?" The ditcher anfwered, "Yes I did, and it is, Sir, but you are not at the bottom yet by a mile."

A French marquis being one day at dinner at Roger Williams's, the famous punfter and publican, was boafting of the happy genius of his nation, in projecting all the fine modes and fafhions; particularly the ruffles, "which, he faid, was de fine ornament to de hand; and had been followed by de oder nation." Roger allowed what he faid, but obferved at the fame time, "that the Englifh, according to cuftom, had made a great impro-

improvement upon their invention, by adding a fhirt to it."

A gentleman called for fome beer at a friend's table, and finding it very flat, gave it back to the fervant without drinking, "What! fays the mafter of the houfe, don't you like the beer? it is not to be found fault with." "No, anfwered the other, we fhould never fpeak ill of the dead."

A lady's age happening to be queftioned, fhe affirmed it was but forty, and called a gentleman who was in company to deliver his opinion. "Coufin, fays fhe, do you believe I am right, when I fay I am but forty?" "I am fure, madam, faid he, I ought not to difpute it; for I have conftantly heard you fay fo for above thefe ten years."

A fenator, who is not efteemed the wifeft man in the houfe, has a cuftom of fhaking his head when another fpeaks; which giving offence to a particular perfon, he complained of the indignity. Hereupon, one who had been acquainted with the firft gentleman from a child, as he told the houfe, affured them it was only the effects of an ill habit; "For, fays he, though he often fhakes his head, there is nothing in it."

A

A gentleman on his travels abroad, for it could not be in England, had lodged at an inn, where they made him a moft extravagant bill for his entertainment, which he difputed with the waiter; but to no purpofe, for he found himfelf obliged to pay it. Juft as the horfes were ordered out, the landlord, with his ufual civility, came to wifh him a good journey; and while they were talking, the oftler ftepped up to his mafter, and complained of what damage the rats had done the preceding night. "Why, are you much troubled with rats," faid gentleman, "Oh, intolerably! faid the inn-keeper, they do me infinite mifchief." "I think, returned the gentleman, I could put you in a way to get rid of them." "Sir, fays the other, I fhould be much obliged to your honour." "There is nothing fo eafy and fo certain as this fcheme I fhall tell you, quoth the gentleman: Only make them fuch an extravagant bill as you have made me, and not one of them will come to your houfe again."

A country 'fquire being in company with his fweetheart, and wanting his fervant, cried out, "Where is my blockhead? "Upon your fhoulders," faid the lady.

A

A drunken fellow having made away with all his goods, except his feather-bed, was at length obliged to part with that too; for which, being reproved by some friends, "Phoo! says he, I am very well, thank heaven, and why should I keep my bed?"

Two gentlemen rode up to an inn on the road, and called for some wine and water: It was brought to them in a foul tankard; which one of them took up, and turning it round, said to his companion, "Sure this is not a silver tankard! it has a very brassy look." Phoo! says the other, it is only the reflection of your countenance."

A man asked Tom Trip how he lived these hard times? "Why, upon my wit," says Tom. "I wonder, replied the other, how you can live upon so small a stock."

A gentleman, who was parting some people in a fray, received so large a cut in his head, that the surgeon told him he could see his brains. "That's impossible, says the gentleman, for if I had any brains, this had never happened to me."

While a scholar was blowing the fire, the nose of his bellows dropped off: "I see, indeed, says he, 'tis cold weather, for the nose of the very bellows drops."

A

A knight of the four knaves, or, in other words, a gamefter, had grown, as it were, by his behaviour, into difufe, and could get no man of character to play with him: Upon which he complained to one of his company, and faid, he thought their diflike to his perfon arofe from his not being fufficiently dreffed; adding, that he would immediately go and buy a new fuit of clothes.— "That you may do, fays his friend, but I think you had better buy a new fet of principles."

One was faying, that his great grandfather, grandfather, and father, died at fea. Quoth another, if I were you, I would never go to fea. "Why, faid the other, where did your great grandfather, and father die?" He anfwered, "In their beds," "Then, faid the firft, if I were you, I would never go to bed."

A gentleman travelling with Mr. Tagg, who had a bad guinea in his pocket, called his fervant to the fide of the poft chaife; "Dick, fays he, here's a guinea, which is too light, and I can get nobody to take it; do you fee and part with it, fome how or other, on the road." "Yes, fir, fays the footman, I'll endeavour to do it." Tagg remon-

remonſtrated againſt this, as both diſhoneſt and cruel; but the gentleman only laughed at his admonition, and ſaid he knew no-thing of the world. When they came to the inn at night, the gentleman called his ſer-vant, to know if he had paſſed off the gui-nea. "Yes, ſir, ſays the man, I did it ſlily." "Aye, Dick, ſaid the maſter, I fanſy thou art a ſly ſort of a fellow; but tell me how." "Why, ſir, ſays the footman, the people refuſed him at breakfaſt, and ſo they did where your honour dined; but as I had a groat to pay at the turnpike, I whipped him in between the half-pence, and the man put it in his pocket and never ſaw it."

C H A P. III.

A Droll fellow, who got a livelihood by fiddling at fairs and about the country, was one day met by an acquaintance that had not ſeen him a great while, who accoſted him thus: "Bleſs me, what, are you alive?" "Why not? anſwer'd the fiddler, did you ſend any body to kill me?" "No, replies

the

other, but I was told you was dead." "Aye, so it was reported, it seems, says the fiddler, but I knew it was a lie as soon as I heard it."

When Tom Tinsel was at the Temple, he was always very fine, and for the most part very poor; which was sufficiently known to many of his acquaintance. One night, at the tavern, Tom desired one of his companions to pay for him, for that he had no silver in his pocket. "Then I am sure, said the gentleman, you have no gold there, for that you always spread upon your coat."

When Colonel H. arrived at K——e, as governor of that place, the officers told him they hoped he would give a ball to the ladies. "Ladies! says he, aye, aye, I'll give them a ball; but it shall be a ball of worsted to mend their stockings."

A schoolmaster asked one of his boys, in a sharp winter-morning, what was Latin for cold? The boy hesitating a little, the master said, "What, sirrah, can't you tell?" "Yes, sir, says the boy, I have it at my fingers ends."

Two country attornies overtaking a waggoner on the roat, and thinking to crack a

joke

joke upon him, afked why his fore-horfe was fo fat, and the reft fo lean? The waggoner knowing them to be limbs of the law, anfwered, "That his fore-horfe was a lawyer, and the reft were his clients."

A perfon of a college put his horfe into a field belonging to Merton in Oxford, and being often warned of it, took no notice thereof; the mafter of the college fent his man to him, bidding him fay, if he continued the trefpafs, he would cut off his horfe's tail. Say you fo, replies the perfon? "Go tell your mafter if he cuts off my horfe's tail, I'll cut off *his* ears." The fervant returned, deliver'd the meffage, and was fent back to bring the perfon to his mafter; who making his appearance, the mafter faid, How now, what mean you by that menace you fent me? "Sir, faid the other, I threatened you not; for I only faid, if you cut off my horfe's tail, I would cut off *his* cars."

A gentleman in King Charles the Second's time, who had paid a tedious attendance at court, in foliciting a place, and after a thoufand promifes feemed as far off as ever, at laft refolved to fee the king himfelf. When introduced, he told his majefty what preten-

fions

fions he had to his favour, and boldly afked for the place juft then vacant: the king,
hearing his ftory, told him the place was
juft given away. Upon this, the gentleman, making a very low obedience to the
king, thanked him many times over. The
king obferving how thankful he was, called him again, and afked the reafon why
he thanked him in fo extraordinary a manner when he had denied his fuit; "The rather, ant pleafe your majefty, replied the
gentleman, your courtiers have kept me here
thefe two years, and gave me a thoufand
put offs, but your majefty has faved me all
that trouble, and gracioufly given me my
anfwer at once." "Gads fifh, man, fays
the king, thou fhalt have the place for thy
downright honefty."

A Scotch bagpiper, travelling into France, opened his wallet by a wood-fide, and
fet down to dinner; he had no fooner faid
grace than three wolves came about him.
To one he threw bread, to another, meat,
till his provifion was all gone; at length, he
took up his bagpipes and began to play;
at which the wolves ran away. "The de'el
faw me, faid Sawney, an I had kenned ye
loved

loved mufic fo, ye fhould have had it before dinner."

King Charles II. in company with the Lord Rochefter and fome others of the nobility, had been drinking the beft part of the night; when Killigrew came in. Now, fays the king, we fhall hear of our faults. "No, quoth Killigrew, I never trouble my head with that which all the town talks of."

A fcholar of Chrift-church that was whimfical, or, as we ufed to fay, magotty, complained that when he eat fifh, they would always *rife in his ftomach.* "No wonder, quoth another, for they rife and leap after the maggots in your head."

One of the rebels having efcaped out of the Tower in the year fifteen, a gentleman frightened out of his fenfes, ran to King George I. to acquaint him of this news, and begged his majefty would tell him what he could do in this cafe. "Really, fir, fays the king, for your part, I don't know what you can do; but for the prifoner's part, I think he could not have done better than he has."

Two gentlemen having words in a tavern, at length fell to fighting with their canes; a

ftander

stander-by, obferving one of them to ftrike his antagonift over the head, while the other only belaboured his fides and fhoulders, after the fray was over, afked the latter why he did not ftrike upon the head alfo; "O fir, faid he, if I had hit him over the head, I fhould have broken me cane."

A certain doctor, having raifed a pretty fortune by irregular practice, was defirous of purchafing a coat of arms to adorn his chariot, and accordingly afked a friend's advice, what he had beft have for them? Oh! doctor, faid he, nothing will fuit you better than three ducks; and let the motto, if you pleafe, be quack, quack, quack.

When the army of Lewis XIV. of France was encamped in Flanders, during his war with the confederates, the kink ufed fometimes to refide at the head quarters himfelf. It happened, that a very fine horfe which he had lately purchafed, was exercifed before his tent, and among others who had gathered round him was a corporal, who, having been that afternoon too free with aqua vitae, was become as great a man as his majefty. He had ftrolled up to the fpot, and getting within the circle, put himfelf into an attitude of confequence, and after having

some

some time made his obfervation with the air
of a profound connoiffeur, he thrufts a quid
of tobacco into his mouth, and fwore it was
as fine a creature as ever he faw, and as
well broke; then tottering up to the groom
who had been riding it, and juft difmount-
ed, afked him who was the owner? At
this moment the king came out from his
tent, and overhearing the corporal's quae-
ftion, with whom he had already been di-
verted, told him courteoufly, that the horfe was his; the corporal made his majefty
a flight compliment by moving his hat, and
then fetting his arms akimbo, told him,
that his reafon for afking was, that he had
taken a liking to the horfe, and was inclin-
ed to buy it. The king faid, he had no
intention to fell it; but, if it would oblige
him, he would treat with him on the fame
fpot the next morning. The corporal, thruft-
ing out his hand, cried, *a match;* to with
the king confented, and rode off, giving
private orders that no punifhment fhould be
inflicted upon the corporal, but that he
fhould be brought before him the next morning. In the morning, when the poor fellow
was told what had paffed, and conducted to
the king's tent, he was feized with a dread-

ful

ful panic, left his infolence and drunkennefs might coft him his life. Into the prefence, however, he was carried: and the king, who intended only fome fport, afked him if he was the man that would laft night have bought his horfe? "No, an't pleafe your majefty, fays the fellow, that man went away at three o'clock this morning." Did he fo? fays the king, who underftood that at three o'clock fleep had fubftituted a fober man for one that was drunk, I am very glad that I have got fo fenfible and decent a perfon as you are in his ftead, and I hope he will never come back; for if I fee him, I fhall certainly refent his behaviour.

C H A P. V.

A Melting fermon being preached in a country church, all the congregation fell a weeping, but one man, who being afked why he did not weep with the reft? "Oh, faid he, I belong to another parifh."

Oliver riding in his coach on a very rainy day, and Hugh Peters on horfeback by him,

him, fays Oliver, "Peters, I'll lend you my coat." "Pleafe you, fir, fays he, I would not be in your coat for a thoufand pounds."

An Irifhman, being at a tavern where the cook was dreffing fome carp, obferved fome of them move after they were gutted and put into the pan, which much furprifed Teague; faid he, "Of all the chriftian creatures I ever faw, this fame carp will live the longeft after it is dead."

A country 'fquire afked a merry-andrew, why he played the fool? "For the fame reafon, faid he, as you do, out of want; you do it for want of wit, I for want of money."

Two fmart fellows riding by a countryman, who was fowing his field, one of them called to him with an infolent air, "You, farmer, faid he, it is your bufinefs to fow, but we reap the fruits of your labour." To which the farmer replied, "It is very likely you may, mafter, for I am fowing hemp."

Mr. Tagg was once propofing a charity fubfcription at an affembly, when Sir William ✝✝✝ was prefent, and after he had delivered a fentence to the company, he repeated
ed

ed it aloud in Sir William's ear. "What doft thou bellow thy nonfenfe in my ears for?" fays the knight. "Becaufe, replied Tagg, on thefe occafions you are generally deaf."

A linen-draper in London had his picture drawn in armour, which he was very fond of fhowing. Two country gentlemen, of his acquaintance coming to fee him, he, according to cuftom, fhows them the picture, afking if it was not extremely like him? "Indeed, faid one of the gentleman, 'tis a good likenefs; but there is a fault in it; for you are drawn in armour, and the painter has given you no head-piece." "Phoo! fays his friend, if he had had a head-piece, he would not have been drawn in armour."

A taylor fent his bill to a lawyer for money; the lawyer bid the boy tell his mafter, that he was not running away, but very bufy at that time. The boy comes again, and tells him, he muft needs have the money. "Did'ft tell thy mafter, faid the lawyer, I was not running away?" "Yes, fir, faid the boy, but he bid me to tell you, that he was."

A Braggadocio, upon a certain occafion, chanced to run away; and being afked by one, what was become of all that courage
he

he ufed fo much to boaft of? "It is got, faid he, into my heels."

Three gentlemen being at a tavern, whofe names were More, Strange, and Wright: fays the laft, "there is but one cuckold in company, and that's Strange;" "Yes, anfwered Strange, here is one More;" "Aye, faid More, that's Wright."

Some gentlemen feeing a fellow ftand ftill when it rained very faft, they afked him why he ftood ftill in the rain? "Why, fays he, you do not think me fuch a fool as to ride in the rain as you do."

A man who had money enough to make him whimfical, on acount of fome imaginary indifpofition, ordered a phyfician to be fent for; who prefently attending, felt his pulfe, and examined his urine; which finding of a good colour, he afked him, "Sir do you eat well?" He anfwered, "Yes." "And do you fleep well?" he faid, "he did." O then, fays the phyfician, I'll find you a remedy that fhall drive away all thefe things."

A perfon being fummoned to appear at the feffions for a witnefs, about a fray that happened in Holborn, being called to ftand up to give in his evidence, the judge faid

to

to him, "Friend, how came thefe two perfons to fall out." "Why, an't pleafe you,
my Lord, fays the fellow, he faid, my Lord,
you are a rogue." The judge perceiving
the people fmile, bid him fpeak to the jury,
"for there were twelve of them."

A caufe being to be tried before a judge,
one of the witneffes, ftanding up for the
defendant, being a plain country fellow in
a leathern jacket, the council for the plain-
tiff thinking to dafh the witnefs out of countenance, faid to him, "How now, you fellow in a leather doublet, what are you to
have for fwearing?" "Pleafe your worfhip,
quoth the fellow, if you get no more by
lying than I do by fwearing, you might go
in a leather doublet as well as I."

Two gentlemen on the road between
Stanftead and Bifhop Stortford, overtook a
miller riding very foberly, and being merri-
ly difpofed, they were refolved to affront
him; fo one rides on one fide, and the other
on the other fide. After they had rode fome
way with him, fays one to the miller, I
prithee, friend, refolve me one queftion.
"Whether thou art moft knave or fool?"
"Truely, fays the miller, I do not know
which

which I am muft, but I am fure I am between both."

Two fellows meeting, one afked the other why he looked fo fad; "I have good reafon for it, anfwered the other, poor Jack fuch a one, the greateft crony and beft friend I had in the world, was hanged but two days ago." "What had he done?" fays the firft. "Alas! replied the other, he did no more than you or I fhould have done on the like occafion; he found a bridle on the road, and took it up." "What! fays the other, hang a man for taking up a bridle? that's hard indeed!" "To tell the truth of the matter, fays the other, there was a horfe tied to the other end of it."

A dyer in a court of juftice being ordered to hold up his hand, which was all black; "Take off your glove, friend," faid the judge to him. "Put on your fpectacles, my Lord," anfwered the dyer.

A gentleman t'other day going to court, was afked by another at the palace, "Where he was going, and whether he wanted a poft?" "No, no, fir, fays the former, if I did I would take you."

A gentleman in company complaining that he was very fubject to catch cold in his feet,

feet, another, not overloaded with fenfe, told him, that might be eafily prevented, if he would follow his directions. "I always get, faid he, a thin piece of lead, out of an India cheft, and fit it to my fhoe for this purpofe." Then, fir, fays the other, you are like a rope-dancer's pole, you have lead at both ends."

An arch prifoner, who had an unfavourable countenance, being brought to the bar to be tried for horfe-ftealing, the judge immediately cry'd, "Oh! here is a noted villain, I'm fure! why firrah, I can fee the rogue in your face." "Aye, my Lord, fays the fellow, I wonder at that; for I did not know that my face was a looking-glafs, till your Lordfhip faw yourfelf in it."

A lady told another fhe had a mind to quarrel with an impertinent teazing young fellow fhe did not like; who was fo very affiduous and fubmiffive, fhe could not tell how to provoke him. "Slife, faid her friend, fpit in his face." "Alas! madam, replied the firft, that won't do! while men are fawning like lap dogs, they'll take that for a favour."

CHAP.

C H A P. V.

ONE meeting his godfon, afked him where he was going? "To fchool, fir," fays the boy. "That's well done, fays he, here is fix-pence for thee, be a good boy; and I hope I fhall live to hear thee preach my funeral fermon.

A certain prince ufed to fay, that to make a married ftate happy, it was neceffary that the hufband fhould be deaf and the wife blind.

A very fat gentleman riding through a town, fome of the ruder fort of the inhabitants fell a jeering him, and told him he carried his portmanteau before when it fhould be behind. "Oh, fays the gentleman, I always carry it before me, but efpecially when I ride through a town where there is nothing but whores, rogues, and pickpockets."

Two men having a difpute together about works of fortification, one faid to the other, "For all your pretended knowledge, I'll lay you a fhilling you don't know what makes a fortification." "Done, fays the other, who was a droll follow, I infift on it that two twentyfications make a fortification."

As Sir Richard Lovewit was forting and burning a parcel of letters, his fervant, who was juft come out of the country, and was ignorant enough, ftepped up to him, and, making a bow, fir, faid he, I wifh you would give me two of thofe letters. "Why, what will you do with them?" fays the knight. "Oh, I would fend them my father and mother, faid the man, it is a great while fince I fent them a letter, and thefe will fave me the expence of writing."

A fool, kept by King James I, upon fome offence done by him to a gentleman, was told, that his fool's coat fhould be no protection to him, for he certainly would beat his head off, if ever he did the like again. The fool ran openmouth'd to the king with his complaint, who bid him not be afraid! for if the gentleman fhould kill him, he would hang him the day after. "I had much rather, replied the fool, you would hang him the day before."

An elderly gentleman was entertaining fome company in a coffee-houfe with the felicities he had enjoyed in the early parts of his life, and lamented he was now grown

fo

fo old; upon which an impertinent young fellow ſtarted up, and aſked what he would give to be as young a he was? "Why, ſir, anſwered the gentleman, I would even ſubmit to be almoſt as fooliſh."

Naſh, ſeeing a gentleman before him in Fleet-ſtreet, whom he took for an old acquaintance, ran after him, and without ſpeaking a word, clapped him on the ſhoulder. However, when the gentleman turned, he diſcovered his error, and aſked pardon; but the other grumbled, and ſeemed diſpleaſed. "Pray don't be angry, ſaid Naſh, I miſtook you for a very honeſt gentleman." "How do you know but I am ſo?" ſaid the other ſurlily. "Why, if you are, ſaid Naſh, I ſhould be a ſecond time miſtaken."

A gentleman was reading to ſome company, in a coffee houſe by St. James's, a ſyſtem of polity, in which a calculation was made of all the inhabitants in Great-Britain; the number ſeemed ſo immenſely great to a beau politician who ſtood by, that he immediately cried, "Sir, if what you ſay be true, there is more people in Great Britain than in all England put together." "That wiſe gentleman, ſays an arch old cuff in the corner, puts me in mind of the mayor of

W——, who, on being informed that a hurrica-
ne had deftroyed many ſhips at ſea, declared,
with the ſagacity and air of a magiſtrate,
"that he believed more miſchief was done by
ſea and land, than in all the world beſide."

As Mr. *Amner* was going through a ſtreet
in Windſor, two boys looked out of a one-
pair of-ſtairs window, and cried. "There
goes Mr. *Amner*, that makes ſo many bulls!"
He hearing them, looked back, and in a paſſion ſaid, "You raſcals! I know you well
enough, and if I had you here, I'd throw
you down ſtairs."

Mr. Pope, who, notwithſtanding his miſ-
ſhapen figure, was a little vain of his perſon,
aſked Dr. Swift what people thought of him
in Ireland. "Why, ſaid Swift, they think you
a very little man, but a very great poet."
Pope retorted with ſome acrimony, "They
think the reverſe of you in England."

What poet ever lik'd his brother?
Wits are game-cocks to one another.

Quin was at Tunbridge a few years ago,
when a certain fantaſtical gentleman burſt out
into ſuch extravagant fits of laughter in the
aſſembly-room, that he drew on him the
obſervation of all the company; when, coming

ing up to Quin, he afked him if he had ever feen a man in fuch fpirits before. "Yes, once, replied Quin, but then he was in Moorfields.'

CHAP. VI.

AS a boy, who lived in my neighbourhood, was keeping fheep on Marlborough Downs a gentleman called to him, and afked him, what it was o'clock. "It is twelve, fir," anfwered the boy. "No, returned the gentleman, it can't be twelve yet." "Then you may ride till it is, if you pleafe" fays the boy. The gentleman, thinking there was fomething droll in the boy's anfwer, after he had rode a little away, fent his fervant back to know if he would come and live with him. "What does your mafter want me for?" faid the boy. "To be his fool," anfwered the fervant. "What, are you going away then? quoth the boy, if you a'nt, I won't come, for your mafter can't afford to keep two of us."

A fea captain, being juft come afhore, was invited by fome gentlemen to a hunting

match.

match. After the fport was over, he gave
his friends this particular account of it: Our
horfes being completely rigged, we man-
ned them, the wind being at S. W. and
twenty of us in company, away we fet
over the Downs. In the time of half a
watch we fpied a hare under a full gale;
we tack'd and ftood after her, coming up
clofe, fhe tacked and we tacked, upon which
tack I had like to have run aground; but
getting clofe, off I ftood after her again;
but as the devil would have it, juft about
to lay her aboard, bearing too much wind,
I and my horfe overfet, and came keel upwards.

Upon the happy return of King Charles
the fecond, one Bull, who had loyally and
learnedly maintained his majefty's rights,
was prefented by the king with a grant for
a very confiderable benefice; but before the
patent was fealed, my Lord Chancellor
Hyde had difpofed of it to another. The
parfon having fpent all his money, put his
hand into his pocket, and finding nothing
but the king's grant there, with his hand
to it, went boldly to his majefty, and told
him he had loft all his money out of his
pocket, and he found none but his majefty's
                                          hand

hand there. The king smiled, and asked him if his business was done: He replied, No; and he was thereon immediately recommended to Chancellor Hyde, to put him into business. Says the chancellor, knowing him to be a wit, "What's your name?" "Bull," says the parson. "Where are your horns?" says my lord. "Please your lordship," replied the parson, "the horns always go along with the Hyde."

Two scholars, passing by a windmill, stood for some time viewing it; the miller, looking out of a little wicket, asked them what they whould have? and what they stared at? "Why, says one of them, we are looking at this thing; I pray, what is it?" "Why, says the miller, don't you see? where are your eyes? it is a windmill." "We crave your mercy, sir, say the scholars, we took it for a gaol, seeing a thief look out of the window."

Some persons pleading their cause before the lord chancellor, and showing, as it were, the boundaries and limits of their land; the council on one side said, "We lie on this side, my lord;" and the council on the other side said, "We lie on this side." The lord chancellor arose and said, "If you lie on both fides, pray which would you have me believe?"

A lady belonging to a wealthy parifh in London, having had the misfortune to bury feveral of her family in a little time, the fexton brought her a bill, which fhe thinking unreafonable, demanded fome abatement, and tendered him five fhillings lefs than he had charged. The fexton eyed the money, and at length took it up, faying. "As you have been a good chap, madam, and I expect more of your cuftom, I'll take it for this time; but I really can't afford it."

One of the Mendicant friars in France and his afs laden with his provifions he had collected, croffing a ferry, the poor beaft, with the weight of his load, and the coldnefs of the feafon, trembled and fhook exceedingly. One in the boat, thinking to be witty, told the friar, his brother trembled. "Aye, fays the friar, if you had a cord round your neck, irons at your feet, and a man of my profeffion at your elbow, you would tremble too."

A Welchman riding with a charge of money was fet upon by a thief, who bid him deliver it prefently, or he would make that piftol bounce through him. "Says hur fo? quoth

quoth the Welchman, well there is, hur master's money, better lose that than hur own
life: but, sir, since hur hath hur money,
let hur have a pounce for hur money." So
the thief to please the Welchman, let off his
pistol. "Splutter hur nails, quoth the fellow, that was a rare pounce indeed; good
fur, let hur have another pounce." So the
thief let off the other; with which the
Welchman seemed to be better pleased than
before, and asked him if he had no more
pounces. "No, says he, I have no more."
"Then, said the fellow, hur has one pounce in store, which hur will make pounce
through hur immediately, if hur deliver not
hur money back presently." On this the
thief, though with much reluctance, was
obliged to give the Welch fox his money
again.

It was an usual saying of King Charles
the second; that sailors got their money like
horses, and spent it like asses; and the following story, I think, is an instance of it.
One sailor coming to another on pay-day,
desired to borrow twenty shillings of him.
The moneyed man fell to telling out the
sum in shillings, but a half crown thrusting
its head in put him out, and he began to

C 5   tell

tell again, when an impertinent crown piece was as officious as his halfbrother had been, and again interrupted the tale: fo taking up a handful of filver, he cried, "Here Jack, give me a handful when your fhip is paid; what fignifies counting it."

A gentleman fent for his carpenter's fer-vant, to drive a nail or two in his ftudy; af-ter the fellow had done, he fcratched his ears, and faid, he hoped the gentleman would give him fomething to make him drink. "Make you drink! faid the gentleman, the-re's a pickle herring for you; if that won't make you drink, I'll give you another."

Lun, the famous harlequin, ufed frequent-ly to fup at Jerry Lucas's, the Sun-Tavern, in Clare-market, which has a door in one ftreet and windows in another. One night after the entertainment, he had got into a hackneycoach, and ordered the man to dri-ve him to the Sun. It happened that as the fellow was driving by the window, Lun per-ceived it to be open, and threw himfelf out of the coach into the room. The coach-man having turned the corner drove up to the houfe, and getting from the box open-ed the coach door, and let down the ftep; then, taking off his hat, he waited fome time

expecting

expecting his fare to alight, but at laft looking into his coach, and feeing it empty, he
beftowed a few hearty curfes on the rafcal
that had bilked him, and remounting his
box, turned about, and was driving the fame
way back. As he paffed by the window,
Lun watched the opportunity, and again
threw himfelf into the coach; he then looked out, and calling to the coachman, afked
where he was going, and bid him turn and
come once more to the Sun Tavern door.
When Lun got out, after reproaching the
fellow for his ftupidity he would have given
him his fare: "No, God blefs your honour,
fays the man, my mafter has ordered me to
take no money to night." "Why then,
fays Lun, he's a fool, and here's a fhilling
for yourfelf." "No, fays the man, who
by this time had mounted the coachbox,
that won't do; I know you too well for
all your fhoes; and fo Mr. Devil, for once
you are out-witted.

————

CHAP

CHAP. VII.

A GENTLEMAN, in the weſt of England, had a preſent made him of an exceeding fine oſtrich, which excited the curioſity of the country; and ſuch numbers went to ſee it, that had he been a man of ſpirit, he might with reputation have ſpent half his fortune; but, as he was an egregious miſer, the hiſtory of that country tells us, it never coſt him a ſingle bottle of wine. Tom Tagg, among others, was taken by a relation of the gentleman's to ſee this uncommon creature. It was in the ſummer-time, and they had travelled a great way without any refreſhment: upon which, Tom deſired his friend to make a motion for ſomething to drink; but he, knowing his couſin's diſpoſition, declined it. While they were viewing the animal, a diſpute aroſe between the two kinſmen, whether the account of its eating and digeſting iron was true or falſe: after much altercation, it was left to the deciſion of Mr. Tagg, who boldly affirmed, that they did eat iron; "And it is my opinion, ſays he, this vile creature
ture

ture has eaten the key of the cellar, or we
should have been asked to drink before
now."

A young fellow, who had made away
with all he had, even to his last suit of clothes, was thus addressed by his friend; "Now
I hope you'll own yourself a happy man,
for you have put an end to all your cares."
"How so?" said the gentleman. "Because,
replied the other, you have nothing left to
take care of."

It has been often observed, with too much
truth, that English gentlemen reap no benefit from travelling. Tom Smart made a pretty use of this, when he told a prating coxcomb, just returned from Italy, "That the
English went out figures, and returned cy-
phers."

Tom Clark, of St. John's, desired a fellow of the same college to send him Bishop
Burnet's history of the Reformation." The
other told him he could not possibly spare
it out of his chambers; but, if he pleased,
he might come there and read it all day
long. Some time after, the same gentleman sends to Tom, to borrow his bellows;
Tom sent him word, "He could not possibly

fibly fpare them out of his chambers, but he might come there and blow all day long if he would."

Jemmy Spiller, as he was going one day through Rag-fair, a place where they fell fecond-hand goods, cheapened a leg of mutton, he faw hung up there at a butcher's ftall. The butcher told him it was a groat a pound. "Are not you an unconfcionable fellow, faid Spiller, to afk fuch a price, when one may buy a new one for that in Clare-market?"

Quin was once upon a journey to Somerfetfhire, and having put up for a few days at a farm-houfe, which he admired for the agreeablenefs of its fituation, he, in the mean while, turned his horfe to grafs, and loft him. Upon enquiring after him of a country fellow, and afking if there were any thieves, or horfeftealers, in his neighbourhood, "No, we be all honeft folk here, quoth the man, but there's one Quin, I think they call him, a ftrolling player from London, mayhap he may have ftolen him."

As the late king was walking one morning in Hampton-court gardens, a mower left

his

his companion, and with his hat off, and scratching his head, thus addreſſed him: "God bleſs you, ſir, I hope your majeſty will give a poor mower ſomething to drink your health this morning?" "I have no money, friend. I have no money" ſaid the king. "Nor I neither, quoth the fellow, rot'em, I can't think what they have done with it all!"

A tradeſman, who could neither write nor read, employed a ſaucy boy to write his letters for him. — It happened one day, that this young rogue was at play when his maſter wanted him to write to one of his cuſtomers; upon which he ſent for him, was very angry, and called him puppy, as he uſually did when out of temper. "Come, ſit down, ſays he, ye puppy you, and write, ye puppy you." "What ſhall I write?" ſays the boy. "Why, returned the maſter, ſay, ſir, ye puppy you, I have ſent the goods, ye puppy you, and ſo on." The boy, in revenge for being chid by his maſter, wrote every word he ſaid, and the letter ran thus:

"Sir, ye puppy you, I have ſent the goods you ordered, ye puppy you, which are very good of the ſort, ye puppy you, and

and very cheap, ye puppy you, which is
all that's needful, ye puppy you, from

Your humble fervant, ye puppy you,
T. Smith, ye puppy you.

Loxdon, Jan. 8. 1767, ye puppy you.

This letter was made up, and the boy
carried it to the gentleman, who being greatly furprifed at the contents, afked if his
mafter could write. The boy blufhed, but
made no anfwer; upon which the gentleman
faw he was guilty, and, calling to his fervant, "Tom, fays he, how many are four
times five?" "Twenty, fir," anfwered the
man. "Then take the horfe-whip, fays the
gentleman, and give this boy twenty ftrokes
for his infolence." Thefe he received and
carried home, and the gentleman followed
with the letter to his mafter, who gave him
twenty more; fo that the young rogue got
twice twenty, which is forty ftripes, for
mifapplying his wit; and this proves "That
wit is *folly*, unlefs a *wife head* hath the
keeping of it."

A tradefman newly made mayor of a little
town in the north, meeting with an old acquaintance while he was mending his hedge,
who

who fpoke to him, and by accident kept his hat off, imagined it was done out of refpect to his new dignity; upon which, bridling and compofing his mufcles with great gravity, he faid, "Put on your hat, fir, put on your hat, I am ftill but a man!"

A Lawyer and his man riding on the road, his man defired to know what was the chief point of the law. His mafter faid, if he would promife to pay for their fuppers that night, he would tell him; which the man agreed to. "Why then, faid the mafter, good witneffes are the chief point in the law." When they came to the inn, the mafter befpoke a couple of fowls for fupper; and when they had fupped, ordered the man to pay for them according to agreement. "Oh, fir, fays he, where's your witnefs?"

A fcholar declaiming in a college-hall, having a bad memory, was at a ftand, and, in a low voice, defired one who ftood clofe by him, to help him out: "No, fays the other, you are out enough already."

We commonly fay fecond thoughts are beft; and young women who pretend to be averfe to marriage, defire not to be taken at their words. One afked a girl, if fhe would have him: "No, John, faid fhe, but you may have me if you will."

One told another, who was not ufed to be clothed often, that his new coat was too fhort for him, "That's true, faid he, but it will be long enough before I get another."

Hippefley, the player, having a large full wig on, which he had not paid for, was told by a friend of his, that it was a very good one. "Faith, fir, faid Hippefley with his ufual humour, I know not how good it may prove in the long run, but at prefent it has run me over head and ears in debt."

A certain lord had a termagant wife, and at the fame time a chaplain that was a tolerable poet, whom his lordfhip defired to write a copy of verfes upon a fhrew. "I can't imagine, faid the chaplain, why your lordfhip fhould want a copy, who have fo good an original."

An arch wag faid, taylors were like woodcocks, for they got their fubftance by their long bills.

CHAP. VIII.

CONUNDRUMS.

WHY is a paffionate man like a gentle-
man's fhirt?
Becaufe he is ruffled.
Why are fleepy eyes like amber?
Becaufe they draw ftraws.
Why is a woman's head like a mountebank?
Becaufe it is often in a mob.
Why is a pretty lady like an oat-cake?
Becaufe fhe is toafted.
Why are moft authors like a fhip juft launch-
ed?
Becaufe they want new rigging.
Why is a man in debt like a nobleman?
Becaufe he has many to wait on him.
Why is a falfe note like a bar of iron?
Becaufe it is forged.
Why is going into the country like learn-
ing to dance?
Becaufe it gives one a good air.
Why is claret like an oath?
Becaufe it is binding.

Why

Why is a bad pen like a wicked man?
  Becaufe it wants mending.

Why is a good fermon like a plumb-pudding,
  Becaufe there are reafons in it.

Why is Ireland like a bottle of wine?
  Becaufe there is a Cork in it.

Why is a drawn tooth like a thing forgotten?
  Becaufe it is out of one's head.

Why is a peevifh man like a watch?
  Becaufe he is often wound up.

Why is fwearing like a fhabby coat?
  Becaufe it is a bad habit.

Why is a parifh-bell like a good ftory?
  Becaufe it is often told.

Why is my Lord Mayor like an almanack?
  Becaufe he ferves but one year.

Why is a looking-glafs like a philofopher?
  Becaufe it reflects.

What is a man like, that is in the midft of
      a great river, and cannot fwim:
  Like to be drowned.

Why is a cook like a woman of fafhion?
  Becaufe fhe dreffes well.

Why is a book like a tree?
  Becaufe it is full of leaves.

Why is an unbound book like a lady in bed?
  Becaufe it is in fheets.

                                    What

Why is a firſt floor like a lie!
 Becauſe it is a ſtory raiſed.
What is a man like, in the midſt of a deſert,
  without meat or drink?
 Like to be ſtarved.
Why is a poor man like a ſempſtreſs?
 Becauſe he makes ſhifts.

———

PART

PART II.

Prudent Maxims and Wife Sayings.

CHAP. I.

SILENCE, when it appears free from affectation, fullennefs, and ignorance, is a fort of ornament to fpeech, and, like authority, procures refpect.

He that blows the coals of others ftrife, may chance to have the fparks fly in his face.

Alexander ufed to fhut up one ear with his hand, when he heard any accufer in criminal matters: thereby, as he called it, referving the other for the defendant.

In fpeaking to men, confider whether what you are about to fay be better than filence; fuitable to times, places, and perfons; befitting both fpeaker and hearer.

Words are arrows that ought not to be fhot at random.

When reafon is beat off its guard, the tongue is apt to run riot.

To

To lie to the prejudice of others, argues malice and villany; to lie in excufe of ourfelves, guilt and cowardice.

By one fingle lie a man lofes all his good name; deceit goes for falfe coin, and the deceiver for the coiner, which is ftill worfe.

Perjury is not only a wrong to particular perfons, but treafon againft human fociety; fubverting at once the foundations of public peace and juftice, and the private fecurity of every man's life and fortune.

Interrupt nobody, even in telling a ftory you had heard before: why fhould you rob one who feeks to divert you of the pleafure of believing he had told you fomething you did not know, or hinder the reafonable diverfions of his friends?

Montagne juftly complains, that inftead of taking notice of others, we make it our bufinefs to have the company take notice of us.

To give your opinion before required, looks like upbraiding others ignorance, or over-valuing your own parts.

In giving your opinion, be neither ftiff nor fingular about things indifferent, nor over confident in doubtful and obfcure.

Cenfu-

Cenfure always with modefty and caution, left you forwardly condemn what you have not fkill to underftand.

Praife no man too liberally before his face, neither cenfure him too lavifhly behind his back. The one favours of flattery, the other of malice.

Condemn nothing out of humour, nor maintain any thing out of faction: never defend a falfe caufe either to revenge a wrong, or do a pleafure.

Be not forward to fpread reports, left your credit be called in queftion, or you chance to kindle a fire you cannot eafily quench.

Contend not with fuperiors: the thread will break where it is weakeft.

Make a virtue of neceffity, and fuffer what you cannot hinder with a refpectful humility.

'Tis next to conquering, wifely to fubmit.

Shun or break off all difputes with infe-riors, left they lofe their refpect.

Take heed of fpeaking when you are an-gry.

Paffion is a fort of fever in the mind, that always leaves us weaker than it finds us.

To

To be angry is to revenge the faults of others upon ourfelves.

Cardinal Mazarine ufed to fay, "Two to one in all things againft the angry man."

Never whifper in company, efpecially of your betters, the more eminent the perfons are the more it is uncivil.

If we have private bufinefs with any one in company, we ought, when nobody is difcourfing, to afk leave, and then take them afide, and carefully avoid eyeing any of the company whilft difcourfing privately, left it fhould be thought we talk of them.

The height of good breeding is fhown rather in never giving offence, than in doing obliging things.

In all debates fpeak laft, to be mafter of others ftrength before you fhow your own.

He that will not hear cannot judge; and he that cannot bear contradiction may with all his wit mifs his mark.

A man that in converfation modeftly queftions much, may learn much, if he wifely applies his queftions to the fkill of the perfons with whom he difcourfes, and puts them upon thofe things they underftand beft; for by giving them the pleafure of fhowing their expertnefs, he may collect at eafe

D 5   the

the choiceſt things that others have acquired by long ſtudy and pains.

Should you be obliged to enter upon an
argument, give your reaſons with the utmoſt coolneſs and modeſty, to the end that
if you appear to have the worſt end of the
ſtaff, you may make an honourable retreat,
with an *I was not poſitive, and am now
glad to be better informed.*

When you have ſaid a pleaſant thing never repeat it, whether the company heard
it or loſt it, let it paſs off as it came on,
careleſsly and eaſily, without laying any
ſtreſs upon it. Why ſhould you ſet up for
a wit, to find laughter for others?

Many, by endeavouring to purchaſe the
reputation of being witty, have loſt the advantage of appearing wiſe; and, by too often trying to excite laughter, made them-
ſelves ridiculous.

To laugh firſt, much, or loud, at ſerious matters, or at what you ſay yourſelf,
is the way to be derided by others.

Upbraid no man with his weakneſs, neither report it to diſparage him or advance
thyſelf. It is a wretched thing to eſtabliſh
ourſelves upon the ruin of others, and a very
ſcandalous way to fame.

Mode-

Modefty makes men amiable to their friends, and refpected by their very enemies. In all places, and on all occafions, it attracts benevolence, and demands approbation.

Seeing there is no protection againft the fting of a malevolent wit and licentious tongue, if at any time you chance to be touched to the quick, turn wittily into a jeft what was rudely faid in earneft.

He that revengeth himfelf by not being offended, retorts upon his adverfary the grief and fmart intended by the affront, with the additional fting of the difappointment.

Socrates being afked, "Who was the wifeft man? anfwered, "He that offends leaft."

If you have erred, perfevere not in it; think it no fhame to fubmit to truth, but rather rejoice that you have found it.

Never fwell a fmall impertinence into a crime by defending it. Be the firft to condemn yourfelf; it is the way to extricate yourfelf out of difficulties with honour.

Ariftippus and Aefchines having fallen out, Ariftippus came and afked Aefchines, whether they would be friends? "Yes, with all my heart," fays Aefchines. "Remem-

ber

ber, says Ariftippus, that I, though your elder, fought for peace." "True, fays Aefchines, I began the ftrife, and you the peace; for which reafon I will always acknowledge you to be the worthieft man."

A man that walks the ftreets in a populous city, muft expect to meet with a joftle in one place, a flip in another, a ftop in a third, the dafh of a kennel in the fourth, &c. &c. Juft fuch are the adventures of life, and with the fame confideration to be undergone.

Difputes commonly begin in miftakes, are carried on with heat and fury, and end in reproach and uncharitable names, and too frequently in blood.

It is the glory of a man to pafs by a tranfgreffion, not tendering evil for evil. Anger refteth in the bofom of fools.

When you have found a friend, be faithful, difcreet, and fincere; bear his little failings; and, fo far as confifts with honour and a good confcience, cultivate his friendfhip, left it expire; yet neither afk nor grant him any thing unjuft or evil. Love him fo as to hate his faults, and never by too great a familiarity expofe yourfelf to his contempt.

The

The many things a man cannot do for himself speak his need of a faithful friend; who, the wife fon of Sirach fays, is the medicine of life.

The blind man bears the lame; what fate denies
The wretched pair, their mutual help fupplies:
One lends his feet, the other lends his eyes.

CHAP. II.

A Man may have a thoufand intimate acquaintances, and not a friend among them all.

Be as folicitous to avoid making enemies as to gain friends.

Injure no man: the meaneft perfon may, once in feven years, have an opportunity of doing you much good or harm.

Though we have a thoufand friends we may lack more, but one enemy is too much.

Whofoever would reclaim his friend, and bring him to a perfect underftanding of himfelf, may privately admonifh, but must never
ver

ver publicly reprehend him.   An open admonition is an open difgrace.

Two perfons will not be friends a long
time if they cannot forgive one another little failings.

All men have their frailties; whoever
looks for a friend without imperfections, will
never find what he feeks.   We love ourfelves with all our faults, and we ought to
love our friends in like manner.

Whoever moves you to part with a true
and tried friend, has certainly a defign to
make way for a treacherous enemy.

A true friend unbofoms freely, advifes
juftly, affifts readily, adventures boldly, takes all patiently, defends courageoufly, and
continues a friend unchangeably.

Harmony of temper begets and preferves
friendfhip; but difagreeing inclinations are
like improper notes in mufic, that ferve only
to fpoil the concert and offend the ear.

There muft be a nice diet obferved to keep
friendfhip from falling fick; nay, there is
more fkill neceffary to keep a friend, than
there is to reclaim an enemy.

Thofe who flight and difoblige their
friends fhall infallibly come to know the
                                                value

value of them, by having none when they shall moſt need them.

Plato, being told that ſomebody had ſpoken ill of him, ſaid, "It matters not, I will live, ſo that nobody ſhall believe him."

The eyes, tongue, and looks are the windows and doors, no leſs than the interpreters of the hearts of man: every paſſion gives a particular caſt to the countenance, and is apt to diſcover itſelf in ſome feature or other.

Any thing that diſturbs our reaſon lets looſe the tongue; which when at liberty, ſeldom keeps within the bounds of prudence.

Be grave, but not formal; brave, but not raſh; humble, not ſervile; patient, not inſenſible; conſtant, not obſtinate; chearful, not light; rather ſweet than familiar; familiar than intimate; and intimate with very few, and upon very good grounds.

Becauſe you find any thing difficult to praĉtiſe, do not preſently conclude you cannot maſter it.

Virtue is never the leſs venerable for being out of faſhion.

If

If it is common to be touched with things rare, how comes it that we are so little touched with virtue?

To relieve the oppreſſed is the moſt glorious act a man is capable of; it is in some meaſure doing the buſineſs of God and Providence.

A forwardneſs to oblige, doubles the intrinſic worth of the obligation: in theſe caſes, whatever is done with pleaſure is always received ſo.

Whenever I find a great deal of gratitude in a poor man, I take it for granted there would be as much generoſity if he were a rich man.

There is no exceſs in the world ſo commendable as an exceſs of gratitude.

A knave leans ſometimes ſo hard upon his impudence, that it breaks and lets him fall.

He is rich enough that needs neither to flatter nor borrow, and truely rich that is ſatisfied.

He that keeps his accounts will keep his family; but he that keeps no account may be kept by the pariſh.

A knave may get more than an honeſt man for a day; but the honeſt man will get moſt by the year.

A

A diligent careful mafter makes a good fervant; but he that is carelefs makes all his people partners.

Abfence leffens fmall paffions, and increafes great ones; as the wind extinguifhes tapers, and kindles fires.

Our paffions are like convulfive fits, which, though they make us ftronger for the time, leave us the weaker ever after.

He that overcomes his paffions, conquers his greateft enemies.

A good-natured man has the whole world to be happy out of. Whatever good befalls his fpecies, a well-deferving perfon promoted, a modeft man advanced, an indigent one relieved, all this he looks upon as a remote bleffing of Providence on himfelf; which then feems to make him amends for the narrownefs of his own fortune, when it doth the fame thing he would have done, had it been in his power: for what a luxurious man in poverty would want, for delicacies, for horfes, and footmen, a good-natured man wants for his friend or the poor.

It is impoffible that an ill-natured man can have a public fpirit, for how fhould he love ten thoufand men who never loved one?

He

He that can be quite indifferent when he fees another man injured, hath a lukewarm honefty that a wife man will not depend upon.

Cruelty is fo contrary to human nature, that it is diftinguifhed by that fcandalous name, inhumanity.

Malice may be fometimes out of breath, envy never. A man may make peace with hatred, but never with envy.

Refufe not to be informed; good counfel breaks no man's head. Solomon brands thofe for fools that defpife inftruction; and Horace laughs at thofe that are afhamed to learn, and not afhamed to be ignorant.

To do nothing amifs is the beft way of being revenged of our enemies.

Stand in awe of yourfelf, if you would not be afhamed before others.

What avails the faculty of reafon without the exercife of it? Where an obftinate *I will* is the preface, *I would I had not* is generally the conclufion.

It is impoffible to be happy without making reafon the ftandard of all our thoughts, words, and actions, and yielding conftant, ready, and chearful obedience to all its dictates.

The

The care of religion, and of our fouls, is the one thing neceffary. He that neglects the fervice of the Almighty, dies without doing that for which he was made to live.

Religion will bear a man up in all eftates and accidents, make his thoughts virtuous, his words difcreet, actions prudent, and life blamelefs; as aiming only at the glory of God, and doing all the good he can to himfelf and others.

True devotion is the fource of repofe; it fupports us in life, and fweetens death.

Chriftianity is the higheft exaltation of nature and right reafon, the only excellent and compendious art of happy living. Piety towards God, juftice and charity towards men, and temperance and chaftity in reference to ourfelves, are tafks that are rewards, and precepts that are a divine fort of alchymy, to fublime at once our natures and our pleafures.

As yefterday cannot be recalled, to-morrow cannot be affured; this day is only ours, which, if loft, is loft for ever.

CHAP.

CHAP. III.

TO laugh at deformed perfons is inhuman, if not impious.

He who makes a jeft of the frailties of human nature, upbraids the god of nature.

Old age is too venerable for raillery, and fhould be reverenced.

The unfortunate are fit fubjects of compaffion, not of raillery.

'Tis monftrous to confider how eafy and pleafed we are when we rally or play upon others; and how angry and choleric when we are rallied or played upon ourfelves.

He that affects always fhowing his wit, feldom fails of letting the world know he has little or none.

Flattery is a fort of bad money, to which our vanity gives currency.

Few are fo wife as to prefer ufeful reproof to treacherous praife.

He that reviles me, it may be, calls me fool; but he that flatters me, if I take not good heed, will make me fo.

If we did not flatter ourfelves, the flattery of others could do us little harm.

A

A beau dreffed out is as the cinnamon-tree, the bark is more worth than the body.

None more impatiently fuffer injuries, than thofe that are moft forward in doing them.

Rife when the cock calls: let not the fun be up before you. Man's life is at moft but a fpan: Why fhould you live but half your days?

Count your very minutes; let no time flip you. Time is life, which wife men lengthen by a right ufe of it from one moment to another.

Be neither mimically in, nor ridiculoufly out of the fafhion: let your apparel be neat, not chargeable; fitted as well to your eftate, years, and profeffion, as to your perfon. "A fool is known by his coat."

There is not in the world a furer fign of a little foul, than the ftriving to gain refpect by fuch defpicable means as drefs and rich clothes; none will depend on thefe ornaments, but they who have no others.

A fine coat is but a livery, when the perfon who wears it difcovers no higher fenfe than that of a footman.

We read in Daniel how pulfe and water made the four childres fairer in countenance,

and

and fatter in flesh, than those who fared on the royal provision.

Men rifle the air, the seas, and the forests, to please their palates, till from excess of meats and drinks proceed dulness of spirits, heaviness of mind, and such vicious humours and crudities, as occasion a long train of diseases, swell the bills of mortality, and prepare a treat for the worms.

When a man is taken sick, his senses are busied about his disease, or distracted between physician, lawyer, and minister, so that his friends are unwelcome, strangers troublesome, visits offend, his own servants cannot please, others discourses tire him; to speak spends, to be silent grieves him; not to be told how he does vexes him, to be told how ill he is discomforts him; to see his wife and children weeping and lamenting, bitterly afflicts him. Thus distressed and distracted with sickness, pain, and grief, and still as death approaches, the worm of conscience gnawing, and evil spirits moving to despair, how miserably disabled and unfit will the heart of a sinner be, to lift up itself to God by a sincere repentance! When surrounded by these deplorable horrours, how wretched is that man, who

who cannot look backward but with fhame, nor forward but with terrour! What comfort will his riches afford him in his extremity; or what will his fenfual pleafures, his vain and empty titles, robes, dignities, and crowns, avail him in that day of his diftrefs?

When I look upon the tombs of the Great, fays Mr. Addifon, every emotion of envy dies in me; when I read the epitaphs of the beautiful, every inordinate defire goes out; when I meet with the grief of parents upon a tombftone, my heart melts with compaffion; when I fee the tomb of parents themfelves, I confider the vanity of grieving for thofe whom we muft quickly follow; when I fee kings lying by thofe who depofed them, when I confider rival wits placed fide by fide, or the holy men that divided the world with their contefts and difputes, I reflect with forrow and aftonifhment on the little competitions, factions, and debates of mankind; when I read the feveral dates of the tombs, of fome that died as yefterday, and fome fix hundred years ago, I confider that Great Day when we fhall all of us be contemporaries and make our appearance together.

E 4   To

To carry inflaming tales between perfons at variance, is as dangerous an office as holding a wolf by the ears.

By taking revenge, a man is but even with his enemy; but in paffing it over he is fuperior. "To err is human, to forgive divine."

True honour will pay treble damages, rather than juftify one wrong by another.

Slanderers are like flies; they leap over all a man's good parts, to light upon his fores.

The worthieft people are moft injured by flanderers; as we ufually find that to be the beft fruit, which the birds have been pecking at.

Slander would not ftick, if it had not fomething to lay hold of.

What mifchief is it the craft and fubtility of a double tongue cannot work upon a credulous fool: tale-bearers ought to be hung up by the tongue, tale-hearers by the ears.

Believe nothing againft another but upon good authority; neither report what may hurt another, unlefs it be a greater hurt to conceal it.

Thofe who are incapable of great crimes do not readily fufpect others of them.

Hear

Hear not ill of an enemy: believe not all you hear, nor report all you believe.

Every man defires to live long, but no man would be old.

It is infolent as well as unnatural to trample upon the venerable decays of human nature: he that acts in this manner does but expofe his own future condition, and laugh at himfelf before-hand.

Cuftom is the plague of wife men and the idol of fools.

Ufe makes every pofture familiar to the body, and every opinion to the mind.

If a man walks lame, he is pitied; if he dances lame, he is laughed at: The one is unavoidable, the other is not.

The defire of appearing perfons of ability often prevents our being fo.

Our humour has more faults than our underftanding.

Familiarity, it is true, breeds contempt; but love is not to be gained without fome degree of it.

The power of fortune is confeffed only by the miferable; for the happy impute all their fuccefs to prudence or merit.

To pardon thofe abfurdities in ourfelves which we cannot fuffer in others, is neither

better

better nor worfe than to be more willing to be fools ourfelves, than to have others fo.

The only way to be revenged on a perfon who talks too much, is not to give him the hearing.

The fhorteft and beft way to make your fortune, is to convince people it is their intereft to ferve you.

He who folicits for others has the confidence of one that demands juftice; and he who fpeaks for himfelf, the confufion and bafhfulnefs of him that implores mercy.

A man throws himfelf down whilft he complaineth; and when a man throws himfelf down, no body cares to take him up again.

Nothing has an uglier look to us than reafon, when it is not on our fide. We quarrel fo often with it, that it makes us afraid to come near it. A man that doth not ufe his reafon is a tame beaft: a man that abufes it a wild one.

———————

CHAP.

C H A P. IV.

YOU muſt labour and climb the hill, if you would arrive at virtue, whoſe feat is upon the top of it; it is a great encouragement to well doing, that when you are once in the poſſeſſion of virtue, it is your own for ever.

Virtue is like precious odours, fragrant by being cruſhed: for proſperity beſt diſcovers vice, but adverſity beſt diſcovers virtue.

If vanity does not overturn all the virtue, it certainly makes them totter.

The ſtrongeſt paſſions allow us ſome reſt, but vanity keeps us perpetually in motion. "What a duſt do I raiſe?" ſays the fly upon a coach wheel.

If we were not proud ourſelves, we ſhould not ſo much complain of the pride of others.

Humility is no doubt a great virtue, but it ceaſes to be ſo when it is afraid to ſcorn an ill thing.

Hope is generally a wrong guide, though it is very good company by the way: It bruſhes through hedge and ditch, till it comes

mes to a great leap, and there is apt to fall.

The reflection upon a holy and virtuous life, and the confcioufnefs of a man's upright-nefs and fincerity, are fprings of joy and peace to him, which refrefh his mind with unfpeakable comfort and pleafure, under all the evils and calamities of death.

The beft philofophy is to ftudy man's mortality, and to meditate frequently upon death.

Death keeps no calender; he turns many pale before age hath made them grey. Far greater numbers are fnatched away in their infancy than live to the age of maturity.

The world owes us all to death. Kind heaven hath concealed the hour, that we might be ever in readinefs for it.

There will come an evening after which we fhall fee no morning; or a morning af-ter which we fhall fee no evening.

Our infancy is full of ignorance and fears; our youth of fin; our age of forrow; and our whole life of danger.

Never think your foul in a good cafe, fo long as you are afraid to think of dying.

Whilft young and in health, ere pains or fears abate the acts of reafon, think often on

the

the great end of your creation, and the proper means to attain that end.

Flatter not yourſelf by the example of the thief upon the croſs; but take warning by the rich fool in the goſpel.

Let not the greatneſs of your guilt, though heightened by ſuch repeated provocations as gall your conſcience, and fill your ſoul with terrour, nor the difficulty of the work, deter you from repentance, much leſs cauſe you to adjourn it to old age.

The hoary fool, who many days
   Has ſtruggled with continued ſorrow,
Renews his hope, and blindly lays
   The deſp'rate bett upon to-morrow.
To morrow comes, 'tis noon, 'tis night.
   The day like all the former flies;
Yet on he runs to ſeek delight
   To-morrow; 'till to-night he dies.

It is madneſs in a buſineſs whereon depends the welfare of the ſoul, to tarry and wait for the worſt diſpoſition of the body.

The good we have received from a man ſhould make us bear with the ill he doth us.

Where diligence opens the the door of the underſtanding, and impartiality keeps it,

truth

truth is fure to find both an enterance and a welcome.

He who defires to live, merely for living's fake, has not a worthy notion of his being. He only puts a right value upon life, who defires it that he may do good.

Every virtue gives a man a degree of felicity in fome kind: honefty gives him a good report; juftice, eftimation; prudence, refpect; courtefy and munificence, univerfal affection; temperance confers on him health of body, and fortitude fuch a fteady and quiet mind as not to be moved, whatever happens.

Fear may keep a man out of danger, but courage only can fupport him in it.

We fhould not judge of a man's merit by his great qualities, but by the ufe he makes of them.

He that laughs at mifchief tells us he is pleafed that it is done, though he is forry he had no hand in it.

He that is in the wrong oftentimes deferves our pity; but he that is unwilling to be in the right, fhould have nothing but our contempt.

Whoever flies to a knavifh lawyer for fuccour, as the fheep to the bufhes in a
storm,

ftorm, muft expeft to leave good part of his coat behind him.

No man is wife or fafe, but he that is honeft.

If he is only rich who wants nothing, a very wife man is a very rich man.

He is a wife man, who, though not fkil-led in fcience, knows how to govern his paffions and affeftions. Our paffions are our infirmities. He that can make a facrifice of his will is lord of himfelf.

When a man owns himfelf to be in an er-ror, he does but tell you in other words, that he is wifer than he was.

There is as much difference between wit and wifdom, as betwixt the talent of a buf-foon and a ftatefman; and yet, in the ordi-nary courfe of the world, one paffes for the other.

Witty men commit the moft fatal errors, as the ftrongeft horfes make the moft dan-gerous ftumbles; a moderate genius goes fair and foftly, and advances flowly, but more certainly to a defign.

Fine fenfe, and exalted fenfe, are not half fo ufeful as common fenfe.

There are forty men of wit for one man of fenfe: and he that will carry nothing
about

about him but gold, will be every day at a
lofs for want of readier change.

The beft way to prove the clearnefs of
our mind, is by fhowing its faults; as when
the ftream difcovers the dirt at the bottom,
it convinces us of the traufparency and purity of the water.

A wife man maintains the ftrength of his
body, not by delicacies, but by temperance: and drinks wine, as fick men take phy-
fick, merely for health. Reafon is his rule,
confcience his counfellor, and his actions
are ever contrary to thofe he finds fault with.
Age renders him neither morofe nor impe-
rious; his knowledge influences and tempers his mind with all the humanity, goodnefs, calmnefs, ftrength, and fincerity of a
found and unaffected philofopher, and makes his converfation fo affable, pleafant, and
inftructive, that both young and old delight
in it, and improve by his councils.

When a true genius appears in the world,
you may know him by this fign, that the
dunces are all in confederacy againft him.

The fituation of the rich differs not con-
fiderably from that of the poor. Want and
fuperfluity may be attended with equal in-
conve-

conveniences; as intenfe cold and heat have equally bad effects.

It is not uncommon to fee dejected coun. tenances in gilt coaches, and merry faces behind them.

He is the richeft man who defires no fu- perfluity, and wants for no neceffary.

Fulnefs breeds forgetfulnefs of God and his works, of men and their miferies.

The fight of a drunkard is a better fermon againft that vice, than the beft that ever was preached upon that fubject.

An habit of idlenefs, or inapplication of mind, contracts a ftagnation of humours, numbnefs of the joints, and dulnefs of the brain, hardly or never to be cured.

There are very few who know how to be idle and innocent: By doing nothing, we learn to do ill.

Bifhop Sanderfon fays, idle gentlemen and idle beggars are the very pefts of the common-wealth.

Solomon notes that from idlenefs and floth come poverty, fervitude, fruitlefs wifhes and defires, hunger, beggary, death.

The pleafure of the body is commonly the poifon of the mind.

Ufe

Ufe ftudy for delight, ornament, and ability: and labour, if not for food, for phyfic.

Books are noble companions; hiftory makes men wife, poetry witty, the mathematies fubtile, natural philofophy deep, morals grave, logick and rhetorick able to contend, &c.

Study and learning refine our minds and manners, make a young man thinking, attentive, induftrious, and wary; an old man chearful and refolved: they are an ornament in profperity, a refuge in adverfity, an entertainment abroad, a companion at home; they chear in folitude and prifon, and moderate our paffions in the height of fortune.

What fculpture is to a block of marble, education is to a human foul. The philofopher, the hero, the faint, the wife, the good, or the great man, very often lie hid in a plebean, which a proper education might have difinterred and have brought to light.

AD,

ADDENDA.

History of the four Ladies, Coquetilla, Prudiana, Profusiana, and Prudentia.

COQUETILLA was the daughter of a worthy baronet, by a lady very gay, but rather indiscreet, who took not the requisite care of her daughter's education, but let her overrun with the love of fashions, dress, and equipage; and when in London, balls, operas, plays, and the withdrawing-room took up her whole attention. She admired nobody but herself, fluttered about, laughing at, and despising a croud of men followers, whom she attracted by gay thoughtless freedoms of behaviour, so nearly treading on the steps of immodesty. Yet made she not one worthy conquest, exciting on the contrary, in all sober minds, that contempt upon herself, which she so profusely would be thought to pour down upon the rest of the world. After she had several years fluttered about the dangerous light, like some silly fly, she at last singed

F 2   the

the wings of her reputation; for, being de-
fpifed by every worthy heart, fhe became
too eafy and cheap a prey to a man the moft
unworthy of all her followers, who had refolution enough to break through thofe cob-
web referves in which fhe had incircled her
precarious virtue, and which were no longer of force to preferve her honour, when
fhe met with a man more bold and enter-
prifing than herfelf, and who was as defign-
ing and as thoughtlefs. And what then became of Coquetilla?— Why fhe was obliged to pafs over fea to Ireland, where nobody knew her, and to bury herfelf in dull
obfcurity.

Prudiana was the daughter of a gentleman who was a widower, and had, while
the young lady was an infant, buried her
mama. He was a good fort of man; but
had but one leffon to teach Prudiana, and
that was, to avoid all manner of converfation with the men; but never gave her the
right turn of mind, nor inftilled into it that
fenfe of her religious duties, which would
have been her beft guard againft all temptations. For provided fhe kept out of the
fight and converfation of the gentlemen,
and avoided the company of thofe ladies,
who

who more freely converfed with the other
fex, it was all her papa defired of her.
This gave her a haughty, fullen, and re-
ferved turn; made her ftiff, formal, and affected. She had fenfe enough to difcover
early the faults of Coquetilla, and in dislike of them, fell more eafily into that
contrary extreme; which her reclufe, education, and her papa's cautions, naturally led
her; fo that pride, referve, affectation, and
cenforioufnefs, made up the effentials of her
character, and fhe became more unamiable
than Coquetilla; and as the other was too
acceffible, Prudiana was quite unapproach-
able by gentlemen, and unfit for any converfation but that of her fervants, being alfo
deferted by thofe of her own fex, by whom
fhe might have improved, on account of
her cenforious difpofition; and what was
the confequence? Why this; every worthy
perfon defpifing her, and fhe being ufed to
fee nobody but fervants, at laft throws herfelf upon one of that clafs: In an evil hour,
fhe finds fomething that is taking to her
low tafte in the perfon of her papa's valet,
a wretch fo infinitely beneath her, but a
gay coxcomb of a fervant, that every body
attributed to her the fcandal of making the

E 3   firft

firſt advances; for, otherwiſe it was pre-
ſumed, he durſt not have looked up to his
maſter's daughter: ſo here ended all her pride. All her reſerves came to this! Her cen-
ſorioufneſs of others, redoubled people's
contempt upon herſelf, and made nobody
pity her. She was, finally, turned out of
doors without a penny of fortune; ſo that
Prudiana became the outcaſt of her family,
and the ſcorn of all who knew her; and
was forced to mingle in converſation and
company with the wretches of her huſband's
degree!

Profuſiana took another courſe to her
ruin: ſhe fell into ſome of Coquetilla's foi-
bles, but purſued them for another end,
and in another manner. Struck with the
grandeur and magnificence of what weak
people call the higher life, ſhe gives herſelf
up to the circus, to balls, to operas, to
maſquerades, and aſſemblies; affects to ſhine
at the head of all company, at Tunbridge,
at Bath, and every other place of public re-
ſort; plays high, is always receiving and
paying viſits, giving balls, and making
treats and entertainments, and is ſo much
above the conduct which moſtly recommends
a young lady to the eſteem of the deſerv-
ing

ing of the other fex, that no gentleman, who prefers folid happinefs, can think of addreffing her, though fhe is a fine perfon, and has many outward graces of behaviour. She becomes the favourite toaft of the places fhe frequents, is proud of that diftinc. tion; gives into the fafhion, and delights in the pride, that fhe can make apes in imitation whenever fhe pleafes. But yet endeavouring to avoid being thought proud, makes herfelf cheap, and is the fubject of the attempts of every coxcomb of eminence; her conduct procures her not one folid friendfhip, and fhe has not in a twelvemonth, among a thoufand profeffions of fervice, one devoir that fhe can attend to, or a friend that fhe can depend upon. All the women that fhe fees, if fhe excels them, hate her; the gay part of the men, with whom fhe accompanies moft, are all in a plot againft her honour. Even the gentlemen, whofe conduct in general is governed by principles of virtue, came down to thefe public places to partake of the innocent freedoms allowed there, and oftentimes give themfelves airs of gallantry and never have it in their thoughts to commence a treaty of marriage, with any acquaintance begun on that

gay

gay fpot. What folid friendſhips and fatis-
factions is then Profuſiana excluded from?

Her name indeed is written -on every
public window, and proſtituted, as I may
call it, at the pleaſure of every profligate,
or fot, who wears a diamond to engrave it:
and that may be, with vile and barbarous
imputations and freedoms of words, added
by rakes, who very probably never ex-
changed a fyllable with her. All this while
makes not the leaſt impreſſion upon one noble
heart; and at laſt, perhaps having run on to
the end of an uninterrupted race of follies,
ſhe is cheated into the arms of ſome vile
fortunehunter, who quickly laviſhes away
the remains of that fortune which her extra-
vagance had left; and then, after the worſt
uſage, abandoning her with contempt, ſhe
ſinks into an obſcurity, which cuts ſhort
the thread of her life, and leaves no rememberance but on the brittle glaſs, and more
faithful bark, that ever ſhe had a being.

But *Prudentia*, like the induſtrious bee,
makes her honey-hoard from every flower,
bitter as well as fweet; for every character
is of uſe to her, by which ſhe can improve her own. She had the happineſs of an
aunt, who loved her and an uncle who
doated

doated on her: for, alas! poor Prudentia
loft her papa and mama almoft in her infancy, in one week; but was fo happy in her
uncle and aunt's care, as not to mifs them
in her education, and but juft to remember
their perfons. By reading, by obfervation,
and by attention, fhe daily added new advantages to thofe which her education gave
her. She faw, and pitied the fluttering
freedoms, and dangerous flights of Coquetilla; the fullen pride, the affectation, and
ftiff referves which Prudiana affumed, fhe
penetrated, and made it her ftudy to avoid.
And the gay hazardous conduct, extravagant temper, and love of tinfelled grandeur,
which were the blemifhes of Profufiana's
character, fhe dreaded and fhunned; fhe
fortifies herfelf with the excellent examples
of the paft and prefent ages, and knows
how to avoid the errors of the faulty, and
to imitate the graces of the moft perfect.
She takes into her fcheme of that future happinefs, which fhe hopes to make her own,
what are the true excellencies of her fex,
and endeavours to appropriate to herfelf the
domeftick virtues, which fhall one day make
her the crown of fome worthy gentleman's

F 5. earthly

earthly happinefs; and which, of courfe, will fecure and heighten her own.

That noble franknefs of difpofition, that fweet and unaffected opennefs and fimplicity, which fhone in all her actions and behaviour, commend her to the reverence and efteem of all mankind, as her humility and affability, and a temper uncenforious, and ever making the beft of what is faid of the abfent perfon, of either fex, do to the love of every lady. Her name indeed is not proftituted on windows, nor carved on the bark of trees in public places; but it is pleafing to every one, dwells on every tongue, and is engraved on every heart. She meets with no addrefs but from men of honour and probity: the fluttering coxcomb, the inveigling parafite, the infidious deceiver, the mercenary fortune-hunter, fpread no fnares for a heart guarded by difcretion and prudence, as hers is. They fee all her amiable virtues are the happy refult of an uniform judgement, and the effects of her own wifdom, founded in an education to which fhe does the greateft credit; and at laft, after feveral worthy offers, enough to perplex any lady's choice, fhe bleffes fome good happy gentleman, more diftinguifhed than

the

the reft, for learning, good fenfe, and true politenefs, which is but another word for virtue and honour; and fhines to her laft hour, in all the duties of domeftic life, as an excellent wife, mother, miftrefs, friend and chriftian; and fo confirms all the ex- pectations of which her maiden life had given fuch ftrong and fuch edifying pre- fages.

To a Robin Red Breaſt, *that lodged in a Gent-*
leman's Houſe.

Written by a Young Lady.

WELCOME pretty harmleſs creature.
 From the cold and bluſt'ring wind;
Here each night thy tender nature
 Safety, warmth, and reſt ſhall find.

When the ſun's returning rays
 Drive night's gloomy ſhades away;
With thy ſoft harmonious lays,
 Here ſalute the cheerful day.

From my chamber when I come,
 Let not fear invade thy breaſt;
Still my houſe ſhall be thy home,
 At my table thou ſhalt feaſt.

Unconfin'd, or go, or ſtay,
 No one e'er ſhall thee moleſt;
All my kindneſs thou'lt repay
 With thy muſic, tuneful gueſt.

END of the SEVENTH VOLUME.

GULLIVER'S LECTURES

Vol. VIII.

CONTAINING

THE

LILLIPUTIAN BIOGRAPHER.

Vol. VIII. A

PREFACE.

WITHOUT the affiftance of Bio-
graphy, which lays before us, in
one view, the actions and conduct of thofe who have lived ages before us, we
fhould be confined to the narrow limits of
our own knowledge, which can be but
very trifling at the age of my little pupils:
I have therefore ranfacked all the libraries
of Lilliput for the materials of this volume; fo that they may be affured they will
here meet with the beft collection of curious lives, that has ever yet appeared in
the Lilliputian republic of letters.

I would advife all my little pupils, whether mafters or miffes, carefully to read
this volume and endeavour to imitate

A 2   every

every thing done by thofe, who, through their induftry, care, and prudence, have made themfelves, beloved and refpected by all, and have thereby raifed themfelves to the moft diftinguifhed honour.

THE
LILLIPUTIAN BIOGRAPHER,

MEMOIRS of a PIOUS HERMIT.

A MONG the ancient records of Lilliput, we read of a certain Hermit,
who had paffed the greateft part of his life
in the middle of a lonely defert, remote
from all mankind, whofe food was the fruits
of the earth, whofe drink was the chryftal
fountain, and who, had not one fingle
doubt arifen, might have ended his days in
devotion and happinefs. This doubt was,
whether Providence guided the actions of
men or not; for, faid he, if heaven does
really intereft itfelf in the concerns of mortals, how happens it, that we fo often fee
vice triumphing over virtue, and the good
man fuffering great injuries from the hands
of the wicked?

In order to clear the matter up, he determined, even in his old age, to leave his
humble cell, and to vifit the world. Accordingly he arofe at break of day, and

after travelling for some time, he perceived a youth come posting over a crofs way; his raiment was decent, his complexion fair, and his hair fell in loofe ringlets down his fhoulders: when they met, "Good-day to you, honoured father," faid the youth, and "Good day to you, young man," replied the Hermit. Words brought on words, and queftions produced anfwers; and the agreeable converfation deceived the length of their journey till night approached. They obferved a ftately palace juft by the road-fide; the knight who refided there was hos-pitable, but very oftentatious; they ftepped up to the door, and giving a gentle knock, were admitted in an inftant; a fplendid fupper was ferved up, and a large train of livery fervants attended, and waited upon the two guefts with as much refpeft as if they had been noblemen: at length they went to bed, being fatigued with their journey, and did not wake till morning. As foon as they were up, however, they were fummoned, by their kind hoft, to breakfaft; the table in the hall was covered with a fumptuous banquet, and rich wines were handed round in a large golden cup. When they had eaten and drank as much as they

pleafed

pleafed, the knight difmiffed them, and they left his door with ten thoufand thanks; the landlord only had reafon to be forry, for the young man was fo ungrateful as to purloin the golden cup.

They had not purfued their journey far, before the youth took an opportunity of fhowing it to the Hermit, and acquainted him of having fecreted it under his cloak. The fage ftood for fome time in aftonifhment and confufion; he wifhed, but did not dare to hint his defire of parting; he turned up his eyes to heaven, and thought it hard, that generous actions fhould be fo ftrangely rewarded.

The weather now became cloudy, a ruftling noife was heard in the air, the cattle in the fields fcudded acrofs the plain in fearch of fhelter, and at length fo violent a fhower fell, that the two travellers were obliged to feek fhelter at a neighbouring feat; it ftood upon a rifing ground, and was built in the old Gothic tafte, with turrets at every corner; it was moreover large and very ftrong; and the uncultivated ftate of the fields round about, befpoke it the refidence of fome penurious mifer.

They

They stood knocking at the door for a long time, driven by the wind, battered by rain, and almoſt blinded by lightning. At length a ſmall gleam of pity warmed the breaſt of the maſter of the houſe, he advanced with ſlow and creeping ſteps, the lock was turned with a ſuſpicious care, and, for the firſt time, his threſhold received the feet of a ſtranger. They were but half welcomed. One frugal faggot only lighted the naked wall; a ſmall pittance of coarſe brown bread was brought out, and a little flat ſmall beer to allay their thirſt; even this refreſhment was not granted without grudging, and as ſoon as the tempeſt ceaſed, a ready warning bid them depart in peace.

The Hermit could not help privately expreſſing his amaze, that a man of ſuch poſſeſſions could lead ſo ſordid a life; and here again he blamed Providence, for ſuffering ſo much wealth to be uſeleſsly locked up, when by an equal diſtribution it might have made thouſands happy. But with what new wonder was he ſeiſed, when he beheld his companion reward ſuch ſtinginefs with the valuable cup, that had before been ſtolen from a more generous benefactor.

Night

Night foon after once more came on, and once more they wanted a place of reft; and looking round, they perceived a manfion not far off; the dwelling was neither mean, nor idly fuperb, and it feemed to befpeak the mind of its owner, a man content and benevolent, not for the fake of idle praife, but from a principle of virtue. Hither they bent their way, and were very kindly received; the hoft gave them a fober, welcome repaft: and they talked upon fubjects of religion and virtue till bed-time.

In the morning, before they departed, the youth drew near to a cradle, where laid an innocent infant, the pride and joy of its aged father, and writhed its neck. But how looked the Hermit, when he beheld the black deed! O ftrange return for fo much hofpitality!

Confufed, and ftruck with horror, the good old man was determined to get rid of fo vile a companion: he fled, but the youth purfued and foon overtook him. As the country laid wide, and the roads were difficult to find, a fervant went before to fhow the way; they had occafion at laft to pafs a river, when the youth, who feemed to watch every opportunity of mifchief, ap-

proached

proached the carelefs guide as he was croffing a wooden bridge, and foufed him into
the river; for fome time he plunged, and
called for help, but being at length worn
out and fuffocated, he funk to rife no more.
.. The Hermit's eyes now fparkled with rage
and deteftation; he overcame his fears, and
wildly exclaimed, "Detefted wretch"——
before he could fpeak another word, his
partner feemed no longer man; a fweet fe-
renity graced his youthful vifage, his robe
turned as white as fnow, and flowed down
to his feet; a radiant crown adorned his
temples, heavenly odours breathed round
about him, and his wings difplayed colours
more beautiful than the rainbow.   The pilgrim ftood aftonifhed; furprife had ftopped
his fpeech, and he knew not what to do.
The beauteous angel at length broke filence,
in the following manner:

"Thy prayers and praifes, O holy Hermit, thy virtue and religion, rife in fweet
memorial before the throne of Grace, and
call even an angel down to calm thy mind.
Then know this truth; the great Creator of
the univerfe juftly claims the world he has
created, and his Majefty depends on ufing
fecond means to work his own good pur-

pofes. The vain man, who fared fumptuouf-
ly, and whofe life was too luxurious to be
good, whofe fideboard difplayed his wealth,
and who forced his guefts to morning
draughts of wine, by lofing the golden cup,
has broke off fo bad a cuftom; and though
he ftill welcomes every ftranger yet he now
does it with lefs pomp and expence.

"As for the fufpicious wretch, whofe
doors were bolted with fo much precaution,
with him I left the cup, that he might
learn, that if mortals will be kind, heaven
can repay their benevolence; confcious of
this, his icy bofom now, for the firft time,
feels the warm touch of compaffion.

"The child of our pious friend had almoft weaned the affections of his father
from the duty he owed to the Almighty;
but Got, to fave the parent, took the child;
to all but thee he feemed to die in fits, and
I was ordained to call him hence. The poor,
humble, fond father now owns in tears,
that the punifhment was juft.

"But had the falfe fervant whom I drowned returned back in fafety, what a fund of
charity would then have been loft! for he
had laid a plot againft the life and poffeffion
of his mafter, and this night, this very night,

it

it would have been put in execution. Thus then, by heaven inſtructed, depart in peace, reſign and ſin no more."

· The viſion vaniſhed. On bended knees the Hermit gazed with holy admiration, and ſaid, "Lord as in heaven on earth thy will be done:" then riſing, ſought his ancient reſidence, and ſpent the remainder of his life in piety and peace; convinced of this great duty, that when men cannot inveſti-gate the Almighty's operations, they ought to truſt to the rectitude of them, without doubting or diſcontent.

ANECDOTES of HELIM the VIR-TUOUS PHYSICIAN.

THE name of Helim is ſtill famous through all the eaſtern parts of the world. · He is called among the Perſians, even to this day, Helim, the Great Phyſi-cian. He was acquainted with all the pow-ers of ſimples, underſtood all the influen-ces of the ſtars, and knew the ſecrets that were engraved on the ſeal of Solomon the ſon of David. Helim was alſo Governor of
the

the Black Palace, and chief of the phyſicians to Alnareſchin, the great king of Perſia.

Alnareſchin was the moſt dreadful tyrant that ever reigned in this country. He was of a fearful, ſuſpicious, and cruel nature, having put to death, upon very ſlight jealouſies and ſurmiſſes, five an thirty of his queens, and above twenty ſons, whom he ſuſpected to have conſpired againſt his life. Being at length wearied with the exerciſe of ſo many cruelties in his own family, and fearing, leſt the whole race of Caliphs ſhould be entirely loſt, he one day ſent for Helim, and ſpoke to him after this manner: "Helim, ſaid he, I have long admired thy great wiſdom, and retired way of living. I ſhall now ſhew thee the 'entire confidence which I place in thee. I have only two ſons remaining who are as yet but infants. It is my deſire that thou take them home with thee and educate them as thy own. Train them in the humble unambitious purſuits of knowledge. By this means ſhall the line of Caliphs be preſerved, and my children ſucceed after me, without aſpiring to my throne whilſt I am yet alive." "The words of my lord the king ſhall be obeyed," ſaid Helim. After which he bowed and went out of the king's presence. He then received the children into his own house, and from that time bred them up with him in the studies of knowledge and virtue. The young princes loved and respected Helim as their father, and made such improvements under him, that by the age of one and twenty they were instructed in all the learning of the East. The name of the eldest was Ibrahim, and of the youngest Abdallah. They lived together in such a perfect friendship; that to this day it is said of intimate friends, that they lived together like Ibrahim and Abdallah. Helim had an only child, who was a girl of a fine soul, and a most beautiful person. Her father omitted nothing in her education, that might make her the most accomplished woman of her age. As the young princes were in a manner excluded from the rest of the world, they frequently conversed with this lovely virgin, who had been brought up by her father in the same course of knowledge and virtue. Abdallah, whose mind was of a softer turn than that of his brother, grew by degrees so enamoured of her conversation, that he did not think he lived when he was not in company with his beloved Balfora, for that

was

was the name of the maid. The fame of
her beauty was fo great, that at length it
came to the ears of the king, who, pretending to vifit the young princes his fons,
demanded of Helim the fight of Balfora his
fair daughter. The king was fo inflamed
with her beauty and behaviour, that he
fent for Helim the next morning, and told
him, it was now his defign to recompence him for all his faithful fervices; and, that,
in order to it, he intended to make his daughter queen of Perfia. Helim, who knew very
well the fate of all thofe unhappy women
who had been thus advanced, and could not
but be privy to the fecret love which Abdallah bore his daughter; "Far be it, faid
he, from the king of Perfia to contaminate
the blood of the Caliphs, and join himfelf
in marriage with the daughter of his phyfician." The king, however, was fo impatient for fuch a bride, without hearing any
excufes, he immediately ordered Balfora to
be fent for into his prefence, keeping the
father with him, in order to make her fenfible of the honour which he defigned her.
Balfora, who was too modeft and humble
to think her beauty had made fuch an impreffion on the king, was a few moments
after

after brought into his prefence as he had commanded.

She appeared in the king's eyes as one of the virgins of paradife. But upon hearing the honour which he intended her, fhe fainted away, and fell down as dead at his feet. Helim wept, and after having recovered her out of the trance into which fhe was fallen, reprefented to the king, that fo unexpected an honour was too great to have been communicated to her all at once; but that, if he pleafed, he would himfelf prepare her for it. The king bid him take his own way, and difmiffed him. Balfora was again conveyed to her father's houfe, where the thoughts of Abdallah renewed her affliction every moment, infomuch, that at length fhe fell into a raging fever. The king was informed of her condition by thofe that faw her. Helim finding no other means of extricating her from the difficulties fhe was in, after having compofed her mind, and made her acquainted with his intentions, gave her a certain potion, which he knew would lay her afleep for many hours; and afterwards, in all the feeming diftrefs of a difconfolate father, informed the king fhe was dead. The king, who never let any

fenti-

sentiments of humanity come too near his heart, did not much trouble himself about the matter; however, for his own reputation, he told the father, that since it was known through the empire that Balsora died at a time when he designed her for his bride, it was his intention that she should be honoured as such after her death, and that her body should be laid in the Black Palace, among those of his deceased queens.

In the mean time Abdallah, who had heard of the king's design, was not less afflicted than his beloved Balsora. As for the several circumstances of his distress, as also how the king was informed of an irrecoverable distemper into which he was fallen, they are to be found at length in the history of Helim. It shall suffice to acquaint my reader, that Helim, some days after the supposed death of his daughter, gave the prince a potion of the same nature with that which had laid Balsora asleep.

It is the custom, among the Persians, to convey, in a private manner, the bodies of all the royal family, a little after their death, into the Black Palace: which is the repository of all who are descended from the Caliphs, or any ways allied to them. The chief

chief phyfician is always governor of the Black Palace, it being his office to embalm and preferve the holy family after they are dead, as well as to take care of them while they are yet living. The Black Palace is fo called from the colour of the building, which is all of the fineft polifhed black marble. There are always burning in it five thoufand everlafting lamps. It has alfo a hundred folding doors of ebony, which are each of them watched day and night by an hundred negroes, who are to take care that nobody enters befides the governor.

Helim, after having conveyed the body of his daughter into this repofitory, and at the appointed time received her out of the fleep into which fhe was fallen, took care fome time after to bring that of Abdallah into the fame place. Balfora watched over him, till fuch time as the dofe he had taken loft its effects. Abdallah was not acquainted with Helim's defign when he gave him the fleepy potion. It is impoffible to defcribe the furprife, the joy, the tranfport he was in at his firft awaking. He fancied himfelf in the retirements of the bleffed, and that the fpirit of his dear Balfora, who he thought was juft gone before him, was the

firft

firft who came to congratulate his arrival.
She foon informed him of the place he was
in, which, notwithftanding all its horrors,
appeared to him more fweet than the bow-
er of Mahomet, in the company of his
Balfora.

Helim, who was fuppofed to be taken
up in the embalming of the bodies, vifited
the place very frequently. His great perplexity was how to get the lovers out of
it, the grates being watched in fuch a manner as I have before related. This confideration did not a little difturb the two interred lovers. At length Helim bethought
himfelf, that the firft day of the full moon,
of the month Tizpa, was near at hand.
Now it is a tradition among the Perfians,
that the fouls of thofe of the royal family,
who are in a ftate of blifs, do on the firft
full moon after their deceafe, pafs through
the eaftern gate of the Black Palace, which
is therefore called the Gate of Paradife, in
order to take their flight for that happy
place. Helim therefore having made due
preparation for this night, dreffed each of
the lovers in a robe of azure filk, wrought
in the fineft looms of Perfia, with a long
train of linen whiter than fnow, which
flowed

flowed on the ground behind them. Upon Abdallah's head he fixed a wreath of the greeneft myrtle, and on Balfora's a garland of the frefheft rofes. Their garments were fcented with the richeft perfumes of Arabia. Having thus prepared every thing, the full moon was no fooner up, and fhining in all its brightnefs, but he privately opened the gate of Paradife, and fhut it after the fame manner, as foon as they had paffed through it. The band of negros, who were pofted at a little diftance from the gate, feeing two fuch beautiful apparitions, that fhow- ed themfelves to advantage by the light of the full moon, and being ravifhed with the odour that flowed from their garments, im- mediately concluded them to be the ghofts of the two perfons lately deceafed. They fell upon their faces as they paffed through the midft of them, and continued proftrate on the earth till fuch time as they were out of fight. They reported the next day what they had feen, but this was looked upon by the king himfelf, and moft others, as the compliment that was ufually paid to any of his family. Helim had placed two of his mules at about a mile diftance from the Black Temple, on the fpot which they had

agreed

agreed upon for their rendezvous. Here he met them, and conducted them to one of his own houses which was situated on mount Khacan. The air on this mountain was so very healthful, that Helim had formerly transported the king thither, in order to recover him out of a long fit of sickness; which succeeded so well, that the king made him a present of the whole mountain, with a beautiful house and gardens, that were on the top of it. In this retirement lived Abdallah and Balfora. They were both so fraught with all kinds of knowledge, and possessed with so constant and mutual a passion for each other, that their solitude never lay heavy on them. Abdallah applied himself to those arts which were agreeable to this manner of living, and the situation of the place, insomuch that in a few years, he converted the whole mountain into a kind of garden, and covered every part of it with plantations or spots of flowers. Helim was too good a father to let him want any thing that might conduce to make his retirement pleasant.

In about ten years after their abode in this place, the old king died, and was succeeded by his son Ibrahim, who, upon the

sup-

suppofed death of his brother, had been called to court, and entertained there as heir
to the Perfian empire.   Though he was for
fome years inconfoleable for the death of his
brother, Helim durft not truft him with the
fecret, which he knew would have fatal
confequences, fhould it by any means come
to the knowledge of the old king.   Ibrahim was no fooner mounted to the throne,
but Helim fought after an opportunity of
making a difcovery to him, which he knew
would be very agreeable to fo goodnatured
and generous a prince.   It fo happened, that
before Helim found fuch an opportunity as
he defired, the new king Ibrahim, having
been feparated from his company in a chafe,
and almoft fainting with heat and thirft, faw
himfelf at the foot of mount Khacan; he immediately afcended the hill, and coming to
Helim's houfe demanded fome refrefhments.
Helim was very luckily there at that time,
and after having fet before the king the
choiceft of wines and fruits, finding him
wonderfully pleafed with fo feafonable a
treat, told him, that the beft part of his entertainment was to come, upon which he
opened to him the whole hiftory of what
had paffed.

The

The king was at once aftoniſhed and tranſported at ſo ſtrange a relation, and ſeeing
his brother enter the room with Balſora in
his hand, he leaped off from the ſofa on
which he ſat, and cried out, *'tis he; my*
Abdallah!——Having ſaid this, he fell upon
his neck and wept. The whole company
for ſome time remained ſilent, and ſhedding
tears for joy. The king at length, after
having kindly reproached Helim for depriving him ſo long of ſuch a brother, embraced Balſora with the greateſt tenderneſs, and
told her, that ſhe ſhould now be a queen
indeed, for that he would immediately make
his brother king of all the conquered nations on the other ſide the Tigris. He eaſily diſcovered in the eyes of our two lovers,
that, inſtead of being tranſported with the
offer, they preferred their preſent retirement
to empire. At their requeſt therefore he
changed his intentions, and made them a
preſent of all the open country as far as
they could ſee from the top of mount Khacan. Abdallah, continuing to extend his
former improvements, beautified this whole proſpect with groves and fountains, gardens, and ſeats of pleaſure, till it became
the moſt delicious ſpot of ground within the

empi-

empire, and it is therefore called the Garden of Perſia. This Caliph, Ibrahim, after a long and happy reign, died without children, and was ſucceeded by Abdallah, a ſon of Abdallah and Balſora. This was that king Abdallah; who afterwards fixed the imperial reſidence upon mount Khacan, which continues at this time to be the favourite palace of the Perſian empire.

The good diſpoſitions of the two brothers Ibrahim and Abdallah, as well as that of the fair Balſora, and the happy conſequences reſulting therefrom, can be imputed only to the advantage of a virtuous education under the wiſe Helim; a proof that nothing has contributed ſo much to the happineſs of perſons of all ranks, and of every age, country, and religion, as pious precepts early impreſſed on the infant mind, and inforced with ſuitable examples.

MEMOIRS of a BASKET-MAKER.

IN the midſt of the ocean, commonly called the South Sea, lie the iſlands of Solomon: in the centre of thoſe lies one, diſtant

ftant from the reft, and larger in proportion.
The prince, who, now reigns abfolute in
this central ifland, has given the Name of
Solomon's Iflands to the whole, by the
effect of that wifdom wherewith he polifhed
the manners of his people.

A defcendant of one of the great men of
this ifland, becoming rich to fuch a degree,
as to defpife the good qualities which had
originally enobled his family, thought of nothing but how to fupport and diftinguifh his
dignity by the pride of an ignorant mind,
and difpofition abandoned to pleafure. He
had a houfe on the fea-fide, where he fpent
great part of his time in hunting and fifhing; but found himfelf at a lofs in purfuit
of a large flip of marfh land, overgrown with
high reeds, that lay between his houfe and
the fea: refolving at length, that it became
not a man of his quality to fubmit to reftraint
in his pleafures, for the eafe and convenien-
cy of an obftinate mechanic, and having often endeavoured in vain to buy it of the
owner, who was an honeft poor Bafket-maker, and whofe livelyhood depended on
working up the flags of thofe reeds in a manner peculiar to himfelf; the gentleman took
advantage of a very high wind, and com-

C 3 manded

manded his fervants to burn down the bar-
rier. The Bafket-maker, who faw himfelf
undone, complained of the oppreffion in
terms more fuited to his fenfe of the injury, than the refpect due to the rank of the
offender; and the reward this imprudence
procured him, was the additional injuftice
of blows and reproaches, and all kinds of
infult, ill ufage, and indignity.

There was but one remedy, and he took
it; for going to the capital, with the marks
of his hard ufage upon him, he threw himfelf at the feet of the king, and procured a
citation for his oppreffor's appearance; who
confeffing the charge, proceeded to juftify
his behaviour, by the poor man's unmind-
fulnefs of the fubmiffion due from the vulgar to gentlemen of rank and diftinction.
But pray, replied the king, what diftinction
of rank had the grand-father of your father,
when, being a cleaver of wood in the palace of my anceftors, he was raifed from
among thofe vulgar you fpeak of with fuch
contempt; his diftinction was nobler than
yours; it was the diftinction of foul, not of
fortune! I am forry I have a gentleman in
my kingdom, who is bafe enough to be
ignorant, that eafe and diftinction of fortune

ne were bestowed on him for any other end,
than that being at rest from all cares of pro-
viding for himself, he might apply his heart,
head, and hand, for the public advantage of
others.

Here the king, discontinuing his speech,
fixed an eye of indignation on a sullenness
which he observed in the haughty offender,
who muttered out his dislike of the encouragement this way of thinking must give to
the commonalty, whom he considered as
persons of no consequence, in comparison of
men who were born with honours. When
reflection is wanting, replied the king, with
a smile of disdain, men must find their de-
fect in the pain of their sufferings. Yan-
humo, added he, turning to a hardy captain of his gallies, strip the injured and the
injurer, and, conveying them to one of the
most remote parts of the island, set them on
shore in the night, and leave them both to
their fortune.

The place in which they were landed was
a marsh, under cover of whose flags the
gentleman was in hopes to conceal himself,
and give the slip to his companion, whom
he thought it a disgrace to be found with;
but the lights in the galley having given

alarm

alarm to the favages, a confiderable body of
them came down in the morning, and difcovered the ftrangers in their hiding-places;
fetting up a difmal yell, they furrounded
them, and advancing nearer and nearer, with
a kind of clubs, feemed determined to defpatch them without fenfe of hofpitality or
mercy.

Here the gentleman began to difcover,
that the fuperiority of his blood was imaginary; for between a confcioufnefs of fhame
and cold, under the nakednefs he had never been ufed to, a fear to the event, from
the fiercenefs of the favages, and the want
of means to foften or divert their afperity,
he fell behind the poor fharer of his calamity, and with an unmanly fneakingnefs, gave
up the poft of honour, and made a leader
of the very man, whom he had thought
it a difgrace to confider as a companion.

The Bafket-maker, on the contrary, to
whom the poverty of his condition had made
nakednefs habitual, to whom a life of pain
and mortification, reprefented death as not
dreadful; and whofe rememberance of his
fkill in arts, of which thefe favages were
ignorant, gaves him hopes of becoming fafe,
from demonftrating that he could be ufeful,
                                                moved

moved with bolder and more open freedom, and having plucked a handful of the flags, fat down without emotion, and making figns that he would fhow them fomething worthy their attention, fell to work with fmiles and noddings; while the favages drew near, and gazed; in expectation of the confequence.

It was not long before he had wreathed a kind of coronet, of pretty workmanfhip, and rifing with refpect and fearfulnefs, approached the favage who appeared the chief, and placing it gently on his head, fo charmed and ftruck his followers, that they threw down their clubs, and formed a dance of welcome and congratulation round the author of fo furprifing a favour.

There was not one but fhowed the marks of his impatience to be made as fine as his captain; fo the poor Bafket-maker had his hands full of employment; and the favages obferving one quite idle, while the other was fo bufy in their fervice, took up arms in behalf of natural juftice, and began to lay on arguments in favour of their purpofe.

The bafket-maker's pity now effaced the remembrance of his fufferings; fo he arofe

and

and fecured his oppreffor; by making fings that he was ignorant of the art; but might, if they thought fit, be ufefully employed in waiting on the work, and fetching flags to his fupply, as faft as he fhould want them.

This propofition luckily fell in with the defire the favages had to keep themfelves at leifure, that they might crowd round and mark the progrefs of a work they took fo much pleafure in; they left the gentleman therefore to his duty in the bafket-maker's fervice; and confidered him from that time forward as one who was, and ought to be treated as inferior to their benefactor.

Men, wives, and children, from all corners of the ifland, came in droves, the men fell to work, gathered boughs and poles, made a fine hut to lodge the Bafket-maker, and brought down daily from the country fuch provifions as they live upon themfelves, taking care to offer the imagined fervant nothing till his mafter had done eating.

Three months reflection in this mortified condition, gave a new and juft turn to our gentleman's ideas; infomuch, that lying awake one night, he thus confeffed his fentiments in favour of the Bafket-maker. I
have

have been to blame, and wanted judgement
to diftinguifh between excellency and accident. When I fhould have meafured nature, I but looked to vanity. The preference which fortune gives is but empty and
imaginary; and I perceive too late, that
only things of ufe are naturally honourable.
I am afhamed, when I compare my malice, to remember your humanity; but if the
gods fhould pleafe to call me to a repoffef-
fion of my rank and happinefs, I would di-
vide all with you in atonement of my juftly punifhed arrogance.

He promifed, and performed his promife;
for the king foon after fent the captain who
had landed them, with prefents to the favages; and ordered him to bring both back
again: and it continues to this day a cuftom
in that ifland, to degrade all gentlemen who
cannot give a better reafon for their pride,
than that they were born to do nothing:
and the word for this punifhment is, *Send
him to the Bafketmaker.*

ANECDOTES of the HUMANE MR. ALLWORTHY.

MASTER William Smith was proud, obstinate, passionate, ill-natured, fretful and whimsical, and in consequence of being a naughty boy, had very few acquaintance or play-fellows; for young gentlemen were ashamed of being seen with him, lest they should be thought to resemble him, and even poor children, who were good, excused themselves from playing with him. Besides, he used them very ill, was quite fretful if he did not win at marbless, cards, &c. wanted them to oblige him in every thing, and yet would never comply with their desires. One day Mr. Allworthy, a gentleman of large fortune, and excellent character, sent messages to all the little boys in the neighbourhood, poor as well as rich, that they should come to his house the next day, and whoever had the best character from his parents, servants, and the neighbours, should receive from him a present of a good collection of entertaining and instructive
tive

tive books, and wear a ribbon with this motto, "This diſtinguiſhes goodneſs."

Maſter Smith no ſooner heard this, than he ran to his mama, his papa was dead, and told her of Mr. Allworthy's intention, that he thought it would be a great honour to gain theſe prizes, and that he did not doubt but he ſhould obtain them. You have too good an opinion of yourſelf, child, ſaid ſhe; I aſſure you I dare not expeſt ſuch a thing; I will go with you, if you deſire it; but it ſhocks me that I am forced to tell you, I can ſay very little in your favour. Maſter Smith was not however diſcouraged by his mama's reproof; but ran out to give orders for the chariot to be in readineſs the next morning. He dreſſed himſelf at the time in his beſt clothes, and ſet out with his mama for Mr. Allworthy's. As they went along, they ſaw ſeveral little boys walking to the ſame place on the ſame occaſion. Maſter Smith laughed at, and deſpiſed them, for their expeſtations of ſucceſs: but his mama bid him remember, that the prizes were not to be given to the richeſt or fineſt child, but to him who ſhould be found to be the beſt.

When

When they alighted at Mr. Allworthy's they saw several little masters, and poor children, assembled. Mr. Allworthy soon entered the room, in which was a handsome bookcase, containing near a hundred books proper for the instruction and entertainment of children. Master Smith looked at them with an air of confidence, as if he was quite secure of a preference in his favour. A little boy, whose name was Charles Nichols, came up to Master Smith, and told him, he remembered he had once the honour of playing with him at Mr. Jones's, and therefore he took the liberty of asking him how he did. The child was perfectly neat and clean: he was not handsome, but there was so much sweetness and good-nature expressed in his countenance, and so much politeness and complaisance in his behaviour, that he gained the love and esteem of every good person. Master Smith thought himself so much superior to this little boy, who happened to be poor, that he scarcely answered him, which Mr. Allworthy observing, said to Charles, I think, my dear, I heard you mention your having had the honour of playing with Master Smith; remember, my love, it can confer no honour on any one to play

with

with a naughty boy; the pooreſt child, if he be good and humble, is far ſuperior to the richeſt who is naughty. He who thinks very highly of himſelf, will certainly be brought to ſhame. Maſter Smith coloured and was aſhamed.

Mr. Allworthy then began his enquiry. Several of the children had indifferent charaĉters, but ſome were tolerably good. Maſter Thompſon was acknowledged to be the beſt boy who had been yet examined; an old ſervant, who had been his nurſemaid, aſſured Mr. Allworthy, that in his mama's abſence, when ſhe had the care of him, ſhe never deſired him twice to do any thing. It was now Maſter Smith's turn: Mr. Allworthy aſked, if he was dutiful to his parent. Mrs. Smith only anſwered with a ſigh; he then deſired to know, if he was fond of his brother and ſiſter, if he ſpoke in an obliging manner to the ſervants, and other inferiors, if he behaved civilly to his viſitors and playfellows? Mrs. Smith then ſhook her head. Of what then, Madam, ſaid Mr. Allworthy, can ſuch a boy be proud? What could make him deſpiſe a child, who ſpoke ſo pretty as Charles Nichols did? Indeed, Sir, anſwered Mrs. Smith, I had no

expec-

expectation of his gaining the reward; but
I brought him, that he might be humbled
into a fenfe of his faults, by comparifon
with others. I pity you fincerely, Madam,
faid Mr. Allworthy, yet I ftill more pity
him, for whoever is naughty, injures himfelf. How miferable, child, added he, muft
you be! Beloved by nobody; vexing every one. How could you poffibly expect a
reward, when you only deferve punifhment? Do not ftand near Mafter Thompfon: he is very good, and therefore cannot
defire to be of your acquaintance.

. Charles Nichols was now the only boy
to be queftioned. He ftood with his eyes
modeftly caft down; Mr. Allworthy afked
his father and mother if he was dutiful.
They both eagerly cried out, Oh! Sir,
this child, though but five years old, is a
real bleffing to us. We never afked him to
do any thing, but he immediately performed it. When we have been fick, he has
attended us with the care and tendernefs of
nurfe, a fpeaking in whifpers, and walking
on tiptoe, to avoid difturbing us. He is
the kindeft, beft of brothers. He never
has any thing given him to eat but he referves for his brother and fifter the largeft
share.

ſhare. He always refuſes to take any fruit, cakes, &c. but what we chooſe he ſhould have, he willingly exchanges playthings with his playfellows, or lends, and frequently gives them away, when his brother, ſiſter, or viſitors, ſeemed to be pleaſed with any of them. We keep no ſervant, but our neighbours and I hope all this company who know him, will give him the character of a good child. The gentlemen and ladies all ſaid, that Charles's behaviour did honour to his parents inſtructions, and was a proof of his excellent diſpoſition, adding, thoſe of us who have children, wiſh to have them imitate Charles Nichols, and thoſe who have none, can ſcarcely help feeling a deſire of being the parents of ſuch. All his poor neighbours ſaid it gave them pleaſure to ſee him, he was ſo induſtrious, ſo fond of his book, ſo attentive to his parents, and ſo deſirous of making every body happy, that there could not be a better example for any children, whether they were rich or poor. They never heard him aſk for any thing, without uſing ſome ſuch expreſſion, as *pray* give me this, or *be ſo good* as to do ſuch a thing, and always received every thing with thanks. He never

fretted nor murmured on a refufal of what he
wifhed to have, but was convinced that his
friends knew what was beft for him.

Mr. Allworthy was fo much delighted
with this information, that he took little
Charles in his arms, kiffed him feveral times, and carrying him to the book-cafe,
told him, that half of thofe books fhould be
his, and the other half he fhould give to
Mafter Thompfon, adding, that he had alfo
a ribbon for each. I thank you, fir, faid the
good boy very modeftly, for your kind intention; but I am afraid I fhould be thought
proud and vain, if I wear your favour.
No, my love, anfwered Mr. Allworthy, you
are as much entitled to wear it as Mafter
Thompfon: every body will know, that it
was not given you as a piece of finery, but
as a mark of your defert. Then turning to
Mafter Smith, who felt afhamed of his own
unworthinefs, You fee child, faid he, it is
not the boy who rides in his coach, nor
who is rich, who gains every ones approbation; but it is he who behaves beft, who
does what is defired by his friends, and
who endeavours to improve his own mind.
Charles Nichols, in a whifper, begged to
know, if Mr. Allworthy liked he fhould
make

make a prefent of a book to each of the mafters and other boys. Mr. Allworthy praif-
ed him for his defign, but told him, he
could not confent, that what belonged by
right to the good, fhould be given to the
unworthy. When thefe children, faid he,
become like you and mafter Thompfon, I
fhall not only be pleafed with you for en-
couraging their improvement, but I will add
prefents to yours, for their inftruction and
entertainment. And now, my dear mafter
Thompfon, let me hear you read a ftory.

Mafter Thompfon immediately did as he
was defired, making every proper ftop, and
pronouncing every word with the utmoft
propriety. Charles Nichols then did the
fame at Mr. Allworthy's defire, they then
ftood up, and fpelled extremely well; and
if either of them happened to forget a word,
he afked the other how it was fpelled, and
thanked him for the information which was
given him, with the utmoft modefty and
good nature.

Mafter Thompfon and Charles Nichols then
went with Mr. Allworthy, to take a walk
in his garden; he told the other children,
he fhould not afk them then to go with him
and the good boys, but that he fhould al-

ways

ways be glad to fee any of them, who improved by an imitation of their examples. Mafter Thompfon afked little Charles to ride home with him in his chariot, which offer he gladly accepted, not fo much, he faid, for the pleafure of the ride, though that would be agreeable to him, as for the enjoyment of Mafter Thompfon's company, which might be an improvement to him.

Mr. Allworthy then gave thefe two excellent children an invitation to his houfe, whenever their parents could part from them, faying, he fhould always fend for them both, whenever any other children came to pay him a vifit. As to Mafter Smith, he was now humbled into fhame and forrow. He and the other children fell on their knees, and promifed amendment; and I have the pleafure of hearing that they became, in a fhort time, worthy of an intimacy with Charles Nichols and Mafter Thompfon.

———————

The HISTORY of MASTER JACKEY and MISS HARRIOT GRACEMORE.

IN the county of Salop, and near the delightful borders of the Severn, lived the Earl of Fairfame, remarkable for his generofity and benevolence to the poor, and affability and good nature to the rich,

The fituation of my lord's was truely charming. There was a village not above half a mile diftant, in which lived Mr. Gracemore, a tradefman of indifferent circumftances; he had a fon whom he named John, after himfelf: when mafter Jackey grew to be about eight years old, his papa, who was exceffively fond of him, fent for his coufin, who was about his own age, to be a companion for him; they went to fchool together, and after fchool hours they would play at marbles.

Mafter Tommy, for that was his coufin's name, was not fo good a boy as mafter Jackey, an inftance of which I will give you.

This young gentleman had fome how or other got into favour with Mr. Brufhem's, his fchoolmafter, cook, from whom, though only a day fcholar, he received many little

knick-

knick-knacks, which the young gentlemen who were boarders but feldom tafted. This encouragement made him a conftant vifitant of the kitchen, where he was oftener found than any other of his fchool-fellows. This raifed a kind of jealoufy among the boarders; and though they bore him no ill will, re-folved to play him an innocent trick, to fhame him, if poffible, from fpending his time among women in a kitchen.

They foon effected this fcheme; for with-out his knowing it, he one morning en-tered the fchool with a dirty difh-cloth hanging to his tail, which raifed a loud laugh from every one, even Mr. Brufhem himfelf had much difficulty to keep his coun-tenance.

Though he was much laughed at in the fchool, he was pitied in the kitchen, and received more favours than ever, and was frequently in the kitchen by himfelf with the pantry unlocked. Mrs. Cook had once or twice given him fome preferved plumbs, which encreafed his defire for a few more. He once faw her take fome out of a jar, and put them into a plate for the next day's ufe; but before fhe had well finifhed, being called away in hafte, ran out with the candle

in

in her hand, and in her hurry threw down
a moufe trap, which had been baited and
fet on a fhelf above. Unluckily the trap
fell among the plumbs, and ftill worfe, unluckily did not go off.

No fooner was the cook out of the kitchen, than Tommy ran into the pantry, and
it being dark, thruft his fore finger and
thumb into the trap inftead of the jar; it
inftantly went off, and caught him faft. Unable to difengage himfelf, he roared out luf-
tily, when Mr. Brufhem, his wife, the
cook, fcullion, and ten or a dozen of his
fchool-fellows, ran to fee what was the
matter, when poor Tommy was dancing
about the kitchen, with the trap hanging
to his fingers; this indeed broke him of
fpending his time in the kitchen, but as
long as he was at the fchool, he went by
the name of trap-fingered Tommy.

Another time he wanted his coufin to ftop
and play when they came out of fchool,
before they had been home; but Jackey,
who was remarkable for his pretty behaviour, never would till he had afked his
papa's leave. One day they faw a boy playing at top, Come, fays Tommy, let us have
a game: No, fays Jackey, not till I have
been

been home. Why? fays he, we won't ftay
long, and my uncle won't know it: fo pulling out his top he began to play.

O fye! fays Jackey, I did not think you
was fo naughty; when you know my papa
always defires us not to ftop as we come
from fchool, therefore, I will make hafte
home; I do not care, fays Tommy, I will
have one game.

Mafter Jackey ftood a little, begging him
not to ftay, but finding it in vain, went
home by himfelf. His papa afked him where Tommy was? He told the truth, for he
knew better than to tell a ftory: Tommy
ftaid fo long, that his uncle went and fetched him home, and fent him fupperlefs to
bed, which had fuch an effect upon him,
that he behaved pretty well for fome time;
but Mafter Jackey was fo conftant in his
good behaviour to every body, that the
whole village talked of nothing elfe, which
at laft reached the ears of the Earl of Fairfame, in the following manner. There was
an old woman who ufed to ferve my lord's
houfe with butter. My lord happening to
fee this old woman one day, fays to her,
well Goody Creamer, what news? Who is
the beft boy in town now? To which the
old

old woman, making a low curtefy, anfwers, an't pleafe you, my lord, Jackey
Gracemore, I think; for though I often
meet him in the ftreet coming from fchool,
yet I never fee him behave rudely, and I
hear he is a fine fcholar. Ah, indeed! fays
my lord, then I muft make him a prefent,
when putting his hand into his fob, he pulled out his fine watch, and bid her give it
to Mafter Jackey, and tell his papa, he would
call at his houfe to morrow, and fee if what
he heard of his fon was true. The old
woman went directly to Mr. Gracemore's,
and delivered the fine watch to Mafter Jackey, and her meffage to his papa; the
next day my lord came, dreffed very grand,
in his ftar and garter, his fword by his fide,
and his gold-headed cane in his hand, and
was received with great refpect.

When he came to Mr. Gracemore's, he
enquired for mafter Jackey, who was then
playing at battledore and fhuttlecock in the
yard with his coufin; but hearing who wanted him, he left play immediately, and
going to the room where my lord was,
he made a very low bow and entered; my
lord took him by the hand, and afked him
a great many queftions all which he anfwer-

ed

ed fo prettily, that his lordfhip was quite
charmed with him, and begged the favour
to have Jackey home with him for a month
or fo, faying, he had a young lady about
his age at his houfe who would ferve him
for a playmate; my lord, fays Mafter Jackey, my papa has been fo good as to provide me a playmate: I have a coufin who
lives with me in the houfe: if my papa
pleafes, I fhould be proud to accept of your
lordfhip's invitation. Then faid Mr. Gracemore, if his lordfhip will be troubled with
you for a month, you may go home with
him now; but I do not know how your
coufin will fpare you. Ah! fays the Earl,
he fhall go with us: whereupon Tommy
being called, they all fet off for my lord's
houfe, where they were kindly received by
Lady Fairfame, who took them out, and
fhowed them fome fine curiofities which
were in the garden: the garden itfelf
was indeed charming, every one who
walked in it, found fome moral couched under the general defign; here you were
taught wifdom as you walked, and felt the
force of fome noble truth, or delicate pre-
cept, refulting from the fine difpofition of
the groves, trees, and grottos.

You

" You defcended from the houfe between two groves of trees, planted in fuch a manner, that they were impenetrable to the eye; while on each hand the way was adorned with all that was beautiful in gardening, ftatuary, and painting. This paffage from the houfe opened into an area furrounded with rocks, flowers, trees, and fhrubs; but all fo difpofed as if each was the fpontaneous production of nature. As they proceeded forward on this fpot, on the right and left hand were two gates, oppofite each other, of very different architecture and defign, and before them lay a beautiful fummer-houfe, built rather with minute elegance than oftentation. The infide was adorned with emblematical paintings, reprefenting the charms of virtue and deformity of vice; there was alfo a painting of Eneas carrying his aged father on his back from the flames of Troy, leading his little fon by the hand; and his wife following them. The outfide was embellifhed in the moft mafterly manner, and adorned with the figure of a Mercury on the top of it.

The right hand gate was planned with the utmoft fimplicity, or rather rudenefs, ivy clafped round the pillars, the baleful cyprefs

prefs hung over it; time feemed to have deftroyed all the fmoothnefs and regularity of the ftone: two champions with lifted clubs appeared in the aft of guarding its accefs; dragons and ferpents were feen in the moft hideous attitudes, to deter them from approaching; and the perfpeftive view that lay behind was dark and gloomy to the laft degree; and Jackey and Tommy were tempted to enter only from the motto: Pervious to virtue.

The oppofite gate was formed in a far different manner; the architefture was light, elegant, and inviting; flowers hung in wreaths round the pillars; nymphs in the moft alluring attitudes beckoned their approach; while all that lay behind as far as the eye could reach, feemed gay, luxuriant, and capable of affording endlefs pleafure. The motto itfelf was contrived to invite them, for over the gate were written thefe words, *The defcent is eafy.*

By this time I fancy you begin to perceive, that the gloomy gate was defigned to reprefent the road to virtue; and the oppofite the more agreeable road to vice.

I is but natural to fuppofe, that our young gentry were tempted to enter by the

gate

gate which offered them fo many allure-
ments; and Lady Fairfame, as was always
her cuftom in thefe cafes, left them to
their choice; and they, like moft others,
took to the left, that promifed moft entertainment.

Immediately upon entering the gate of
vice, the trees and flowers were difpofed
in fuch a manner as to make the moft pleafing impreffion; but as they walked on, the
landfcapes began to darken, the paths grew
more intricate, they appeared to go downwards, frightful rocks feemed to be over
their heads, gloomy caverns, unexpeded
precipices, aweful ruins, heaps of bones, and
terrifying founds, caufed by unfeen waters,
began to take place of what at firft feemed fo lovely; it was in vain to attempt returning, the labyrinth was fo perplexed.
When Lady Fairfame difcovered they were
fufficiently impreffed with the horrours of
what they heard and faw, fhe took advantage of it, and thus addreffed them: "My
dears, you now fee the terrible termination
of the road to vice, I would have you learn
from what you now fee before you, that,
vice, how fpecious foever at its firft appearance, terminates in endlefs mifery:" And
then

then taking them by the hand, she brought them by an hidden door, a shorter way back into the area.

The gloomy gate now presented itself before them, and though there seemed little in its appearance to raise their curiosity, yet encouraged by the motto, they were tempted to enter. The darkness of the enterance, frightful figures which seemed to obstruct their way, and trees of mournful green, conspired at first to disgust them; however as they proceeded, all began to open and wear a more pleasing appearance, beautiful cascades, beds of flowers, trees laden with fruit, and arbours of jessamine and roses improved the scene: they now found they were ascending, and as they proceeded, all nature grew more beautiful, the prospect widened as they went higher, and Lady Fairfame at last led them to an arbour, from whence they might view the garden and the whole country round. Now, my dears, said she, from this little walk you may learn, that, The road to virtue terminates in happiness.

When they came back, my lord introduced them to Miss Harriot, which was the
young

young lady the Earl had proppſed for a companion for Maſter Jackey: her papa was a grocer at Shrewſbury, and my lord brought her home to live with him on account of the good charaƈter he heard of her; my lord left them together, when Miſs Harriot ſhowed them a fine rocking horſe my lord had bought her.

Thus the young folks lived very happily together, only Maſter Tommy would ſometimes be unlucky; for one day he tied a rope to two trees, and perſuaded Miſs Harriot to ſwing: ſhe had ſcarce ſat down on the rope, when he ſwung her with violence, that ſhe fell off and hurt herſelf ſadly; my lord was very angry, and I believe would have beat him, had not Maſter Jackey and Miſs Harriot interceded for him; however, the next day he got into miſchief again; for in getting up a tree into which he had ſeen a bird fly, he thinking, to be ſure, it had a neſt there, and trying to deprive the poor bird of its young, tore his breeches, which was a nice new pair, in ſuch a manner, that he never could wear them again; at length he grew ſo naughty, that he would ſcarce ever play with Jackey and Harriot, but get into the kitchen, and

play

play at cards with one of the maids, who was not so good as she should be to suffer it.

One day, being at play with Jackey at whipping top, he without any provocation catched up the top and threw it at his head; Miss Harriot, who sat on the side of a new wheel-barrow to see them play, and seeing Tommy's ill-nature, cries out, O fye, Tommy, I'll tell my lord of your ill usage to your cousin: the naughty boy directly runs to her, takes hold of the barrow and threw her down. Now my lord happening to see this from a window, sent a servant home with him, but bought Jackey a fine horse. Sometimes he let him ride after the deer in the park.

Sometimes he would play on the fiddle to Miss for an hour or two together; at other times, he would play on the flute whilst Miss Harriot sung, which she did very prettily.

One day Jackey was told my lord was very ill, and desired to see him; whereupon he ran into his bed chamber, and falling on his knees prayed to God to restore his health; my lord said he found his end approaching, that he had provided for him

when

and Harriot, and begged God to blefs them; and in a few hours refigned his breath. The next day my lady fent for them, and fhowed the will, in which he had left them five hundred pounds each. They lived with my lady eight years after my lord's deceafe, when fhe dying likewife, left them joint heirs to her vaft eftate.

After the time of mourning was over, Jackey and Harriot agreed to be married. Accordingly the happy day being arrived, they went to church, where they were married by the Reverend Mr. Trueman, who had formerly been chaplain to Lord Fairfame.

Thus Jackey and Harriot were now the richeft, as they were before the beft, people in the county of Salop, and lived many years in the greateft harmony, beloved by all the country round.

This little hiftory will, I hope, be a fufficient inducement to make all girls and boys behave themfelves in a proper manner to every body: If they hope to be rich and happy, let them take care to follow the example of Jackey and Harriot.

The HISTORY of MASTER PETER
PRIMROSE.

MASTER Peter Primrose was a boy of
such uncommon abilities, that he was
admired by every body. When he was
but seven years old, he could say all his ca-
techism perfectly, and repeat the greatest
part of his Prayer-book and Testament by
heart; then he could answer any question
in the Bible, and had also obtained some
knowledge of men and things; Master Peter's fame was founded thro' the whole
kingdom, and though his father was only
a shepherd, and he bred up among the flocks,
the king sent for him to court, and placed
him among the wise men of the nation.
Here he lived in great splendour for some
time; for the king gave him a little pranc-
ing horse, clothed with purple and gold,
and caused him to ride out every day in
company with his only son. How uncer-
tain are riches and honours, and indeed how
frail is all human felicity! Master Peter had
not been at court above two years, before the good old king and his son were ex-
pelled the kingdom, by an unaccountable
                                    faction

faction that' arose in the state. Duty and gratitude obliged this young gentleman to take the part of his king and his prince; for which he was persecuted by the oppo-site party with great fury, and one day forced into the woods to shield himself from their hatred. Here he lay securely all day, but in the evening, his fears were conti-nually alarmed by the roaring of lions, ty-gers, wolves, and other beasts of prey, and his compassion excited by the groans and cries of the tender part of the animal creation, who, not being endowed by na-ture with strength and fierceness to oppose their enemies, easily became victims, and were devoured. This called up in his mind the cruelties which had been exercised on his poor master's family and himself, the thoughts of which so robbed him of his re-solution, that he grew heedless of his safe-ty, and sitting down on the green turf, re-signed himself to the mercy of the beasts; "Ah! why should these creatures, says he, fill me with horrour, who are more merci-ful than men? These spare their own, and slay only those of another species; but men, more savage men, are bent against each other, and seek their own destruction. Let me

fall

fall then by the lion, the tyger, or other animals less cruel, and who act confiftently with the dictates of nature." As this was delivered with great emotion, he was overheard by a hermit, whose cave was concealed under a thicket, by which he lay. The good old man ftartled at the found of the human voice, which he had not heard before for years, and fuppofing it came from one in diftrefs, kindled a brand, for fear of the wild beafts, and ran to his affiftance. He found Mafter Primrofe ftretched on the ground, and by forrow rendered infenfible of any danger. The old man reproached him for defpairing of God's providence and mercy. "Is it for this, fays he, that man is endowed with fuperior reafon, and fo highly favoured of the Almighty? Shall the dove, fhall the lamb, and other creatures fly for refuge, and feek their own fafety, and fhall man bafely and ungratefully difregard, and throw away the life that has been given him? Arife and fhake off this fhameful floth, nor longer defpair of God's protection. Do your duty, and you will always meet with the favour of heaven."

The young man, fenfible of the juftnefs of this reproof, arofe and bowed refpectful-

ly

ly, and was led by the hermit into his cave, and refreſhed with a ſimple repaſt the good old man provided for him, and then repoſed himſelf till the morning on a couch of flocks, that here ſeemed more ſoft than the down-bed he had been ſo long uſed to.

In the morning, when he awoke he related to the old man the hiſtory of his life; and the hermit, after giving him ſuch things as were neceſſary to ſupport him in his journey, deſpatched him with this advice: "You ſee, my ſon, what miſchiefs attend the ambitious. The love of riches and of power drew you from a ſtate of innocence, from a delightful place, where your paths were paved with violets and primroſes, to a court where your road was planted with thiſtles and thorns. True greatneſs conſiſts in being good, in promoting the happineſs of mankind, and not in wealth and power, as is vainly imagined; for he who hoardeth up treaſure, hoards up trouble, and he who aſpires to the higheſt office of ſtate, makes himſelf a public mark for the multitude to throw their envious arrows at. Retire, my ſon, to thy former peaceful abode, there worſhip thy God, comfort thy neighbours, and tend thy innocent flock, and leave the

E 3 affairs

affairs of ſtate to thoſe who have leſs virtue and more experience." Contentment is the only ingredient that can render life happy, and that is ſeldom to be found in the palaces of princes.

MEMOIRS of the VIRTUOUS CITIZEN.

AN eminent Citizen, who had lived in good faſhion and credit, was, by a train of accidents, and by an unavoidable perplexity in his affairs, reduced to a low condition. There is a modeſty uſually attending faultleſs poverty, which made him rather chooſe to reduce his manner of living to his preſent circumſtances, than ſolicit his friends, in order to ſupport the ſhow of an eſtate when the ſubſtance was gone. His wife, who was a woman of ſenſe and virtue, behaved herſelf on this occaſion with uncommon decency, and never appeared ſo amiable in his eyes as now. Inſtead of upbraiding him with the ample fortune ſhe had brought, or the many great offers ſhe had refuſed for his ſake, ſhe redoubled all the inſtances of her affection, while

her

her hufband was continually pouring out his heart to her in complaints, that he had ruined the beft woman in the world. He fometimes came home at a time when fhe did not the leaft expect him, and furprifed her in tears, which fhe endeavoured to conceal, and always put on an air of chearfulnefs to receive him. To leffen their expenfe, their eldeft daughter, whom I fhall call Amanda, was fent into the country, to the houfe of an honeft farmer, who had married a fervant of the family. This young woman was apprehenfive of the ruin which was approaching, and had engaged a friend in the neighbourhood to give her an account of what paffed from time to time in her father's affairs. Amanda was in the bloom of her youth and beauty, when the lord of the manor, who often called at the farmer's houfe, as he followed his country fports, fell paffionately in love with her. He was a man of great generofity, but from a loofe education, had contracted a hearty averfion to marriage. He therefore entertained a defign upon Amanda's virtue, which at prefent he thought fit to keep private. The innocent creature, who never fufpected his intention, was pleafed with his perfon; and

E 4   having

having obferved his growing paffion for her, hoped, by fo advantageous a match, fhe might quickly be in a capacity of fupporting her impoverifhed relations. One day, as he called to fee her, he found her in tears, over a letter fhe had juft received from her friend, which gave an account that her father had lately been ftripped of every thing by an execution. The lover, who with fome difficulty found out the caufe of her grief, took this occafion to make her a propofal. It is impoffible to exprefs Amanda's confufion, when fhe found his pretenfions were not honourable. She was now deferted of all her hopes, and had no power to fpeak; but rufhing from him in the utmoft difturbance, locked herfelf up in her chamber. He immediately defpatched a meffenger to her father, with the following letter.

" Sir,

"I have heard of your misfortune, and have offered your daughter, if fhe will live with me, to fettle on her four hundred pounds a year, and to lay down the fum for which you are diftreffed. I will be fo ingenuous as to tell you, I do not intend marriage; but if you are wife, you will
ufe

ufe your authority with her, not to be too nice, when fhe has an opportunity of faving you and your family, and of making herfelf happy.

I am, &c."

This letter came to the hands of Amanda's mother; fhe opened and read it with great furprife and concern. She did not think it proper to explain herfelf to the meffenger; but defiring him to call again the next morning, fhe wrote to her daughter as follows.

"Deareft child,

"Your father and I have juft now received a letter from a gentleman who pretends love to you, with a propofal that infults our misfortunes, and would throw us to a lower degree of mifery than any thing which is to come upon us. How could this barbarous man think, that the tendereft of parents would be tempted to fupply their want, by giving up the beft of children to infamy and ruin? It is a mean and cruel artifice to make this propofal, at a time when he thinks our neceffities muft compel us to any thing; but we will not eat the

E 5

bread

bread of fhame; and therefore we charge
thee not to think of us, but to avoid the
fnare which is laid for thy virtue. Beware of pitying us: it is not fo bad as you
have perhaps been told. All things will
yet be well, and I fhall write my child better news.

"I have been interrupted. I know not
how I was moved to fay things would mend.
As I was going on, I was ftartled by a
noife of one that knocked at the door, who
hath brought us an unexpected fupply of a
debt which had long been owing. Oh!
I will not tell thee all. It is fome days I
have lived almoft without fupport, having
conveyed what little money I could raife to
your poor father.——Thou wilt weep to
think where he is, yet be affured he will
foon be at liberty. That cruel letter would
have broken his heart; but I have concealed it from him. I have no companion at
prefent, befides little Fanny, who ftands
watching my looks as I write, and is crying for her fifter: fhe fays, fhe is fure you
are not well, having difcovered that my
prefent trouble is about you. But do not
think I would thus repeat my forrows to
grieve thee: no it is to intreat thee not to
make

make them infupportable, by adding what would be worfe than all. Let us bear chearfully an affliction which we have not brought on ourfelves, and remember there is a Power who can better deliver us out of it, than by the lofs of thy innocence. Heaven preferve my dear child.

Thy affectionate mother, —."

The meffenger, nothwithftanding he promifed to deliver this letter to Amanda, carried it firft to his mafter, who he imagined would be glad to have an opportunity of giving it into her hands himfelf. His mafter was impatient to know the fuccefs of his propofal, and therefore broke open the letter privately to fee the contents. He was not a little moved at fo true a picture of virtue in diftrefs. But at the fame time was infinitely furprifed to find his offers rejected. However, he refolved not to fupprefs the letter, but carefully fealed it up again and carried it to Amanda. All his endeavours to fee her were in vain, till fhe was affured he brought her a letter from her mother. He would not part with it, but upon condition that fhe fhould read it without leaving the room. While fhe was perufing it,
he

he fixed his eyes on her with the deepest
attention: her concern gave a new foftnefs
to her beauty, and when fhe burft into tears,
he could no longer refrain from bearing a
part in her forrow, and telling her, that he
too had read the letter, and was refolved
to make a reparation for having been the
occafion of it. My little reader, will not
be difpleafed to fee the fecond epiftle, which
he now wrote to Amanda's mother.

"Madam,

"I am full of fhame, and fhall never forgive myfelf, if I have not your pardon for what I have lately written. It was
far from my intention to add trouble to the
afflicted; nor could any thing, but my being
a ftranger to you, have betrayed me into a
fault, for which, if I live, I fhall endeavour
to make you amends as a fon. You cannot be unhappy while Amanda is your
daughter, nor fhall be, if any thing can
prevent it, which is in the power of,

Madam,

Your moft obedient
Humble fervant, —."

This

This letter he fent by his fteward, and foon after went up to town himfelf, to complete the generous act he had now refolved on. By his friendfhip and affiftance, Amanda's father was quickly in a condition of retrieving his perplexed affairs. To conclude, he married Amanda, and enjoyed the double fatisfaction of having reftored a worthy family to their former profperity, and of making himfelf happy by an alliance with their virtues.

A patient refignation to the Divine Will, under fuch calamitous circumftances as our own honeft endeavours are incapable of relieving, is not only our duty, but our intereft; whereas, on the contrary, the ufe of unlawful means to extricate ourfelves from difficulties, may, perhaps, afford a fhort and temporary relief; but will moft certainly render us offenfive to God, and to all good men, as well as deprive us of that greateft of all human bleffings, a confcience void of offenfe.

In this piece are evidently feen the happy effects of a virtuous and good education. The fair Amanda appeared more amiable, even in the eyes of a libertine, while fhe was thus nobly ftruggling with her adverfe fortune;

fortune; and her purity, which was tried, as it were, in the fire, her firm attachment to the good principles she had imbibed from her parents and teachers, together with the tender concern expreſſed for her innocence in her good mother's letter, awakened in the heart of her lover a proper ſenſe and deteſtation of his own folly, and made him, who was before abandoned to ſenſual delights, a convert to religion and virtue.

ANECDOTES of MASTER BENTLEY.

MASTER BENTLEY was the ſon of a gentleman of moderate fortune: He was a remarkable lively youth, poſſeſſed of great ſweetneſs of diſpoſition, and ſhowed a very ſtrong attachment to thoſe who had the care of him.   He had no faults that proceeded from the heart; but his ſpirits were ſo high, that they frequently wanted reſtraint.

. This livelineſs prevented his making any progreſs in learning.   He had quick parts, but did not improve them by application. The ſlighteſt difficulty diſcouraged his further attempts, and his inattention was frequently

quently miftaken for ftupidity. His father
and mother took all imaginable pains to make
pleafure the vehicle of inftruction, but were
difcouraged by the little advancement he
made. He wifhed to be always at play.
He was reftlefs, difturbed others, and was
generally diffatisfied with himfelf. His parents endeavoured to make him fenfible, in
the moft familiar manner, that idlenefs is
the foil in which every vicious weed fprings
up, and chokes the feeds of virtue.

Mafter Bentley ftole out one evening, unknown to his parents, and entered into a
game at trap-ball with fome children he found
there.

His heedleffnefs, however, had prevented him from acquiring any degree of excellence even at thefe fports. The boys finding him an interruption, at laft turned him
out of the company. His heart was full,
he went and fat down at a fhop door and
burft into tears—The woman of the houfe
came up to him. "What mafter Bentley,
faid fhe, are you rambled from home? Your
good papa and mama don't know where
you are, I am afraid. Come in a moment,
let us hear what is the matter, and I will
ftep home with you." "They won't let
me

me play with them, answered he, with a
burst of indignant grief, and I think I can
play as well as they. I am sure I play as
much as any boy, and therefore I must
know how to play."

"I believe it would be better for you if
you played less, sir, said the good woman, —
I never heard any body speak of your
reading your book — there is a proper time
for all things — those boys have been at
school, and learned their lessons before they
went to play." — "I am sure all of them
have not, replies he, — there is Sam Rogers,
and Dick Giles, they do not learn to read;
they do nothing but play." "You are very
much mistaken, master, said the old woman,
those boys help their father to pull turnips,
and their mother to spin! — Only think of
John Meadows, he was never taught to
work, nor keep his church, and therefore,
as he was poor, he learned to steal, and
at last came to a bad end. Poor peoples
children are made useful, and I am sure rich
ones were not born to do nothing, though
they have different employments. It is expected that Master Bentley should be able
to read better than Sam Rogers, or Dick
Giles;

Giles; but it has been whispered in my ear, that Master Bentley cannot read at all."

The boy was really abashed. "Let me go home, dame, said he, I can go by myself." She went home with him, however, and as he passed the boys, they called out—

"O what a thing it is to say,
"That boy can neither read nor play."

He tried to hide himself behind Mrs. Spilman. The good woman told his mother what had happened. Mrs. Bentley hoped for a good effect from it, but dared not expect it. The next morning, when she went into his chamber, she found him with a book in his hand, and he was asking his elder brother some questions. She was much pleased, and did not interrupt him. After breakfast he asked her to let him read, telling her, he was so laughed at the night before, for not being able to read nor play well, that he was resolved not to be idle any more. He continued to give such attention to his books, that he soon lessened all difficulties, and he endeavoured to excel in playful exercises as well as in learning.

A year or two after, his father became acquainted with a neighbouring baronet, and Master Bentley was invited to pass a day with his son. The family lived in great taste and elegance.—He went, and was amazed at the grandeur and opulence of every apartment, and could not help thinking, that where there was so much magnificence, there muft be a vaft deal of happinefs. He looked up to Mafter Grandville as to a being of a fuperior order. His joy was increafed at the fight of the variety of dishes at table. He had been ufed to eat only of one kind of meat. He wanted to tafte of every thing he faw, and yet, when he had begun with one dish, he was unwilling to refign it for another.

After dinner, inftead of being lively and fit as ufual for a walk, he found himfelf fleepy and difpirited. He had eaten fuch a variety, that when the defert appeared, he had no relish for it. Mafter Edward Grandville foon defired him to leave the company and take a walk with him. By degrees his fpirits returned; but, when they were called in to tea, he felt much lefs inclination for rich cake he faw prepared, than towards his ufual food. The young gentlemen, in a short

short time, returned his visit; but the behaviour of the younger son troubled him exceedingly.

Mr. Bentley's house and gardens were perfectly neat and convenient, though not grand nor elegant. Master Grandville declared the apartments were scarcely fit to sleep in: there was no room to breathe. They both, however, eat very heartily of the genteel dinner provided for them, and seemed not to regret the delicacies and variety of their own table. After their wholesome repast was ended, they walked into the garden.

Mr. West, the tutor of the young gentlemen, followed them. Master Edward would not be drawn from the fruit trees, therefore his brother and Master Bently walked on without him.——"I am afraid, sir, said the latter, you have made a very indifferent dinner——you are not used to live in such a manner as we do.——You will not come to see me any more, I doubt." "Indeed but I will, Master Bentley, answered the other, with a good natured smile, and an affectionate shake by the hand, what do you think I cannot dine without two courses? I never past a day more agreeably than

F 2　　　　　　this."

this."——"What not at home, in your charming houfe, fir, faid he, and were you have
fuch a plenty of every thing you can wifh
for? You muft be vaftly happier than we
are."

Mafter Grandville fmiled.   He was feveral years older than Mafter Bentley, had a
good natural underftanding, improved by diligent application, and he had been accuf-
tomed to keep the beft company. He had
in confequence acquired great eafe of manners, with a becoming prefence of mind:
he had a natural politenefs, which flowed
from the benevolence of his heart.   "Can
you really think, my dear Mafter Bentley,
that I am happier than you, becaufe I have
a finer coat, a larger houfe, and a greater
variety of difhes at table? I have been
thought to thank Providence for every inftance of his bounty, and I endeavour to
imitate my parents in making the beft ufe
of the grandeur and opulence I poffefs. It
is indeed a moft delightful power to relieve
mifery, and to promote happinefs; but you
can enjoy this fatisfaction as well as myfelf, and if not in an equal degree, you
have no more reafon to complain than I have,
fince were lefs is given lefs is required; and
                                    from

from thofe who received more than we, more will certainly be expected."

"You talk vaftly well, fir, anfwered Mafter Bently; but it is a charming thing to do juft as we pleafe. To read when we like, and to play, or walk, or ride, or fifh, juft as we choofe." Mr. Weft now joined them. He heard Mafter Bentley, and fmiling, "When any perfon pleafes to do what is right, faid he, there is no danger in his purfuing his own inclinations; but young people are generally happieft when they are under the direction of their parents, or fome experienced perfon; and as to walking, riding, fifhing, &c. they are very agreeable amufements; but they were never defigned for the bufinefs of our lives.—If youth is the time, in which we are moft capable of enjoying pleafure, it is alfo the feafon in which we muft fow the feeds of inftruction, if we expect to reap the fruits of improvement. My pupil always paffes his mornings in a regular fucceffion of ufeful employments—writing themes, letters, reading, Latin exercifes, French, mufic, drawing, &c. are each taken in turn, and he enjoys every ftudy that tends to make him wifer, and every accomplifhment that can render

him

him more agreeable, and in confequence more ufeful. "

"You feem, my dear Mafter Bently, added Mafter Grandville, to think it an happy circumftance to be able to eat of a great variety, when, I affure you, my mother always makes it a general rule to dine upon one difh of meat, as muft falutary to health. I fuppofe fhe practifed fome felf-denial at firft, but her health required it, and cuftom has now made it not only eafy but preferable." "Her enjoyments, faid Mr. Weft, are not thofe peculiar to a dignified ftation; but fuch as are the eafy and natural gratifications of every rational mind."

As they were talking, they drew near the court-yard gate; from whence they faw a pretty little girl of nine or ten years old, with a bafket on her arm.

Mafter Bentley afked her how her grandmother did. She fhook her head, and anfwered fhe was very full of pain, and fhe doubted never would be better. Then, after making a low curtfey, walked on.

Mafter Grandville enquired what was the matter with her grandmother, and was told by Mafter Bentley, that fhe had a cancer in her breaft, which was extremly painful,

and

and it was thought would foon occafion her
death; that it was become very offenfive;
that her neighbours did not know how to
be with her, or affift her; that the mother
of this little girl, who had lived with the
friends of her deceafed hufband, and been
provided for, as well as her child by them,
on hearing her mother's deplorable fituation,
left them immediately, and devoted herfelf
to the care of her poor parent. The child
alfo begged fhe might go with her mother,
that fhe might fpin, knit, and few for them
both, and that fhe was the moft induftrious
creature of her age in the village.

The young gentleman called her back,
and gave her fomething for her grandmother.
Mr. Weft afked her if fhe did not wifh herfelf again with her father's friends, and if fhe
had not been happier with them. "What
and leave my grandmother, poor dear foul!
faid the little innocent, no, I am fure my
mother and I would work our fingers to
the bone, rather than fhe fhould want any
thing we could do for her; and though we
often fit and cry to fee her in pain, and
that we cannot prevent it, yet there is a vaft
comfort, as my mother fays, in thinking,
that we are doing our duty, and keeping

her

her fweet and clean; and we feel us happier in that thought, than when we lived in great plenty at my uncle's.

Mr. Weft and Mafter Grandville were delighted with the little girl. They afked if her grandmother was not afraid to die. The child looked aftonifhed. "Afraid fir, faid fhe, what, fhould fuch a good woman be afraid to die? She is fo patient, and always did her duty. fo well, that fhe may be glad to go and receive her reward. But I muft not ftay any longer, for my mother will want the eggs." She then made her curtfey, and tripped away.

"You find, my dear Mafter Bentley, happinefs is not confined to fplendour and greatnefs. This little girl has higher enjoyments in her prefent fituation, in the difcharge of fuch an effential duty, than fhe had while fhe poffeffed a greater plenty of thofe things the world think defireable. Believe me, it is not the part we act on the ftage of life, but the manner in which we fupport the character allotted us, which conftitutes our merit, and fecures our happinefs. The buftle we make in the purfuit of the good things of this life, would almoft lead us to imagine, that people expected to live for ever.
Remem-

Remember, my dear pupil, you once longed for a drum. How pleasing was the noise it afforded you while in the possession of another; but even the very day after you became master thereof, you grew sick of the noise, and laid it aside in disgust. So is it in the common occurrences in life. We sicken for what others possess, and often envy those who stand most in need of our pity. Sumptuous living impairs our health, renders our lives full of complaints, and much shortens our course here. Fine clothes may attract the eye of the vulgar and unthinking, but learning, virtue and wisdom, are the only sure marks, by which the amiable youth is distinguished from the indolent and slothful.

The HISTORY of MASTER TOMMY THOROUGHGOOD.

MASTER Thomas Thoroughgood, the younger son of a country gentleman, was put out apprentice to an eminent tradesman in Cheapside. The master, finding his business increase, was obliged to take

another

another about two years after, whofe name
was Francis Froward.

Thomas had behaved exceedingly well,
was very diligent and honeft, as well as
good; he ufed to fay his prayers conftantly every morning and night; he never went
to play when he fhould be at church or
about his mafter's bufinefs; never was
known to tell a lye, nor ever ftaid when
he was fent on an errand. Thefe rare qualifications had gained him the affeftions of
his mafter and miftrefs, and made him a favourite in the family before Francis came
to them. It was in a great meafure owing
to Mafter Tommy's charaƈter in the neighbourhood, that Mr. Froward was induced
to comply with the mafter's demands; not
doubting but his fon, in fuch a happy fituation, and with a companion of fo fweet a
difpofition, would one day turn out to his
fatisfaƈtion, and be a comfort to him in his
old age.

Francis, in the firft year of his apprenticefhip, began to difcover the natural bent
of his inclination. He chofe to affociate
himfelf with naughty boys in the ftreets,
and feemed to place his whole delight in
loofe and idle diverfions; he neglefted the
                                    bufi-

bufinefs of the fhop when at home, and entirely forgot it when he was abroad. Thefe;
and many more indifcretions of the like nature, Tommy Thoroughgood concealed at
firft from his mafter, though not without
fome inward uneafinefs.

In the fourth year's fervice, our young
fpark, who was an only child, and heir to
a pretty fortune, gave further proofs of his
vicious turn of mind, and frequentiy launch-
ed out into follies of a more heinous nature;
for now he made no fcruple of abfenting
himfelf from church on the Lord's day: always ftaid out late when he knew his mafter was engaged in company, and at fuch
times very rarely returned home fober; nay,
he had fometimes the affurance to lie out of
his mafter's houfe all night. In order to deter him from purfuing this wicked courfe
of life, Mr. Thoroughgood threatened to inform his mafter of his fcandalous behaviour,
and to acquaint his parents of his mifcon-
duct. But, alas! all thefe menaces proved
ineffectual, and inftead of working out his
reformation, ferved only to heighten his
refentment, and to raife daily fquabbles and
animofities between them. Hereupon Mr.
Thoroughgood, finding all his good offices
hither-

hitherto thrown away, at length determined no more to meddle in the affair, or even to offer his brotherly advice: but to leave the unhappy youth to follow the dictates of his own perverfe will; being refolved at the fame time to take particular care; that he fhould not, in any of his mifchievous frolics, defraud his mafter, and thereby caft an odium upon his fellow-apprentice.

The mafter was chofen alderman of the ward, and Mr. Thoroughgood was out of his time in the fame year; and from his faithful fervice, and unblameable conduct, had now the whole management of the trade, as well abroad as at home, committed to his care and infpection. This great charge obliged him to keep a ftricter eye over Francis's behaviour, who was juft entering into the laft year of his apprenticefhip, and imagined his actions were above the cognizance of one, who, the other day, was but his equal; and on this account would neither bear his reproof, nor hearken to his admonition; but continued to riot in all the follies and degeneracies of human nature, till his apprenticefhip was expired: So true is it, that "the wicked hateth reproof, but the wife man lendeth his ear to inftruction."

Mr.

Mr. Francis having been for a long while impatient of a fervile life, was now become his own mafter, and feemed eager of putting himfelf upon a level with his late companion. To effect this, he goes down to his father, and prevails upon him to fet him up in the bufinefs, that he might trade for himfelf. The reins were no fooner laid on his neck, then he gave a loofe to his fenfual appetites, and in little more than four years had a ftatute of bankruptcy taken out againft him. The unexpected news of this fatal event inftantly broke his mother's heart, nor did the old gentleman furvive her long. Hereupon our heir was obliged to fell the perfonal and mortgage the real eftate, to procure his liberty, and to fatisfy the affignees. In this finking fituation, after the days of mourning were over, he let the houfe his father lived in, and returned again to London, where he purchafed a handfome equipage, commenced the fine gentleman, frequented the balls, mafquerades, playhoufes, routs, &c. &c. and cut as good a figure as the beft of them. But here let us leave him for a while, and turn our eyes to a worthier object.

In

In the fame fpace of time which Mr. Froward took to fquander away a good eftate, Mr. Thoroughgood had, by his own induftry, and from a fmall fortune, gained one confiderable better, and was in a fair way of encreafing it. The former made pleafure his bufinefs, but the latter made bufinefs his pleafure, and was rewarded accordingly. The alderman, who by his own application, and Mr. Thoroughgood's affiduity, was grown very rich, had no child now living but a daughter, of whom both he and his lady were extremely fond; they had nothing fo much at heart as to fee her well fettled in the world. She was the youngeft, and juft now turned of twenty. She had many fuitors; but refolved to encourage none without the confent of her parents, who would often, when by themfelves, tell her that it was their joint opinion fhe could not difpofe of herfelf better than to Mr. Thomas, and would frequently afk how fhe liked him? for they would be unwilling to marry her againft her own inclination. Her ufual anfwer was, "Your choice fhall be mine; my duty fhall never be made fubfervient to any fenfual paffion." This reply was not fo full and expreffive as they expected;

pected: and as mothers are commonly very
dexterous in finding out their daughters ma-
ladies, madam had a good reason to believe, from some observations she made on
miss's behaviour, that her affections were
already fixed, and that she was deeply in
love with somebody else, which was the
cause of her unusual anxiety. Hereupon, as
she was sitting at work one evening in a melancholy posture, they called her, and desired to be informed whether the husband
they proposed was disagreeable to her, if so,
she should choose for herself.

The young lady, after some hesitation,
with blushes confessed her regard for Mr.
Thoroughgood; which gave infinite satisfaction to the alderman and his lady, who
were overjoyed at the prospect they had of
marrying their daughter to a person of such
prudence, integrity, and honour.

The next day, as soon as dinner was over,
the alderman and his lady withdrew, and
left the two lovers together all the evening;
from this interview they became sensible of
each other's approaching happiness, and
about a month after were joined together,
to the great satisfaction of all parties concerned. From this day the bridegroom was
taken

taken into partnership, and transacted the whole business himself. In process of time his father-in law died, and left him in possession of all his substance. He succeeded him also in his dignity, and after having served the office of sheriff, was in a few years called to the chair.

Mr. Froward, whom we left a while ago pursuing his pleasures and wicked inclinations, had long before this time been reduced to poverty; and, like many other thoughtless wretches, betook himself to the highway and gaming-table, in hopes of recovering a lost fortune. He had followed this destructive trade with some success, and without being discovered, above three years; but was at length taken near Enfield, and brought to his tryal at the Old-Bailey, during his fellow-prentice's mayoralty, and cast for his life. When he was brought to the bar to receive sentence, his lordship recollecting Mr. Froward's name, examined who he was, and asked if he was not the same person that served his time with Mr. Alderman ⁑ ⁑ ⁑, in Cheapside. This he positively denied; but notwithstanding he used all possible means to disguise himself, his person and speech betrayed him. My lord,
animated

animated with the principles of compaffion and benevolence, and imagining that his de. fign of concealing himfelf in his wretched fituation might very probably proceed from fhame or defpair, took no further notice of it in court, but, forgetting his prefent dif- grace, as well as his former arrogance and indifcretion, privately procured his fenten- ce to be changed into tranfportation for life.

The fhip in which Mr. Froward embark- ed, by ftrefs of weather drove into a cer- tain port in Jamaica, where he, in lefs than ten days was fold to a noted planter, and doomed to perpetual flavery. You may ima- gine how fhocking this profpect muft appear to a gentleman, who had juft before fquan- dered away a good eftate in indolence and pleafure, who never knew what it was to work, nor had ever given himfelf time to think upon the nature of induftry. How- ever, he no fooner began to reflect upon his prefent wretched fituation, and his late pro- vidential deliverance from death, than he alfo began to repent of his former tranfgref- fions; and finding himfelf in a ftrange coun- try, unknown to any perfon about him, he patiently fubmitted his neck to the yoke, and endured his fervility with an uncommon fortitude of mind. In the firft place, he determined, during all the time of his labour, to offer up continual thanksgiving to God Almighty for his manifold mercies beftowed on fo unworthy a creature, and to devote all his leifure hours to the duty of repentance. His next refolution was to obey his mafter's commands, to ferve him faithfully, and to perform whatever bufinefs was impofed on him, fo far and fo long as health and ftrength would permit; not doubting but the fame God, who had preferved him hitherto, in fuch a wonderful manner, would accept the oblations of a contrite heart, and enable him to go through it with courage and chearfulnefs.

The firft month's fervice, went very hard with him. His hands bliftered, his feet grew fore and raw, and the heat of the climate was almoft infupportable; but, as cuftom makes every ftation familiar, before three months were expired, all thefe grievances were at an end; and he, naturally indued with a fpirit of emulation, would not fuffer himfelf to be outdone by any of his fellow flaves. The fuperintendant obferving his extraordinary affiduity, could

not

not help taking notice of him, and would frequently give him encouragement, either by calling him off to go on a trivial errand, or by thrusting some money into his hand. He behaved in this manner near two years, when his master was informed of his good disposition, and removed him from that laborious employment to an easier, where he had more frequent opportunities of paying adoration to that Almighty Being, who supported him under his afflictions. In these intervals, he was generally found with a book in his hand, or on his knees, from which practice he received great consolation.

At the expiration of three years, Sir Thomas Thoroughgood, who made previous enquiry after his fellow-prentice's behaviour abroad, sent orders to his agent in Jamaica, to purchase Mr. Froward's freedom; and to advance him 100l. that he might he enabled to get his own livelyhood; but at the same time gave strict orders to his friend, not to let Mr. Froward know who was his benefactor, and to lay his master under the like injunction. In a short time after Mr. Froward was discharged from slavery; but did not express so much joy on the occa-

sion,

fion, as might have been reafonably expected. From the good ufage he met with in
fervitude, and the unufual favours he received from the fuperintendant, as well as the
planter, he had conceived a great liking for
the latter, and feemed to part with him not
without fome inward reluctance, though
with apparent furprife; which was much
heightened by the additional favour of a note
for a hundred pounds payable upon fight to
Mr. Francis Froward or order, delivered to
him by the fame hand, foon after he received the difcharge before mentioned. During
this confufion, the gentleman, who really
had a value for his late fervant, told him,
he was welcome to be at his houfe till he
was fettled, and that he would do all the
good offices in his power; to promote his
future welfare. Mr. Froward replied, "Sir,
you cannot do me greater fervice than to
let me know who is my generous benefactor; becaufe it is incumbent upon me to
make fome acknowledgement." The mafter pofitively refufed to do this, and turned off the difcourfe, by afking how he intended to difpofe of himfelf and his money.
"Sir, fays he, I am not unacquainted with
the nature of trade, and labour is now be-

come

come habitual to me, and as I am well skil-
led in the cultivation of the sugar-cane, I
would willingly rent a small plantation of
that kind, and work upon it for myself."
The planter approved of this design, and
promised him assistance.

In about a month after, Mr. Froward met
with a bargain, agreeable to his substance,
and worked upon it as hard as if he had
been a real slave, with this difference only;
that he could now spare more time in the
service of his allpowerful Redeemer. In the
interim, his lade master procured him a
wife with a handsome fortune, who had a
sugar-work of her own, and some negroes;
he purchased more, and, by his industry,
thrived a main, and in a few years laid up
100l. in specie.

In this comfortable state, nothing gave
him uneasiness, but that he could not come
to the knowledge of his kind benefactor;
never was man more anxious to show his
gratitude: or more sollicitous to find out his
friend! One day as he was at his devotions,
a strange gentleman came to his habitation,
and desired to see him. He was no sooner
admitted, than he accosted him in the following manner: "Mr. Froward, I am com-

mander

mander of the Dove frigate, whofe princi-
pal owner is Sir Thomas Thoroughgood,
and am juft arrived from England: By Sir
Thomas's orders I am to inform you, that
his Jamaica agent is dead, and he has made
choice of you to fucceed him here in that
ftation. I have a commiffion from him, for
you, in my pocket, do difpofe of my cargo, and to freight me again for my voyage home. He never would own it, but
I am well affured, he is the perfon who
faved your life, who redeemed you from
bondage, and was the fole inftrument of
your prefent profperity." Nothing could
have given Mr. Froward fo great pleafure
and fatisfaction, as this laft piece of intelligence; he knew not how to make the captain welcome enough, he kept him all night,
and in the morning made him a prefent of a
hogfhead of rum. He made all the poffible
defpatch in difpofing of his cargo, and
freighted him out with the utmoft expedition. With the reft of the goods, he fent
Sir Thomas ten hogfheads of fugar, and as
many of rum, for a prefent, with the following letter:

"Honoured

"Honoured Sir,

"Tranſported with joy, and drowned in tears, I ſend this teſtimony of my eſteem, of which I humbly hope your acceptance, as well as of thoſe ſmall tokens of my gratitude, with which it is accompanied. Next under God, it is to you, dear ſir, that I owe my life, my liberty, and my all. Happy me, had I liſtened to your advice in my nonage! happy ſtill as by your means, I have been directed to the paths of virtue. It is to you I am indebted for my preſent confortable ſituation and the dawning proſpect of future happineſs; the bills of lading, &c. are ſent by Mr.——, and all your buſineſs here, with which I am entruſted, ſhall be executed with the utmoſt diligence and fidelity. I have only to add my prayers for the continuation of your life and health, who have been ſo beneficial to many, but more particularly to, honoured ſir,

Your moſt humble, moſt obliged,

Though moſt unworthy ſervant.

Francis Froward."

Sir

Sir Thomas was highly pleafed with the purport of his letter, though he rallied the captain for letting him know to whom he was obliged for his freedom. The fame fhip was fent the next feafon on the fame voyage, when the captain was ordered to pay Mr. Froward a full price for the rum and fugar he had fent to the knight, and to deliver him a letter, in which he gave him a receipt in full for all the favours he had conferred on him.

To be fhort, in a few years afterwards, Mr. Froward died, and, having no children, left the whole of his eftate to Mr. Thoroughgood's family, who thus received with intereft the rewards of a generous and humane action.

ANECDOTES of MISS POLLY MEANWELL.

POLLY Meanwell's parents died when fhe was very young, and left her to the care of an uncle, who was an old rich bachelor, covetous to the laft degree, and one

one who cared for nobody but himſelf. He
put her to ſchool a little after her parents
death, but finding that by a flaw in ſome
writings, he had the power of taking every thing to himſelf, he did ſo, and deprived poor Polly of what her father and mother left for her ſubſiſtence, and turned her
out of doors.

Polly was at firſt very uneaſy at loſing
all her fine clothes, and at being obliged to
go to hard work, which Mr. Williams, the
parſon of the pariſh, obſerving, that good
man came to her one day, and comforted
her in this manner. "Don't be caſt down,
Polly, at your fine clothes being gone,
thoſe ragged ones will keep you warm,
and that is the only uſe of clothes; for
people are not a bit the better for wearing
fine garments. It is true, you cannot have
your tea and your coffee, your tarts and
your cheeſecakes, your cuſtards and ſylla-
bubs as uſual, but what does that ſigni-
fy? You can by your labour get other victuals: then your working for it makes it
go down the ſweeter, and at the ſame time
keeps you in health; the bed you lie upon
ſeems as ſoft, after a hard day's work as

your

your down beds, I fuppofe, ufed to be; why then fhould you be uneafy? Be a good girl, fay your prayers, and put your truft in God Almighty; and he will give you what his all-knowing wifdom fees you want." Polly was fo pleafed with this fpeech, that fhe dropped Mr. Williams a courtefy, and, for the future, refolved to mind nothing but her duty, and not repine at Providence.

As fhe went to church conftantly, and was very devout there, every body took notice of her, and one merchant's wife in particular, fent to the fexton to know what little ragged girl that was who came to church fo conftantly, and behaved fo well there. The fexton anfwered, that it was Polly Meanwell; and, Madam, faid he, "though Polly is fo poor and fo ragged, fhe is the beft girl in the Parifh." "Is fhe fo? fays the lady, then pray give her this new Bible, and this piece of money;" and put into his hand a crown for her. Some time afterwards, this lady, who was very rich, dropped, as fhe was ftepping into her coach, a green purfe full of guineas, and a fine diamond ring, which Polly had the good fortune to pick up. Now fome naughty

girls

girls would have kept all this money, and not have carried it to the lady; and indeed one of her neighbours advifed her to do fo. But Polly was angry with her, and told her, fhe was a wicked woman to put fuch naughty things into a little girl's head. "How can I go to church and fay my prayers to God Almighty, fays fhe, and at the fame time be guilty of fuch a difhoneft thing? and what good do you think this money will do me? why none, it will only corrupt what little I get by my labour, and make God Almighty angry with me." So fhe got a paper wrote, and nailed it up at the church door, to let every body know that Polly Meanwell, the little ragged girl, had found a large fum of money, and a fine diamond ring, and that the owner might have it on defcribing the purfe and ring.

The lady hearing of this, fent for Polly and defcribed the purfe and ring, which Polly returned to her, who gave her ten guineas. "And now Polly, fays fhe, as I know you are a very honeft, religious, and good girl, I will provide for you. Go into the next room, and ftrip off your ragged clothes, and put on thofe new ones you will

will find on the great chair, and you shall
wait on my daughter to the East-Indies;
where, if you behave in the same manner
you have hitherto done, you will become a
great woman; for God Almighty will certainly bless you."

Some years after this, and when Polly
was grown a woman, the lady set off for
the East-Indies, and Polly with her. But
in their passage they were taken by Angria
the pirate; and poor Polly, being a beautiful girl, was again reduced to great distress;
for Angria made several attempts on her
virtue, and because she would not comply
with his wicked desires, he put her into a
dark prison, and would not suffer her mistress to see her. Now this happened at a
time when Kolan-mi Dolan, a very rich
king in India, came to visit his dominions;
for part of which Angria the pirate paid him
a tribute; and she having been punished on
account of her virtue, he procured her freedom of Angria, and took her with him to
his palace of Ilstohan.

King Kolan-mi Dolan intended to make
her one of his concubines; but Polly was
determined not to be guilty of any thing

so

fo wicked, fhe therefore fell on her knees
to him and faid, "O king! you have done
a glorious action in delivering me from that
wicked man Angria, for which I hope God
Almighty will amply reward you; for he
hath promifed to be a friend to thofe who
defend the innocent, and fupport the helplefs. Do not therefore, O king, lofe the
blefling of the Almighty, and fully your
own honour, by depriving me of my virtue, which I hold more dear than life itfelf. Ah! why fhould you for a fenfual
gratification, a momentary pleafure, make
me miferable for ever? Confider, I befeech
you, before whom you ftand; God Almighty takes notice of your actions as well as
mine, nor can thefe things be hid from his
fight; for the darknefs is no darknefs with
him: but the night is as clear as the day.
You and all your hofts are but as nothing
with refpect to him. Look in the charnel-
houfes of your fathers, where is now their
power, their pomp, their grandeur? they
are now but duft, and mingled with the
drofs of mankind. Why then fhould pride
tempt you to provoke God, or wickednefs
prompt you to commit a fin, which perhaps
may be your overthrow? Kill me you
may,

may, but you fhall never deprive me of my virtue and honour."

Kolan-mi Dolan was fo furprifed at this heroic anfwer, that for a confiderable time he could make no reply: he was dumb with amazement, and fixing his eyes on the belov-ed objeft, he revolved in his foul the infta-bility of human grandeur, the majefty of the deity, the dignity of virtue, and the power and perfuafive force of kneeling art-lefs innocence. He then raifed Polly from the ground, and addreffed himfelf to her in thefe words; "O my divine creature! thou art marked out by Providence to read me the lefture I moft wanted, to teach me to turn my thoughts to their proper centre, and to fearch the bottom of my heart. Am-bition, pride, luxury, and revenge had plant-ed themfelves there; but thou haft, by thy prudence and angelic virtue, banifhed them thence. I now fee myfelf, and admire and adore thy fuperior fenfe and virtue. Be my companion for life, and I will this moment difcharge all my concubines, the creators of my luxury and folly, and make myfelf for ever happy with thee only." He then mar-ried Mifs Polly in the moft folemn manner,

accord-

according to the ceremonies of her religion, and built for her a palace of jafper, the front of which was overlaid with pure gold, the floor paved with pearls and emeralds, the walls bedecked with the brighteft diamonds, and the cielings adorned with the moft curious paintings of facred hiftory. She had a large garden richly decorated with the fineft grottos, groves, mazey walks, fountains, and purling ftreams. Here fhe every evening recreates herfelf with thofe ladies of her court who are moft diftinguifhed for their virtue and good fenfe; but her mornings are always fpent in hearing the complaints of her people, and promoting their happinefs.

Virtues or vices fly from the court, and difperfe themfelves through a country, in the fame manner as the fafhions and garbs of drefs; what is worn by the great will be affected by the meaner fort. Hence it followed, that the morality and good principles cultivated at court, by Mifs Polly the queen, were foon fpread throughout all the kingdom, and it became fafhionable for people to be virtuous and honeft. And what was at firft introduced through fafhion, is now maintained through prudence;

ce; for as it became unfashionable to be wicked, the murthers, adulteries, robberies, thefts, &c. with which the nation was continually plagued before, were now not so much as heard of, and the people found, that in consequence of being VIRTUOUS they became happy.

END of the EIGHTH VOLUME.

GULLIVER'S LECTURES
VOL. IX.

CONTAINING

THE

ENTERTAINING MEDLEY.

VOL. IX.   A

PREFACE.

AS I have already given, in the firſt volume of this work, the Hiſtory of a Prince Chery, it may be neceſſary to acquaint my little and learned readers, that I have examined the records of Lilliput, and cannot find, that the hero of the firſt part of this volume was in any manner related to the Prince Chery, whoſe Hiſtory has been already given. There is ſo great a difference between the adventures of the one Prince and the other, that I need make no apology for laying this before my pupils. The many pretty adventures they contain, and the good moral reflections that may be derived from

A 2 them,

hem, are motives that induce me, without
he leaſt ſcruple, to recommend them to
the ſerious peruſal of all my little Maſters
and Miſſes.

THE
RENOWNED HISTORY
OF
PRINCE CHERY
AND
PRINCESS FAIR-STAR.

CHAP. I.

Some Account of the three Daughters, ROU-
SETTA, BRUNETTA, and BLONDINA.

THERE was a princess, who having
undergone several great misfortunes,
had nothing left of all her past grandeur, but
two rich suits of clothes; the one of velvet
embroidered with pearls, and the other of
cloth of gold covered over with diamonds,
which she kept as long as she could: but
the extreme necessity she was reduced to,
obliged her often to sell a pearl or diamond
privately, to support her equipage. She
was a widow, and had three daughters, all

A 3   very

very handfome: fhe thought, if fhe brought
them up in the grandeur and ftate fuitable to
their rank, they would become afterwards
more fenfible of their misfortunes. Thereupon fhe determined to fell that little fhe had
left,' and go and fettle in fome country where they might live cheap; but by the way,
going over a large foreft, fhe was robbed
of almoft all fhe had. This poor princefs,
after this laft misfortune, which was greater than all that had befallen her before,
knew fhe muft now either earn her bread,
or ftarve: and as fhe all her life had taken
great delight in cookery, and having a fmall
kitchen furnifhed with golden plate, which
fhe ufed to divert herfelf in, that which fhe
ufed to do before for her pleafure, fhe was
now forced to undertake for her livelyhood.
She took a pretty little houfe nigh a great
city, and made the beft fricaffees and ra-
gouts imaginable; infomuch that fhe had a
confiderable trade, and acquired great fame
of being an excellent cook. In the mean
time her three daughters grew up, and their
beauty, without doubt, had reached the
ears of the court, had not their mother kept
them up in their chamber. When one day
there came a little old woman, who feemed

to be very much tired, and leaning on a
stick, her body very feeble, and her skin all
wrinkled and shrivelled: " I am come, said
she, to make one good meal before I leave
this world, that I may brag I have had one;
therefore, said she again to the princess,
drawing herself a chair to the fire-side, get
me something nice, and make haste." As
she had at that time her hands fully employed, and could not do all herself, she called her three daughters down, whose names, in relation to the colours of their hair,
which were red, brown, and fair, were
Roufetta, Brunetta, and Blondina; who
were dressed like country-girls in bodice and
petticoats, all of different colours; but the
youngest was the handsomest and best-natur-
ed. The princess their mother ordered one
to go take some pigeons, another to kill
some pullets, and the third to make some
paste. In short, two or three courses were
presently served up, and set before the old
woman with clean linen, good wine, and
every thing in nice order; which made her
eat and drink with an extraordinary appetite.
When she had done, she got up, and said
to the princess, "Honest friend, had I any
money, I would pay you; but I have been

A 4   poor

poor these many years, and wanted so kind
an entertainment as you have given me; all
that I can do, is to wish you better custom-
ers than I have been." The princess smiled,
and replied, "Well, mother, do not trouble yourself, I am always well rewarded if
I can but please. And said Blondina, "We
are glad it was in our powers to serve you;
if you will sup here too, you shall be welcome." O! cried the old woman, how
happy are they who have such generous
souls! but don't you think of receiving some
recompence? Well, continued she, assure
yourselves, that the first wish you make
without thinking of me, shall be completed." Then she went away, leaving them
some reasons to believe her to be a fairy.

This adventure surprised them; they had
never seen a fairy before, and were frightened. Insomuch that for six months after,
they could not forbear talking of her; and
whenever they wished for any thing, she
was always present in their thoughts, so
that they came to nothing, which made
them very angry with the fairy. When
one day the king going a hunting, resolved
to call at their house to see if the princess
was as notable a cook, as she was represent-
ed

ed to him. The three fifters were in the garden gathering ftrawberries when he paffed by. "Ah! faid Roufetta, was I fo happy as to marry the Admiral, I boaft that I could fpin thread enough to make fails for his whole navy." "And I, faid Brunetta, was my fortune fo good that I fhould marry the king's brother, I could work lace enough with my needle to hang his palace." "And I, faid Blondina, would the king have me, boaft at the end of nine months to bring him forth two fine boys and a girl, with ftars in their foreheads, and a chain of gold about their necks; from whofe hair, hanging on curious rings, fhould drop valuable jewels." One of the king's favourites overhearing their difcourfe, went and informed the king thereof, who ordered them to come to him. When they entered the room where the king was, which they did with all refpect and modefty, he afked them, whether what he had been told of their difcourfe about hufbands was true, or not? At which they blufhed, and hung down their heads: but upon his preffing them further, they owned it was. "Certainly, faid he, I know not what power influences me, but I will not ftir from hence, until I have married

ried the fair Blondina." Then, fir, faid his brother, you will give me leave to marry. the lovely Brunetta." "And I live not without hopes, faid the Admiral, but your majefty will confent to my happinefs, in efpoufing Roufetta, with whom I am charmed." The king, pleafed that two of the greateft perfons in his dominions fhould follow his example, approved their choice, and afked the mother's confent; who anfwered, it was too great an honour and happinefs for her to refufe: and then the king, prince, and admiral, kiffed her.

The king pulled a ring off his finger, and put it on Blondina's; and the prince and admiral did the fame: after which all the king's retinue faluted, as became them, both the queen and princefs: but for Roufetta, fhe had not fo much refpect fhown her; for though fhe was the eldeft fifter, fhe was the worft married.

When the coaches came, the king invited his mother-in-law to go along with them; affuring her, that fhe fhould be looked upon with all manner of diftinction. But fhe, comparing a court to the rolling of the waves in a rough fea, told him fhe had had too much experience of the world, to forfake

fake a quiet life. "Why, replied the king, you don't intend to follow your bufinefs?" "No," replied' fhe. "Then, added he, give me leave to appoint you an equipage and attendants." "I thank you, fir, anfwered fhe, when I am alone, I have none to difturb my repofe; and had I a large family of domeftics, there would not fail of fome to incommode me." The king admired the fenfe and difcretion of a woman, who both thought and fpoke like a philofopher. But while he was preffing his mother-in-law to go along with him, Roufetta went and hid all the veffels of gold that were in the Beaufet, in the bottom of the chariot; all which the fairy turned into earthen ware, when fhe arrived at court, and came to put them into her clofet.

The king and queen embraced the prudent princefs with all tendernefs, and affured her fhe might command whatever lay in their power; and leaving this rural abode, came to town, preceded by trumpets, hautboys, and kettle-drums.

——————

CHAP.

C H A P. II.

Roufetta grows envious of her Sifter.　Its Con-
fequence.

THE fair queen, and the princefs Brunetta, were united by a ftrict friendfhip; but Roufetta hated them mortally for
their good fortune.　What, faid fhe to herfelf, muft I, who am the elder, and think
myfelf a thoufand times handfomer than
either of them; muft I be only the wife of
an admiral, who perhaps loves me not fo
well as he ought! and fhall they be, one a
queen and the other a princefs, and be ador-
ed by their hufbands! Ye Gods, it is intolerable!"

The queen and princefs both proved with
child, and by ill fortune a war happened,
which obliged the king to put himfelf at
the head of his troops.　The young queen
and the princefs, finding that they muft be
left in the power of the queen-mother, who
hated the thoughts of this low marriage,
but diffembled her anger, defired they might
return home to their own mother, which
would be fome comfort to them, for the

lofs

lofs of their dear fpoufes: but the king could not be brought to confent to it; he conjured his beloved Blondina to ftay at her palace, and affured her his mother fhould ufe her well. The king, through his defire of a quick return, hazarded his troops in all rencounters; and his happinefs was, that by his rafhnefs he fucceeded: but before he could finifh his campaign, the queen was brought to bed, as was alfo the princefs her fifter, on the fame day, of a lovely boy; but fhe died in the birth. Roufetta's thoughts were wholly employed how fhe might injure the queen; and when fhe faw fuch charming children, and that fhe herfelf had none, her rage increafed, and fhe refolved to fpeak foon to the queen-mother for there, was no time to lofe. "Madam, faid fhe, I am fo deeply touched with the honour your majefty has done me, by letting me fhare fome part of your efteem, that I willingly would do any thing, though againft the intereft of my own family, to obey you. I am not ignorant of the great difpleafure you have conceived at the bafe marriages of the king and prince; and here are four children born to perpetuate the crime; our mother is but a poor country woman,

man, who had scarcely a bit of bread to put in her mouth, when she betook her to be a cook.   Take my advice, Madam, let us make a fricassee of these brats, and put them out of the world, before they make you blush."   "Ah! how much I love thee, my dear Rousetta, said the queen, for being so equitable and partaking with me in my just grief? I had already determined to execute what you now propose, but then, the manner how, perplexes me."   Never let that trouble you, replied Rousetta, I have a little bitch that has just pupped two little dogs and a bitch, with stars on their foreheads, and rings about their necks: we must make the queen believe that she has been delivered of these creatures, and make away with her three children, and that of the princess deceased."   This project was approved of by the inhuman queen, who ordered Feintisa, one of her maids of honour, to fetch the whelps, and dress them in as fine linen and laces as the queen's children should be, and put them into the cradles; then she, followed by Rousetta, went and paid the queen a visit: "I am come to wish you joy, said she, of the heirs you have brought forth to my son; methinks, hold-

ing

ing up the whelps, their head will become a crown: Now I am not amazed at the promife you made my fon, of bringing two fons and a daughter, with ftars on their foreheads, and collars of gold about their necks. Here take them, and nurfe them yourfelf, for no woman, that I know of, will ever give their breafts to them to fuck.

The poor queen, furprifed at the relation of this misfortune, had like to have died away with grief, and when fhe perceived it was true, feeing the whole litter lie yelping upon her bed, cried moft bitterly: then clafping her hands, faid, "Alas! madam, add no reproaches to my affli&tion, which of itfelf is already too great: had the gods permitted me to die, rather than be the mother of fuch monfters, I fhould have thought myfelf too happy. Alas! what will become of me; the king will hate me as much as he loved me before." Here her fighs and fobbings interrupted her, and her fpeech failed her; when the queen-mother continuing her reilections, had the pleafure of paffing away three hours by her bed-fide, and then went away. Her fifter, who pretended to partake of her grief, told her fhe was not the firft that had had fuch misfortunes; that

fhe

she plainly saw it was a trick of the old fairy's, who had promised such wonders; and that, as it might be dangerous for her to see the king, she advised her to go home to her mother with her three whelps. The queen returned no answer, but by tears, which might make the most hardened heart relent, to think she must be forced to suckle nasty whelps, and believe herself the mother of them. The old queen ordered Feintisa to take the four children and strangle them, and after that bury them carefully, that she might not be discovered; but just as she was going to execute that fatal commission, and had the cord about their necks, she looked some time earnestly upon them, and seeing the stars in their foreheads, which she thinking might portend something extraordinary, she durst not lay criminal hands upon them, but put them in their cradle aboard a little boat, and with some jewels committed them to the mercy of the seas. The boat was soon forced from the shore by the wind, which at that time was very boisterous, and was got presently out of sight: the waves swelled as high as mountains, the sun was darkened by thick clouds, and the air was rent by violent claps of thunder, attended

with

with great lightnings; infomuch that Feintifa doubted not in the leaft but that the boat
was caft away, and thefe infants perifhed;
at which fhe conceived no fmall joy, fhe
having had all along a dread, left fomething
fhould happen in their favour.

The king, whofe thoughts were always
on his dear fpoufe, and the condition he left
her in, having concluded a truce for fome
time, returned with all fpeed home, and arrived about twelve hours after her delivery.
The queen-mother met him, and with a compofed air, full of grief, held him a long
time in her arms, wetting his face with her
tears, and feeming as if her forrow prevented her fpeech. The king, all trembling,
durft not afk her what had happened, for he
doubted not but it was fome very great misfortune. But at laft, fhe making as if fhe
ufed fome great effort on herfelf, told him
that his queen was brought to bed of three
whelps, which Feintifa immediately prefented to him; and Roufetta, falling on her
knees, begged of him not to put her fifter to
death, but to fend her back to her mother;
which, fhe faid, fhe fhould take as a great favour. The king was fo ftruck and confounded, that he could hardly breathe, and look-

ing

ing on the whelps, and obferving, with furprife, the ftar on their foreheads, and the white ring about their necks, he fell into a fwoon, and rolling a thoufand things in his imagination, could not refolve on any, 'till the queen-mother preffed him fo much, that he pronounced his innocent queen's banifh-ment: who was that minute put into a litter with her whelps, and fent to her mother's, where fhe arrived almoft dead.

But heaven looked with a more favoura-ble eye on the boat the three princes and the princes were in; for the fairy, who pro-tected them, rained milk into their mouths, and preferved them in this fudden and terri-ble ftorm; they floated feven nights and days, and were met out at main fea by a corfair, the captain of which, feeing the ftars on their foreheads, though at a great diftance, thought the boat was full of jewels, which he found to be true in the end. But what touched him moft, was the beauty of thefe four charming children, the defire of preferving which made him turn back again, to give them to his wife, who ne-ver had any, and was very defirous of them. She, for her part, was frightened to fee him return fo foon, he ufing to ftay out a long time, but was overjoyed when be put fo valuable a treafure into her hands. They both wondered at the ftar, the chain of gold, which could not be taken from off their neck, and their fine hair; but what increafed it the more, was; when the good woman came to comb them, there fell out diamonds, rubies, emeralds, and pearls, of feveral fizes, fome whereof were very large and beautiful. The hufband feeing this, told his wife he was weary of the feas, and that if thofe children continued to beftow fuch treafures, he would go no more, but might ftay at home, and live as well as the greateft captains they had; at which refolution of her hufband, the wife, whofe name was Corfina, was overjoyed, and grew every day fonder of thefe children. The princefs fhe called Fair-Star, the elder brother Bright-Sun, the fecond fon Felix, and the princefs's fon Chery, who was much, more beautiful than the others, for all he had neither a ftar nor chain, and was beft beloved by Corfina.

After the firft years of their infancy, the corfair applied himfelf ferioufly to cultivate the natural parts, with which heaven had fo largely endowed them. And he made no doubt, but that some great mysteries were concealed in their birth, and his finding them as he did; therefore he resolved to make the Gods an acknowledgment for this present, by his extraordinary care of their education: insomuch, that after having enlarged his house, he hired masters to instruct them in all manner of learning and qualifications, who were amazed at the great geniuses of their pupils. The corsair and his wife never divulged this adventure, but the children passed for their own, though in all their actions they plainly showed they were of more illustrious blood. There was a strict unity among them; and as they grew up, their mutual tenderness encreased, and they lived with all imaginable pleasure and satisfaction. "Dear brother, said Fair-Star to Chery, one day, if my wishes could make you happy, you should be one of the greatest monarchs upon earth." "Alas! sister, replied he, envy me not the blessing I enjoy, in being nigh you; one moment of which time I prefer to all the grandeur you can wish me." If she said the same things to her other two brothers, they only thanked her in a careless manner, and said no more.

CHAP.

, C H A P. III.

Fair-Star discovers herself to be in love.

WHEN she was alone, she examined into the differences of love, and found her heart to be somewhat disposed like theirs; for though Bright-Sun and Felix were both dear to her, she could not wish to live with them all her life: but for Chery, she was all in tears at the least thought of his father's senting him to sea or into the army.

One day the three princes being gone a hunting, Fair Star went up into a little dark closet, which she loved to sit and think in, which was separated only by a thin partition from Corsina's chamber; where she heard her, thinking she was gone a walking, say to the Corsair, "It is now time to think of marrying Fair-Star: if we knew who she was, we should endeavour to marry her suitable to her rank: or if we could believe that these, who pass for her brothers, were not so, we might bestow her on one of them; for where can we find one more deserving of her? When I found

B 3   them,

them, faid the Corfair, I faw nothing that could inform me of their birth; but knew by the jewels that were faftened to their cradles, that they were no mean perfons: and what is more fingular, you know they feemed all of an age, and four are too many for one birth." "I fufpected fo, faid Corfina, that Chery is not their brother, for he has neither a ftar nor collar." "That is true, replied the hufband, but jewels fall out of his hair as well as the others: yet after all the riches we have amaffed together by them, I could wifh to know whofe they are." "That we muft leave to the gods, faid Corfina, who gave them us, and when they fhall think fit, will let us know." Fair-Star liftened attentively to their difcourfe, and could not exprefs her joy, that fhe might hope fhe was born of illuftrious parents, though fhe had never failed any ways in refpect to thofe fhe thought to be hers; and yet was not over well pleafed at her being a Corfair's. But what flattered her imagination moft, was to think that Chery was not her brother; which thought made her impatient to fee him, to tell him of this extraordinary adventure. Hereupon fhe went and took horfe, and followed them

by

by the found of the horn. Chery, as foon
as he faw her, came to meet her before the
other two. "How agreeable a furprife is
this, Fair-Star, faid he, to fee you a hunting, who are never to be drawn away from
your mufic and other amufements?" "I
have fo many things to tell you, replied fhe,
that I came to feek you, to talk in private with you." "Alas! fifter, faid he fighing, what is it you would have with me to
day, for it is a long time fince you have
taken any notice of me?" At that fhe blufhed, and caft down her eyes, and remained
fome time thoughtful, without ever returning any anfwer. At laft, when her two
brothers came to them, fhe, like one awakened out of a lethargy, jumped from off
her horfe, and went, followed by them, to
a little hillock, furrounded with fhady trees;
where fhe faid to them, "Sit down here,
and I will tell you what I have heard."

And accordingly fhe told them word for
word, the Corfair's, and his wife's difcourfe, and how that they were not their children. Nothing can be faid to exprefs the
furprife of the three Princes: they debated
among themfelves what they had beft to do;
One was for going without faying any

thing;

thing; another was not for going at all; and the third was for going and acquainting them with it. The firſt maintained his was the fureſt way, becaufe the advantage they made of them would induce them to keep them; the ſecond faid, it was not proper to leave them, unleſs they had fomewhere to go, where they might be well received, for that he could not bear the thoughts of being called wanderers; the third alledged the ingratitude of leaving them without their confents; that it was folly to ſtay any longer with them in a defert part of the world, where they could never learn who they were, and that therefore the only way was to tell them of their defign, and get their confents. This opinion at laſt prevailing, they all took horfe again, and returned home to the Corfair.

Chery's heart was flattered with all that hope can offer moſt agreeable to comfort an afflicted lover; his love made him guefs at what was to come: He no longer looked upon himfelf as brother to Fair-Star, and his conftrained paſſion taking wing a little, permitted a thoufand ideas that charmed him. They addreſſed themfelves to the Corfair and his wife with a vifible joy, and yet uneafi-

nefs

nefs in their faces: "We come not, faid Bright-Sun, to deny the friendfhip, gratitude, and refpect we owe you, though we are informed how you found us on the fea, and that you are not our father and mother. The piety with which you faved us, the noble education you have given us, and the care and bounty you have fhown, are fuch indifpenfable ties, that nothing in this world can free us from. We are come now to renew our fincere thanks, and to beg of you to relate to us fo rare an event, and to advife us, that guided by your wife counfels, we may have nothing to reproach ourfelves withal." The Corfair and his wife were very much furprized, that a thing which they had concealed with fo much care, fhould be difcovered. "You are too well informed, faid they, and we can no longer hide from you, that you are not our children, and that fortune alone put you into our hands. We have no knowledge of your birth; but, by the jewels that were found in your cradles, guefs your parents to be people of quality, or very rich. What can we advife you more? If you confult the friendfhip we have for you, you will, without doubt, ftay here with us, and com-

Tort

fort us in our old age by your prefence. If
you do not like this houfe or abode, we
will remove where you fhall think fit, provided it be not to court, which a long experience has made us difrelifh; and will make
you too, if you knew but the continual
trouble and care, the difguifes and diffimula-
tions, the envy and ftrife, the falfe happinefs, and all the mifchiefs attending there;
I could tell you more, but that you may
think my counfels too much interefted,
which they really are my dear children: we
only defire to detain you in this peaceable
retreat; yet you are your own mafters, to
go when you will. Confider, now you are
in the haven, and are going to fail in a boi-
fterous fea; the trouble exceeds the pleafure: the courfe of man's life is limited, and
oftentimes is cut fhort by one half; the
grandeurs of this world are like falfe ftones;
the moft folid happinefs is to know how to
fet bounds to our defires, to be wife and
live in a perfect tranquillity."

The Corfair had not made an end of thefe
his remonftrances fo foon, but that he was
interrupted by prince Felix: "We have too
great a defire, dear father, faid he, to make
fome difcoveries of our births, as to live buried
here

here in a defert; the morals you have laid
down are excellent, and I wifh we were
able to follow them; but I know not what
fatality guides us; let us fulfil our deftiny,
we will come and fee you again, and give
you an account of our adventures." At
thefe words the Corfair and his wife burft
out in tears; the princes very much relented, and particularly Fair Star, who was of
a fweet difpofition, and would never have
thought of going away, had fhe but Chery
to ftay with her. After this refolution,
their thoughts were wholly bent upon their
equipage and their embarkation; for they
hoped, when at fea, to get fome light of
what they wanted to know. They put four
horfes a-board; and after having combed
their heads to give Corfina as many jewels
as poffibly they could, they defired her in
exchange to give them the chains and diamonds that fhe found in their cradle; who
went immediately and fetched them out of
her clofet, where fhe kept them fafe, and
tied them all upon Fair-Star, whom fhe embraced with all motherly affection, wetting
her face with her tears.

Never was any feparation more melancholy: The Corfair and his wife were ready

to die with grief. But their sorrows proceeded not from interest; they had already
amassed too much riches to desire any more.
In short, Bright-Sun, Felix, Chery, and
Fair Star, went a-board a vessel which the
Corsair had fitted out with all magnificence,
and fine paintings. The course they steered
was to the same degrees of latitude where
the Corsair found them; and he prepared a
great sacrifice for the gods and fairies to obtain their protection, and guide them to the
place of their birth. They took a Turtle
Dove, and were going out to sacrifice it;
but that the compassionate princess thought
it so beautiful, that she saved its life, and
let it fly, saying, "Go thou pretty bird of
Venus, if I should ever want thy assistance,
remember what I have done for thee."
Away went the bird, and when the sacrifice was over, there was heard such a charming concert of music, that all nature seemed to keep a profound silence to listen to it;
the seas were calm, and the winds only
breathed gentle zephyrs, which disordered
the princess's veil and hair; and a Syren
arose out of the water, and sung, while the
princess and her brothers admired her. After
some airs, she turned herself towards them,

and

and faid, "be not uneafy; let your veffel drive before the wind; and where it ftops, there difembark; and let thofe who love, love ftill on."

Fair Star and Chery were fenfible of an extraordinary joy at thefe words of the Syren, never difputing but that they related to them; and by figns gave each other to underftand as much, without Bright-Sun and Felix perceiving them in the leaft. They were full three months out at fea, during which time the amorous prince had a great deal of converfation with his beloved princefs.

The days were then very long and hot; towards the evening the princefs and her brothers went upon the deck, to fee the fun repofe himfelf in the breaft of his beloved Thetis; and taking their inftruments, began a very agreeable concert. In the mean time, a frefh gale of wind arifing, they foon doubled a point, which concealed from their eyes a beautiful city, the profpect of which amazed and pleafed our lovely youths fo much, that they wifhed their veffel might enter the port; but doubted left there fhould not be room; there being fo many in before them, that the mafts looked like a floating

ing

ing foreſt. Their deſires were accompliſh-
ed; the ſhores were preſently crouded to ſee
the magnificence of the ſhip.

C H A P. IV.

Containing ſeveral wonderful Incidents.

ALL that ſaw the ſtars on the princes
were filled with admiration; and ſome
ran to inform the king of it, who as he could
not believe it, and as the large great terraſs
belonging to his palace looked to the ſea,
he came preſently and ſaw the princes Bright-
Sun, and Chery, taking the princeſs in their
arms, and carrying her aſhore; and after
that unſhipping their horſes, the richneſs of
whoſe accoutrements were anſwerable to
the reſt.

The princes, hearing the people ſay,
there's the king, there's the king, lifting up
their eyes, beheld in him an air of ſo much
majeſty, that they no longer diſputed but it
was true; and paſſing by him, made him
each a low bow, fixing their eyes on him
all the time; while he looking no leſs ear-
neſtly

neftly upon them, was charmed with the
incomparable beauty of the princefs, and
the good mien of the three princes. He
fent the firft gentleman of his bed-chamber
to offer them his protection, and whatever
they fhould want, they being perfect ftrangers. They accepted of the honour the
king did them, with a great deal of refpect
and acknowledgment, and told him that they
only wanted an houfe where they might
live private; and that they fhould be glad
if it could be two or three miles from the
city, becaufe they took great delight in
walking. He accordingly did as they defired, and lodged them and their train com-
modioufly. The king, whofe thoughts
were full of what he had feen, went immediately into the queen-mother's apartment,
and told her what he had been feeing, and
how much he admired the youths and the
young lady. At this news fhe ftood as it
were thunder-ftruck: but recovering herfelf
afked in a carelefs manner, of what age
they might be, and he anfwering about fifteen or fixteen, her uneafinefs encreafed;
and fhe apprehended with fear that Feintifa
had betrayed her; while the king walked
about the room, in fome paffion and concern,

cern, often faying, "How happy muſt that father be, who is bleſſed with ſuch an off-ſpring! and how miſerable am I to be a king and father to three whelps, and have no heirs to my crown."

. The old queen heard theſe words with a deadly dread; the ſtars and the nearneſs of their age, with the princes and their ſiſter, gave her great ſuſpicions that Feintiſa, in-ſtead of making away with the king's chil-dren, had preſerved them. But as ſhe was a woman that had a great command over her-ſelf, ſhe diſcovered not in the leaſt what agitated her ſoul; and would not ſend that day tho inform herſelf of what ſhe deſired ſo much to know; but the next day ſent her ſecretary under pretext of giving ſome or-ders for their entertainment, to examine and enquire into what was ſo neceſſary to her re-poſe. The ſecretary went early the next morning, and arrived juſt as the princeſs was ſet down to her toilet, and was comb-ing her hair, which hung down in fine rings below her waiſt, which was hung round with baſkets to catch the jewels ſhe combed out: her ſtar ſhined ſo bright that it dazzled him, and the chain of gold about her neck ſeemed no leſs extraordinary than the dia-monds

monds, &c. rolling down from the top of her head. The secretary could hardly believe his eyes; when the princess making choice of a large pearl, such as the kings of Spain esteem so much by the name of *peregrina*, or the pilgrim, as it came from a traveller, she desired him to accept of it, that thereby he might remember her. He, confounded by so much liberality, took his leave of her, and went to pay his respects to the three princes, with whom he stayed some time to inform himself of what his mistress desired so much to know; and after that returned back to the queen, with an account that confirmed what she so much feared. He told her Chery had no star, but diamonds, &c. fell out of his hair; and that in his opinion he was the handsomest: that they were come a great way off; and that their father and mother had prefixed a time for them to finish their travels in.

This article put the queen a little to a stand, and she imagined sometimes that they were not the king's children. Thus she wavered between hope and fear; when the king hunting one day by their house, the gentlemen of his bed-chamber told him as they passed by, that it was there the princefs and her brothers lived. "The queen has advifed me, replied the king, not to fee them, fearing left they may have come from fome place where the plague rages, and may bring fome infection with them." "Indeed, replied the gentleman, it is very dangerous; but I believe there's more to be feared from the eyes of this young ftranger than any infection of the air." "I am of your opinion," faid the king, and fpurring his horfe went forward; when prefently hearing a found of inftruments, he ftopped at the hall windows, which where open; and after having admired the fweetnefs of this fymphony, went on. The noife the horfes made, engaged the princes to look out; who, when they faw the king, faluted him very refpectfully, and made all hafte to come out, and accofting him with a gay countenance and much fubmiffion, they embraced his knees, and the princefs kiffed his hand. The king careffed them with a pleafing fatisfaction, and found his heart fo touched, that he could not guefs at the caufe. He bid them not fail of coming to court, telling them he fhould be very glad to fee them there, and that he would prefent them to his mother. They thanked him for the

honour

honour he did them, and affured him, that as foon as their clothes and equipage were got ready, they would make their appearance there. After this the king left them to purfue his game, and fent them one half of what he killed, and carried the other with him to the queen his mother; who faid to him, "How comes this about? you ufed to kill three times as much as this." "Indeed, replied the king, I have regaled the beautiful ftrangers with fome; and I have fo ftrong a fancy for them, that were you not fo much afraid of fome contagion, I would lodge them in the palace."

The old queen very much vexed, accufed him of want of refpect to her, and reproached him for expofing himfelf fo rafhly; and when he was gone, fent for Feintifa into her clofet, and catching hold of her hair with one hand, and clapping a poynard to her throat with the other, faid, "I know not, bafe wretch, what remains of kindnefs hinder my facrificing thee to my juft refentment; thou haft betrayed me, and haft not killed the four children I put in thy hands for that purpofe: own thy crime, and perhaps I may forgive thee." Feintifa half dead with fear, caft herfelf at her feet and

told

told her all she had done; that she thought
it impossible that they should be alive, because there arose just then such a terrible
tempest, that in all probability they must be
cast away; adding, that if she would but
give her time, she would find out a way to
destroy them one after another, without the
least suspicion. The queen, whom nothing
but the promise of their death could appease,
bid her to lose no time; and indeed Feintisa who saw her life in great danger, neglected nothing that lay in her power: she
watched the time when the princes were
gone out a hunting, and carrying a guittar
under her arm, went and sat over against
the princess's window, and sung these
words:

    Happy they, the use who know
    Of blessings the kind Gods bestow;
        Beauty fades,
        Age invades,
  And blights the fairest flower;
        Too great's the grief,
        When past relief,
  And charms have lost their power;
        Then to our cost,
        We find we've lost,
  And miss'd the lucky hour.

                     Fair

Fair ones, beware, your charms improve,
While in your bloom, and fit for love;
    Beauty fades,
    Age invades,
And blights the faireſt flower;
    Too great's the grief,
    When paſt relief,
And charms have loſt their power:
    Then to your coſt,
    You'll find you've loſt,
And miſs'd the lucky hour.

Fair-Star liking the words, came into her balcony to ſee who the perſon was that ſung them, and Feintiſa appearing in a dreſs ſuitable to her deſign, made her a very low courteſy. The princeſs, as ſhe was gay, returning the ſalute, aſked her if thoſe words were made upon herſelf. "Yes, charming lady, they were, replied Feintiſa, but that they may never be applied to you, I am come to give you ſome good advice, which you ought not to negleƈt." "What's that?" ſaid Fair-Star. "Let me come into your chamber, and I will tell you." replied the other. "Come up then," ſaid the princeſs. And immediately thereupon, the old woman roſe up, and came into her chamber

with

with a courtly air, which when once at-
tained, is not eafily laid afide. "Dear lady,
faid fhe, without lofing any time, for fhe
was afraid of being interrupted, heaven has
formed you charming and lovely, you are
adorned with a bright ftar upon your forehead, and feveral wonders are reported of
you: but you want one thing that is effen-
tially neceffary; and if you have it not, I
pity you." "And what is it?" replied fhe.
"The dancing-water, added the wicked Feintifa, if I had had it in my youth, you fhould
not have feen a grey hair in my head, nor
a wrinkle in my brow. I fhould have had
now the moft charming white teeth: but,
alas! it was too late when I knew this fecret; my charms were decayed before.
Profit by my misfortunes, dear child, it
will be fome comfort to me, for I have a
tendernefs for you." "But where fhall I
get this dancing-water?" replied Fair-Star.
"In the Burning Foreft, faid Feintifa.
You have three brothers, do none of them
love you well enough to go and fetch it for
you?" "My brothers, faid the princefs,
love me tenderly; and I am fure there is one
of them will refufe me nothing; and I will
certainly, if this water does what you fay,
give

give you a recompence fuitable to your deferts." The perfidious Feintifa retired in
hafte, overjoyed that fhe had fucceeded fo
well, telling Fair-Star, fhe would be fure
to come and fee her again.

When the princes came from hunting,
one brought a boar, another a hare, and the
third a ftag, and laid them at their fifter's
feet; which homage fhe looked upon with
difdain; her thoughts were fo much employed on the advice Feintifa had given, that fhe
feemed uneafy; and Chery, whofe whole
ftudy was to obferve her humour and mo-
tions, was not long before he obferved it.
"What is the matter, my dear Star? faid
he, perhaps you like not the country where
we are; if fo, we will go away immediately; perhaps you are not pleafed with our
equipage, it is not fine enough; fpeak, and
tell me, that I may have the pleafure of
obeying you firft." "The confidence which
you give me, faid fhe, to tell you what
paffes in my mind, engages me to declare to
you, that I cannot live without the dancing-
water which is in the Burning Foreft: had
I that, I need not fear any thing from the
power of time." "Trouble not yourfelf,
my lovely Star, added he, I will go and

C 4   fetch

fetch it you, or let you know by my death, that it is impoffible to have it." "No, faid fhe, I would rather renounce all the advantages of beauty, and be horridly frightful, than hazard a life fo dear. I conjure you never to think more of this water; and if I have any power over you, I forbid you." The prince feemed to obey; but as foon as he faw her engaged and bufy, he mounted his white horfe, and furnifhed his pockets plentifully with money, and for jewels his head fupplied him fufficiently. He took no attendants with him, that he might be more at his own liberty; and that if any dangerous adventure prefented, he might not be troubled with the remonftrances of an over-zealous and timorous fervant.

CHAP. V.

Chery fets out on an Expedition to the Burning Foreft.

WHEN fupper-time came, and the princefs faw not her brother Chery, fhe was fo much troubled, that fhe could neither eat nor drink, but ordered the fervants

to

to search every where for him. The other two princes, who knew nothing of the dancing-water, told her she was too uneasy, and that he could not be far off; that she knew he loved retirement sometimes, to indulge his thoughts, and that without doubt, he was amusing himself in a little wood that was hard by. This made her easy for some time; but then again she lost all patience, and told her brothers, crying, that she was the cause of his absence, by expressing a desire to have some of the dancing-water in the Burning Forest, and that without doubt he was gone thither. At this news, they resolved to send after him; and she charged the messengers to tell him, that she conjured him to come back. In the mean time, Feintisa, who was not without her spies, to know the effect of her advice, when she learned that Chery was gone, was overjoyed; not doubting in the least, but he would make more haste than those that followed him, and that some mischief would befal him. Big with these hopes she ran to the queen-mother, to give her an account of all that had past.

The contrivance, of the Prince Chery's destruction was one of the most certain; for

the

the dancing-water was not easily to be got; the reports of the misfortunes that attended all those who had gone for it, had made the way known almost to every body. The prince never spared his white nag, who went at an incredible swiftness, so willing was he to return soon to Fair-Star, to give her all the satisfaction she could promise herself from his journey. He was eight days and nights without taking any repose, but what he got under a tree in a wood or forest, while his horse was grasing; and lived on what fruits he found on the trees. The ninth day, he found himself very much incommoded by the excessive heat of the air, and not knowing what cause to attribute it to, since he was certain it was not the sun, when he gained the top of a hill, he perceived the Burning Forest; where the trees were always in flames, without ever consuming; which cast such a heat, that all the country about was a dry desart. In this forest, the prince heard the hissing of adders, and the roaring of lions, which very much amazed him, who could not believe that any thing but a salamander could live in a kind of furnace. After having considered on so dreadful a thing, and thought on what

was

was to be done, he gave himfelf up for loft; when going higher to this great fire, and being ready to die with thirft, finding a fountain, he alighted from off his horfe, and ftooping to take up fome water into a golden veffel he brought with him, to carry that the princefs defired in, he perceived a turtle drowning, and taking pity on it, faved it; and after having held it fome time by the heels, and wiped its wet feathers, put it in his bofom, where the poor turtle recovered. "Prince Chery, faid it, in a foft tender voice, you never could have obliged any creature more full of acknowledgment than myfelf; this is not the firft time I have received moft fignal favours from your family; I am glad that I now can, in return, be ferviceable to you. Think not that I am ignorant of the caufe of this your journey, which you have too rafhly undertaken, fince it is almoft impoffible to tell how many have perifhed here. The dancing-water is the eighth wonder of the world; it beautifies ladies, makes them young again, and enriches them: but if I am not your guide, you can never get to it: the fource of the water falls with fo great an impetuofity into a deep abyfs. In
the

the road is a blockade of trees, laid fo clofe,
and fo entangled by their branches and briars,
that I fee no way but to go under ground.
Reft yourfelf here, and be not uneafy, I
will go and take proper meafures about
it."

Then the turtle left him, flying back-
wards and forwards, and taking feveral
flights about: and towards the clofe of the
day, came and told the prince all was ready:
who took the loving bird in his hand, kiffed it, careffed it, and thanked it; and
after that, followed it upon his white horfe.
They had not gone many hundred yards,
before the prince feeing a great number of
foxes, badgers, moles, and other creatures
that burrowed, and wondering how they
came to be fo affembled together, the turtle
told him it was by her means, and that
they came to work for his fervice. Chery,
when he came to the mouth of the vault,
pulled the bridle off his horfe's head, and
tied it to the faddle, and turned him loofe;
and then followed the turtle, who conducted him to the fountain, the falling of whofe
water made fuch a noife as would have dea-
fened him, had not the turtle given him two
of her white feathers. He was ftrangely

furprifed to fee the water dance with fo
much juftnefs to the warblings of fome birds,
who, flying in the air, formed a band of
mufick. He filled his veffel of gold, and
pulled two hearty draughts, which made
him a thoufand times more beautiful than
he was before, and refrefhed him fo much,
that he was able to bear the heat of the
foreft. He returned the fame way he came,
and finding his horfe again at the cavern's
mouth, mounted him again, and taking the
dove in his hand, faid, "Loving turtle, I
know not by what prodigy you have fo
much power here; what you have done for
me demands all my gratitude: and as liberty is the greateft of all bleffings, I give you
yours, to fhow fome token of my good-
will." As he faid thefe words, he let her
go; fhe flew away with as fullen an air,
as if he had kept her againft her will. Upon
which he faid to himfelf. "How fickle art
thou! thou haft more of a man than a turtle in thee; the one is inconftant, the other
is not." To this the turtle mounted high
in the air, faid, "And do you know who
I am?"

Chery, amazed that the turtle fhould
anfwer thus to his thoughts, fufpected her

to be fomething very extraordinary, and was
forry he had let her fly, faying to himfelf
that fhe might be very ufeful to him, and
he might have learned of her feveral things,
that might have contributed very much to
his repofe. But then again, he confidered
with himfelf, that he ought never to regret
a good action, and that he was indebted to
her, when he thought on the difficulties
fhe had fmoothed out for him, to get the
dancing-water. His golden veffel or bottle,
in which he put it, was fo clofe ftopped up,
he could not fpill one drop, nor the fpirit
of the water evaporate; fo that all the way,
he entertained himfelf with the thoughts,
how agreeable he fhould pleafe his Fair Star,
and the joy fhe would receive, to fee the
water and him again: when prefently he
fpied feveral men on horfeback, galloping
at full fpeed, who no fooner perceived him,
but they gave a halloo, and pointed to him.
Though his intrepid foul was fo void of fear,
as not to be alarmed at any danger, yet
was he vexed to think he fhould be ftopped; he fpurred on his horfe, and made
boldly towards them: but how agreeable
was his furprife, to find them to be his do-
mefticks, with a letter from the princefs,
charging

charging him not to expofe himfelf to the dangers of the Burning Foreft! he kiffed the writing, fighed feveral times, and made all poffible hafte to eafe her of her fears.

When he came home, he found her fitting under fome trees, abandoned to her grief; but when fhe faw him at her feet, fhe knew not what reception to give him; fhe could both chide him, for going contrary to her orders, and thanked him for his prefent: at laft, her tendernefs prevailing, fhe embraced her dear brother, and received him with all poffible demonftrations of joy. The reftlefs Feintifa knew by her fpies, that Chery was returned, and more beautiful than when he went, and that the princefs, by wafhing her face with the dancing-water, was become fo exceffive beautiful, that no body could behold her without admiration. She was very much amazed and vexed; for fhe made account that the prince would perifh in the attempt: but recollecting, this was no time to defpond, but feeking an opportunity, when the princefs went to the temple of Diana unaccompanied, fhe accofted her with an air of friendfhip, and faid, "I congratulate you, madam, on the happy fuccefs of my advife; your looks difcover

too

too plainly that you have used the dancing-water: but, if I durst advise you once more, you should think of getting the singing-apple, which is as great an embellishment to the wit: would you persuade, would you appear in publick, make verses, write prose, make people to laugh or cry, it is smelling, it has all these virtues; and besides, sings so fine, that it ravishes all that hear it." "I will have none of it, cried the princess, my brother had like to have lost his life, in fetching the dancing-water, your counsel is too dangerous." "What! madam, replied Feintisa, would you not be the most learned and witty lady in the world?" Sure you do not think so." "Alas! what would have become of me, if my brother had been brought back dead, or dying!" "Then let him go no more, said the old woman, let the other two oblige you in their turns, this enterprise is not so dangerous." "No matter for that, said the princess, I will not expose them to it." "How much I pity you, replied Feintisa, to let so advantageous an opportunity slip you; but consider upon it; farewel, madam." And then left her, very much unsatisfied with the success of her harangue. Fair-Star staid

at

at the feet of Diana's ftatue, irrefolute what
to do; fhe loved her brothers, but fo earneftly defired the finging-apple, that fhe
fighed and fell a crying. Bright-Sun coming
into the temple, and feeing the princefs's face
covered with her veil, becaufe fhe was afhamed to be feen blear-eyed; but he guefling
fhe was in tears, and going up to her, conjured her inftantly to tell him why fhe cried.
But fhe refufed, telling him fhe could not
for fhame; and the more fhe denied, the
more earneft he was to know. At laft fhe
faid, that the fame old woman that advifed
her to fend for the dancing-water, had been
telling her of the finging-apple, which was
more wonderful; becaufe it created as much
wit as to make the perfon poffeffed of it a perfect prodigy, and that fhe would almoft give
her life for fuch an apple, but that fhe feared
there was too much danger in going for it.
" You need not be afraid of me, replied the
brother, I affure you, for I am not fo fond
as that comes to: what have you not wit
enough already? Come, come, do not vex
yourfelf about fuch a foolifh ftory."

Fair-Star followed him from thence home,
not a little melancholy at the manner of his
receiving the confidence fhe repofed in him,

and the impoffibility of her having the finging-apple. When fupper was fet upon the
table, fhe could not eat. Chery, the lovely Chery obferved it, and helped her to the
niceft bits, preffing her to tafte thereof: but
all he could fay proved ufelefs, the tears
came in her eyes, and fhe rofe from the
table. O heavens! how heafy was Chery,
ignorant of what was the caufe? when
Bright-Sun told him in a fort of raillery, dis-
obliging enough to his fifter, who was fo
much piqued thereat, that fhe retired to her
chamber, and would fee nobody all that
night.

CHAP. VI.

Prince Chery fets out in Purfuit of the Singing-
Apple.

WHEN Bright-Sun and Felix were in
bed, Chery mounted his white nag
again, and without faying any thing to any
one, fet out on his journey for the finging-
apple, though he knew not one foot of the
way, leaving a letter behind him, to be
given to Fair-Star the next morning; who

when

when she received it, felt all the difquiet and torments conceivable upon fuch an oc-cafion. She ran into her brothers chamber, to let them partake fomewhat of her grief; who prefently fent after him, to oblige him to return, without attempting an adventu-re wherein there was fo much hazard. All this time the king, who never had thefe four ftrangers out of his thoughts, as often as he went a hunting, called upon them, and reproached them for not coming to his court.

They excufed themfelves, firft, that they had not completed their equipage; and then, that their brother was abfent: affuring him, that upon his return, they, after the leave he gave them, would pay their muft hum-ble refpects to him.

The prince Chery, who was too much urged on by his paffion, not to make all poffible hafte, fome time after day break, found a handfome young man fit under a fhady tree, reading a book he held in his hand; to whom he addreffed himfelf in a civil manner; and faid, "Give me leave to interrupt you, to afk if you know where I may find the finging-apple." The young man looking up and fmiling, afked him if

he

he intended to obtain it. "Yes, replied the
prince, if it is possible I will." "Ah! sir,
added the stranger, you know not all the
dangers! here is a book that speaks of them,
and the very reading of it is enough to
make one tremble." "No matter for that,
said Chery, the danger is not capable of
dismaying me; tell me only where I may
find it." "This book, continued the man,
says, in the deserts of Lybia, that we may
hear it sing eight leagues off; and that the
dragon, which guards it, has already devoured above five hundred thousand people."
"I shall make one more," said the prince
smiling; and then taking his leave, set forward for the deserts of Lybia. After several days journey, he listened if he could
hear the apple, afflicting himself with the
length of the way; when perceiving in the
road a turtle almost dead; and seeing no
one nigh that could have wounded it, he
believed that it might belong to Venus;
and that having escaped her court, the little archer, to try his bow and arrows had
let fly at her; and taking pity on it, alighted off his horse, took it up, and wiped its
bloody feathers, took out of his pocket a
little golden box of an admirable ointment,
                                    and

and no sooner applied it to the wound of the poor turtle, but it opened its eyes, raised up its head, ſtretched out its wings, and then looking at the prince, ſaid, "Good-morrow, Chery, you are deſtined to ſave my life, and I may perhaps do you no leſs ſignal ſervices. You are come for the ſinging-apple, the enterpriſe is difficult, and worthy of you; for it is guarded by a terrible ſcaled dragon, with three heads and twelve feet." "Ah! my dear turtle, ſaid the prince, how overjoyed am I to ſee you again, and at a time when your aſſiſtance is ſo neceſſary. Do not deny it me, my pretty creature, for I ſhould die with grief, if I ſhould return without the ſinging-apple; and ſince that I got the dancing-water by your means, I hope you will find out ſome expedient whereby I may ſucceed as well in this undertaking." "Follow me, anſwered the turtle, and I hope all will be well."

The prince let her go; and after following her all the day, arrived at a great mountain of ſand, into which the turtle told him he muſt dig; which he accordingly did, ſometimes with his hand, and ſometimes with his ſword. After ſome hours hard

work-

working, he found a headpiece, breaft plate,
and, in fhort, a complete fuit of armour
for man and horfe, all of glafs. "Arm yourfelf, faid the turtle, and fear not the dragon;
for when he fhall fee himfelf in all thefe
glaffes, he will be fo frightened, thinking
his own refemblance, in fo many mir-
rours, to be as many fuch monfters as
himfelf, that he will run away." Chery
approving this contrivance, armed himfelf,
and taking the turtle in his hand, they travelled all that night, and at day-break heard
a moft ravifhing melody; and the prince
afking what it was, the turtle told him, fhe
was perfuaded that nothing but the finging-
apple could be fo agreeable, for that it performed all parts in mufick, and feemed as
if all manner of inftruments were played
upon, which made them ftill keep advancing towards it. The farther they advanced,
the more charming the mufick feemed; and
whatever dread the prince might be in, he
was fometimes fo ravifhed, that he ftopped
almoft infenfible of any thing elfe: but the
fight of the dragon, who appeared fudden-
ly, foon recovered him out of this kind of
lethargy. He had fmelt the prince a great
way off, and expected to devour him, as
he

he had done by all the reft. He came jumping along, covering the ground as he came
with a poifonous froth. Out of his infernal throat there iffued fire and little dragons,
which he ufed inftead of darts, to throw
into the eyes and ears of all the knights-
errant that came to fetch away the finging-
apple. But when he faw his own terrible
figure, multiplied a thoufand times, in the
prince's glafs-armour, he ftopped; and looking hard upon him, bearing fo many no
lefs horrid monfters than himfelf about him,
was frightened, and ran away. Chery perceiving the happy fuccefs of his armour,
purfued him to the mouth of a deep cavern,
which he clofed up, to prevent his returning again. After that, fearching about, he
difcovered, with admiration, the beautiful
tree, which was all amber, except the apples, which were topazes; but that which
he fought after with fo much pains, and
great danger, was a ruby crowned with a
diamond. The prince, tranfported with
the joy of having it in his power to beftow
fo great a treafure on his beloved Fair-Star,
made hafte to break off the bough; and
proud of his good-fortune, mounted his horfe again, but faw no more of the turtle,

who,

who, when there was no further need of her affiftance, was flown away. In fhort, the prince returned to his princefs with the prize, who had never enjoyed one moment's repofe fince his abfence: fhe continually reproached herfelf for her ambition of wit, dreading Chery's death far more than her own. No afflicting, tormenting thought efcaped her imagination, when, in the middle of the night, fhe heard fuch ravifhing mufick, that fhe could not lie in bed, but got up, and went to the window to hear it more plainly, not knowing what to think of it. At laft, it being moonlight, fhe difcovered the prince; upon which fhe retired, feeing a gentleman, not knowing who it might be: when he ftopped under her window, and the apple fung an air the beginning of which words were, or fomething like it, "Awake, you fleeping fair."

At this the curious princefs prefently looked out, and knowing her brother again, was ready to jump out of the window to him. She talked fo loud, that the whole family were prefently alarmed, and came and opened the doors; which Chery entered ed with all imaginable hafte, holding in his hand a branch of amber, with the wonderful fruit upon it: and as he had fmelt on it often, his wit was fo much increafed, that nothing was comparable to it. Fair-Star ran to meet him with great precipitation, crying with joy, and faying, "Do you believe I thank you, dear brother? No, there's nothing that I do but buy too dear, when I expofe you to fetch it." "And there are no dangers I would not hazard, anfwered he, to give you the leaft fatisfaction. Accept, Fair-Star, of this fruit, none deferves it fo much as you." Bright-Sun, and his brother, came juft then, and interrupted their converfation, and were glad to fee their brother again, who gave them an account of his journey, which lafted till morning.

The wicked Feintifa having left the queen, after having acquainted her with her projects, was juft retired home; and got to bed, but could not fleep, through her uneafinefs, one wink. When fhe heard the fweet finging of the apple, and not doubting but that he had obtained it, fhe cried and bewailed her condition, fcratching her face, and tearing off her hair. Her grief

was

was extremely great; for inftead of doing the princes the mifchief fhe projected, fhe did them all the fervice imaginable. As foon as it was day, fhe was too well inform- ed of the prince's return, and upon that hurried away to the queen-mother: "Well, Feintifa, faid that princefs, do you bring me any good news, are they deftroy- ed?" "No, madam, replied fhe, cafting herfelf at her feet, but let not your majefty be impatient; I have a thoufand ways yet left." "Ah wretch! faid the queen, thou intendeft to betray me, and therefore fpareft them." Feintifa protefted to the contrary: and when fhe had appeafed her, returned home, to think of what was to be done next. She let fome days pafs without un- dertaking any thing; when being informed by her fcouts, that the princefs was walking in the foreft alone, expecting her brothers, fhe went thither; and addreffing herfelf to her, faid, "Charming Star, I have been in- formed that you have got the finging-apple, and was overjoyed to hear of it; for I have fo great an inclination for you, that I am in- terefted in whatever tends to your advanta- ge. And, continued fhe, I cannot forbear advifing you to one thing more." "Ah, cried

cried the princefs, getting from her, keep your advice to yourfelf, for though the benefits I receive be great, yet they make not amends for the trouble and uneafinefs they have caufed me." "Uneafinefs is not fo great an evil, anfwered fhe with a fmile, there is a fweetnefs and tendernefs fometimes in it." "Forbear, faid Fair-Star, I tremble when I think on it." "Indeed, faid the old woman, you are very much to be pitied, to be the moft beautiful and wittieft lady in the world." "I defire once more, replied the princefs, to be excufed, I know too well the condition the abfence of my brother reduced me to." "You muft notwithftanding be told, faid Feintifa, that you want the little green-bird, that tells every thing, by which you will be informed of your birth, and your good and ill-fortune; there is no particular thing he does not difcover; and when the world fhall fay, that Fair-Star has the dancing-water and the finging-apple, and wants the little green-bird, they had as good fay nothing."

After having, in this manner, uttered what fhe intended, fhe retired, leaving the princefs melancholy and thoughtful, and fighing, as if there was fomething fhe defired:

ed: "This woman is in the right, said she,
what am I the better for the dancing-water
and singing-apple, if I know not who I am,
who are my parents, and by what fatality
my brothers and I were expofed to the fury
of the waves? There muft be fomething
extraordinary in our births, that we fhould
be abandoned in the manner we were, and
receive fo evident a protection from heaven.
How great a pleafure would it be to me to
know my father and mother, to love them
if they be alive, and to honour their memory if dead?" Thereupon tears trickled down
her cheeks, clear as drops of morning dew,
diftilling upon lilies and rofes. Chery, who
was always more impatient to fee her again
than the other two, made the moft hafte, after the fport was over, to return home:
that day he was a foot, his bow hung ne-
gligently by his fide, fome arrows he held in
his hand, and his hair was tied with a rib-
band behind him; and in this warlike drefs
he looked charmingly pleafing. When the
princefs faw him, fhe retired to a dark fhady
walk, that he might not perceive thofe cha-
racters of grief in her face. But nothing can
efcape a lover's eye; for the prince looking
upon her, foon knew fomething was the
matter.

matter. Whereupon he was difturbed, and defired her to tell him what it was; but fhe refufing with obftinacy, he turned one of his arrows againft his breaft, and faid, "Since you love me not, Fair-Star, I have nought to do but die." By this means he, as I may fay, extorted the fecret from her; but on thefe conditions, that be fhould not with the hazard of his life feek to fatisfy her defires: all which he promifed. But as foon as fhe was retired to her chamber, and her brothers to theirs, he went into the ftable again, and mounting his horfe, fet out without faying a word to any one.

C H A P. VII.

Prince Chery fets out on the dangerous Purfuit of the little Green Bird.

WHEN it was known the next morning, the whole family was in the utmoft confternation. The king, who could not forget, fent to invite them again, and they returned the fame excufe again of their brother's being abfent, and that they could

have

have no pleasure and satisfaction without him; that upon his return they would not fail to pay their devoirs. The princess was inconsoleable; the water and apple could not charm her, for nothing was agreeable without Chery.

The prince wandered up and down, asking all he met where he might find the little green bird; but nobody could tell him, till he lit on an old man, who taking him home with him, took the pains to look over his books and a globe, which he had made the study of his life; and then told him it was in a frozen climate, on the point of a frightful rock, showing him all the roads to it. The prince, by way of return, presented him with a purse of jewels he had combed out of his hair: and taking leave of him, pursued his journey. To be short, one morning by sun-rise, he perceived the rock, which was very high and craggy, and on the top of it the bird talking like an oracle, telling most strange things. He thought he might catch it with little trouble, since it appeared to be very tame, hopping from one place to another. He alighted off his horse and climbed up without making any noise, promising himself and Fair-Star the

most

moſt ſenſible pleaſure; when, all on a ſudden, the rock opened, and he fell as motionleſs as any ſtatue into a large hall; ſo
that he could neither bemoan nor complain
of his deplorable adventure. There he found
three hundred knights, who having made
the ſame attempt as himſelf, were in the
ſame condition, being only able to look at
one another.

The time of his abſence ſeemed ſo long
to Fair-Star, that ſhe fell extraordinary ill;
and the phyſicians pronounced her to be devoured by deep melancholy. Her brothers,
who loved her tenderly, would often tell
her the cauſe of her illneſs; upon which ſhe
confeſſed, that ſhe reproached herſelf night
and day for Chery's departure; and that ſhe
was ſure ſhe ſhould die if ſhe heard no news
of him. Bright-Sun, moved by her tears,
reſolved to go and ſeek his brother; and accordingly knowing where the bird was, ſet
out, approached it with the ſame hopes,
was ſwallowed up by the rock, and fell into
the great hall, where the firſt objeĉt he fixed his eyes on was Chery; but could not
ſpeak to him. In the mean time Fair-Star
grew better, hoping every minute to ſee
her two brothers return; but being deceived
therein,

therein, her grief renewed, and she complained incessantly, accusing herself for the disasters that befel her brothers: When Prince Felix, having no less compassion on her, and concern for his brothers, resolved to go and find them; and acquainted her therewith. She at first seemed to oppose it; but he replyed, that it was just that he should expose himself for those who were so dear to him; and then set out, after taking his leave of the princess, whom he left a prey to the most piercing grief.

When Feintifa knew that the third prince was gone, her joy had no end, but away she ran to the queen, and promised her with more assurance than ever, to destroy this unfortunate family. Felix fared the same with Chery and Bright-Sun; he found the rock, saw the bird, and fell into the hall, where he knew the princes he sought, and saw them ranged in niches. They never slept, nor eat but remained in that sad condition, having only their thoughts at liberty. Fair-Star seeing none of her brothers return, was inconsoleable, and reproached herself for staying so long after them; and without any longer hesitation ordered their servants to stay six months: and if neither she nor her

her brothers returned in that time, to go and acquaint the corfair and his wife with their deaths. Then dreffing herfelf in men's clothes, as moft fitting to fecure her from all infults in her journey. Feintifa, had the pleafure to fee her go upon her Ifabella-horfe; and immediately after ran full of joy to the palace to regale the queen with the news. She only armed herfelf with an head-piece, the vifor of which fhe never lifted up, becaufe her beauty was fo perfect fhe would not otherwife have paffed for a man. She fuffered very much by the rigour of the weather; for that country where the green-bird lived, in no feafon ever received the happy influence of the fun, but cold: nor nothing could difmay her. In her way fhe faw a turtle no lefs white nor cold than the fnow it lay upon, which, notwithftanding her impatience of arriving at the rock, fhe could not fee perifh; but alighting off her horfe, took it up, warmed it with her breath, and put it into her bofom, where it never ftirred. Fair-Star thinking it dead, pulled it out, and looking forrowfully upon it, faid, "What fhall I do, lovely turtle to fave thy life?" To which the little creature made anfwer,

"One

"One fweet kifs, Fair-Star, from your mouth, will finifh what you have fo charitably begun." "Not only one, faid the princefs, but a thoufand if need be:" and fell a kiffing it. Upon which the dove replied, "I know you, notwithftanding your difguife, and muft tell you, that you undertake a thing which will be impoffible for you to effect without my affiftance; but do as I advife you. When you come to the rock, inftead of attempting to climb it, ftay at the bottom, and fing the moft melodious fong you can think of; the green bird will hear you, and obferve from whence the voice comes, then you muft pretend to be afleep, and I will ftay by you: When he fees me, he will come from the rock to peck me, and then you muft take your advantage, and catch him."

The princefs overjoyed at this hope, arrived foon at the rock, where fhe found her brothers horfes grafing, which fight renewed all her grief, and fhe fat down and cried bitterly, but the little green-bird faid fuch fine comfortable things to thofe who were afflicted, that fhe dried up her tears, and fung fo loud and charming, that the princes in the hall had the pleafure of hearing her,

her, which was the firſt moment they be-gan to hope. The little Green-bird heard her alſo, and looked to ſee from whence the voice came, and perceiving the princeſs, who had pulled off her maſk, that ſhe might lie down to ſleep with more eaſe, as alſo the turtle hopping by her, he came down to peck her, but had not pulled off three feathers before he was taken himſelf. "Ah! ſaid he, what would you have with me? What have I done to engage you to come ſo far to make me miſerable? Give me my liberty, I conjure you, and I will do what-ever you deſire in exchange." "Reſtore my brothers, ſaid Fair-Star, whom, by their horſes feeding here, I know thou de-taineſt ſomewhere hereabouts." "I have a red feather, ſaid he, under my left wing, pull it out, and touch the rock with it." The princeſs made haſte to do what he had bid her; but at the ſame time ſaw ſuch flaſhes of lightning, and heard ſuch claps of thunder, together with the roaring of the wind, that ſhe was very much frigh-tened; but notwithſtanding held the Green-bird faſt, that he might not eſcape her: then touched the rock again the ſecond and third time, at which laſt it ſplit from the top to

E 2 the

the bottom, and ſhe with an air of victory
entered the hall, where the three were,
with a great many others. She ran to Chery, who knew her not in that dreſs, and
in a helmet; for then the enchantment was
not deſtroyed, inſomuch that he could neither ſpeak nor ſtir. The princeſs ſeeing
that, aſked the bird more queſtions; to
which he made anſwer, that ſhe muſt rub
the eyes of all thoſe ſhe would free from
the enchantment, with the ſame red feather;
which good office ſhe did to ſeveral kings
and princes, as well as her three brothers:
who in return for ſo great a benefit, fell
down on their knees, and called her the
deliverer of kings.

Fair-Star then perceiving that her brothers,
deceived by her dreſs, did not know her,
pulled off her helmet, and holding out her
arms, embraced them a thouſand times, if
poſſible, and afterwards aſked the other princes civilly who they were; every one told
his own particular adventure, and offered to
accompany her wherever ſhe went: To
which ſhe anſwered, that though the laws
of knighthood might give her ſome right
over their liberty, ſhe waved it, leaving
them to purſue their own pleaſures; and
then

then retired with her brothers, that they
might give each other a particular account
of what had befallen them fince their feparation. The little Green-bird often interrupted them, to defire Fair-ftar to give him
his liberty; upon which fhe looked for the
dove to afk her opinion: But not finding
her, told the bird he had coft her too much
trouble and uneafinefs to enjoy fo little of
her conqueft. There upon they all four
mounted their own horfes, leaving the other
kings, &c. to go a-foot, their equipage, &c.
being all loft and dead, during the many
years of their enchantment.

CHAP. VIII.

In which Virtue is rewarded, and Vice punifhed.

THE queen mother, eafed of all the difquiet with which the return of the
princes and princefs had burthened her, renewed her inftances to the king to marry
again; and importuned him fo much, that
he made choice of a princefs, one of his relations. But as he muft firft difannul his

marriage with the queen Blondina, who had lived all that time at her mother's with the three whelps, the old queen fent a coach for her and them. She came according to her commands, and was dreffed in black, with a long veil that reached down to her feet; in which apparel fhe appeared as beautiful as the morning-ftar: though fhe was become lean and pale by not fleeping nor eating, but juft to fuftain nature, and out of complaifance to her mother, who was pitied by all, the king relented fo much, that he durft not caft his eyes on her; for he confented to this fecond match purely out of the hopes of heirs. The marriage day being appointed, the old queen, urged thereto by Roufetta, who always hated her unfortunate fifter, would have the queen Blondina appear at the feaft, which was to be very magnificent: and the king to fhow his grandeur to ftrangers, fent the firft gentleman of his bedchamber to the princes and their fifter to invite them to it.

The gentleman went accordingly, and knowing the extreme defire the hing had to fee them, finding them not at home, left one of his attendants to wait for them without any delay. The night before this banquet,

quet, Fair-Star and the three princes arrived, to whom the perfon that was left delivered his meffage, telling them withal the hiftory of the king's life; how that he had married a young beautiful damfel, who had the mis. fortune to be delivered of three whelps; and that upon that account he had put her away, though he loved her tenderly: that he bad lived fifteen years before he would hearken to any propofals of marriage; but being preffed thereto by the queen-mother and his minifters of ftate, he had determined to ef- poufe a young princefs of his court, to who- fe nuptials they were invited.

Fair-Star dreffed herfelf in a rofe-coloured velvet, bedecked on the robings with dia- monds, her hair hanging on her fhoulders in fine curls, but tied together with a bunch of ribbons, by means of which the gold chain on her neck appeared more vifible; the ftar on her forehead fhined with all imaginable luftre; and in fhort, fhe feemed too beautiful for a mortal. Her brothers came not far fhort of her; and Prince Chery bad fomething that diftinguifhed him moft advantageouf- fly. They went all four into an ivory and ebo- ny chariot, drawn by twelve white horfes, their equipage every way fuitable. The

E 4

king,

king, overjoyed to see them, received them at the stair-head; the apple sung wonderfully fine, the water danced, and the Green-bird talked like an oracle. They all fell on their knees, till the king raised them up with his hand, which they kissed with all respect and affection. After that he embraced them, and said, "I am obliged to you, lovely strangers, for your company to-day; your presence gives me a sensible pleasure." Then he led them into a large hall, where there were several tables set out with all manner of rarities and dainties, and music playing all the time. Soon after came the queen-mother with her new daughter in-law that was to be, accompanied by Rousetta, and a great number of ladies, and with them the poor queen led by a brass chain about her neck, to which the three dogs were fastened; who, together with them, was carried to a great bowl of bones and offal meats that was set out by the old queen's command, in one part of the hall.

When Fair-Star and the princes saw this unhappy princess, tears came in their eyes; either because they were sensibly touched with the vicissitudes and changes of this world, or by instinct of nature. But how
outra-

outrageous were the old queen's thoughts at
fo unexpected a return, fo contrary to her
defigns? She caft fo furious a look at Feintifa, that fhe wifhed the earth would open,
and fwallow her up; fo much did fhe dread
her. The king prefented the princefs and
her brothers to his mother, faying the moft
obliging things of them; and fhe, notwithftanding her inward hatred and concern, received them with a favourable compliment,
and a fmile; for at that time diffimulation
was as much in vogue as now. No mirth
was wanting during the feaft, though the
king was not very well pleafed to fee his
wife eat with dogs, as the meaneft of all
creatures; but having refolved to fhow all
manner of complaifance to his mother, fhe
ordered every thing as fhe thought fit.

When the repaft was over, the king, addreffing himfelf to Fair-Star, faid, "I hear
you are poffeffed of three incomparable
things, I wifh you joy of them, and defire
you to tell me how you got them. "Sir,
replied fhe, I fhall obey your pleafure. I
was told that the dancing water would make
me handfome, and the finging-apple infpire
thofe who had it with wit; which were the
two reafons made me defirous of them. For

E 5 the

the little green-bird, who tells every thing, our fatal ignorance of our births made me covet him, fince we were children abandoned by our parents." "To judge of your birth by your perfons, replied the king, it muſt be illuſtrious; but tell me fincerely who you are." "Sir, faid fhe, my brothers and my-felf deferred that enquiry till our return, and then we received the honour of an invitation to your wedding, and have brought thefe rarities to divert you." "I am very glad of it, faid the king, therefore let us not defer fo agreeable an entertainment." "What, faid the queen-mother, in a paſſion, can you amufe yourfelf no better than with fuch idle ſtories, and fuch filly chits and their rarities; I am forry your credulity fhould be fo much abufed, and that they fhould have the honour to fit at my table." Fair-Star and her brothers knew not how to behave them-felves at this difobliging expreſſion, but were confufed and vexed to be affronted before fo much company: but the king telling his mo-ther that this proceeding of hers very much difpleafed him, defired them to take no no-tice of it, and held out his hand as a fign of his friendfhip. Fair-Star called for a glafs-bafon, and pouring the dancing-water into

it;

it; which, by its fkipping and jumping, fometimes forming waves like a rolling fea,
and fometimes changing its colour, filled all
the company with admiration, by its forc-
ing the bafon along the table to the king,
caft out fome drops into the firft gentleman's
of the king's bedchamber face; who being
a man of good mien, but of a difagreeable
face, though a man of merit, having but
one eye, the water made him beautiful,
and reftored his eye again. The king,
whofe favourite he was, feemed as much
pleafed with this adventure, as the queen-
mother was vexed to hear the applaufes of
the whole company. After that Fair-Star
produced the ruby apple upon its branch of
amber, which began as melodious a concert
as if there had been a hundred muficians;
which ravifhed the fenfes of the king and
whole court; whofe admiration increafed
when fhe fhowed the little green-bird in a
golden cage, out of which fhe took him
gently, and fet him upon the apple, which
out of refpect left off finging, to give him
time to fpeak: his feathers were fo bright,
that when the eyes were fhut, they
gliftened, and were of all manner of fhades
of green. He addreffed himfelf to the king,

and

and afked him what he pleafed to know. "We want to be informed, replied the king, who this lady and three gentlemen are." "O king, anfwered the bird, with a plain and intelligible voice, fhe is thy own daughter, and two of thefe princes are thy fons; the third, whofe name is Chery, is thy nephew." Thereupon, with an unparalleled eloquence, he told the whole ftory, without omitting the leaft circumftance.

The king melted into tears, and the afflicted queen leaving her dogs, came foftly forwards, crying for joy; for fhe no longer difputed the truth of the ftory, when fhe faw all the tokens. The three princes rofe up at the end thereof, caft themfelves at the king's feet, embraced his knees, and kiffed his hand: he, with open arms, clapped them to his heart; and at that time, there was nothing heard but fighs and cries of joy. When at laft the king feeing his queen ftanding fearful by the wall-fide in an humble pofture, ran to her, and embraced her a thoufand times: then took her by the hand, and made her fit down by him; but not before her children and fhe had embraced one another as often. Never was fight more tender and moving; they were all in tears, lifting up
their

their eyes and hands to heaven to return thanks. The king made the princefs he was to marry a compliment, and withal, a prefent of jewels. But for the queen-mother, Roufetta, and Feintifa, they could expect nothing but the utmoft refentment. The thunder of his anger began to grumble, when the generous queen, her children, and Chery, conjured him not to put himfelf into a paffion, but to pafs a more exemplary than fevere fentence. The queen-mother he made a clofe prifoner for life in a ftrong caftle, and Roufetta and Feintifa were caft into a deep nafty dungeon, there to remain all their days with the three dogs."

After thefe three wicked perfons were carried away, the mufic began to play, and all joy and mirth went forward; but none came up to that of Chery's and Fair-Star's, who were as happy as they wifhed to be; for the king, fenfible of his nephew's merit, completed the happinefs of that day, by marrying him to his daughter. The prince, tranfported with joy, caft himfelf at his feet; and Fair-Star difcovered no lefs fatisfaction. But, not to forget the old princefs; who had in a kind of folitude fpent fo many years, but to let her partake of the joy,

the

the fame fairy that had been fo entertained
by her, at the fame moment went and told
her all that happened at court, and afked
her to go with her thither.   The grateful
princefs went with her in her chariot of
blue and gold, preceded by all manner of
warlike inftruments, and followed by five
hundred body-guards, richly clothed; and
by the way, the fairy told her the hiftory
of her grand-children, how fhe had never
forfaken them, but had protected them under the fhape of a fyren and turtle, and all
upon the account of the charitable reception
fhe gave her.   The good princefs was every moment for kiffing her hand, to fhow
her acknowledgment, and could not think
of expreffions to declare her joy.   When
they arrived at court, the king received
them with a thoufand teftimonies of friendfhip.   The queen Blondina, and her children
were glad to fee the princefs, and earneft
to exprefs their gratitude and obligations to
that illuftrious lady, whom the old princefs
told them was the kind turtle that guided
them; who, to complete the king's fatisfaction, told him, that his mother-in-law,
whom he always took for a poor country
woman, was a fovereign princefs: which
was

was the only thing perhaps wanting to that monarch's happinefs. And to conclude, the corfair and his wife were fent for, that they might receive a noble recompence, for the extraordinary education they beftowed on them.

———————

THE

STORY *of the* PIGEON *and* DOVE.

CHAP. I.

Account of the Birth and Education of the Princess CONSTANTIA.

THERE was formerly a king and queen, who lived in that strict union and love, that they were an example to all the families in their own kingdom, which was the kingdom of deserts; where the subjects lived together in that harmony, that they were the surprise of their neighbours. The queen had had several children, but could rear up but one; which was a daughter of such incomparable beauty, that if any thing could comfort her for the loss of her other children, it was the charms that appeared in this. The king and queen educated her as their only hope. But the felicity of this small family lasted not long: the king being one day a hunting upon a fiery starting horse, and some people being a shooting, the horse

was

was fo frightened at the noife of a gun, that he ran away with the king and fell with him down a great precipice, where he died immediately.

This difmal news reduced the queen to the utmoft extremity; fhe was too fenfible of grief to moderate or refift it, and thought of nothing but fettling her affairs, that fhe might die with fome fort of quiet; and having a friend, who was called, the Sovereign Fairy, becaufe of her authority over all kingdoms, and her great power, fhe wrote a letter to her with a dying hand, defiring her to come, that fhe might expire in her arms, and to make hafte if fhe would find her alive, becaufe fhe had fomething of confequence to fay to her.

Though the fairy had at that time matters of great concern upon her hands, fhe left them all unfinifhed, and mounting upon her fiery camel, that went fwifter than the fun, came to the queen, who waited for her with the utmoft impatience: firft, fhe acquainted her with feveral things relating to the government of the kingdom, defiring her to accept of it, and withal to take care of the little princefs Conftantia.

The

The Sovereign Fairy promifed what fhe defired, and the queen having embraced her dear Conftantia with all the tendernefs of a loving mother, died in great tranquillity.

Thefe fairy, who read with great eafe whatever was foretold by the ftars, faw plainly, that the princefs was threatened with the fatal love of a giant, whofe dominions lay nigh to the kingdom of Defarts; therefore fhe thought the beft way to avoid him, was to remove her charge to a part the fartheft off from that giant, where they might be in no likelihood of his difturbing their repofe. Whereupon, fhe went one night into Conftantia's chamber, and, without waking her, took her in her arms, and carried her on her fiery camel into a fertile country, where fhe might live free from ambition and trouble; it being a true reprefentation of the valley of Tempe, where fhepherds and fhepherdeffes lived in little huts of their own building. The fairy knowing, that if the princefs lived to fixteen years of age, without feeing the giant, that fhe might return in triumph back to her own dominions, took all the care imaginable to conceal her from the eyes of all the world; and that fhe might not appear fo beautiful,

beautiful, dreffed her like a fhepherdefs, with her coifs, and hat hanging over her eyes; but that charming princefs, like the fun, breaking out from a dark cloud, could not be fo difguifed, but that fome of her charms muft appear; and notwithftanding all the fairy's care, Conftantia was every where mentioned as the chief work of the Gods, and the ravifher of all hearts. Befides, her beauty was not the only thing for which fhe was admired; the fairy had endowed her with a delicate voice, and the knowledge of all inftruments, that fhe might be faid even to excel Apollo and the Mufes. In this folitude fhe lived without the leaft repining, for the fairy had acquainted her with the reafons of bringing her up in fo obfcure a manner; which, as fhe had a great fhare of wit and good fenfe, fhe relifhed extraordinary well: in fhort, fhe was the admiration of the fairy for her docility and aptnefs of apprebenfion. But as her prefence, at that time, was abfolutely neceffary in the kingdom of Deferts, fince the minifters fhe had appointed acted not according to their inftructions, fhe was obliged to leave Conftantia, enjoining her not to ftir out till fhe returned.

The

The princess had a favourite ram, which having strayed away from her, she, contrary to the strict orders given her, left the house, and went in pursuit of it, when, passing by a wood, there came out of it a terrible giant, who opened a great sack and put her into it. The first thing she perceived was the wolf and the ram, which the giant had taken as he was hunting. "Alas! said the princess to the sheep, kissing it, thou must die with me, my dear Rufon, the name of her ram, but that's but a small comfort; would it not have been much better for us to have staid at home?" This melancholy reflexion made her cry most bitterly; she sighed and sobbed, Rufon bleated, and the wolf howled, which awakened a dog, a cock, a parrot, and a cat, that were fast asleep, and they all together made such a noise, that the giant tired therewith, thought once to kill them; but at last contented himself with only tying them up in the sack, and hanging it upon a tree while he went to fight a duel with another giant.

The princess, however, took out her scissars, and ripped up the sack, and let out her Rufon, the dog, the cock, the cat, and parrot; and after them got out herself; leaving the

wolf

Wolf behind. The night was very dark, and the princefs a ftranger to the place where fhe was, and knew not which way to go, being in the midft of a large foreft, and not a ftar appeared in the heavens that might afford her the leaft light, and fhe always in fear of meeting the giant; notwithftanding all this, fhe went forwards, and had fell a thoufand times, but that the animals fhe had fet at liberty, out of gratitude, ftaid with her, and were very ferviceable to her in her journey. The cat's glaring eyes ferved for a flambeau; the dog as a centinel, to give notice by his barking; the cock by his crowing, to frighten the lions; and the parrot, by his talking, fecured her againft thieves, by making them believe there were twenty people; and the ram by going juft before, picked out her way, that fhe might not ftumble.

CHAP.

CHAP. II.

CONSTANTIA's *Progress in the Passion of Love.*

AT day-break she found herself by the
side of a river, that watered a most
agreeable meadow, and looking about, saw
neither dog, cat, cock, or parrot, but only
Rufon, who kept her company: and the
princess being fatigued and weary, sat herself down on the banks, where the shade
of some trees securing her from the heat of
the sun, invited her to lie down to take a
short sleep, while Rufon, who served for
her guard, walked around her. She had
not been long in a found sleep, before Rufon bleated so loud, that he awakened her;
but then how great was her astonishment,
to observe at twenty paces off a young man
behind some bushes; the beauty of his shape and face, the nobleness of his air, and
the magnificence of his dress, equally surprised the princess, that she started up all
on a sudden, with a resolution to be gone;
but what secret charm detained her, I know
not. She looked upon the stranger with as
much concern as if he had been the giant;
but

but her apprehenfions proceeded from different caufes; their looks and actions difcovered too well the fentiments they entertained
of each other, and they perhaps might have
remained for fome time before they had
fpoken, had not the prince heard the found-
ing of the horn, and the dogs approaching
them. Perceiving fhe was furprized, he
addreffed the lovely fhepherdefs in the tendereft manner, and fhe anfwered with becoming decency and modefty; but, as the
company was coming up, he advifed her
to take fhelter in a neighbouring cottage;
for he could not endure the thoughts of
any one feeing her but himfelf. He took
his leave of her with the utmoft regret; but
promifed to recommend her to the queen as
a fhepherdefs.

He foon found means to procure her this
place; and, as he perceived himfelf paffionately in love with her, he was glad at her
being thus removed from court, where her
beauty would undoubtedly procure him
many rivals,

He avoided the fight of his fhepherdefs as
much as poffible, and followed his diverfion
of hunting and other fports; and whenever
he faw any fheep, turned his head away,

as if they were fo many vipers, infomuch
that in a little time he was infenfible of the
wound he had received: when one day, it
being the hotteft of the dog-days, fatigued
with fevere hunting, and being alone by
the river's fide, he retired under fome wil-
lows and ofiers, which by the uniting their
branches formed a pleafant fhade, and invited him to fleep; when all on a fudden he
was awakened by an heavenly voice, and
agreeably furprifed to hear thefe words:

Why, alas! have I then vow'd
　　To live all free from love,
Since it is the God's decree,
　　That he will me perjur'd prove.

How from fuch a killing wound
　　Shall I free each tender part,
Since Conftantio is become
　　Mafter of my eafy heart.

T'other day I faw him walk
　　To this folitary glade,
Wearied with the pleafing toil,
　　That invites men to its fhade.

Nothing

Nothing, fo charming had I feen
  To rob me of my reft;
'Twas then Love drew his bow,
  And aim'd it at my breaft.

The dart pierc'd in too deep,
  So large a wound it made;
My paffion burns up to a flame,
  No cure is to be had.

His curiofity, at the hearing of his name
mentioned, prevailing over the pleafure of
liftening to the fine finging, he rofe up, and
went to a little eminence, furrounded with
trees to look about. He was no fooner at
the top, but he perceived the fair Conftantia at the foot thereof, fitting by the fide of
a brook, the precipitant fall whereof, feemed, by the agreeable noife it made, to agree
with her voice. Her faithful fheep lay on
the grafs by her fide, while fhe frequently
patted him with her crook, and he in acknowledgment, looking her in the face, kiffed her hand. He gazed on her in filent
amazement, and envied her fheep the caref-
fes they received. She rofe from her feat,
and, accidentally driving her flock by the

F 5

spot where the prince stood, accosted her, and begged to know to whom her song was addressed: "For, said he, you are in love." She blushed, and, turning from him, went away suddenly.

The prince being driven to despair, employed one of his courtiers, in the dress of a shepherd, to communicate his love to Constantia; but she, supposing herself to be only a shepherdess, and he a great prince, would not give ear to his words. She wished her ram Rufon to be her only companion, to whom she would frequently tell the tale of her love, though she knew he could not understand her, and he was the only witness of her tears.

The prince, however, found means to pay her a visit; but she was so fearful of being deceived, and no less fearful of disclosing her own passion for him, that she affected to treat him with coolness and indifference, which threw him into so dangerous an illness that his life was despaired of.

The physicians having given him over, one of the prince's favourites, to whom he had entrusted the secret of his passion, undertook to answer for the ability of the youg shepherdess to cure him, by means

of

of a composition of herbs known only to herfelf. She was immediately fent for to court, where the fight of the lovely Conftantia foon recovered the prince, to the amazement of the whole court. They were now frequently together, and, having mutually confeffed their love for each other, they fwore to an eternal friendfhip.

The queen, however, having by fome accident difcovered the paffion of thefe two faithful lovers, was violently enraged with her fon for falling in love with a fimple fhepherdefs, and contrived an excufe for fending him on a vifit to fome neighbouring court, in order to feparate them. The prince was no fooner gone, than the queen began to meditate in what manner fhe fhould difpofe of Conftantia, and foon came to a refolution. She privately ordered enquiry to be made what fhips were in the port, and hearing there was one bound to a very diftant quarter, fhe caufed Conftantia to be conveyed there by night, and fold as a flave. She then dreffed up a wax-work figure, and caufed it to be interred with funeral pomp, as the remains of the haplefs Conftantia; after which fhe fent her fon the news of that terrible event.

He

He immediately left the court where he was, and returned home with incredible speed.

C H A P. III.

The prince goes in Purſuit of CONSTANTIA.

IT is not eaſy to conceive how great was his grief; but, after a little time, he began to ſuſpect that the relation of his Conſtantia's death was only a contrivance of his mother. The vigilance of love ſoon found out the deception, and he determined to go in purſuit of the dear object of his heart. He accordingly went on board a ſhip, and ſailed in queſt of her, though but with little hopes of ever being able to find her. One night, coming to an anchor behind a large rock, he went on the ſhore as uſual; but as they knew not the country, and the night was very dark, thoſe that were along with him, would not venture any farther for fear of danger. The prince, who valued not his life to find out the object of his wiſhes, kept going forwards, often falling and

getting

getting up again, till at laſt he heard a ſoft ſymphony that raviſhed his ſenſes; and looking towards a furnace, ſaw the moſt beautiful child Fancy could ever repreſent, brighter than the fire he came out of. When he conſidered his charms, the bandage over his eyes, his bow and quiver by his ſide, he no longer doubted but that it was Cupid; who cried out to him, "Stay, Conſtantio, you burn with too pure a flame for me to refuſe my aſſiſtance: I am called Virtuous-Love; it was I that wounded you with Conſtantia, and defended her againſt the giant that perſecuted her. The Sovereign Fairy is my intimate friend; we have engaged to protect her; but I muſt make a trial of your paſſion, before I diſcover where ſhe is." "Command, Love, command what you think fit, cried the prince, I will not diſobey thee." "Then throw yourſelf into this fire, replied the child, but remember, if you love not faithfully, you are loſt." "I have no reaſon to fear that," ſaid Conſtantio, and immediately threw himſelf into the furnace, where he loſt all ſenſe preſently; he ſlept thirty hours, and when he awaked, found himſelf changed into a moſt beautiful pigeon, and inſtead of being in the terrible furnace

furnace, on a nest of roses, jessamines, and
honeysuckles. Never was any surprize greater than his, to see his rough feet, his skin
stuck full of feathers of various colours, and
his eyes, as he beheld them in a brook, as
red as fire: he attempted several times to ut-
ter his complaints, but found he had lost the
use of his speech, though he had recovered
his senses. He looked upon this metamor-
phosis as the completest of all misfortunes;
he flew to the top of a high mountain, and
from thence cast himself down; but forgot,
having not been long a pigeon, that his
wings and feathers would keep him up: thereupon he resolved to unplume himself, and
accordingly put this design in execution. As
soon as he had quite stripped himself, he
walked up to the top of a high rock, to attempt his destruction once more, where he
was surprised by two young damsels, who
came suddenly upon him; who, finding him
so tame and familiar, they resolved to bring
him up, and keep him alive; to which end
the elder put him into her work-basket she
had in her hand, and so they pursued their
walk.

Some days after, one of these damsels
said to the other, "Methinks our mistress
has

has a great deal of bufinefs upon her hands, fince fhe is never from off her fiery camel, but goes night and day from one pole to the other." "If you can be difcreet, replied the other, I will tell you a fecret fhe had entrufted me with; the princefs Conftantia, of whom fhe is fo very fond, is perfecuted by a giant that would marry her, and has put her in a tower; and fhe is doing fome furprifing things to prevent this marriage." The prince liftened to this converfation, and thought till then nothing could add to his troubles; but found, to his grief, he was much deceived; for we may judge by his paffion, and by the unhappy circumftances he lay under, of being a pigeon, at a time when the princefs ftood in moft need of his affiftance, that his anguifh of foul was great; his imagination, always ready to torment him, reprefented to him, that Conftantia was fecured in a difmal tower, and there expofed to the importunities and violences of a barbarous giant; and was always in apprehenfion, left fhe, through fears, might confent to marry him; and then again, left by refufing fhe fhould hazard her life, through the rage of an unfuccefsful lover. One day the young maid, that
carried

carried him in her bafket, having been abroad,
and returning back with her companion to
their miftrefs at the fairy's palace, found her
walking in a fhady walk of the garden, went
and caft herfelf at her feet, and told her,
that fhe had found a pigeon that was fo tame
and familiar, that her companion and fhe defigned to keep it in their chamber; that if
fhe liked it, it was at her fervice, it being
very diverting.   The fairy took the bafket,
opened it, and feeing the pigeon at the bottom, and knowing, who it was, for that
metamorphofis was owing to her, fell into
a ferious and deep reflection, moralizing on
the viciffitudes and changes of this life, and
above all on thofe of Conftantio.   She careffed the pigeon; and he, for his part, neglected no little artifice to gain her attention,
that fhe might give him fome comfort in this
melancholy adventure.   The fairy carried
him into her clofet, and there faid to him.
"Prince, the miferable condition you are at
this prefent in, makes me, that I cannot
forbear owning and loving you for my beloved Conftantia's fake, who, I can affure
you, is no lefs indifferent than yourfelf;
blame no body but me for this metamorphofis; I did it to try your paffion, which

is

is both pure and lasting; and will tend to
your own honour." The pigeon bowed his
head three times in acknowledgment, and
listened attentively to what the fairy told
him.

"The queen, your mother, said she, had
no sooner received the money for the princess, but she sent her aboard with all imaginable violence; and the ship set sail for the
Indies, where they were sure to make a
considerable advantage of the precious jewel
they carried with them. After having been
some months at sea, a great storm arose,
and the princess, oppressed with grief, and
fatigued with the sea, was at the point of
death; when they, to preserve her, put her
into the first port they could make; but as
they were disembarking, a great giant, followed by several others, came down upon
them, and would see what they had in their
vessel; where the first object he fixed his
eyes on, was the young princess; and
knowing her again, as well as she knew
him, cried out, Ah! little runaway, the
just and merciful Gods have put thee in my
power again: do not you remember how I
found you, and you cut my sack? But I
shall be very much mistaken, if you serve

me fo any more. And without any more
words, took her away in his arms from the
whole fhip's crew, and carried her to his
great tower, which is fituated upon a high
mountain, and built by enchanters, who
neglected nothing to make it fine and curious. When the giant had the charming
Conftantia in his poffeffion, he told her he
would marry her, and make her the happieft woman in the world; that he would
give her a year's time to confider on it; and
if fhe did not then come to a refolution, he
would marry her againft her will, and then
kill her.

"In fhort, the poor princefs feeing no
likelihood of any fuccours, and the year
being expired all but one day, defigns to
throw herfelf from off the top of the tower.
This, prince, is what fhe is reduced to,
and the only remedy I know of, is for you
to fly to her with a little ring, which, as
foon as fhe fhall put it on her finger, will
change her into a dove, and fo you may
fave yourfelves together." The pigeon was
in the utmoft impatience to be gone, and
taking the ring, he arrived by break of day
at the tower.

CHAP.

CHAP. IV.

Containing a very singular Conclusion.

HE perched upon an orange-tree with the ring in his mouth, and in extreme anguish of mind; when the princess came into the garden in a long white robe, and her face covered with a black veil embroidered with gold, which hung all upon her shoulders, the amorous pigeon could not have been certain that it was her, but by the noblenefs of her shape, and her majestic air, which too plainly discovered who she was. But when she came and sat under the orange-tree, and lifted up a veil, he remained some time dazzled. "My regret and sad melancholy thoughts, cried she, are now uselefs, my afflicted heart has lived a whole year betwixt hope and fear, but now the fatal time is come; this day, some few hours hence, I must die, or marry the giant. Alas! is it possible that the sovereign fairy, and the prince Constantio, should thus abandon me? What have I done? But what need all these reflexions? I had better execute my noble design." Hereupon she got on

the

the top of the tower to throw herſelf of; but as the leaſt noiſe frighted her, and hearing the pigeon ſtir in the trees, ſhe lifted up her eyes to ſee what it was; when he taking that opportunity, flew upon her ſhoulder, and put the ring in her breaſt, which ſhe placed upon her finger, without knowing its effect, and was immediately changed into a dove, and flew away with her faithful pigeon.

Never was ſurpriſe equal to that of the giant's, who, after having ſeen his miſtreſs metamorphoſed into a dove, and traverſing the open air, remained ſome time motionleſs; then he made moſt dreadful outcries and howlings that ſhaked the neighbouring mountains, and with them ended his life. The charming princeſs flew after her guide; and when they had taken a long flight, they lit in a thick ſhady wood, rendered very agreeable by the graſs and flowers that grew therein. Conſtantia knew not that the pigeon was her beloved prince, and he was grieved that he could not ſpeak, to tell her; when ſuddenly he felt an inviſible hand unlooſe his tongue, and ſaid to the princeſs; "Charming dove, your heart hath not informed you, that you are with a pigeon

who

who burns always with the flames your bright eyes firſt kindled." "My heart, replied ſhe, has ever wiſhed for this happineſs, but never durſt flatter itſelf: Alas! who could imagine it? I was at the very brink of deſtruction, and you came and ſnatched me out of the arms of death, or from a monſter much more terrible." The prince, overjoyed to hear theſe words of his dove, and to find her as tender as his deſires could wiſh, ſaid whatever the moſt delicate and lively paſſion could inſpire, and told her all that had happened ſince the ſad moment of their ſeparation. "If you love me with an equal flame, ſaid he, I have one propoſal to make, not to change our forms; we may burn, you a dove, and I a pigeon, with a paſſion as ardent as Conſtantio and Conſtantia; and I am perſuaded, that being free from the cares of crowned heads, we may live only for each other in this delightful ſolitude." "Ah! cried the dove, how delicate and great is this deſign!" At that inſtant, Cupid deſcending from heaven, cried out, "I am your guide, a deſign ſo full of tenderneſs deſerves my protection." "And mine too, ſaid the Sovereign Fairy, who appeared all on a ſudden, I come to

partake

partake in your joy." The pigeon and dove' were as much pleafed as furprifed, and put themfelves under the care of the fairy. Cupid invited them to Paphos, where he told them his mother was worfhipped, and doves admitted; but Conftantia told him, they defired to have no commerce with men, but were happy they could enjoy a pleafant folitude.

END of the NINTH VOLUME.

GULLIVER'S LECTURES
VOL. X.

CONTAINING

LILLIPUTIAN FRAGMENTS

OR,

WISDOM AND MIRTH UNITED.

VOL. X.   A

PREFACE.

I AM now entering on the preface to the last volume of my Lilliputian Library, in which I muſt take leave of all my little pupils, whether miſſes or maſters; and doubt not, that, by this time, if they have properly attended to the matters contained in this *important* work, they have become great proficients in the moſt uſeful of all ſciences, that of *Human Knowledge.*

After I had finiſhed the nine preceding volumes, I found I had left on my hands a number of very curious articles, which I could not find room for in their proper places; and, as they were communi-

cated

cated to me by some of the most capital little ones in Lilliput, I have inserted them without regard to order; hoping however, that they will not prove the less valuable or entertaining on that account.

———

LILLIPUTIAN FRAGMENTS;

OR

WISDOM AND MIRTH UNITED.

GENERAL RULES *for* BEHAVIOUR.

FEAR God, honour the king, reverence your parents, submit to your superiors, and despise not your inferiors.

Pray daily, converse with the good, avoid the wicked, and attend to instruction.

At coming into company always bow, and remain uncovered, especially in presence of your parents or elders.

When you speak to your parents, begin with sir, or madam; never delay to do as they shall order or bid you, nor enter the room where they are, if strangers be there, till sent for.

Never quarrel or dispute with any one, especially your brothers or sisters, but be loving and obliging to all.

Never

Never come to table till wafhen and combed, nor meddle with any thing till helped,
and whatever it be, content yourfelf therewith, and not find fault.

Feed yourfelf decently without greafing
the table-cloth, your clothes, or fingers, as
little as poffible.

Make no noife in eating, nor eat greedi-
ly, neither fpit, cough, or blow your nofe
at table, unlefs you cannot avoid it, then
do it with as little noife as poffible,

Lean not on the table or back of your
chair, nor ftare any one in the face.

Never drink or fpeak without emptying
your mouth: and on quitting the room make
a handfome bow or courtefy.

To look at one and whifper another at
the fame time is unmannerly, as it is to
whifper at all in company.

To whomfoever you fpeak, in afking a
queftion or returnig an anfwer, remember
to ufe the proper title of refpect, as fir,
madam, my lord, my lady, &c.

Never attend to fuch as whifper, or fpeak
in fecret, nor correct your fuperiors though
you know they are wrong; when any thing
immodeft is fpoken in your hearing, feem

not

not to hear it; and beware of saying any
thing that will hardly be believed. . .

Always give the wall to your elders and
superiors, and leave to pass into any room
or narrow paffage, where only one can pafs
at a time, unlefs you are ordered to go before. And keep company with none but
what are good; "Evil communications corrupt good manners."

　　Tell me with whom thou goeft,
　　And I'll tell thee what thou doeft.

Thefe my dears are the rules; and now
follows a letter in verfe, from a celebrated
poet to a young and noble lady.

My noble lovely little Peggy,
Let this, my firft epiftle beg ye,
At dawn of morn, and clofe of ev'n,
To lift your heart and hands to heav'n,
And, deareft child, along the day,
In every thing you do or fay,
Obey and pleafe my lord and lady,
So God fhall love, and angels aid ye.
If to thefe precepts you atttend,
No fecond letter need I fend,
And fo I reft your conftant friend.

The STORY of FORTUNATUS.

THE island of Cyprus has long been re-
nowned for many things, and particularly for giving birth to Fortunatus. He
was the son of a wealthy merchant; but the
family, by living too freely, were a length
reduced. The young man imagining himself to be now but an incumberance to his
father, determined with himself to leave his
home and seek his fortune. He had not travelled long before he lost his way in a
wood; night came on, and he could not
tell what to do. At mitnight the wild beasts
began to howl and roar about him, and for
his security he was forced to get upon a
tree. At the dawn of the day a bear made
towards him, and was mounting up the tree,
but Fortunatus made so gallant a defence
with his sword, that he cut off one of the
bears paws, so that it was impossible for
him to keep his hold, and down he fell:
But though Fortunatus rejoiced at the success
of his adventure, new sorrows came now
upon him; for though it was day-light, and
he travelled on in tolerable safety, yet hunger and weariness overtook him.

But

But all of a fudden a lady, with a bandage upon her eyes, met him and accofted
him; fhe held in her hand a purfe, and of-
fering it to him, told him her name was Fortune. And this purfe, fays fhe, which I
give you, will never be empty; as often as
you thruft your hand into it, you will be
able to take out a handful of gold and filver.
He thanked her, and was doubtlefs extremely glad of this moft noble prefent.

Getting into the high road, he came to
a great city, where he bought himfelf fine
clothes, horfes, and fervants, and lived like
a prince; for he never put his hand into his
purfe, but he always found money enough
to pay for what he wanted. He now took
a fancy to travel over the world. To this
end he furnifhed himfelf with every thing
proper for that purpofe in the moft fplendid
manner imaginable, and thus he went to all
the princes coorts in Europe. He came at
laft to the court of the Grand Turk at Con-
ftantinople, who paid him great refpect, and
fhowed him the rarities of his palace, which
abounded with diamonds and rich things of
all forts. Laft of all he drew him into a
room, and faid he could now fhow him the
greateft curiofity in the world; Where is it?
said

said Fortunatus; for my part I see nothing here but an old hat. That is the very thing, said the Grand Turk. This, continued he, is a wishing hat, and I no sooner clap it on, but I am conveyed in a trice wherever I desire, let the distance be what it will, over hills, vallies, rivers, or oceans. Fortunatus was surprised at the account of this hat. Lord! thinks he to himself, could I but get that hat to my purse, what man alive would be so happy as I? Pray, said Fortunatus, is not this same hat heavier than ordinary hats? No, said the Grand Turk, put it upon your head and try. Fortunatus put it on, and presently wished himself at home in his own country, and in a moment flew out of the window, and left the Grand Turk in the utmost rage.

Who was then so happy as Fortunatus? If he wanted money, it was only putting his hand into his purse, and he always found enough for his purpose: If he wanted to be conveyed any where, it was only clapping on his wishing hat, and he was instantly there.

He now heard that the king of England had a beautiful daughter, and he determined to see her; so putting on his hat he wished
himself

himfelf at London, and prefently found himfelf there. He went to court, and his clothes, which were all embroidered with gold
and diamonds, were the admiration of all
the ladies, and what added to their aftonifhment was, that he appeared every day
in a different drefs, but all equally fine.
He foon found an opportunity to declare his
love to the king's daughter. She told him
fhe would return his love if he would tell
her how he came by his great riches. He
could not deny her, and told her the fecret
of his purfe. She then promifed to admit
him the following night into her chamber;
but in the mean time fhe had procured a purfe to be made perfectly like his, and contrived a fleepy potion, which fhe mixed
with the wine he drank with her, which
caufed him to fall faft afleep. During this
fleep fhe changed purfes with him. Fortunatus waking, was ignorant of all that
happened; but taking his leave, and wanting to make the fervants a handfome prefent,
he put his hand into his purfe, but was ter-
ribly difappointed, for he found nothing in it.
Sufpecting what had been done, he catched
the princefs in his arms, and wifhed himfelf
in fome folitary wildernefs, with her alon

which immediately came to pafs. The lady was fadly terrified and faint, both with her journey and with the horrour of the wildernefs; but looking up and feeing fome fruit on a tree, fhe begged of him to climb up and get her fome. He, willing to oblige her, got up into the tree, but left his hat upon her head. As fhe fat mufing, Oh! fays fhe, that I was but once more at home with my dear father! The very inftant fhe fpoke this fhe was gone, and left poor Fortunatus deprived of both hat and purfe.

: Fortunatus defcending from the tree, knew not what he fhould do. He fat down very penfive and melancholy: at length beginning to eat one of the apples the princefs had defired him to gather, he found a pair of great horns fprouting from his head; but an old hermit meeting him, informed him, that if he would only eat fome apples of another tree, which grew near the place, his horns would drop off. He did fo, and it fell out as the hermit faid. A fudden thought now came into his head, that he would carry fome of both thefe forts of apples to court, and fo manage matters that one of them fhould be left in the chamber of the king's daughter. This plot he executed with

with fuccefs; and when the princefs entered her apartment, and beheld a very fine apple lying on the table; fhe took and eat it; and immediately a pair of great horns fprung from her forehead. Help and advice was fent for from every quarter, but no phyfician was found able to remove thefe horns. Fortunatus now thought it was high time to play his game, and perfonating a phyfician, undertook the cure of the princefs's ftrange diforder. The firft thing he caft his eyes upon after entering the princefs's chamber, was his old wifhing hat; it hung there difregarded, and not a creature dreamt of the virtues of it. Now, thinks he, could I but be equally fatisfied that fhe had the purfe about her, I fhould know how to proceed. In order to try whether fhe had or no, he acquainted her that his fee came to a thoufand pounds. She was contented to give it him. He then pulled out of his pocket an apple of the tree the hermit had fhowed him, and bid her eat it; which fhe had no fooner done, but her horns dropped off. Rejoiced at the doctor's fuccefs, fhe took out the purfe to fatisfy his demand; but Fortunatus efpying his purfe, clapped on his hat, and clafping her in his arms, wifhed himfelf at

B 2 home

home with her in the ifland of Cyprus; where when they arrived, he reproached her for her deceitful ufage, and put her into a nunnery to fpend the refidue of her days. After this he began to think what vexation and trouble he had undergone by means of his hat and purfe, and being thoroughly perfuaded in his own mind, that riches were a burthen, and that enjoying our wifhes is often the caufe of much mifery, he refolutely took both hat and purfe and flung them into the fire, which foon confumed them; and ever after this he lived a quiet, happy, and contented life.

FLÓRIO *and* FLORELLA.

THERE was a country woman, who upon her intimacy with a fairy, defired her to come and affift at the birth of her daughter; when the fairy, taking the infant in her arms, faid to the mother, make your choice; the child, if you have a mind, fhall be very handfome, excel in wit even more than beauty, and be queen of a mighty empire, but withal unhappy; or if you had rather,

ther,

thier, fhe fhall be an ordinary, ugly country creature, like yourfelf, but contented with her condition. The mother immediately chofe wit and beauty for her daughter, at the hazard of any misfortunes.

As the child grew, new beauties opened daily in her face, till in a few years fhe furpaffed all the rural laffes that the oldeft people had ever feen, her turn of wit was genteel, polite, and infinuating; fhe was of a ready apprehenfion, and learned every thing fo faft, as foon to excel her teachers. Every holiday fhe danced upon the green with a fuperior grace to any of her companions. Her voice was finer than any fhepherd's pipe; and fhe made the fongs which fhe ufed to fing. For fome time fhe was not apprifed of her own charms; till diverting herfelf with her playfellows on the green flowery borders of a fountain, fhe was furprifed with the reflexion of her face. She obferved how different her features and her complexion feemed from the reft of her companions, and admired herfelf greatly. The country flocking from day to day to obtain a fight of her, made her more fenfible of her beauty. Her mother, who relied on the predictions of the fairy, began

already

already to treat her as a queen, and spoil-ed her by flattery. The young damsel would neither sow nor spin, nor look after the sheep: her whole amusement was to ga-ther flowers to dress her hair with, to sing, and be in the shade.

The king of the country was a very pow-erful king, and he had but one son, who-se name was Florio; for which reason his father was impatient to have him married. The young prince could never bear to hear the mentioning of any of the princesses of neighbouring nations, because a fairy had told him, that he should find a shepherdess more accomplished than all the princesses in the world. Therefore the king gave orders to assemble all the village nymphs of his realm, who were under the age of eigh-teen, to make choice of her who should ap-pear most worthy of so great an honour. In pursuance of the order, when they came to be seated, a vast number of virgins, whose beauty was not extraordinary, were refus-ed admittance, and only thirty picked out, who infinitely surpassed all others. These thirty virgins were ranged in a great hall, in the figure of a half moon, that the king and his son might have a distinct view of

them

them together. Florella, our young heroine, appeared in the midſt of her companions like a lily amongſt marigolds; or as an orange tree in bloſſom ſhows amongſt the mountain ſhrubs. The king immediately declared aloud, that ſhe deſerved his crown; and Florio thought himſelf happy in the poſſeſſion of Florella. Our ſhepherdeſs was inſtantly deſired to caſt off her country weeds, and accept of a habit richly embroidered with gold. In a few minutes ſhe ſaw herſelf covered with diamonds and pearls, and a number of ladies were appointed to wait on her. Every one was attentive to prevent her deſires before ſhe ſpoke, and ſhe was lodged within the palace in a magnificent apartment, where, inſtead of tapeſtry, there were large pannels of looking glaſſes from the floor to the cieling, that ſhe might have the pleaſure of ſeeing her beauty multiplied on all ſides, and that the prince might admire her, whterever he caſt his eyes. Florio in a few days quitted the chaſe, and all the bold exerciſes in which before he delighted, that he might be always with his miſtreſs. The nuptials were concluded, and ſoon after the old king died. Thereupon Florella becom-

ing queen, all the councils and affairs of
ftate were directed by her wifdom. The
queen mother, whofe name was Envy, grew
jealous of her daughter-in-law: fhe was an
artful, perverfe, cruel woman; and age had
fo much aggravated her natural deformity,
that fhe refembled one of the furies. The
youth and beauty of Florella made her appear yet more frightful; fhe could not bear
the fight of fo fine a creature. She likewife dreaded her wit and underftanding, and
gave herfelf up to all the rage of malice.
"You want the foul of a prince, fhe would
often fay to her fon, or you could not have
married this mean creature. How can you
be fo abject as to make an idol of her?
Then fhe is as haughty as if fhe had been
brought up in the palace where fhe lives.
You fhould have followed the example of
the king your father, when you thought
of taking a wife. He preferred me, becaufe I was the daughter of a monarch equal
to himfelf: Send away this infignificant fhepherdefs to her hamlet, and take to your
bed and throne fome young princefs, whofe birth is anfwerable to your own." Florio continued deaf to all the entreaties of his
mother. But one morning Envy got a bil-
let

let into her hands, which Florella had writ to the king; this she gave to a young courtier, who by her instructions showed it to the king, pretending to have received a letter from the queen with such marks of affection as were due only to his majesty. Florio blinded by jealousy, and the malignant insinuation of his mother, immediately ordered Florella to be imprisoned for life, in a high tower built upon a rock which stood in the sea. There she wept night and day, not knowing for what supposed crime she was so severely treated by the king, who had so passionately loved her. She was permitted to see no person but an old woman, to whom Envy had intrusted her, and whose business it was to insult her upon all occasions.

Now Florella called to mind the village, the cottage, the sweet privacy, and the rural pleasures she quitted. One day, as she sat in a pensive posture, overwhelmed with grief, and to herself accused the folly of her mother, who chose rather to have a beautiful unfortunate queen, than an ugly contented shepherdess; the old woman who was her tormentor, came to acquaint her, that the king had sent an executioner to take off

her

her head, and that she must prepare to die.
Florella replied that she was ready to receive the stroke. Accordingly the executioner,
sent by the king's order at the persuasion of
Envy, apeared, with a drawn sabre in his
hand, ready to perform his commission,
when a woman stepped in, who said she
came from the queen-mother, to speak a
word or two in private with Florella before
she was put to death. The old woman,
imagining her to be one of the ladies of the
court, suffered her to deliver her message:
but it was the fairy who had foretold her
misfortunes at her birth, and who had now
assumed the likeness of one of Envy's attendants; she desired the company to retire a
while, and then spoke thus to Florella in
secret: "Are you willing to renounce that
beauty which has proved so fatal? Are you
willing to quit the title of queen, to be put
in your former habit, and to return to your
village?" Florella was transported at the offer; thereupon the fairy applied an enchanted mask to her face; her features instantly became deformed, all the symmetry vanished,
and she was now as disagreeable as she had
been handsome. Under this change it was
impossible to know her; and she passed without

out difficulty through the company who came to fee her execution. In vain did they fearch the tower, Florella was not to be found. The news of this efcape was foon brought to the king and Envy, who commanded diligent fearch to be made after her throughout the kingdom, but to no purpofe.

The fairy at this time had reftored Florella to her mother, who would never have been able to recollect her altered looks, had fhe not been let into the circumftance of her ftory. Our fhepherdefs was now contented to live an ugly, poor, unknown creature in the village, where fhe tended fheep. She frequently heard people relate and lament over her adventures; fongs were made upon them which drew tears from all eyes; fhe often took a pleafure in finging thofe fongs with her companions, and would often weep with the reft. But ftill fhe thought herfelf happy with her little flock, and was never once tempted to difcover herfelf to any of her acquaintance.

The

The EFFECT *of* GOOD-NATURE.
A FAIRY-TALE.

THERE was in my country a widow, who had two daughters: the eldeſt was juſt like her mother, croſs, ſurly, and proud; but the youngeſt, a beautiful girl, was all meekneſs, complaiſance, and good-nature. As people, however, are generally fond of their own likeneſs, the mother deſpiſed this pretty young creature, and obliged her to drudge in the kitchen, whilſt her favourite, the eldeſt, ſat primmed up in the parlour, and was indulged in every thing.

As this little girl was obliged to do all the houſehold work, it was her buſineſs, among other things, to go twice every day to a well, near two miles from the houſe, to draw water. One day, juſt as ſhe was going to fill her pitcher, there came to her a poor woman, and begged that ſhe would let her drink. "O! ah, goody, with all my heart, ſays ſhe, and accordingly rinced her pitcher, took ſome of the cleareſt

water

water; and held it up to her mouth, that she might drink with the more eafe; and, after the pitcher was returned, dropped her a fine curtefy, notwithftanding she was fuch a poor ragged woman, and afked if she would pleafe to have auy more? "No, I thank you, my pretty dear, faid the wo-man; but fince you are fo good-natured, and behave with fuch good manners, I can-not help beftowing a blefling upon you; and from henceforth, whenever you fpeak, there shall come out of your mouth either a flower, a jewel, or a piece of gold." For you muft know this was a fairy all the while, who had only taken the form of a poor countrywoman, to fee how this little girl would behave.

When she came home, her mother began to fcold at her for ftaying fo long; "Where have you been all this time, Hufl'y?" fays she. "Dear mamma, fays the girl, I beg your pardon for ftaying fo long, for she never told a lie, but I met with"——and was going on with the ftory, when inftant-ly flew out of her mouth two rofes, two pinks, two pearls, two diamonds, and three pieces of gold. "Blefs me, fays her mother, quite aftonished, what do I fee! Rofes, and
pinks

pinks, and pearls, and diamonds, and gold,
come out of the girl's mouth. How happens this, child?" The pretty creature
told her mother the whole ſtory, during
which time there dropped from her mouth
ſuch a vaſt variety of flowers, pieces of gold,
and precious ſtones, that the houſe was
ſtrewed from one end to the other. "Bleſs
my eyes, cried the mother, I muſt ſend my
child thither; Fanny, come hither, and
ſee what drops from your ſiſter's mouth
when ſhe ſpeaks. Take the pitcher, and
go you for ſome water, my dear, and obtain the ſame bleſſing." "Yes, I will warrant you, ſays the ill-bred minx, it would
be a fine ſight indeed to ſee me draw water."
"You ſhall go, huſſy, ſaid the mother, and
this minute." So away ſhe went, but
grumbled and growled all the way; and inſtead of the pitcher, took the beſt ſilver tankard in the houſe.

As ſoon as ſhe arrived at the fountain,
there came out of the wood juſt by, a lady
dreſſed in the moſt ſplendid manner, and
aſked leave to drink. This was, you muſt
know, the ſame fairy, who had now taken
the air and dreſs of a princeſs, to ſee how
far the girl's pride and ill-nature would carry
                                        her.

her. "Am I come hither, quoth the faucy flut, to ferve you with water? Pray what do you take me for, a waiting-maid? I did not bring the filver tankard here for your ladyfhip, as I know of: but however you may drink, if you will."

"You are not over and above mannerly, replied the fairy, without putting herfelf in a paffion, and fince you are furly and dif-obliging, whenever you fpeak a word hereaf-ter, a fnake or a toad fhall fly out of your mouth." As foon as the mother faw her coming home, fhe cried out, "Well, daughter!" "Well, mother!" anfwered the pert huffy, and out of her mouth leaped two vipers and a toad. "O mercy, cried the mother, what do I fee! All this is occafion-ed by the witch her fifter; but fhe fhall pay for it;" and immediately ran to beat her, but the poor child fled away, and hid herfelf in a foreft that was in the neighbour-hood.

The king's fon being on his return from hunting, accidentally caft his eye on this fair virgin, and being enchanted with her graceful features, afked her what fhe did there alone, and why fhe cried? She told him what had happened, and faid her ma-

ma's

ma's rage was fo great fhe was afraid to
return home. The young prince feeing fo
many brilliant diamonds drop from her mouth,
which were equalled in brightnefs by nothing but her eyes, promifed her his royal
protection; conducted her to his father's
court, and having obtained his permiffion,
married her the next day, and built for her
a ftately palace, the front of which was
overlaid with pure gold, the floors paved
with pearls, and the cielings and walls bedecked with the richeft diamonds. The turf
in her garden bears a continual verdure, the
moft delicious fruits bow down their labour-
ing branches to falute the enchanted eye,
and the odoriferous never-fading flowers
pay an eternal tribute to her virtue and good-
nature. In this ftate of happinefs fhe fuffers
none to approach her but thofe who are
efteemed for their piety, virtue, and good
manners; and perfons of every ftate and condition who come thus recommended, are
admitted. She is bleffed with a numerous
offspring, who all inherit her amiable virtues, and every thing profpers in her houfe,
and in the ftate. The prince, her hufband,
thinks himfelf bleffed above all men in the
world,

world, and she is the happiest woman upon earth.

But how different from this was the fate of her sister! She, by her pride and ill-nature at last rendered herself disagreeable even to her own mother, who being unable to bear with her intolerable temper, turned her off; and seeing herself thus despised and hated by all mankind, she retired into a wood to avoid being seen, and was there torn in pieces by a wolf.

AIRY *and* PRUDENCE.

THERE was an old man, whose name was Lenity, who had two children, a son, and a daughter. The name of the son was Airy, the daughter was called Prudence. It happened, that as these two were one day playing together, they found a looking-glass, which was in their mother's bed-chamber; and looking into it, they discovered that Airy was extremely handsome, but Prudence very deformed.

The boy was not a little proud of this: he immediately began to entertain a very

high

high opinion of himself, and to defpife his fifter. He was always talking of his own beauty, and putting Prudence in mind of her deformities. He would run to the glafs every minute, and call upon his fifter to ob⸗ ferve how differently they appeared in it; in fhort, he omitted nothing which he thought might create a mortification to his fifter, or improve the opinion, which he thought every body entertained of the co⸗ melinefs of his perfon.

Prudence, grieved to find herfelf the con⸗ ftant fubject of her brother's mirth, at length complained to her father of his behaviour. The old man, who had a tender affection for both, and was forry to find there was any quarrel between his children, thought this was a proper occafion to beftow fome good advice on them. After having kiffed them both, "If, faid he, Airy, you find, by looking into the glafs, that nature has beftowed a handfome face upon you, I would have you by all means endeavour to ren⸗ der your inward accomplifhments anfwera⸗ ble to fuch an outfide; let your actions be handfome as well as your perfon; and you, faid he, my dear Prudence, if you cannot recommend yourfelf by your beauty, you may

may by your behaviour; the world will pardon the defects of your perfon, if they find you are not wanting in the perfections of the mind."

The PERSIAN SULTAN'S EXEM-PLARY JUSTICE.

AS one of the fultans lay encamped on the plains of Avalá, a certain great man of the army entered by force into a peafant's houfe, and finding his wife very handfome, turned the good man out of his dwelling, and went to bed to her. The peafant complained the next morning to the fultan, and defired redrefs; but was not able to point out the criminal. The emperor, who was very much incenfed at the injury done to the poor man, told him, that probably the offender might give his wife another vifit, and if he did, commanded him immediately to repair to his tent, and acquaint him with it. Accordingly, within two or three days, the officer entered again the peafant's houfe, and turned the owner out of doors; who thereupon applied him-

felf

self to the imperial tent, as he was ordered. The sultan went in person, with his guards, to the poor man's house, where he arrived about midnight. As the attendants carried each of them a flambeau in their hands, the sultan, after having ordered all the lights to be put out, gave the word to enter the house, find out the criminal, and put him to death. This was immediately executed, and the corpse laid out upon the floor by the emperor's command. He then bid every one light his flambeau, and stand about the dead body. The sultan approached it, looked upon the face, and immediately fell upon his knees in prayer. Upon his rising up, he ordered the peasant to set before him whatever food he had in the house. The peasant brought out a great deal of coarse fare, of which the emperor eat very heartily. The peasant seeing him in good humour, presumed to ask him, why he had ordered the flambeaus to be put out before he had commanded the adulterer to be slain? Why, upon their being lighted again, he looked upon the face of the dead body, and fell down in prayer? And why, after this, he had ordered meat to be set before him, of which he now eat so heartily? The

sultan,

sultan, being willing to gratify his hoft, anfwered him in this manner: Upon hearing
the greatnefs of the offenfe which had been
committed by one of the army, I had reafon to think it might have been one of my
fons, for who elfe would have been fo au-
dacious and prefuming? I gave orders, therefore, for the lights to be extinguifhed,
that I might not be led aftray by partiality
or compaffion from doing juftice to the criminal. Upon lighting the flambeau a fecond
time, I looked upon the face of the dead
perfon, and, to my unfpeakable joy, found
it was not my fon. It was for this reafon
that I immediately fell on my knees, and
gave thanks to God. As to my eating heartily of the food you have fet before me,
you will ceafe to wonder at it, when you
know that the great anxiety of mind I have
been in upon this occafion, fince the firft
complaints you brought me, has hindered
my eating any thing from that time till this
very moment.

The tranfgreffor here met with the punifhment juftly due to his demerits, for vio-
lating the chaftity of the poor man's wife;
but the juftice of the fultan is deferving of
the higheft applaufe, who determined, we

fee,

fee, not to fpare even his own fon, had he found him guilty of a crime of fo black a dye: nor is his piety lefs to be admired, who, confidering himfelf as God's vicere-gent on earth, was refolved to do juftice even to the deftruction of his own family; and, when his anxiety was at an end, of-fered up his heart to the Almighty for his deliverance.

The HISTORY of KING ALLGOOD.

THERE was a king, whofe name was Allgood, feared by all his neighbours, and loved by all his fubjects. He was wife, juft, good, valiant; and deficient in no qua-lity requifite in a great prince. A fairy came to him one day, and told him, that he would foon find himfelf plunged into great difficulties, if he did not make ufe of a ring, which fhe then put on his finger. When he turned the ftone of the ring in the infide of his hand, he became invifible, and when he turned the diamond outwards, he became vifible again. He was mightily pleafed with the prefent, as foon as he grew fenfible of

the

the ineftimable value of it. When he fufpected any one of his fubjects, he went into
that man's houfe and clofet, with his diamond turned inward, and heard and faw all
the fecrets of the family without being perceived; when he miftrufted the defign of
any neighbouring potentate, he would make
a long journey unaccompanied, to be prefent in his moft private councils, and learn
every thing without the fear of being difcovered. By this means, he eafily prevented
every intention to his prejudice, he fruftrat-
ed feveral confpiracies formed againft his perfon, and difconcerted all the meafures of his
enemies for his overthrow. Neverthelefs,
he was not thoroughly fatisfied with his
ring; and he requefted of the fairy the power of conveying himfelf in an inftant from
one country to another, that he might make
a more convenient and ready ufe of this ring.
The fairy replied, "You afk too much; let
me conjure you not to covet a power
which, I forefee, will one day or other be
the caufe of your mifery, though the particular manner thereof be concealed from me."
The king would not liften to her intreaties,
but ftill urged his requeft. "Since then you
will have it fo, faid fhe, I muft neceffarily

C 4   grant

grant you a favour of which you will dearly repent. Hereupon, she chafed his shoulders with a fragrant liquor, when immediately he perceived little wings shooting at his back. These little wings were not discernable under his habit, and when he had a mind to fly, he needed only to touch them with his hand, and they would spread so as to bear him through the air, swifter than an eagle. When he had no further occasion for them, with a touch again they shrunk to a small size, so as to be concealed under his garments. By this project, Allgood was able to convey himself in a few minutes wherever he pleased. He knew every thing, and no man could conceive how he came by his intelligence; for he would often retire into his closet, and pretend to be shut up there the whole day, with strict orders not to be disturbed; then making himself invisible, he would enlarge his wings, and traverse vast countries. By this power he entered into very extraordinary wars, and never failed to triumph. But as he continually saw into the secrets of men, he discovered so much wickedness and dissimulation, that he could no longer place confidence in man; the more powerful he grew the less

he

he was beloved; and he found that even they, to whom he had been moſt bountiful, had no gratitude nor affection towards him.

In this difconfolate condition he refolved to fearch through the wide world, till he found a woman complete in beauty and all good qualities, willing to be his wife; one who ſhould love him, and ſtudy to make him happy. Long did he fearch in vain; and as he faw all without being feen, he difcovered the moſt hidden wiles and failings of the fex. He vifited all the courts where he found the ladies infincere, fond of admirers, and fo enamoured of their own perfons, that their hearts were not capable of entertaining any true love for a hufband. He went likewife into all the private families; he found one was of an inconſtant volatile difpoſition, another cunning and artful, a third haughty, a fourth capricious; almoſt all vain, faithlefs, and full of idolatry to their own charms.

Under thefe difappointments, he refolved to carry his enquiries even to the loweſt clafs of mankind; whereupon, he found the daughter of a poor labourer, fair as the brighteſt morning, but fimple and ingenuous

in

in all her beauty, which she difregarded, and which in reality was the leaft of her perfections; for fhe had an underftanding and virtue, which outfhone all the graces of her perfon. All the youth in the neighbourhood were impatient to fee her, and more impatient after they had feen her, to obtain her in marriage, not doubting of being completely happy with fuch a wife. King Allgood beheld her, and he loved her; he demanded her of her father, who was tranfported with the thoughts of his daughter's becoming a great queen. Clarinda, fo fhe was called, went from her father's hut into a magnificent palace, where fhe was received by a numerous court; fhe was not dazzled, nor difconcerted at the fudden change. She preferved her fimplicity, her modefty, her virtue, and forgot not the place of her birth, when fhe was in the height of her glory. The king's affection for her increafed daily, and he believed he fhould at laft arife to perfect happinefs, neither was he really far from it; fo much did he begin to confide in the goodnefs of his queen. He often rendered himfelf invifible, to obferve her, and to furprife her; but he never difcovered any thing in her, that was not worthy of his admiration;

fo

so that now there was but a very small remainder of jealousy blended with his love.

The fairy, who had foretold the fatal consequences of his last request, came so often to warn him, that he thought her importunity troublesome; therefore, he gave orders that she should no longer be admitted into the palace; and enjoined the queen not to receive her visits for the future. The queen promised to obey his commands, but not without much unwillingness, because she loved this good fairy. It happened one day, when the king was upon a progress, that the fairy, desirous to instruct the queen in futurity, entered her apartment under the appearance of a young officer, and immediately declared in a whisper who she was; whereupon the queen embraced her with tenderness.

The king, who was there invisible, perceived it, and was instantly fired with jealousy. He drew his sword, and pierced the queen, who fell, expiring in his arms. In that moment the fairy resumed her true shape; whereupon the king knew her, and was convinced of the queen's innocence. Then he would have killed himself: but the fairy withheld his hand, and strove to comfort

fort

fort him: when the queen, breathing her laſt words, ſaid, "Though I die by your hand, I die wholly yours."

Too late now Allgood curſed his folly, that put him upon wreſting a boon from the fairy, which proved his miſery. He return-ed the ring, and deſired his wings might be taken from him. The remaining days of his life he paſt in bitterneſs and grief, knowing no other conſolation, but to weep perpetual-ly over Clarinda's tomb.

The HISTORY of CLARINDA and CLOE.

CLARINDA and Chloe, two very fine women, were bred up as ſiſters in the family of Romeo, who was the father of Chloe, and the guardian of Clarinda. Phi-lander, a young gentleman of good perſon and charming converſation, being a friend of old Romeo, frequented his houſe, and by that means was much in converſation with the young ladies, though ſtill in the preſence of the father and the guardian. The ladies both

both entertained a fecret paffion for him, and could fee well enough, notwithftanding the delight which he really took in Romeo's converfation, that there was fomething more in his heart which made him fo affiduous a vifitant. Each of them thought herfelf the happy woman; but the perfon beloved was Chloe. It happened; that both of them were at a play in a carnival evening, when it is cuftomary, in moft countries in Europe, both for men and women, to appear in mafks and difguifes. It was on that me-memorable night, in the year 1679, when the playhoufe by fome unhappy accident was fet on fire. Philander, in the firft hurry of the difafter, immediately ran where his treafure was, burft opon the door of the box, fnatched the lady up in his arms, and, with unfpeakable refolution and good fortune, carried her off fafe. He was no fooner out of the croud, but he fet her down; and grafping her in his arms, with all the raptures of a deferving lover: "How happy am I, fays he, in an opportunity to tell you I love you more than all things, and of fhowing you the fincerity of my paffion at the very firft declaration of it." "My dear, dear Philander, fays the lady, pulling

off

off her maſk, this is not a time for art: you are much dearer to me than the life you have preferved; and the joy of my prefent deliverance does not tranſport me ſo much as the paſſion which occaſioned it." Who can tell the grief, the aſtoniſhment, the terror, that appeared in the face of Philander, when he faw the perſon he ſpoke to was Clarinda. After a ſhort pauſe, "Madam, fays he, with the looks of a dead man, we are both miſtaken;" and immediately flew away, without hearing the diſtreſſed Clarinda, who had juſt ſtrength enough to cry out, "Cruel Philander! why did you not leave me in the theatre?" Crowds of people immediately gathered about her, and after having brought her to herſelf, conveyed her to the houſe of the good old unhappy Romeo. Philander, was now preſſing againſt a whole tide of people at the doors of the theatre, and ſtriving to enter with more earneſtneſs than any there endeavoured to get out. He did it at laſt, and with much difficulty forced his way to the box where his beloved Chloe ſtood, expecting her fate amidſt this ſcene of terror and diſtraction. She revived at the ſight of Philander, who fell about her

T 3   neck

neck with a tendernefs not to be expref-
fed, and amidft a thoufand fobs and fighs
told her his love and his dreadful miftake.
The ftage was now in flames, and the whole houfe full of fmoke: the entrance was
quite barred up with heaps of people, who
had fallen one upon another as they endeavoured to get out; fwords were drawn,
fhrieks heard on all fides; and in fhort, no
poffibility of an efcape for Philander himfelf
had he been capable of making it without
his Chloe. But his mind was above fuch a
thought, and wholly employed in weeping,
condoling, and comforting. He catches
her in his arms. The fire furrounds them,
while — I cannot go on —

Were I an infidel, misfortunes like this
would convince me, that there muft be an
hereafter; for who can believe that fo much
virtue could meet with fo great diftrefs without a following reward. As for my part,
I am fo old fafhioned as firmly to believe,
that all who perifh in fuch generous enter-
prifes, are relieved from the further exercife
of life; and Providence, which fees their
virtue confummate and manifeft, takes them
to an immediate reward, in a being more
fuitable to the grandeur of their fpirits. What

A   elfe

elfe can wipe away our tears, when we contemplate fuch undeferved, fuch irreparable diftreffes? it was a fublime thought in fome of the heathens of old, "That the fame employments and inclinations which were the entertainment of virtuous men on earth, make up their happinefs in Elyfium."

A DIALOGUE.

Between Mafter Billy, *aud his Tutor Mr.*
Aimwell.

A. PRAY, how do you like the company
your papa introduced you to yefterday?

B. Oh! mighty well, Sir.

A. They are gentlemen and ladies of exceeding good fenfe; but did you obferve
how fond they were of Mafter Meanwell?

B. Yes, Sir, and I wonder a it; for he
is no pretty boy, nor is his papa a rich
man.

A. That is nothing to the purpofe. Little
boys and girls are not beloved for their beauty or riches, but for their *good nature,
good manners*, and *good fenfe.*

B. Pray, fir, do you think he is a good-
natured boy.

A. Yes, indeed; for he is never crofs nor
out of humour, but always chearful and ready to give an anfwer to any body that
fpeaks to him. If you give him but an apple or an orange, he will part with any fhare of it to thofe that are with him, whether

they are ftrangers or playmates; for which reafon he is greatly admired by all his acquaintance.

B. I fhould like to be taken notice of in this manner. But, pray, fir, is this goodnature, as you call it, and a readinefs to run of an errand, or part with any thing, all that is neceffary to make people love me?

A. No, you muft alfo behave with goodmanners, and do every thing with an eafy genteel air; for it is the graceful behaviour that diftinguifhes pretty young gentlemen from ignorant boys who mind nothing but fpinning of tops. You muft alfo behave with becoming refpect to all thofe who are older, and fuppofed to be wifer than yourfelf. When you are afked any queftion, you muft not anfwer bluntly, yes, or no; but yes, or no, fir; yes, madam, or no, madam: and look full in the gentleman or lady's face, when you fpeak; for it is a mark of meannefs to look fhy; and that boy is always counted a booby, who hangs down his head and is afhamed to be feen. When you want any thing, you muft not fay, give me this, or I'll have that; but afk in this manner: Pray, fir, give me that apple; pray, madam, oblige me with that orange;

or,

or, pray do me the favour of that nut, that plumb, that pear, &c.

B. Why, now I think on't, Master Meanwell always says so.

A. Yes, my dear boy; but Master Meanwell not only speaks in this pretty manner, but behaves as prettily also. When he enters the room, he adresses himself to the whole company with a graceful bow, and when he goes out, takes his leave with another bow.

At dinner he sits upright in his chair, and never asks for any thing, but receives what is given him with complaisance and thankfulness; and when he drinks, bows to the most considerable person at the table, and afterwards to all the rest of the company; and if at any time he is sent out of the room, he takes care to pull the door softly, so as not to give them any disturbance. In short, Master Meanwell comes when he is called, does as he is bid, and shuts the door after him, and by that means he has gained the good-will of every body. Then he takes off his hat to all the people he meets, and while he is talking to a gentleman or lady, holds it under his arm.

B.

B. Why, fir, Mafter Dicky de Coverly don't do fo.

A. That booby; No, he does nothing as he ought; but you are not to take example from fuch ill-bred naughty boys as he. Why, it was but the other day his father fent him with a meffage to Mr. Friendly, who, you know, is a polite gentleman, and he bolted into the parlour among all the company, without taking off his hat or paying his refpects to any of them. With that Mr. Friendly afked him where his hat was? " *Why, on my head,*" quoth Dick, and walked off without any more ceremony. When he came home, his father afked how Mr. Friendly did, "Why rarely well, father, quoth Dick, but only I doubt he is blind." "Blind! why doft think fo?" fays the father. "Why! becaufe when I came into the parlour, quoth Dick, he afked me where my hat was? I told him upon my head; but thouf'n I told'n fo, he wou'dn't believe me; and I am fure if a hadn't been blind, he might a feed'en plain enough." This ftory hath made both father and fon the jeft of the whole country; and as Sir Roger de Coverly was fo great a man, every body is

furprif-

furprifed that his fon and grandchild fhould turn out fuch blunderbuffes.

B. But, fir, you was faying juft now, that *good fenfe* would make me agreeable to every body; pray, what do you mean by *good fenfe?*

A. Why, I mean *judgement* or *under-ftanding*. A boy who is endowed with good fenfe, will do nothing but what is honeft, juft or right; and will diftinguifh between fuch things as are idle and trifling, and fuch as are of moment, and worth his knowing.

B. And pray, fir, what muft I do to get this judgement or underftanding? for this feems to me harder to learn than good manners.

A. When you meet with any thing you do not underftand, you muft enquire of thofe who are older and wifer than yourfelf: you muft alfo read fuch books as are moft like-ly to improve your mind; and laftly, how the better fort of people fpeak and behave; for by imitating other great men, you will become a great man yourfelf.

B. A *great man!* ah! that I fhall like indeed. But then, fir, I muft have a fine coach and horfes, and money; for this good

nature,

nature, good manners, and good fenfe, won't make me a great man, unlefs my papa gives me a great deal of money.

A. Your obfervation, my dear child, is not amifs, according to the idle notion the common people have of a great man. But you muft know, a man cannot be truely great unlefs he be truly good. A rich man may be a mifer, and not make ufe of his money; or a fool, and know not how to make ufe of it; and if a man has ever fo many fine houfes, coaches, or fine clothes, or fervants, yet if he fpends more than he is worth, and runs into debt with his tradefmen, without taking any care to pay them, he is fo far from being a great man, that he is only a great knave, and deferves to be thrown into a jail, which is too often the confequence of living extravagantly.

B. If then neither riches nor fine clothes, nor a great number of fervants, are figns of a great man, I fhould be glad to know who is a great man?

A. He only is a great man, who, by his prudence and good conduct gains the efteem and favour of all who know him. But if you want a living example of a great man,

or

or in other words a wife man, turn your eyes on Mr. Friendly. That gentleman has, by his generosity and good management, made all the people, who live round about him, and yet his estate is not half so large as Sir Timothy Trifle's.

B. How muft I do to be as great a man as Mr. Friendly?

A. You muft, as I told you before, be very good, and keep company with none but thofe who are admired for their good behaviour. You muft not only read the books I recommend to you, but you muft remember the good precepts and morals that are contained in them. When you read the life of any good man, you muft endeavour to copy after all thofe great qualities by which he became so famous. You muft learn to write and read well, endeavour to get a habit of fpeaking with elegance and eafe. But above all, you muft love God, and be thankful to him for all the bleffings he hath beftowed upon you, and never forget to offer up your prayers to him morning and evening, not for yourfelf only, but alfo in behalf of your friends, relations, and all mankind. You muft take the part of the poor and diftreffed, relieve thofe who are in want, and

make

make peace between thofe who are at variance. You muft alfo be employed in fome
bufinefs, fo as to make yourfelf ufeful to the
commonwealth; and be afhamed of doing
nothing but what your confcience tells you
is idle, wicked, or difhoneft.

The ADVICE *of a* FATHER *to his* CHILDREN.

THIS inftant is thine; the next is in the
    womb of futurity, and thou knoweft
not what it may bring forth.

Whatfoever thou refolveft to do, do it
quickly; defer not till the evening, what
the morning may accomplifh.

Idlenefs is the parent of want and pain;
but the labour of virtue bringeth forth pleafure.

The hand of the diligent defeateth want;
profperity and fuocefs are the induftrious
man's attendants.

Who is he that hath acquired wealth,
that hath rifen to power, that hath clothed
himfelf with honour, that is fpoken of in the
city with praife, and that ftandeth before
                                        the

the king in his counfel? Even he that hath
fhut out idlenefs from his houfe, and that
hath faid unto floth, thou art mine enemy.

Boaft not of thyfelf, for it will bring contempt upon thee; neither deride another,
for it is dangerous.

From the experience of others, do thou
learn wifdom, and from their failings correct thine own faults.

It behoveth thee, O child of calamity!
early to fortify thy mind with courage and
patience, that thou mayeft fupport, with a
becoming refolution, thy allotted portion of
human evil.

The neareft approach thou can'ft make to
happinefs on this fide of the grave, is to enjoy from heaven underftanding and health.
Thefe bleffings, if thou poffeffeft, and would-
eft preferve to old age, avoid the allure-
ments of voluptuoufnefs, and fly from her
temptations.

In all thy undertakings, let a reafonable
affurance animate thy endeavours; if thou
defpaireft of fuccefs, thou fhalt not fucceed.

Confider how few things are worthy of
anger, and thou fhalt wonder that any but
fools fhould be wrath.

Be

Be grateful to thy father, for he gave thee life; and to thy mother, for fhe fuf- tained thee. Hear the words of his mouth, for they are fpooken for thy good; give ear to her admonition, for it proceedeth from love.

Fear the Lord all the days of thy life, and walk in the paths which he hath opened before thee. Let Prudence admonifh thee, let Temperance reftrain thee; let Juftice gui- de thy hand; Benevolence warm thy heart; and Gratitude to heaven infpire thee with devotion. Thefe fhall give happinefs in thy prefent ftate; and bring thee to the man- fions of eternal felicity in the paradife of God.

The BENEFITS *of* DISAPPOINT- MENTS.

CHILDREN, let me advife you not to murmur at difappointments. Frequent occafions of difcontent will unavoidably oc- cur; but you muft fubmit to be taught by your parents, to improve every circumftan- ce that fhall happen.

Mr.

Mr. Nelſon had a family of three ſons and four daughters: both he and Mrs. Nelſon took great pains, not only to form their un-derſtandings, but to regulate their tempers, and to improve their hearts. They were inſtructed to cultivate the tendereſt diſpoſi-tions, not only towards each other, but to every perſon whatever. Every ſelfiſh incli-nation was carefully checked on its firſt ap-pearance; and they were early taught, that by giving pleaſure to others, they increaſed their own happineſs.

To give ſome inſtances of their behaviour, will be an uſeful leſſon to my little readers. A gentleman, who one day dined at Mr. Nelſon's, and who took every opportunity to exerciſe the diſpoſitions of children, made the following experiment on one of theſe lit-tle gentry. Mrs. Nelſon had given an apple to her younger ſon: Mr. Felton, the gentle-man above-mentioned, who ſat next him, ſnatched it out of his hand. The child look-ed rather confuſed for a few moments; but ſoon recovering himſelf, "Indeed, ſir, ſaid he, you did not take the apple in a very pretty manner. If you had aſked me for it, you ſhould have had it with all my heart." — "I had a mind to try your temper,

Wil-

William, anſwered the gentleman, you are a good boy, I like you; and to be praiſed is a greater ſatisfaction than eating a ſorry apple."——"The apple was a very good one, I believe, Sir; but you may have it, if you pleaſe." He then went to play. The gentleman putting his hand into his pocket, "Well, my boy, ſaid he, as you have treated me ſo kindly, I will endeavour to be as civil to you. There is a fine peach for you." Maſter Nelſon thanked him; and, calling his brothers and ſiſters about him, diſtributed the fruit into equal ſhares between them and himſelf.

Another time, when one of the young ladies was confined to her chamber by illneſs, Mrs. Nelſon produced a box of curioſities, which were never taken out but when ſhe was preſent. Miſs Nelſon was rejoiced at the ſight of it, and, ſitting down by her mamma, waited the opening of the box with great eagerneſs; when, juſt as the key was put in, a chariot drove up to the door with unexpected company. Mrs. Nelſon was vexed at the interruption, and looking at her daughter, "I am ſorry for your diſappointment, my dear, ſaid ſhe, it is one to myſelf, that I cannot give you the intended

ed pleafure."—"My dear mama, anfwered
fhe, how very good you are! I can fee
them another time, you know, when you
are at leifure. I am forry to lofe your company too; but it cannot be avoided. My
fifter will be fo kind as to come and read
me a ftory." Mrs. Nelfon kiffed her, and
left her with unwillingnefs.

Soon after Mifs Nelfon was recovered,
her brothers were invited to go upon the
water with a party on pleafure. They were
very happy in the expectation: the morning
appointed was very fine, and the two children in readinefs to go, when, on the arrival of the gentlemen who were to accompany Mr. Nelfon, they found two more
than were expected, and that there would
not be room for the brothers. Mr. Nelfon
was much concerned; he then propofed taking the elder only, but was unwilling to
part them; and the elder, on knowing his
intention, faid, he had rather ftay at home,
unlefs his brother could go with him; to
which his father agreed. A little cloud of
melancholy overfpread their countenances for
a few minutes; but not the leaft appearance
of fullennefs or ill-nature.

About

About two hours after the gentlemen's departure, an unexpected storm arose; and, though its violence soon abated, yet a settled rain followed, to the entire destruction of the pleasure proposed in the voyage. Mrs. Nelson made use of this opportunity to read a lesson of instruction to her children. "How frequently, my loves, said she, will you experience, that the disappointment of your wishes is a real blessing!— You see, that had you gone, you would have had no pleasure; you would even have been in some danger, and your dear papa would have been more distressed on your account."— "I hope papa is in no danger, cried the elder boy, I should not mind being wet, if I could help papa." Mrs. Nelson catched the child in her arms, and could not forbear letting fall a tear. The gentlemen returned in safety the next day, but had an uncomfortable voyage, and rejoiced that the children had not been of the party, as they would have been alarmed for their safety. "Well, papa, said the younger boy, I was in hopes ·you would come to no hurt; for you know Mr. Selby's boat is called a pleasure boat, and that it would not have proved such, if any body had been lost in it."

This

.This remark drew a fmile from the compa-ny; and the praifes the two boys received for their manner of fupporting a difappoint-ment, gave them more fatisfaction than they could have enjoyed from the moft pleafant voyage.

When any of the young Nelfons forgot themfelves and tranfgreffed their duty, it was their punifhment to be excluded from the prefence of their papa and mama, and their good brothers and fifters. As they felt the utmoft filial and fraternal love they fuffered greatly by this punifhment; but it was very feldom that there was occafion to inflict it.

. The children took it by turns to vifit with their parents, and Mifs Emely was dreffed one afternoon to accompany her mama; when, being at play in the nurfery, fhe faw her doll in her little fifter's hands. She ran eagerly to take it from her; but little Lucy holding it, faid, "nay, fifter, you did not want it before; I will not hurt it; but you know, Mifs Clement broke mine, and I had a mind to nurfe this a little while." Mifs Emely, however, was not difpofed to be good; fhe fcuffled, and endeavoured to pull it away in this manner.

Mifs

Miſs Lucy, in playfulneſs, detained it, when the former, angry on being oppoſed, gave her ſiſter a ſlap on the hand. Miſs Lucy, unuſed to ſuch treatment, ſhrieked and cried aloud.

Mrs. Nelſon, who was in her own room, which was adjoining, inſtantly entered the nurſery, and deſired to know the cauſe of this confuſion. All were ſilent, the nurſe-ry-maid had gone down juſt before the affair happened; Mrs. Nelſon therefore addreſſed herſelf to her eldeſt daughter, and inſiſted on her telling the cauſe of Miſs Lucy's tears. Miſs Nelſon was viſibly unwilling to ſpeak; but her mama's commands were not to be diſputed: "I am ſorry, madam, that I am obliged in truth to ſay, that my ſiſter Emily has been to blame; but I dare ſay ſhe is very ſorry for her fault, and perhaps Lucy ſhould not have taken it without leave." She then related all that had paſt, and con-cluded with ſaying, it was the firſt time ſhe ever knew her ſiſter do ſuch a thing, and ſhe dared to anſwer for her, that ſhe would do ſo no more.

Mrs. Nelſon ſtood for a few moments ſi-lent, "You are a very good girl, Suſannah, ſaid ſhe at laſt, to be ſo concerned for your

ſiſter's

fister's fault. She is very naughty; go, continued she, go, Emily, and stand in that corner for an hour. Reflect on what you have done, and pray God to forgive, and enable you to be better. As you are not good enough to be my companion, it is Lucy's turn to visit with me; and remember, Emily, she loses the favour of her mother, who is unkind to her brothers and sisters." Mrs. Nelson then left the room, and Miss Lucy was dressed to attend her mama; but her little heart was divided between joy for being permitted to pay a visit, and grief for her sister's punishment. She went to her, and taking her hand, "indeed, Emily, said she, I am sorry I did not give up the doll, and I wish you had not been angry; I thought you had been only in jest till you hit me." Mrs. Nelson that instant called her, and she left her sisters with a smile dimpling her cheek, and a tear glistening in her eye.

As soon as the chariot drove from the door, Miss Nelson went to her sister, whom she found with her handkerchief up to her face, and sobbing most piteously. "Come, my dear Emily, do not cry any more, said

she,

she, I find you are very sorry for your fault, and that was all mama desired; you will ask her's and Lucy's pardon, and all will be well again."

Miss Emily's pride had prevented her for some time from feeling a proper sense of her fault.

A false shame made her unwilling to own she had done wrong, and to ask pardon; but her sister Lucy's forgiving temper, and the kindness of Miss Nelson's expressions, convinced her of her offence. She could return no answer to her sister but sobs and tears, till fearing Miss Nelson should mistake her silence for obstinacy, "You are too good to me, sister, said she, I do not deserve your love; how kind poor Lucy was! how could I hit her, and I know I have vexed my dear mama too! and then Mrs. Graves will ask the reason why I did not go, and will hear that I am naughty, and she will not love me. I am a sad naughty girl, and I am very, very sorry for my fault."

"Well, my dear, you can do no more than be concerned for your fault, ask God's
pardon,

pardon, and he will receive you to his favour. I am going to take a little walk with
Edward, and I will come to you again."

Whilſt Miſs Nelſon was walking with
her brother, a Miſs Smyth, who was very
intimate in the family came in, and finding
no one in the parlour, ran up ſtairs. On
ſeeing Miſs Emily, well, my dear, ſaid ſhe,
where is your mama, and where are your
brothers and ſiſters?" Miſs Emily hid her
face, and ſobbing, "O! Madam, cried ſhe,
pray do not take any notice of me; I am
in diſgrace, and you muſt not ſpeak to a
naughty girl." "I am ſure you are very
good now, anſwers the lady, but I will
break through no rules. I ſhall tell your
mama how prettily you have behaved, and
dare ſay, I ſhall ſee you in favour again
to-morrow."

Miſs Nelſon, after her walk, returned
with impatience to her ſiſter, and the clock
ſtriking as ſhe entered, "Come, my dear
ſaid ſhe, your time is out, and you have
been ſo much concerned, that I am ſure my
mama will not be offended, if you now
play with us."—"I thank you, ſiſter, an-

E 2 ſwered

fwered Emily, but I am not good enough to play with you. I will fit down, and read fome of the ftories in Mrs. Teachum; thofe miffes, efpecially Mifs Jenny Peace, are good examples for me."

When Mrs. Nelfon returned, her eldeft daughter eagerly told her how well her fifter had behaved, and Mifs Emily made the moft proper fubmiffions to her mama and fifter Lucy. She then infifted, that the latter fhould accept of her doll, which Mifs Lucy with great fweetnefs declined; but Emily was fo concerned at her refufal, that Mrs. Nelfon defired her to take it. "Now, my Emily, faid the fond parent, you are as dear to me as ever. You have been faulty, but your concern has been at leaft equal to your offence. Recover your fpirits, for peniten-ce reftores us to the favour of heaven." The account Mifs Smyth gave of Emily con-firmed her mama's good opinion of her.

A ftrict conformity to reafon and religion had been the foundation of their obedience in childhood; and thefe principles fupported in them through every feafon and condition of life. One of the fons, by the carelefs-
nefs

nefs of his nurfe, had received a confiderable
hurt, which, by her imprudent conceal-
ment, paffed unnoticed, till the effects appeared in the alteration of his fhape. Though
his health fuffered by this deformity, his
difpofition was not warped. He made ufe
of the misfortune in his own perfon to guard
his brothers and fifters againft inattention to
their carriage. "Look at me, he would fometimes fay, when he faw any of them
ftooping or carelefs in their gait, would you
wifh to be diftorted as I am? Mine is a misfortune. Be cautious, left you fuffer by
your own fault. A perfonable figure is a
great recommendation, and where it has
pleafed God to give a well made form, furely it is very faulty to injure it by our ne-
glect."

This young gentleman was one day walking with another, when a rude boy, running paft him, called out laughing, "My
lord! my lord! what fhall I give you for
the bunch at your back?" Mafter Watfon,
the companion of Mafter Nelfon was fhock-
ed. "You young knave, cried he, in the
warmth of his refentment, I have a great
mind to lay my ftick upon your back!" "You

are

are very kind to me, faid Mafter Nelfon, but let him alone: he does not hurt me by this fpeech—Let him be merry—I only wifh he had a more propcr fubject for his mirth."

This young gentleman was of a very be-nevolent difpofition: he and his eldeft fifters took great delight in teaching poor children to read. Mifs Nelfon alfo taught feveral girls to work, and frequently gave them fome of her own linen, out of which fhe in-ftructed them to make neceffaries for them-felves. Mr. Nelfon's was a family of love and happinefs. The latter was interrupted by a misfortune which happened to the third fon, an exceeding promifing youth. A humour broke out at the corner of his mouth, which fpread very faft. The father, being advifed by eminent furgeons to have part of the bone of the cheek taken away, as the only means of faving his life, deter-mined on having the operation performed. He informed the child of the defign, telling him, that he hoped he would bear the pain like a good boy, as it was intended to pre-vent a ftill greater, and would foon be over. The poor child looked at him earneftly; he

saw

faw the grief and trouble his father laboured to conceal, and burft into tears: but foon recovering himfelf, "I will be cut, faid he, I will fubmit to any thing you think ought to be done. I am fure papa and mama would not let me fuffer any pain but what is for my good."

The father could not help weeping as he embraced him. However, he encouraged him to bear it with patience. The operation was performed, and the child, who was not ten years of age, behaved with uncommon refolution and patience. The effect was not conformable to their hopes. The diforder foon broke out again; it fpread with greater rapidity, and the poor child was foon unable to receive fufficient fuftenance.

As he lay languifhing on his death-bed, his mother and fifters fat weeping by him. "Do not cry for me, mama, faid he, do not cry for William, fifter, I do fuffer a great deal; but I hope my pains will foon be over. I am loth to leave you, and papa, and all my brothers and fifters, but I fhall go to God Almighty, my beft friend; and then I fhall never cry any more, but be for ever happy, and I fhall meet you all again in heaven.

He was foon releafed from a ftate of exquifite fuffering; and though the lofs of fo excellent a child increafed for a while a heart-piercing affliction, yet the confideration of his excellence became in time a fource of confolation.

In every circumftance they looked up to heaven with thankfulnefs or refignation; being convinced, that an all-wife and all-gracious Being could not miftake, nor withhold the means of fecuring the eternal happinefs of his creatures.

ANDROCLES *and the* NUMIDIAN LION.

ANDROCLES was the flave of a noble Roman, who was proconful of Africa. He had been guilty of a fault, for which his mafter would have put him to death, had not he found an opportunity to escape

escape out of his hands, and fled into the defarts of Numidia: as he was wandering among the barren fands, and almoft dead with heat and hunger, he faw a cave in the fide of a rock; he went into it, and finding at the farther end of it a place to fit down upon; refted there for fome time. At length to his great furprife, a huge overgrown lion entered the cave, and feeing a man at the upper end of it, immediately made towards him. Androcles gave himfelf for gone; but the lion, inftead of treating him as he expected, laid his paw upon his lap, and with a complaining kind of voice fell a licking his hand. Androcles, after having recovered himfelf a little from the fright he was in, obferved the lion's paw exceedingly fwelled by a large thorn that ftuck in it. He immediately pulled it out, and fqeezing the paw very gently, made a great deal of corrupt matter run out of it, which probably freed the lion from the great anguifh he had felt fome time before. The lion left him upon receiving this good office from him, and foon after returned with a fawn, which he had juft killed. This he laid down at the feet of his benefactor, and went off

again

again in purfuit of his prey. Androcles, after having fodden the flefh of it by the fun, fubfifted upon it till the lion had fupplied him with another. He lived many days in this frightful folitude, the lion catering for him with great affiduity. Being at length tired of his favage fociety, he was refolved to deliver himfelf up to his mafter's hands, and fuffer the worft effects of his difpleafure, rather than be thus driven out from mankind. His mafter, as was cuftomary for the proconfuls of Africa, was at that time getting together a prefent of all the largeft lions that could be found in the country, in order to fend them to Rome, that they might furnifh out a fhow for the Roman people. Upon his poor flave's furrendering himfelf into his hands, he ordered him to be carried away to Rome as foon as the lions were in readinefs to be fent, and that for his crime, he fhould be expofed to fight with one of the lions in the amphitheatre, as ufual, for the diverfion of the people. This was alfo performed accordingly. Androcles, after fuch a ftrange run of fortune, was now in the area of the theatre, amidft thoufands of fpectators expecting eve-

ry,

ry moment that his antagonift would come out upon him. At length a huge monftrous lion leaped out from the place where he had been kept hungry for the fhow. He advanced with great rage towards the man, but on a fudden, after having regarded him a little wiftfully, he fell to the ground, and crept towards his feeth with all the figns of blandifhment and carefs. Androcles, after a fhort paufe, difcovered that it was his old Numidian friend, and immediately renewed his acquaintance with him. Their mutual congratulations were very furprifing to the beholders, who, upon hearing an account of the whole matter from Androcles, ordered him to be pardoned, and the lion to be given up into his poffeffion. Androcles returned at Rome the civilities which he had received from him in the deferts of Africa. Dion Caffius fays, that he himfelf faw the man leading the lion about the ftreets of Rome, the people every where gathering about them, and repeating to one another, " *Hic eft leo hofpes hominis; hic eft homo medicus leonis.* This is the lion who was the man's hoft; this is the man who was the lion's phyfician. "

The

The grateful returns made by this animal to his benefactor, may ferve as a leſſon to many of the rational part of the creation; who, though they boaſt of advantages far fuperior to inſtinct, yet are too often found wanting in the exercife of gratitude for benefits received.

SULTAN MAHMOUD *and his* VISIER.

THE Sultan Mahmoud, by his perpetual wars abroad, and by his tyranny at home, had filled his dominions with ruin and defolation, and half unpeopled the Perfian empire. The vifier to this great fultan, whether an humouriſt, or an enthuſiaſt, we are not informed, pretended to have learned of a certain dervife to underſtand the language of birds, fo that there was not a bird that could open his mouth but the vifier knew what it was he faid. As he was one evening with the emperor, in their return from hunting, they faw a couple of

owls

owls upon a tree, that grew near an old
wall upon a heap of rubbish. "I would fain
know, fays the fultan, what thefe two owls
are faying to one another; liften to their
difcourfe, and give me an account of it."
The vifier approached the tree, pretending
to be very attentive to the two owls. Upon
his return to the fultan, "Sir, fays he, I
have heard part of their converfation but dare
not tell you what it was." The fultan
would not be fatisfied with fuch an anfwer,
but forced him to repeat word for word
every thing the owls had faid. "You muft
know then, faid then vifier, that one of
thefe owls has a fon and the other a daughter, between whom they are now upon a
treaty of marriage. The father of the fon
faid to the father of the daughter, in my
hearing, brother, I confent to this marriage,
provided you will fettle upon your daughter fifty ruined villages for her portion. To
which the father of the daughter replied,
inftead of fifty I will give you five hundred,
if you pleafe. God grant a long life to Sultan Mahmoud; whilft he reigns over us,
we fhall never want ruined villages."

The

The ſtory ſays, the ſultan was ſo touched with the fable, that he rebuilt the towns
and villages which had been deſtroyed, and,
from that time forward, conſulted the good
of his people.

Advice and reproof conveyed in this in-
direct manner, is not only the moſt ſafe,
but the moſt effectual; for, as it ſeems to
come without deſign, it betrays no ſuperio-
rity of judgement, nor diſinclination to the
perſon; who is left to make the application
himſelf, and if accuſed, is accuſed by his
own conſcience. This was well known to
the fabuliſts of old, who always conveyed
their ſentiments in this concealed and indi-
rect manner.

The HISTORY of the MERCOLIANS.

THE Mercolians, a people who poſſeſſed an iſland in the Lilliputian ſeas,
had, by their induſtry, trade, and commerce, acquired immenſe riches. By their ſhip-
ping

ping they made the product of all nations
their own, and the inhabitants of the neighbouring isles, and on the continent, were
their slaves and dependents. Nothing, however, is so difficult to manage as too much
wealth; and a state may be crushed under
the weight of its own power, which was
the fate of the Mercolians. They grew
proud, infolent, and idle. The only ufe
they made of their riches was to purchafe
them new-invented pleafures. They funk
in down beds, and grew effeminate; exercife, which ftrings the nerves, and preferves health, was a ftranger to them; they
turned day into night, and night into day,
and wafted their moft valuable and precious
time in routs and riotous affemblies; but
fee at once the force of human folly, and
the end of human grandeur! They made a
law to naturalize the flaves and refufe of
other nations; they took counfel of ftrangers; they chofe their generals and officers
from a foreign people, and were at laft plun-
dered and difpoffeffed of their property by
their own dependents. Such was the fete
of the Mercolians; and may this be a warning to all future ftates.

In

In this confufion, fome of the beft families left Mercolia, and took poffeffion of an
ifland uninhabited in the fame feas, but
were followed by their enemies, who drew
up in battle array to deftroy them. At this
inftant of time, when no profpect of fafety
remained, and every man expected his fate,
Mafter Turvolo, a lad of about fourteen
years, arofe, and thus addreffed himfelf to
the Mercolians:— "Brethren, and you men
of Mercolia! let not fear drive you to mad-
nefs? you have lives, you have families,
you have effects worth preferving, and the
means is in your hands to do it. Let every
man deliver to me his money, the only fource and caufe of his misfortune, and I will
deliver you from thefe people, who, from
being your flaves and dependents, are now
become your lords and dictators. "He then
took a large heap of money, which he divided into three hundred bags; untied, and
diftributed thofe bags to the fame number of
men, to each man his bag; and placed them
behind thofe of his friends, who were armed; and when the purfuers came upon them,
thofe men, as they were directed, fcatter-
ed the money upon the ground, which di-
verted

verted the foldiers from their duty, and fet
them to fighting among themfelves; and the
Mercolians ftood at a diftance and beheld
them deftroying one another, till fuch time
as their forces were fufficiently weakened,
and then they turned upon them and over-
threw them with great flaughter. After
this Mafter Turvolo was placed at the head
of the people, and made their king; and,
in order to eftablifh in them virtuous and
good principles, he erected two temples,
one whereof was called the temple of Fame,
and built on the top of a high hill, fortified
round with a ftrong wall and deep ditch;
and the other was placed in the middle of
the road, leading to that on the hill, fo that
there was no coming to the other temple, but through it; and this was called the temple of Virtue. The firft por-
tal of this temple was dignified with this
infcription, namely, *The road to the Temple of Fame is through the Temple of Virtue.* And after paffing through a fpacious
court, a beautiful portico prefented itfelf,
on which was written, in azure and gold,
the following letters: *Thou fhalt love the
Lord thy God with all thy heart, with all*

*thy foul, and with all thy strength, and
thy neighbour as thyself.*

In the temple of Fame were regiftered
the names of all thofe who were good men,
whether ploughmen, tradefmen, or whatever elfe; for worth and honour are confined to no particular clafs of people, and feals
were given them at the public expence, as
a teftimony of their efteem; but to thofe
who were lazy, indolent, and did nothing
for the fervice of the community, no feals
were given, nor were they fuffered to enter the temple.   And if at any time thofe
who had procured that honour degenerated,
that mark of efteem was taken from them,
and a badge of infamy placed on their backs,
which they were obliged to wear, or abandon their friends and country.   Nor did
either honour or infamy defcend from the
father to the fon, for every man was to
win his own laurels, and be accountable for
his own actions *only.* Befides this, as the
ill-ufe of money had corrupted the morals
of the people, rendered them effeminate,
and overthrowh them before, he obliged all
the inhabitants every four years to bring
their money into the public treafury, from
which

which an equal diftribution was again made, to each perfon his fhare; and thofe who had multiplied their ftock by honeft means, had the thanks of the community, and fome marks of royal favour from the king.

Thus did little king Turvolo raife a ruin- ed ftate, and make a miferable people hap- py; for in a few years peace reigned in every breaft, and plenty fmiled in every valley; they had no ambition but of excel- ling in virtue, and no contentions, but who fhould be moft religious and moft juft. Locks, bolts, and bars, they had no occa- fion for, fince thieves there were none, nor did they need any of the dreadful inftruments of war:——*For every man loved the Lord his God with all his heart, with all his foul, and with all his ftrength, and his neighbour as himfelf.*

The AMERICAN MERCHANT.

A Merchant, who fettled in the Weft-In- dies, meeting with good fuccefs, in a few years acquired a handfome fortune, and two children, a boy and a girl; the fon, whofe name was John, was about four years old, and Molly a year younger. Seeing himfelf in fo happy circumftances he refolved to go over to old England and fpend there the remainder of his days. Accordingly he went with his whole family aboard a fhip, but when they were about half-way on their paffage, a dreadful ftorm arofe, and the pilot faid they were in imminent danger of being loft; on hearing this, the merchant took a large plank, and faftened his wife and two children to it, but before he had time to fix himfelf to the fame, the fhip ftruck on a rock, and fplit to pieces. The plank with the wife and two children kept the fea like a little boat, and the wind carried them to an ifland. The mother untied the cords with which they were faftened, and went up into the country, in hopes of difcovering fome houfes, but fhe foon perceived that the ifland was uninhabited: fhe now began to be apprehenfive that herfelf and her children muft perifh for hunger; but advancing farther into the ifland, fhe found feveral trees laden with fruit, and a number of birds nefts with eggs in them; there being no probability of their ever getting off

the

the ifland, fhe was refolved to fubmit to
the Divine Will, and do her beft for the
education of her children. She very fortu-
nately had in her pocket a bible, by which
fhe taught them to read, and inftructed them
in the knowledge of their Maker. At the
end of two years the poor mother fell fick,
and being aware fhe could not long furvive,
fhe called her children to her, and told
them fhe was at the point of death, and
muft foon leave them, but bid them remember that they were not left alone, and God
would fee all; they muft not forget to pray
to him every night and morning, and muft
never quarrel nor fight, but live in love
and amity with one another. The children
obferved punctually the directions they received from their dying mother; no day
paffed without putting up their morning and
evening prayers to God, and they read their
book over fo often, that they had it by
heart. Jacky and Molly had now been eleven years on this ifland: as they were one
day fitting on the fea fhore, they obferved feveral black men coming towards them
in a boat. The blacks were furprifed to
fee thefe children of a different colour from

F 3 them-

themfelves; they furrounded them and fpoke
to them, but Jacky and Molly underftood
nothing of their language; at length four
black men fhowed them their boat, and defired them by figns to ftep in. Molly at
firft was afraid, but by the perfuafion of her
brother, went into the boat; which carried
them into an ifland not far off, inhabited
by favages, who all received them very
kindly. The king could not keep his eyes
off Molly, and often put his hand to his
breaft to let her know he loved her: Molly
and Jacky foon learned their language, and
underftood that they were at war with the
people of fome neighbouring iflands, and
that they eat their prifoners. The king
was now refolved inftantly to make Molly
his queen, who told her brother fhe had rather die than marry him, becaufe fhe thought
him a very wicked man, for inftead of forgiving his enemies, as their book inftructed them, he put his prifoners to death, and
devoured them. The favages were fo ex-
afperated at Molly's refufal to marry their
king, that they tied her and her brother to
piles of wood, and were preparing to fet
fire to them, when they heard that a great
number

number of their enemies were come afhore.
They all ran to fight the invaders, and being
overcome, the victorious enemy cut the
chains of the victims deftined to the flames,
and carried them to their iflands, where
they became flaves to the king of the country. Thofe favages were alfo frequently
engaged in wars, and like their neighbours,
devoured their prifoners. On a certain occafion they took a great number; and among
the reft was a white man; the favages finding him very lean, determined to fatten him
for their eating. He was kept chained in
a hut, and Molly was charged with the
the care of bringing him foot. The white
man, who was furprifed at the fight of a
woman of the fame colour as himfelf, was
much more fo when he heard her fpeak his
own language, and pray to the fame God.
He afked her, who taught her to fpeak
Englifh, and inftructed her in the knowledge of God? She replied, fhe did not know
before the name of the language fhe fpoke;
that her mother fpoke it and taught it her;
that fhe had learned much about God out
of a book which her mother gave her, and
prayed to him daily. The white man then

afked

aſked to ſee the book, on opening which, and finding on the firſt leaf, "This book belongs to John Maurice;" he broke out in the following words: "Ah! my dear children! have I found you once more! Come and embrace your poor father, and give me ſome account of your mother." Jacky and Molly where ſo overjoyed at ſeeing their father again, that it was ſome time before they could ſpeak: at laſt, ſays Jacky, "My heart tells me you are my father, though I cannot conceive how it is poſſible, for my mother told me you went to the bottom of the ſea. It is true, ſays the man, I actually fell into the ſea, but catching hold of a plank, I came aſhore upon an iſland, and concluded you were loſt." Jacky then gave a particular account of all he could remember; the white man was much afflicted, when he heard that his poor wife was dead; "and, alas! ſays he, what avails it, my dear children, that we have met again, if in a few days I am to be ſlaughtered and devoured." But Molly deſired him to leave that to her, for ſhe had thought of an infallible means to ſave his life. She then left her father, and went and threw

herſelf

herself at the king's feet, telling him, she had one request to make, which she hoped he would not deny; the king promised her he would not. She then told him, that the white man was Jacky's and her father; and as he had determined that he should be eaten, her request was that she might suffer in his stead. The king was so moved with Molly's dutiful affection for her father, that he not only promised her own and her father's life, but told her he expected a ship soon which came with white men, and they should have his leave to depart. Molly returned the king her most grateful thanks for his kind compassion, and ran immediately to her father to acquaint him with the good news. The ship mentioned by the black king arriving a few days afterwards, they all went on board, and returned safe to England, where they spent their days in great happiness, often reflecting with wonder on the mysterious and wise providence of God, who only permitted the daughter to be a slave as a means to save her father's life.

An

An ADVENTURE *of* MASTER TOM-MY TRUSTY.

MISS Biddy Johnfon was a pretty girl, and learned her book very well, but fhe was too fond of herfelf. Her beauty made her proud and difobedient to her parents, and, by not taking their advice, and doing as they bid her, fhe had almoft loft her life.

As fhe was their only child, her papa and mama were remarkably fond of her, and thought nothing too good for her either to eat, or drink, or wear. She was always dreffed as fine as a little lady, but her papa and mamma ordered her never to go out but in their company, or with their confent; however fhe did not mind what they faid, but, whenever fhe had any. thing new on, away fhe ran to fhow it her playmates. Pride makes us do many filly things. One day, when her new coat and ftays were brought home, fhe got her maid, who was a filly girl, to put her bobs in her ears, and away fhe ran, forfooth, without any body with her, to fee Mifs

Fanny

Fanny Tinfel. Mifs Fanny was as proud a little girl as any in London; fhe hated every
body that was finer than herfelf; and becaufe
Mifs Biddy was dreffed out fo, fhe would not
play with her: upon which Mifs Biddy huf-
fed, and left her. As fhe was going home,
fhe miffed her way; and, travelling over
Londonbridge, fhe got as far as St. George's
church, and there fat down upon a ftep,
and cried. A woman, who was juft by,
came up to her, and gave her an orange,
and afked her whofe little girl fhe was. "I
am, anfwered fhe, Mifs Biddy Johnfon and
I have loft my way." "Oh, fays the woman, you are Mr. Johnfon's little girl, are
you? My hufband is looking after you, to
carry you home to your papa and mama;
and here, fays fhe, beckoning to a man
that ftood by, do you carry this little mifs
home, and I will go along with you;" fo
they took her up, and Mifs Biddy did not
cry, becaufe fhe thought they came from
her papa and mama. When they got out
of town, fhe knew that was not the way
home, and began to cry: but the man
ftuffed a nafty rag into her mouth, and tied
a black crape hat-band over that, to prevent
her

her making a noife, and then gave her to the woman, who carried her under her cloak. They conveyed her in this manner over the fields to Norwood, and there ftripped her of her clothes, and were going to kill her. Mafter Tommy Trufty, as it was a holiday, happened to be in the wood a nutting, and hearing a child cry, made up towards the noife, and looking through a bufh, he faw Mifs Biddy, and the man with a large knife in his hand, juft going to murther her. Mafter Trufty was a little boy of very good fenfe, and great courage, and of a good-natured merciful difpofition. He was willing to fave Mifs Biddy, but how to do it was the queftion: "I am alone, fays he, reafoning with himfelf, but they do not know it. I have innocency and God Almighty on my fide, and thefe wretches have only the devil and guilt on theirs; which will naturally make them afraid; for their confciences will fly in their faces. I will make a noife, fays he; fo, juft as the villain was about to murther Mifs Biddy, he called out, "Here they are! here they are! and going to kill her!" He then popped a whip he had in his hand, which made the

thieves

thieves conclude that they were purfued by men on horfeback, and they ran away as faft as poffible, leaving Mifs Biddy's clothes behind them. Mafter Trufty watched them out of the wood, and then returned to Mifs Biddy, whom he found with her hands tied, and crying fadly; but as foon as fhe faw him, fhe jumped for joy. Mafter Tommy untied her hands, and, putting on her clothes, he found that one of her ear-rings and bobs were wanting; but fhe did not mind that, for, fays fhe, "I will never be proud any more, but go home to my papa and mama, and do every thing they bid me, and be a very good girl." Mafter Tommy went with her. It was night when they came home, and her papa and mama, thinking fhe was loft, were ready to devour her with kiffes. They prefented to Mafter Trufty a fine library of books, and a pretty little horfe, as a reward for his courage, and the care he had taken of their daughter; and he has now the fatisfaction of having preferved the life of one of his play-fellows, and of being careffed and efteemed by Mr. Johnfon, and all who have heard this ftory. Mifs Biddy, from being a proud naughty

girl

girl, is become exceedingly dutiful to her parents, obliging to all her play mates, and charitable to the poor: she now despises fine clothes, and says, " that virtue and good-nature are the best ornaments a young lady can wear."

The HISTORY of MR. ASHFIELD.

MR. SYLVANUS ASHFIELD was born in the county of Durham; at the age of twenty-one he became possessed of an easy fortune, and thought immediately of settling in the world. He married a lady of equal rank and fortune with himself, by whom he was blessed with three children; he was extremely fond of his little off-spring, and whenever they were assembled around his knees, he thought himself happier than a king. He had a good library, and when he was not with his wife and children, his time was spent in study. Though he had a general taste for all sorts of books, his inclination chiefly directed him to the poets, and particularly those of the

the dramatic kind. He had a ftrong paffion for Shakefpeare's tragedies; he read them over and over without ceafing; and fome-times he thought how happy the people in London muft be, who had opportunities of going to the playhoufes, where thefe ex-cellent pieces were exhibited. This notion which occurred frequently to his mind, grew up to a moft violent defire. He might indeed have taken a journey to London as no body could have hindered him; but whenever he confidered the matter feriouf-ly, reafon oppofed fo abfurd an excurfion, and he was confcious that all his friends would blame him for taking a journey of upwards two hundred miles, merely for the pleafure of feeing a play. He conti-nued two whole years in this diftreffed condition; and became melancholy and pen-five.

Juft at this time, however, he received a letter from town, with an account; that an aunt of his was dead there, who had appointed him her fole executor. It was therefore now become abfolutely neceffary that he fhould come up to London, to fet-tle her affairs. All his friends were furprifed

ed at the joy which he expreſſed on hearing this news, as he always had been
eſteemed a diſintereſted perſon. He was
really uneaſy that they began to think him
covetous, but he could not bring himſelf to
declare the true cauſe of his ſatisfaction. A
French author obſerves very judiciouſly, that
we are more jealous of the opinion others
form of our underſtanding, than we are with
reſpect to what they think of our morals,
and we chooſe rather to be thought immoral than ridiculous, or of a weak capacity.
At leaſt he then acted upon this principle:
He left all the world at liberty to think as
they pleaſed, and his whole care was in haſ-
tening every thing for his departure. He
ſcarce allowed Mrs. Aſhfield time to put up a
few ſhirts in a cloak bag; and though he had
the tendereſt love for his family, the tears
they ſhed when he took horſe were by him
totally diſregarded; his mind was wholly agitated by the pleaſures he hoped to find in
the exhibition of a play. When he alighted at the inn, the firſt queſtion he aſked
was, at what o'clock they opened the play-
houſe? and he was anſwered, about five.
As the time drew nearer his impatience increaſed.

creafed. When he came to the play-houfe-
door it was exactly four o'clock. He was
enraged at the porter, and believed he delay-
ed opening the door for the purpofe. However, it was fet open at laft, and in he rufhed.
He furveyed with eagernefs the place he had
fo long and fo often wifhed to fee; and at
laft feated himfelf. Mean while the company crowded in, and feemed to fhare
with him in impatience; fome by bawling,
others by thumping their fticks upon the
floor, and fome by whiftling. At laft the
long-wifhed for moment comes, the curtain
is drawn up, and, what do you think?—A
man of an enormous fize comes in and feats
himfelf juft before our hero, and almoft ob-
ftructed a fight of the ftage. This incon-
venience however he remedied by leaning on
one fide, till his back was almoft broken.
The actors at laft appeared, and for a time
he feemed to have loft his faculties.

He only came to himfelf again at the clofe of the firft act. He then began to confider the pleafure he had received by this no-
velty; it was really great, but far from
anfwering his expectations. This difappointment occafioned a difguft; however,

he was ſtill determined to examine the play, and to remark its defects; ſo that at laſt he found fault with the author, the players, the decorations, and even thought that every particular fell ſhort of that perfection to which they might have been carried to make the whole complete.

The farce, which was a pantomime, was ſtill more diſagreeable, being in itſelf extremely indecent and immoral. The exhibition at laſt was at an end, and he returned to the inn very penſive and diſcontent. While he was in this melancholy mood, he made the following pertinent reflections.

My caſe, ſaid he to himſelf, is very common. A young lady at fourteen or fifteen, hears of what I may call the grand play or comedy of the world; ſhe longs to be ſeen at this public ſpectacle, and endeavours to haſten the long deſired hour; at length ſhe appears at aſſemblies. What forecaſt! what care is had to be in a proper place to ſee and be ſeen in a manner the moſt likely to ſooth and flatter her vanity! but when ſhe has ſucceeded, and that ſhe is fixed to her content, in comes a taller perſon,

perſon, that is, a lady of greater beauty, a finer ſhape, more wit, and poſſeſſed of talents which ſhe wants; ſhe ſeiſes and fixes every eye in the company, and eclipſes the young perſon that thought herſelf ſo happy, and who, in order to catch a ſide glance, and ſome ſhare in the admiration of the ſpectators, is forced to be upon the rack, and in the moſt uneaſy poſture, where this rival ſhines with ſuperior endowments. — Tho' the conſtraint is greatly troubleſome, ſhe keeps up her heart, and bears her preſent ſituation with the proſpect of the pleaſure ſhe hopes to find in this meeting. How great is her ſurpriſe, and how affecting her concern to ſee, that the pleaſure does not anſwer her expectation; ſhe is fruſtrated, ſhe does not meet with half, no not a quarter of that ſatisfaction ſhe propoſed to herſelf; ſhe grieves, ſhe begins to loath the world, that requires ſo much and returns ſo little, but the diſguſt fails too often of bringing a love of retreat, and ends in being out of temper with the faults of the play, and the performers; that is, the incidents of life; the perfidiouſneſs of indifferent perſons, and the ingratitude of thoſe who were thought friends.

One

One is deceived on all sides, obliged to take
a share in the trouble of this person, and to
suffer the unjust proceedings of that other;
this is not all. This comedy, or universal
pantomime, which is not very entertaining,
is very scandalous; what is heard and what
is seen disposes generally to evil. Who has
the holy fear of the Lord dreads being sullied
with this filth; he must be ever on his guard,
always resisting, and engaged in an endless
struggle. Here the eyes and the ears must
be constantly shut; the tongue must be almost
under a perpetual restraint. What a pity!
In fine, the play draws to an end, night,
that is old age, comes on. What remains,
but that very little pleasure, great uneasiness, unprofitable desires, and tormenting
remorses? Happy those, who like myself,
disgusted with the first representation, take
a handsome resolution, and follow my example.

ＥＮＤ of the ＴＥＮＴＨ and ＬＡＳＴ
ＶＯＬＵＭＥ.